CRAIG RUSSELL

LENNOX

Quercus

First published in Great Britain in 2009 by

Quercus
21 Bloomsbury Square
London
WC1A 2NS

A CIP catalogue record for this book is available
from the British Library

ISBN 978 1 84724 966 1 (HB)
ISBN 978 1 84724 965 4 (TPB)

10 9 8 7 6 5 4 3 2 1

Typeset by Ellipsis Books Limited, Glasgow

Printed and Bound in Great Britain by Clays Ltd, St Ives plc

For Colin

PROLOGUE

In my life, I have had to explain my way out of a lot of tight corners, but this one tops them all.

I am leaning against the wall of an upper-storey room in an empty dockside warehouse. I am leaning against the wall because I doubt if I can stand up without support. I am trying to work out if there are any vital organs in the lower left of my abdomen, just above the hip. I try to remember anatomy diagrams from every encyclopaedia I ever opened as a kid because, if there are vital organs down there, I am pretty much fucked.

I am leaning against a wall in an empty dockside warehouse trying to remember anatomy diagrams and there is a woman on the floor, about three yards in front of me. I don't need to remember childhood encyclopaedias to know that there is a pretty vital organ in your skull, not that I seem to have made much use of it over the last four weeks. Anyway, the woman on the floor hasn't got much of a skull left, and no face at all. Which is a shame, because it was a beautiful face. A truly beautiful face.

Next to the woman without her face is a large canvas bag that has been dropped onto the grubby floor, spilling half of its contents, which comprise of a ridiculously large quantity of used, large-denomination banknotes.

I am leaning against a wall in an empty dockside warehouse with a hole in my side trying to remember anatomy diagrams, while a dead woman without her beautiful face and a large bag of cash lie on the floor. That should be enough of a pickle to be in, but there is also a large bear of a man looking down at the girl, the bag and now, at me. And he is holding a shotgun: the same one that took her face off.

I have been in better situations.

I think I need to explain.

CHAPTER ONE

Four weeks and a day ago, I didn't know Frankie McGahern. I also didn't know that this was a state of affairs much to be desired. My life was, admittedly, not without its ups and, more often, downs, and I knew a lot of people that others would cross the street to avoid, but Frankie McGahern was a bright star that was yet to cross my sky.

I knew the name McGahern, of course. Frankie was one of a matching pair: the McGahern Twins. I had heard of Tam McGahern, Frankie's older brother by three minutes, who was a well-known middleweight gangster in Glasgow, one of those whom the big guys left alone, mainly because it was more trouble than it was worth.

The funny thing about the McGahern Twins – depending on how you define funny – is that although they were outwardly identical, the similarity ended there. Unlike his brother, Tam McGahern was smart, hard and truly dangerous. And he was a life-taker. The viciousness he had learned in the back streets and closes of Clydebank had been professionally honed during the war in North Africa and the Middle East. Tam the alley rat had become a decorated Desert Rat.

Frankie McGahern, on the other hand, had evaded military service courtesy of a dodgy lung. While Tam had been away on active service, his less capable brother had been left in charge of the McGahern business. Frankie's nose had been put out of joint when Tam took back full control on his return from the

Middle East. With Tam's brains behind it once more, the little McGahern empire began to grow again.

But while the McGahern operation wasn't to be sneezed at, it didn't make much of an impact on the Three Kings: the tetrarchy of Glasgow crime bosses who controlled almost everything that went on in the city. And who provided, between them, a fair amount of my workload. The Three Kings set the limits for Tam McGahern but other than that left him and his brother alone. Tam was more than a sleeping dog they let lie: he was an evil, rabid, vicious psycho of a dog that they let lie. But on a short chain.

Until eight weeks and two days ago.

Eight weeks and two days ago, Tam McGahern was spending the evening in a grubby flat above a bar in Maryhill servicing a nineteen-year-old girl, no doubt with the direct, no-nonsense disregard for finesse that has made Scotsmen the envy of every Latin lover. McGahern owned the bar below, and, to all intents and purposes, the girl above as well.

At about two thirty in the morning, the coitus was interrupted by someone banging loudly on the downstairs door of the flat. The caller had also, apparently, shouted obscenities through the letterbox, mainly casting doubt on Tam McGahern's dimensional capability to satisfy his companion. McGahern had come running down the stairs, dressed only in a Tootal shirt and monogrammed socks and clutching a kitchen knife. But as he had flung open the door, he had been faced with two large, sharp-suited gentlemen, each with a sawn-off shotgun. Slamming the door shut, McGahern turned to clamber back up the stairs. His callers, however, had shouldered in the door and let McGahern have it with both barrels times two.

A lead enema, they call it in Glasgow.

I found out all of this from Jock Ferguson, a friend I have in the City of Glasgow CID. Well, more of an acquaintance than a friend. And probably more of a contact than an acquaintance. Ferguson also told me that Tam McGahern had still been alive when the first police Wolseley 6/90 patrol car arrived. The two PCs apparently found that the retreating McGahern had been blasted more or less up the backside, and his buttocks and groin were reduced to a bloody mass of raw flesh. All blood and snotters, as my police chums are fond of saying.

In a classic and inspired piece of police intelligence gathering, one of the attending constables asked the injured gangster if he had recognized the men who had shot him. When Tam McGahern asked: 'Am I gonna be okay?', the police constable replied, despite McGahern's balls now being roommates with his Adam's apple: 'Aye . . . of course you will.' At which point McGahern said, 'Then I'll get the bastards myself.' And died.

In much the same way as the story was being told in bars across Glasgow, it was related to me over a whisky and a pie in the Horsehead Bar by my police contact. There was a lot of talk across the city about Tam McGahern's demise; the one big difference was that with killings like this it was usual to whisper the list of names in the frame. But there were no names with this one. Although McGahern had his fair share of enemies, he had removed most of them from Glasgow and many from this life. If Tam had recognized the gunmen at the door, he had taken their identities to his grave.

Everyone knew that none of the Three Kings was involved. There was talk of an outside job. Of an English connection. There was even mention made of Mr Morrison. Mr Morrison, which certainly wasn't his real name, had the same kind of arrangement with the Three Kings that I had: he worked for them all in total confidence and his impartiality and independence was valued. But, unlike me, Mr Morrison didn't investigate things for the Three Kings. He was in the removal business: specifically removing people from this vale of tears. No one knew what Mr Morrison looked like, or anything about him. Some doubted that he even existed, or thought that he was just a bogeyman invented by the Three Kings to keep the rank and file in line. Rumour was that if you ever did come face-to-face with Mr Morrison, then the next countenance you'd be looking at was St Peter's. But even Mr Morrison was out of the frame. The killing had been professional, but too public and messy. Anyway the Three Kings had made it clear Mr Morrison wasn't involved. And that made it official. Nevertheless, the conjecture and rumour continued, but it was just the morbidly excited speculation of minor players in a game they did not understand.

Me, I didn't give a toss. I didn't think of McGahern's murder much at all until four weeks and a day ago, when his brother, Frankie, made my acquaintance.

It was no accidental encounter: in Glasgow, anyone who wants to find me can. Officially, I had rented a one-room office in Gordon Street, but my main regular consulting hours – between seven thirty and nine in the evening – took place at the Horsehead Bar. And that was where Frankie McGahern found me. My first impression of Frankie was of a Savile Row suit hung on the wrong hanger. Despite the expensive tailoring and the chunks of gold jewellery, he had the typical Glasgow look: small, dark, with bad skin and weighed down by the chips on each shoulder.

'You Lennox?' Frankie posed the question as if it were an invitation to a fight.

'I'm Lennox.'

'My name's Frankie McGahern. I want to talk to you.'

'I'm always amenable to conversation,' I said, with my usual disarming smile. In a city where most of the punters you come up against have anything from a razor to a .45 stashed in a handy pocket, it pays to make your smiles disarming.

'Not here.'

'Why not?'

'Don't fuck me about. You know why.'

And I did. More than a few of the bar grazers were working too hard at looking as if they weren't straining the blue-grey cigarette haze for every word exchanged. Many were probably not seeing Frankie, but the ghost of Tam McGahern. The McGaherns were the hottest gossip. Frankie approaching me made me part of that gossip. Which I didn't like. It was, in fact, a surprisingly clumsy and visible thing for Frankie to have done. The joke was that after Tam's shooting, Frankie now answered every knock at the door with: *Who goes there, friend or enema?*

'Where then?'

He handed me a printed business card with the address of a garage in Rutherglen.

'Meet me at the garage tomorrow night at nine thirty.'

'What's this about?'

'I've got a job for you. Your kind of job. Finding out things.'

'There are some things I avoid finding out,' I said. 'What I think you want me to find out is one of them.'

The small shoulders squared inside the Savile Row. The pock-marked skin on his face went tight, like a cat pulling its ears back before leaping on a mouse. Except I was a big mouse. He leaned forward.

'You can decide whether you turn up or not. But if you don't come looking for me, I'll come looking for you. *Capiche?*'

There's something about Italian or any other Latin language spoken with a Scottish accent that I find hilarious. Frankie picked up on my twitch of a smile and he took another step closer to me and to violence.

'Then we have a problem, friend,' I said, turning from the bar to face him square. It was usually at this point that Audie Murphy or Jack Palance reached for their holsters. If there had been a honky-tonk piano in the corner, it would have stopped playing. As it was, our little dance had muted the talk around us. McGahern's small eyes seemed to become even smaller. Rat small. Hard and bright with hate. He suddenly seemed to sense we had an audience and looked less sure of himself.

'We're not finished with this, Lennox.'

'Oh, I think we are.'

'My money's as good as any of the Three fucking Kings' . . . as good as anyone's. You'll do this job for me. I'm not asking you. I'm telling. Be there tomorrow night.' He turned abruptly and walked out.

I ordered another whisky and weakened it with water from the brass tap on the counter. I realized I still had McGahern's card in my hand and slipped it into my jacket pocket. Big Bob the barman leaned Popeye forearms swirled with blue-grey tattoos on the bar.

'Yon's a bad wee gobshite.' He nodded in the direction of McGahern's wake through the smoke-thick air. 'You would maybe have been better doing whatever it was he wanted you to do. Less trouble.'

I laughed. 'He wants me to find out who snuffed his brother. Walking that line would bring me more trouble than he's capable of bringing. All of Glasgow knows that Frankie's nothing without Tam. And I'm not interested in messing with gangland's process of natural selection.'

Big Bob shrugged. 'Just watch your back, Lennox. McGahern's a treacherous wee rat.'

*

Things tended to get a bit crazy at chucking-out time. Scotland's Presbyterian licensing laws encouraged a culture of against-the-clock drinking. Not that Glaswegians needed much encouraging. And when men who have drunk too much too quickly are thrust out into the night air full of murderous cheer, it's like an explosive chemical reaction. So, after another couple of whiskies, I hit the street about nine thirty to get home before the raging began.

Glasgow was inky sleek with rain that had stopped falling. The Second City of the Empire was a black city, its impressive buildings made shadows with the dark grime of its toiling; there were children here who thought that the natural colour of stone was black. The rain, which was heavy and frequent, never washed the city but oil-rag smeared it.

I saw the black Humber parked across the street and a couple of hundred yards back. Oh, Frankie, I thought, why do we have to dance? I made as if I hadn't noticed the Humber and started to walk towards my Austin Atlantic. When I reached it, I looked across again. The Humber hadn't moved.

There are some things you learn in war that stick with you. Being aware that an attack doesn't always come from the direction you expect is one. Frankie, who unlike his brother hadn't served in the war, made the mistake of taking a step to the side to improve the angle of his assault while still in the shadow of the doorway behind me. He was as predictable as he was clumsy and I recognized the bright arcing flash in the streetlight as a razor. You don't fuck about when someone comes at you with a razor, so I spun round and kicked him in the centre of his chest. Hard. I heard the air pulse out of him and swung the leather sap I always carried in my jacket pocket. It caught him on the side of the head. I swung the sap again and deadened his wrist and the razor dropped with a clatter.

I knew it was already over, but I was pissed at Frankie for not letting it go when I told him I wasn't interested. I pocketed my sap, grabbed a handful of Brylcreem-slick hair, and snap-punched him hard and square in the face. Three times, rapid succession. The punches hurt my hand, but I felt the cartilage of his nose crack with the impact of the second blow and his expensive shirt turned black-red in the streetlight. I punched him again, this time on the mouth to split his lips. I was done. I pushed him against the wall, wiped my hands on his Savile Row, and let him slide down the wall and into unconsciousness.

'Do we have a problem here, gentlemen?'

I turned to see that the black Humber had drawn alongside. The passenger was a huge, thick-set man in his fifties, dressed in a grey suit and with a wide-brimmed hat tight over bristle-cropped white hair. McNab.

'No problem at all, Superintendent.' I took a deep breath and smiled charmingly. Not charmingly enough to stop McNab and his uniformed driver getting out of the unmarked Humber. McNab looked down from an altitude of six-and-a-half feet at Frankie's crumpled figure.

'Well, well. The brother of the recently deceased Mr McGahern. Now what, Lennox, could you possibly have to do with a wee piece of shite like this?'

'You know him? I'm afraid I don't . . . I was just passing and I noticed he needed some assistance. Think he's had a dram or two too many . . . must've fallen over.'

'Funny that . . . he seems to have broken the fall with his nose.' McNab leaned down and turned Frankie's face to the light. His nose had an ugly break in it, right enough. And a welt of black-red blood creased his swollen lip. But, there again, Frankie had been no matinee idol beforehand.

'It happens, Superintendent. I'm sure in your career in the City of Glasgow Police you've encountered many such unfortunate accidents in the cell block.'

McNab took a step towards me and eclipsed Glasgow. He was silent for a couple of seconds, obviously a practised intimidation technique. I tried not to show how good he was at it. Thankfully, his attention was drawn back to Frankie, who started to make groaning and gurgling noises. The uniformed constable hauled him upright.

'What happened, McGahern? You want to make a complaint?'

Frankie looked at me with a dull, unfocused hate, then shook his head.

'On your way, Lennox,' said McNab. 'But make sure you stay easy to find.'

'It's good to know that an officer of your experience and rank is patrolling Glasgow's streets, Superintendent.'

McNab glowered.

'Goodnight, Mr McNab.'

I got back to my flat about ten thirty, poured myself a Canadian Club and watched the trams, the odd car and the throngs of pedestrians on Great Western Road. I was not happy. I'd given Frankie McGahern more of a slap than I should have: maybe he wasn't the gangster his brother Tam had been, but he was connected enough and dangerous enough for me to have to worry.

But there was something else that was getting to me. Detective Superintendent Willie McNab. Twenty-five years' service with the City of Glasgow Police, two sons in the force, prominent figure in the Masonic and Orange Orders. And a complete bastard of the first water. McNab had started his police career as one of Sillitoe's Cossacks, the mounted gang-busters created in the nineteen thirties by the then City of Glasgow Chief Constable, Percy Sillitoe. Sillitoe was now, rumour had it, the head of MI5. In the post-war world of suspicion and mistrust, Sillitoe had become a persecutor of communists and foreigners instead of Glasgow razormen. But back in the late thirties, Sillitoe's Cossacks had been as notoriously violent as the razor gangs they had fought.

So Willie McNab had begun his career fracturing the skulls of members of the Bridgeton Billyboys, the Norman Conks and the Gorbals Beehive Gang. Since then he had worked his way up to second-in-command of Glasgow's detective force.

He wasn't someone you routinely encountered patrolling the streets of Glasgow.

McNab had been there for a reason and the only reason I could think of was Frankie McGahern. Shit. The one thing I had spent the evening trying to avoid was getting involved in whatever gangland squabble was behind Tam McGahern's death. Now I had been caught smacking his twin brother around.

I drank two more whiskies and lay on my bed smoking with the lights out and the curtains open, watching the shapes cut on the ceiling by the streetlamps and passing car headlights. I felt bad about the hiding I'd given McGahern. Not bad for him. Bad for me. And not because of the trouble it could bring. I felt bad because I had enjoyed it. Because that was who I had become.

Post-war me.

To start with I thought it had been a thunderstorm that had woken me up. I switched on the bedside lamp, checked my watch and saw that it was just before three a.m., and recognized the thunder as the flat-fisted thudding of a copper's knock. I started to cough the rheumy cough that always came when I awoke, grumbled something obscene and unlocked the door. I didn't get a chance to count how many of them were outside on the landing before the fist that had been knocking on the door knocked on my face, sending me crashing back into my flat and onto the floor.

The City of Glasgow Police has a history of recruiting from the Highlands. Highlanders tend to be tall and hefty, towering above the average Glaswegian, although their impressive physical stature tends not to extend to their intellects. Ideal qualifications for a copper. Highlanders also have a pleasant, lilting accent, and the red-haired bear who hauled me to my feet seemed to serenade me with foul oaths. Another copper twisted my hands behind my back and snapped shut the bars of a set of handcuffs. I felt sick from sudden wakefulness and the taste of blood in my mouth. The large frame of McNab filled my doorway.

'What the fuck is this all about, McNab?'

McNab nodded to a plainclothesman, who swung an eight-inch sap at my head and my sudden wakefulness ceased to be a problem.

CHAPTER TWO

The large police cell I came to in had the regulation smell of disinfectant, musty blankets and stale piss. I found myself sitting on a chair, my hands still cuffed behind me. I was dressed in just my vest and trousers and either I had been caught in a sudden downpour on the way to the station or someone had thrown water over me to wake me up.

McNab sat on the tiled bunk of the cell. There was a younger, mean-looking cop standing beside me with an empty bucket. His big farm-boy face was ruddy from too much of his childhood spent in a Hebridean field looking into the wind. He was jacketless, had his sleeves rolled up and his collar loosened. As if anticipating some hard physical work. I resigned myself to a tough beating.

'Exactly what is it I'm supposed to confess to?' I asked McNab, but watched the other cop as he wrapped a soaked piece of cloth around the knuckles of his right hand.

'Don't play funny buggers with me, Lennox. You know why you're here.' He punctuated his statement with a nod at the younger cop and a fist slammed into the nape of my neck. There's an art to beating a confession out of a suspect. The neck blow is an old favourite: it causes intense pain in the head, and for weeks after you're reminded of it every time you turn your head, but it doesn't leave a bruise that's visible to a judge or jury. The wet rag around the fist further inhibits bruising. Mainly to the hands of the hard-working and underpaid public servant administering the beating. McNab said something, then waited till I shook the bells out of my ears before repeating it.

'Why did you kill Frankie McGahern?'

I stared at McNab in confusion. 'What are you talking about? He wasn't dead. You were there. You spoke to him after he came round.'

Another nod. More lightning in my skull. Bells in my ears.

'But then you came back later to finish the job. I'm surprised at you, Lennox. No finesse. You really did turn him into mince. We had a probationer puking all over the place. What did you use, Lennox? Just the tyre iron?'

I looked at McNab for a moment. He kept me fixed with small, grey eyes set in a too-broad face. I couldn't tell whether he really believed that I had killed McGahern or not, but the beating I was getting suggested he thought I knew more than I was telling. Which was a problem, because I hadn't a clue what he was talking about. I told him so in fluent Anglo-Saxon and got it in the neck. Again. The pain made me feel sick and I fought back the urge to retch.

'Your neck sore, Lennox?' McNab stood up and took a position that suggested I was in for a game of doubles. I looked down at his feet. Brown brogues, polished. Heavy tweed trouser cuffs pressed knife-sharp. 'Well your neck won't bother you after they break it dropping you through the hatch at Barlinnie. That's two murders we're looking at you for. A matching McGahern pair.'

'I didn't know Tam McGahern at all, and I didn't know Frankie until he introduced himself to me in the Horsehead Bar last night.'

'What did he want?'

'He didn't say. Mainly because I didn't let him say. But he did tell me it was my kind of job. Finding things out. I reckoned he wanted me to look into his brother's death.'

'That's your kind of job is it, Lennox? Solving murders? I was under the impression it was ours.'

'Some people can't come to you. Frankie McGahern, for example. But whatever he wanted me to find out, I told him to take a long walk off a short pier. That's why he was waiting for me outside. Hurt pride. What I can't work out is what you were doing there. You must have been watching him.'

'I don't answer to the likes of you, Lennox. All that's important is for you to tell us why you went back to McGahern's place and finished the job you started.'

'I don't even know where McGahern's place is.'

'Oh no?' McNab reached into some tweed and produced the card Frankie had given me. And I had forgotten about. 'We found this at your place. In your jacket.'

'I had Frankie's card because he gave it to me in the Horsehead Bar. Ask Big Bob, the barman. Anyway, it doesn't have his address on it. Just some garage—'

'That's where we found McGahern. In the repair shop of his garage. His head pulped with a tyre iron.'

'You got the weapon? There must be prints.'

'No prints. You wore gloves.'

I gave a sigh. 'We both know you don't think I did it. And I *know* I didn't. What's this all about?'

'Don't tell me what I think.' McNab grabbed a handful of my hair and snapped my head back. The sudden jerk sent another pulse of pain through my neck. He pushed his big moon-face into mine and bathed me in stale Player's and Bell's breath. 'Why don't *you* tell *me* what it was all about, Lennox? Frankie work out that it was you who killed his brother? Or is it about the money?'

I said nothing. McNab let go of my hair and I waited for the next blow. It didn't come. McNab sat back down on the bunk and indicated the cell door with a nod of his head. The shirt-sleeved copper unwrapped his fist and left.

'Tea break?' I asked with a smile.

The heavy took a step back into the cell but slunk out when McNab shook his head. After he was gone, McNab unlocked my handcuffs. He took a packet of Player's out and lit up, sitting back down on the bunk. We were getting pally.

'I don't like you, Lennox,' he said without malice, as if commenting on the current weather. Maybe we weren't getting pally. 'I don't like anything about you. The people you know. The way you stick your nose where it's not wanted. I don't even like the Yank way you talk.' He picked up the buff file that had been sitting next to him on the bunk. 'I've been looking into your background. Nothing fits with you. A Canadian. An ex-officer. Rich parents. Fancy private school. And then you turn up here. Why should someone like you want to live here and mix with the kind of people you do?'

'I was born here. But brought up in Canada. My father was from Glasgow.' I was out of wisecracks. I had a past that was best left buried and I didn't like McNab rooting about in it.

The truth was that I'd been demobilized in the United Kingdom and handed a ship ticket to Halifax, Nova Scotia. But coming out of the war was kind of like coming out of prison and, as I stood blinking in the cold daylight, Glasgow was waiting for me, like a dark and brooding thug hanging on a street corner. And here I was, eight years later, in the Second City of the British Empire. Glasgow suited me: it offered a dense, dark comfort. The kind of city where you could hide in the crowds. Even from yourself.

'There was a bit of trouble, as far as I can see,' said McNab, thumbing through the file. 'You came a ball-hair away from being court-martialled.'

'I was honourably discharged.' My mouth was dry and I felt sick. My neck and head throbbed. McNab was riling me and I wanted to smack his big, round, stupid face. But, of course, I couldn't.

'Only because they couldn't nail anything on you. It's funny ... the army were reluctant to hand over any information on you, but when the Military Police found out that I was going to be able to nail you with something, they became very cooperative. The redcaps don't like you much, do they, Lennox?'

'What can I say? You can't be popular with everyone.'

'Something to do with the black market in the British Zone in Germany. Selling army medical supplies to civilians. Quinine to prostitutes for abortions, penicillin for syphilis and gonorrhoea. Nice business.'

I didn't say anything.

'Aye,' continued McNab, 'a nice business indeed. But the rumour is that you fell out with your German partner – who ended up floating face down in Hamburg harbour.'

'That had nothing to do with me.'

'Just like Frankie McGahern's death has got nothing to do with you.'

'Just like.'

'And you say you never met Tam McGahern? Not even in the army during the war?'

I frowned. My confusion was genuine. 'Different armies. Different wars, for that matter. I heard that Tam McGahern was a Desert Rat.'

There was a pause. McNab and I stared at each other. For such a big man, he was fastidiously neat. Crisp white shirt beneath the brown tweed, burgundy tie perfectly knotted. I was unshaven, sitting in a wet vest, trousers and no shoes. McNab's neatness was a psychological weapon and the only way I could counter it was to focus on the angry red line where his perfect collar had rubbed the skin on his neck. There was such a thing as too much starch.

'You asked me about money. What did you mean?' I asked.

'I ask the questions, Lennox. You answer them,' he replied without anger. I laughed at the movie line cliché and managed to restore McNab's anger. 'Okay, smart-arse, the money that went missing when Tam McGahern was murdered. Several thousand if the rumours are to be believed.'

McNab dropped the butt of his cigarette onto the floor and crushed it under the toe of his brogue, twisting it into the concrete in a 'tea break's over' kind of way. 'Now I'm going to have to ask Fraser to join us again,' he said, almost apologetically, which disturbed me more. 'You're not telling me everything. There's more to this than you hurting Frankie McGahern's pride. He came at you with a razor. And personally, not one of his boys. Frankie may not have been half the man his brother was, but he was still in charge of a sizeable team. For him to want to deal with you personally tells me that you two had something more going on. What you're telling me doesn't make sense.'

I could see his point. I had expected trouble with Frankie McGahern. But it had turned uglier than I had expected, quicker than I had expected. There again, in Glasgow, things turned ugly all the time, fast and for no good reason. McNab waited a moment for me to answer. When I didn't he made his way to the cell door to summon back the fine farmer's lad with the sore knuckles.

'Wait . . .' I said, not really knowing what to say next. 'I'm giving you all that I've got. It doesn't make sense to me either, but I'm telling you the truth. I didn't have anything to do with either of the McGaherns before Frankie came up to me in the bar last night.'

'I find that difficult to believe, considering the circles you move in, Lennox.'

'I don't move in any "circles", Superintendent. My work means that I have contact with some characters – including some coppers, I have to say – that other people would cross the street to avoid. But Frankie McGahern was not one of my contacts. Nor was his brother.'

Another pause. McNab didn't call in his thug. But he didn't sit back down again either.

'Anything more I tell you,' I continued, 'is just going to be invented to avoid a beating.'

Another copper appeared in the cell passage. I recognized him. I tried to suppress any expression of relief, but at that moment I felt like the last survivor of the wagon train when he hears the bugle call of approaching cavalry.

'What is it, Inspector?' McNab made it clear he was annoyed by the interruption. The detective in the hall looked pointedly at me, at my wet vest and naked feet, before answering.

'I've spoken with Mr Lennox's landlady, sir. She confirms that he arrived home about ten fifteen and didn't leave again until we came and arrested him.'

The collar-roughened skin on McNab's neck reddened more. There's nothing more infuriating than being told what you knew all along but had conveniently and indefinitely filed in pending.

'As far as she can tell . . .' said McNab. 'She would have been asleep.'

'She says there's no way he could have left the building without her hearing. Says she's prepared to stand up in court and say so.'

McNab's collarline blemish was subsumed into the general angry red that bloomed across his thick neck. He glowered at the younger detective for a moment before turning to me and telling me I could go.

Jock Ferguson was waiting for me in the reception area of the station. McNab's reluctant release of me hadn't extended to a ride home, and I was relieved when Ferguson handed me a shirt, my suit jacket and some shoes.

'No socks?' I asked and Ferguson shrugged.

Jock Ferguson was the more-of-a-contact-than-acquaintance-than-friend who had first told me about Tam McGahern's demise. He was one of the cops that I had dealt with over the last five years. He was about my age, thirty-five, but looked older, as did many men who had passed from adolescence straight into middle age during the war. Maybe that was how I looked to other people. Ferguson was smarter than the average copper and knew it. Coppers generally like things to be simple and straight-forward, and Jock Ferguson was neither. I got the feeling that he had always been something of an outsider in the force. The brains would have done that all right. I also recognized him as someone who was haunted by the person he had once been. Maybe that was why he bothered with me. I couldn't work it out otherwise.

'Thanks for that,' I said. 'That was all getting a little too cosy.'

Ferguson didn't answer me and I saw that we had the full cheerless attention of the Station-Sergeant who was leaning his stripes on the counter. Ferguson led me out of the station and into the street.

'I'll give you a lift home,' he said. Glasgow was grey-black in a sulky dawn and I felt its chill breath around my naked ankles. 'Wait here and I'll bring the car around.'

'What's going on with the McGahern thing?' I asked as we drove in Ferguson's Morris through the city. 'McNab was digging for something. And he was pissed off that he was digging in the wrong spot.'

Ferguson offered me a cigarette. I shook my head and he lit his own. 'You know this city,' he said. 'Two, maybe three million people crammed into it and it's still a village. Everyone knows who's who, who does what . . . and who to. But the McGahern killing . . .' Ferguson corrected himself, 'the McGahern *killings* have shaken everyone up. No one knows who did them or why. McNab's been under pressure to get it cleared up. Big pressure, from above. And the problem with pressure from above is that it tends to continue downwards.'

'I know,' I said, 'right onto the back of my neck.'

'But McNab hasn't a clue. That's why he's clutching at straws. It's just that you were unlucky enough to be one of those straws.'

'You any ideas?' We were the only car on the streets and we passed a horse and cart laden with coal, and a stream of flat-caps cycling into their early shift. I turned my head a little and was reminded with a jolt of pain of my encounter with McNab's ruddy-cheeked farmhand.

'Me?' Ferguson snorted. 'No. My ignorance is truly blissful. I'm trying to stay out of this one. Just like you. More trouble than it's worth.'

We didn't say much more until Ferguson pulled up outside my digs. As I got out he leaned across the passenger seat.

'Lennox . . . I'd lie low for a while if I were you. If you've got any ideas about sticking your nose in, forget them.'

I watched Ferguson's Morris head along Great Western Road. I trusted him as much as I could any copper. So why was it that something nagged at me? And why did I feel that he had just delivered the punchline for McNab?

*

My digs were in the upstairs of a reasonably substantial Victorian villa on Great Western Road. I shared the main door with my landlady, Fiona White, who lived with her kids downstairs and it would have been she who had admitted the police in the wee small hours.

She was waiting for me when I opened the front door. 'You look like you could do with a cup of tea,' she said, unsmiling.

I followed her into the kitchen of her flat. She stood leaning against the kitchen counter, her arms crossed.

'You look rough,' she said without solicitude. 'Mr Lennox, I can't have the police knocking on my door at all hours of the night.'

'You want me to leave, Mrs White?'

'I didn't say that. But this is a decent neighbourhood. I've already had a stream of neighbours at my door asking what was wrong. They've already got you down as an axe-murderer.'

'How do you know I'm not?'

'Presumably they wouldn't have let you go.' She lit a cigarette for herself and threw the packet onto the kitchen table. 'Help yourself. I've got my children to think about, Mr Lennox. This is not the kind of thing I want them exposed to.'

'I was a witness, Mrs White. Not a suspect.'

'I wasn't aware that the police dragged witnesses semi-conscious from their homes in the middle of the night.'

'It took them a while to work out that I was a witness.' I sipped my tea. It was sweet and hot and eased the throbbing in my head. I wasn't in the mood for the third degree from my landlady too.

A baker's van sounded its horn out on the street and she excused herself in a 'we haven't finished' way, grabbed her purse and trotted out. I watched her go. She was slim, maybe a little too slim. She was an attractive woman, with Kate Hepburn cheeks and eyes and would have been prettier had it not been for the perpetual wraith of sad tiredness that haunted her face. Fiona White would have been no more than thirty-five or -six, but looked older.

I had grown attached to the sad little White family, who had acknowledged that father and husband lay at the bottom of the Atlantic, yet still seemed to be waiting for his return from a war long-ended. I drank my tea.

'So . . . would you rather that I left?' I asked again when she returned.

'I don't want this kind of thing to happen again. That's all I'm saying for now, Mr Lennox. If it does, then I think you should look elsewhere for somewhere to stay.'

'Fair enough.' I drained my cup and stood up. 'It won't, Mrs White. By the way, thanks for telling the police I was here last night. That saved me a lot of . . . awkwardness, you could say.'

'I only told them the truth.'

The police had been busy in my digs and it took me a half-hour of housekeeping to get things back into order. My flat was really the two upstairs bedrooms and a bathroom of the original house layout. They were good-sized rooms and had big sash windows that let in a lot of light and a view along Great Western Road. The biggest of the bedrooms had been converted into a living room-cum-kitchen. Mrs White was fair with rent, but it was still pricey.

The first thing I checked was the copy of H.G. Wells's *The Shape of Things to Come* I had jammed in the middle of my bookshelves. I opened it and made sure that the hollowed-out section was still full of large, white, crisp Bank of England five-pound notes. It was. My *Niebelungsgold* from Germany, to which I'd been able to add during my time in Glasgow. I had a lot of books and it had seemed a pretty safe hiding place: policemen tend not to be the most literary bunch. The next thing was to check that the floor beneath the bed hadn't been disturbed. I lifted up the section that I had cut out and reached in underneath the floorboards. My hand cupped the heavy, hard object wrapped in oilcloth.

Still there. If I needed it.

CHAPTER THREE

I slept most of that day, but the next I rose early, had a bath, shaved and put on one of my smarter dark suits. I needed to feel clean and fresh. The pain in my neck still nagged at me and I borrowed a couple of sachets of aspirin from Mrs White. But something else was nagging at me and I couldn't quite pin it down. The papers were full of Frankie McGahern's murder and I had sensed an even deeper chill in my landlady's demeanour.

Petrol rationing had ended two years before but I'd gotten into the habit of leaving the car at home if I was just going into the office. I took the tram into town and unlocked the door of my one-room office in Gordon Street. I had often thought about dumping my office, seeing as most of my business was conducted from the Horsehead Bar, but it made sense to keep it for legal and tax reasons. It also provided me with the odd missing person, divorce case or factory theft case: some legitimate sleaze to show the coppers and the revenue.

It was my office that disturbed me most.

Whereas the police had gone through my flat with their usual ham-fistedness, there was no outward sign that someone had been in my office, far less searched it. But I knew they had. The angle of the 'phone on my desk. The position of the inkwell. The fact that my chair was pushed squarely and neatly into the desk. This was a truly professional job. Whoever did this was skilled in searching without detection. Not something the police had to worry about.

After going through every drawer and every file, I was certain nothing had been removed from the office. I checked the door, paying particular attention to the keyhole. No sign of forced entry or even of someone fiddling with the lock. And I had the only set of keys. Whoever had done this was good. Very good. And I had no doubt that if it had been them who'd gone through my home then they would have found both my nest egg and my stash hidden beneath the floorboards. But I had the feeling I wasn't dealing with common thieves and in any case it would be much more difficult to get in and out of my place while Mrs White was in.

I tried to put it out of my mind and focused on the missing-person case I'd been working on. Jobs like these were essential: a client who was legitimate and who gave and asked for receipts meant I had something convincing to show the tax inspector. At least fifty per cent of my clients didn't like to trouble the taxman and, I have to admit, I liked to ease his workload a little myself. The case I had spent the last week on was that of the missing wife of a Glasgow businessman. She was young, pretty and lively and he was middle-aged, paunchy, with bad teeth and definitely no Robert Taylor to look at. It was a clear mismatch based on money and I knew I wasn't going to give the client the happy end he was looking for.

I decided to focus my attention on the missing wife. Maybe if I pretended the whole McGahern thing wasn't there it would go away. I 'phoned the husband, John Andrews, at his office and arranged to meet him at his home at six that evening.

Glasgow was a sleeves-rolled city. For a hundred years its sole reason for being had been to serve as the Empire's factory. The industrial revolution had been born here with a scream of metal and thundering mills. Britain's mercantile and military ships were built here. The vast machines that powered the British Empire were assembled here. The fuel to drive those machines was hewn from the earth here. Glasgow was a city where pretensions of gentility rang false, where the villa of the mogul had to rub grubby shoulders with the tenement. Bearsden lay to the north of the city and dressed itself up as Surrey, yet was within soot-flecked spitting distance of run-down, violent Maryhill. John Andrews's home was set back from the sweep of the street in a large, wooded garden. I didn't fully understand what it was Andrews did; it was one of these occupations that were dismissed with a vague generalization: 'import-export, that kind of thing'. Whatever it was he did, it paid well. Ardbruach House, Andrews's home, was three floors of Victorian villa, built as much to impress as to accommodate. The truth was I had nothing new to tell Andrews, mainly because I had dropped the ball on his wife's case with all that had happened since my encounter with Frankie McGahern.

Andrews had been brusque on the 'phone. He didn't like me 'phoning his office, despite the fake name and company he had given me as a code for his receptionist. But when I pulled up at his mansion, he was waiting for me at the door with what looked like a practised smile. The kind that quivers at the corners.

Andrews was a small, tubby man with whitish-grey hair and a wattle of fat beneath his weak jaw. He wore a fresh carnation in the buttonhole of his sixty-guinea suit. When he shook my hand, his fleshy palm felt moist. 'I'm sorry you've had a wasted journey, Mr Lennox. I didn't get a chance to call you. Mystery solved!' He made a big shrug with his small shoulders and it was as fake as the smile. I was getting all kinds of bad feelings about this. And after the McGahern episode, I could have done with something straightforward.

CRAIG RUSSELL | 29

'Mr Andrews, is there something wrong?'

'Wrong?' He laughed but didn't hold my gaze. 'Quite the contrary. I'm afraid this has all been a terrible misunderstanding. Lillian telephoned me this afternoon, not long after you and I had spoken. She was called on at short notice to visit her sister in Edinburgh. Her sister took ill very suddenly you see. Lillian had left me a note all along, but it had slipped behind the bureau. It was only when she 'phoned that she realized that I'd been so worried.'

'Oh, I see,' I said. He was talking nonsense, or as the locals were wont to call it, shite.

'Here, Mr Lennox.' Andrews made no attempt to invite me in: instead he took a cheque from his pocket and handed it to me. It was for much more than I was due. 'I feel guilty about your wasted effort. I hope this covers the inconvenience.'

This was so wrong. But I pocketed the cheque.

'Do you mind if I have a look at the note your wife left?' I asked.

Andrews's relief faltered and he looked flustered. 'The note? Why? Oh . . . I'm afraid I threw it away after I found it. There seemed little point in hanging on to it.'

'I see.' I lifted my hat an inch. 'Well, I'm glad things are settled. Goodbye Mr Andrews.'

Something flickered in his expression. A faint doubt, or hope. Then it was gone.

'Goodbye, Mr Lennox.'

Maybe it was because I was at a loose end that I didn't go straight home. There are more ways than 'import-export' to make the kind of money to afford a home in Bearsden. I headed north through Glasgow's leafy suburb and turned into another lengthy drive through manicured bushes and trees. But when

I reached the top, it wasn't a short, fleshy businessman who stood outside the small mansion. Instead there was a huddle of thugs in cheap suits, maliciously eyeing my procession up the drive.

'And what can I do for you?' The Glasgow accent was as thick as the macassar on the hair of the heavy who came over to the car window. He was dressed in tight drainpipe trousers and a mid-thigh-length jacket. It was the latest fashion, apparently. It was supposed to look 'Edwardian' and I'd heard followers of it called themselves 'Teddy Boys'.

'I'd like to see Mr Sneddon.'

'Oh you would, would you? Do you have an appointment?' He pronounced every consonant of 'appointment' as if he'd been practising it.

'No. Tell him Lennox is here. I want to talk to him.'

'What about?'

'That's between me and Mr Sneddon.'

The goon in the drainpipes opened the car door and led me into Sneddon's mansion. Like some thug parody of a butler, he told me to wait in the mock-Gothic hall. Sneddon let me stew for half an hour before he emerged from the snooker room. He was making a point. I was now at his pleasure and could not leave without his permission.

Willie Sneddon was one of the Three Kings who ran Glasgow. The Bearsden mock-baronialism that surrounded us may have been Sneddon's castle, but his kingdom sat on the South Side. He was not a particularly big man, and he was expensively and surprisingly tastefully dressed. But at the very first glance you could tell that this man was all about violence. His build was stocky but not heavy. Muscular. Sinewy, as if he had been woven from rope. Added to that, someone had in the distant past permanently creased his right cheek with a razor.

'What the fuck do you want, Lennox?' He fired the greeting over his shoulder as he led me into a study lined with books he would never and probably could never read. I was not invited to but I sat down anyway.

'I had a run in with Frankie McGahern,' I said, lighting a cigarette.

'I heard it was him that had a run in with you,' answered Sneddon with perfect Govan grammar. 'You kill him, Lennox?'

'I'm in the clear for that. Someone else did him. Who, is the big question. And that's what I want to talk to you about. I wanted to ask you if you knew anything about what happened to his brother.'

'You accusing?'

'No, Mr Sneddon. Not accusing, just asking. I can't see any reason why you would have Tam McGahern killed. Or Frankie. But no one knows this town like you . . .'

'Oh aye? I suppose you've not talked to the other Kings?'

'As a matter of fact I haven't. I came to you first.' It was the truth and he knew it. He could check it out easily enough. Although he tried to hide it, I could tell he liked the idea that I somehow rated him above the other two Kings. I failed to mention that I just happened to be in the neighbourhood.

'I know fuck-all about Tam McGahern's killing. Of course I wouldn't tell you if I did and normally I wouldn't give a fuck if you believed me or not. But I really don't know and I don't like not knowing. I don't need to tell you that knowledge is power in this town. I'm not the kind of man that appreciates the lack of either. Who's paying you to look into this?'

'No one.'

Sneddon raised an eyebrow dubiously. This could easily turn into another beating for information I didn't have.

'I mean it. No one. I think that Frankie McGahern wanted

me to find out who killed his brother but I wasn't interested. That's why things turned ugly. I've been warned off by the police. I guess I'm contrary that way, but when someone tries to warn me off with a beating, I tend to get stubborn.'

Sneddon nodded slowly, a cold appraising glint in his eyes. He seemed to make up his mind about something.

'Well, you're being paid now. You find out who snuffed Tam and Frankie and I'll pay you.'

'Like I said, I'm looking into this for myself—'

'Not any more.' Sneddon's tone informed me that the discussion was over. He reached into a drawer of his walnut desk and pulled out a dense, neat roll of fivers. 'This'll keep you going. There's a hundred there. I'll pay you another two hundred if you deliver the name to me first.'

I took the money. 'You know I can't guarantee I'll succeed. I never guarantee results. You know that.'

'Then I'll be a hundred quid poorer. But you only get the other two hundred if you deliver the name.'

'Okay,' I said as if I had a choice in the matter. 'Thanks. I'll see what I can find out. But I'll have to talk to the other two Kings. Things may get complicated.'

'We'll cross that bridge when you come to it, Lennox. Just remember who's paying you. You find out something, I hear it first. And if I say no one else hears about it, that's the way it'll be.'

'Fair enough,' I said. 'Maybe we can start with you telling me something more about Tam and Frankie. I don't know much about them at all. Never had to come across them.' I rubbed the back of my neck, remembering how difficult it had been to convince McNab of that fact.

'Not much to tell,' said Sneddon. 'Couple of wee Fenians on the make. You know the type: one generation away from shiteing in a Galway peat bog. They were trying to carve themselves a wee empire. More Tam than Frankie. Tam was hard, ambitious and sharp as a tack. Frankie was just . . .' Sneddon frowned as he sought an appropriate comparative. 'Frankie was just a wee cunt.'

'I would have thought that they'd have divided the action up equally, being twins and all.'

'Aye, you would have thought that. But the brains weren't divided equally. Tam and Frankie were only identical twins in the way they looked. Like I said, Tam was the brains . . . and the muscle . . . of the operation. He was a clever wee fucker, by all accounts. Frankie wasn't. Tam ran things and looked after Frankie. Threw him scraps from the table.'

'So they were close?'

'How the fuck am I supposed to know? Not my type of people, if you catch my drift. But I did hear one story about how Frankie leaned on some whore who was operating her business independently. Tam found out and gave Frankie a real hiding. But then there's another story about how Tam paid a fucking fortune to have some nobody take a rap and do six months inside for Frankie. Just so Frankie didn't have a record.'

'Frankie's got no criminal record?'

'None.' Sneddon lit a cigarette without offering me one. 'Neither of them has. Tam because he was smart. Frankie because it was as if Tam went out of his way to keep Frankie's record clean. But, like I say, he wasn't above giving Frankie a hiding.'

'What operations did they run?' I asked.

'Three bars – the Highlander, the Imperial and the Westfield – and a couple of bookies; they did a few half-decent hold-ups and they ran security for a whore-house. And they had a small-time protection thing going on. But, like I say, Tam McGahern was a cunning wee shite. He always had some kind of scam going on. We tried to keep track of what he was up to but he always was too slippery.'

'Okay,' I said and stood up, lifting my hat from Sneddon's ornate desk. 'I'll see what I can find out. But it may be tricky. A lot of people are nervous about the whole McGahern thing. Reluctant to talk.'

Sneddon leaned to one side in his chair and shouted 'Twinkletoes!' past me and out into the hall.

Suddenly the light in the study dimmed, as if the door had been closed. I knew, without turning, that it hadn't: it was just that Twinkletoes McBride was standing in the door frame.

'You've met Twinkletoes before, haven't you Lennox?'

'Not in a professional capacity.' I smiled weakly and turned to nod a greeting to the beast in the doorway.

'Hello, Mr Lennox,' Twinkletoes said in his troll baritone, smiled and sat down on the chair by the door. He was a friendly cuss. Not too bright. Read comic books. Occasionally quoted from the *Reader's Digest*. Tortured people for Sneddon.

'This is going to be a tough nut to crack, Lennox,' said Sneddon. 'People aren't keen to talk. I want you to use Twinkletoes if that happens.'

'Listen, Mr Sneddon . . . that's not really my style. No offence, Twinkletoes.'

Twinkletoes McBride sat smiling silently, a dark mass of friendly menace in the corner. Conversation was not his strong point: his reputation was for getting other people to talk. The origin of the epithet 'Twinkletoes' lay in his methods as Sneddon's torturer. These involved the removal of the victim's socks and shoes, the use of a pair of bolt cutters and McBride's recitation, with a surprising use of ironic humour, of 'this little piggy went to market'. Apparently Twinkletoes would leave the big toe of each foot until last.

'I give them the chance to talk before I do the big toe,' the normally laconic McBride had once explained to me. 'Unless Mr Sneddon has said he doesn't want them to walk again. You can't balance without your big toe, you know.'

'That's a really interesting fact,' I had said.

'Aye ...' Twinkletoes's vast, battered moon of a face had shone with an almost child-like pride in his learning. 'I read it in the Reader's Digest.'

I smiled to myself on the way out of Sneddon's mock-baronial, mock-Gothic, mock-respectable mansion. I had managed to become unemployed and employed within an hour. And between John Andrews's cheque and Sneddon's bundle of fivers, I was already two hundred pounds richer.

The only down side was that I hadn't a clue where to start looking, I had the City of Glasgow Police breathing down my already bruised neck, someone highly professional had given my office a thorough going over, and the Neanderthal chiropodist from hell was shadowing me.

CHAPTER FOUR

The first thing I set about doing was finding out who the girl was that Tam McGahern had been giving the seeing-to immediately before his untimely demise. No name had been mentioned. Normally I would have bought Jock Ferguson a pint in the Horsehead Bar and teased it out of him. But every time I thought about his parting shot in the car, it was like touching an electric fence around the police. It was one source – usually my most important and reliable – that I wouldn't be able to use this time. I had no choice but to dive right on in there and go round to McGahern's bar in Maryhill.

The Highlander Bar was surprisingly free of any cultural reference to the Highlands or Highlanders. No grand paintings on the walls of 'Stag at Bay' or 'The Bonnie Prince'. Nor was there a comprehensive array of the fine single malts of Scotland behind the bar. No aroma of rain-washed heather, unless rain-washed heather smells like smoke and piss. Instead the Highlander Bar was typical of the kind of spit-and-sawdust Glasgow pubs that turned over a huge profit. This was a drinking factory. The men who came here – and there was no snug or lounge for the ladies – worked harder at their consumption of beer, fortified sherry or the cheapest blended Scotch they could find than they did in the shipyards or steelworks they had come directly from. I arrived just after opening and the Highlander Bar was already heaving. I am just shy of six foot but still felt awash in an ocean of chest-high flat caps, wreathed in a sea fog of tobacco smoke.

There were three barmen working the bar with a joyless, industrial efficiency. One seemed to be in charge, barking sideways orders to the others as he worked the pumps and the optics. He was a short, angry-looking man in a striped shirt with elasticated sleeve-garters to keep his white cuffs clear of his wrists. He spotted me across the mass of customers and frowned. He disappeared out of sight for a moment and the next thing I knew there were two cap-less thugs in cheap suits flanking me.

'You all right, pal?' said one with a yellow-toothed grin. He was a short, ugly youth with dirty blond hair sleeked back in panels at the side that arced into a 'DA' hairstyle. He was trying too hard to project friendly menace.

'I'm fine. You?'

'Oh the best, pal. If you don't mind me saying, you're not one of the usuals here.' His companion was also smiling with the same insincere friendliness. 'What brings you here, if you don't mind me asking?'

I made a 'you got me' face. 'I'm a reporter. To be honest I'm here because of that murder. You know, the one upstairs.'

A third thug came in through the doors behind me. He was bigger than the other two. But, like them, he was trying too hard to look tough.

'It was a fucking liberty. A fucking liberty,' said the short blond thug. 'Mr McGahern was a gentleman. Treated everybody right. Listen pal, we used to work for Mr McGahern. We still do, in a way. We can give you all the gen you need.'

'You can?'

'Oh, aye . . . no problem at all. Anything you need to know.'

'And why would you do that?'

'Because we'll do anything to help catch the bastards that did it,' the taller, dark-haired one said. 'Get it all in the papers and that.'

Most of the customers were ranged four deep at the bar. In Glasgow drinking was a business so serious you did it standing up. Or standing up till you fell down. It was mostly the older men who sat at the scattered, scratched tables

'Okay. Let's sit down and talk.' I pointed to an empty table. 'First I'll get a round in.'

I took their orders and went up to the bar. When I came back they broke up their huddled conference. The smiles were back in place. This was going to be fun. The youth with the dirty yellow hair introduced himself as Bobby. His friends were Dougie and Pete. We drank warm, sour stout and talked about the night of the killing. Bobby and his pals made a big show of being reluctant to go into detail in a public place.

'We've got the keys to the flat upstairs. We could take you up there, pal. Show you where it all happened, like,' said Bobby conspiratorially. No one had yet asked me what newspaper it was that I was supposed to work for. He glanced around the bar and paused as a man of about seventy staggered past. 'We can't talk here.'

'Okay,' I said and we made our way out the open side door of the pub and into an alley that stank of urine and worse. As soon as we were outside, the three thugs blocked my way. This was the move they had been telegraphing from our first encounter. I turned square on and looked down on them, my hand closing around the sap in my pocket.

'You're not a reporter,' said Bobby. The smile was gone and his movements had the jerkiness of someone hyped up and ready for action. 'You're that Yank Lennox. You're the one that killed Frankie.'

'If you want to play, you wee shite,' I said, moving towards him and forcing him to step back, 'we'll play. And it doesn't matter how many of your little pals you've got with you; it's you I'm going to hurt. Bad. You understand? I don't like the way you look. And I don't like the way you smell.'

I took the sap from my pocket and shoved him in the chest with my other hand. He staggered back another two paces. His back was against the alley wall and his confidence was gone. I could see the other two move in on me and I turned.

'As for you two . . . I'm here working for Willie Sneddon. So back the fuck off or you'll end up like your bosses.'

The small blond one narrowed his eyes at me, trying to regain some credibility. I slapped him. Hard. Strands of oily blond hair fell across his brow. A few flat caps inside the pub turned in our direction. 'What you going to do now, shitface?'

The other two didn't make their move. Instead they glared hatred at their colleague, who had lost face for them all.

'I'll tell you what you're going to do,' I continued. 'Fuck all. Because that's what you are . . . fuck all. Nothing. Your boss is dead. His brother is dead. You're about to be eaten up by the big boys, so don't pretend you're here to defend anything.'

I waited for them to make their move. They didn't. Instead they looked at each other indecisively. I was in charge now.

'What you three wee poofs are going to do now is take me upstairs, just like you said, show me the flat and tell me everything I need to know. I mean *everything*. And there isn't going to be any trouble and you're not going to hold back on me. Because if you do, I'll be back. And I won't be alone. Willie Sneddon has given me a loan of Twinkletoes McBride if I feel you're not cooperating.'

That would be the clincher.

'We can talk upstairs,' Bobby with the greasy blond hair and the slapped-red face said. 'In the flat.'

I made the three would-be goons go ahead of me. We went out of the alley, into the street and through a door immediately next to the bar's main entrance. It opened straight onto a hall so small it only just accommodated the arc of the opening door. A stairway led steeply up to an equally small landing and a door to the left. This was where Tam McGahern had taken it up the ass in the worst way. There were smeary hints of where someone had half-heartedly cleaned up the mess. As we climbed I could hear the noise and smell the smells of the pub. The three Neds were ahead of me and took the opportunity to exchange mumbled words. When we got to the top, Bobby opened the door.

'This is it.'

'You girls go first,' I said.

As I stepped through the door I slammed my elbow into the face of the largest of the three, then swung my sap hard against the temple of the second. The biggest guy recovered enough to take a poke at me. It was a clumsy swing and I dodged it easily, using his momentum to drive him out of the still-open door, slam his face into the wall hard enough to leave a red smear and tip him sideways so that he fell all the way down the stairs. Bobby, the little blond guy, just stared at me. His pal was cupping his nose to try to stem the flow of blood. I swung a kick straight and hard into his groin and he stopped worrying about his nose. When he went down I kicked him in the side of the head and his lights went out. Bobby backed away from me.

'What the fuck was that for?' he wailed indignantly, but slipped his hand into the outside pocket of his bum-freezer jacket.

'That was for whatever it was you were planning in the bar and on the stairs. It's also to show you that I'm not here to play games.'

I took a step towards him and he pulled a razor from his pocket and slashed at the air in front of himself.

'Stay back. I'll fuckin' cut you.' His voice was shrill and shaky.

I looked around. There wasn't much to choose from so I snapped up a wooden chair and swung it full force onto his arm. He dropped the razor and I jabbed the chair at him, hitting him below the eye with the end of one leg. He stumbled back and I threw the chair to one side. I punched him twice on the face where the chair leg had hit him and was already swelling up. He didn't have the weight to stay on his feet and when he went down I dropped on him, my knee on his sternum, squeezing air from his narrow chest. I snatched up the open razor and held it to the eye that was still open, the blade almost kissing the white. He started to squeal.

'You ever killed someone, Bobby?' I hissed at him. 'I mean really killed someone?'

He shook his head energetically, but in movements small enough that the blade of the razor, gleaming bright and sharp, didn't cut him.

'I have,' I said. 'Fucking dozens. In the war. Up close too. Like now. You understand?'

He croaked something which I took as agreement.

'I could do you now, you wee shite. Or I'll maybe just blind you. Pop your eye. It wouldn't cost me a thought. You get used to killing, you see. To hurting people. Like a habit.' I paused. 'But I'll tell you something now . . . I'll tell you two people I didn't kill: Tam and Frankie McGahern. And I'm getting really pissed with people saying that I did. You got it?'

'Got it.'

I kept the blade to his eye for a second to punctuate my point then I stood up and slipped the razor into my pocket.

I took in the flat. We were in the main room which served as a living room and kitchen. The only other room was the bedroom. No bathroom or toilet. I guessed the facilities were out the back and shared with the bar. Romantic.

The greasy windows were half-covered with grime-grey lace. The wooden floor was bare, the furniture old and spartan. A pile of beer crates stood in one corner. When it came to picking a venue for seduction, it was clear Tam McGahern had been no George Sanders.

Bobby made a move to get up from the floor but I pushed him back down with my foot.

'You're not going to give me any more trouble, are you, Bobby?'

He shook his head vigorously.

'Sit down over there.' I indicated an old and worn club chair. 'And stay.'

I went over to the door, where Bobby's colleague was beginning to stir. I hoisted him to his feet, told him to pick up his friend at the bottom of the stairs and to fuck off. He nodded dully and slunk away.

After they had gone I went through to the bedroom. The bed was old and the iron bedhead was rusted, as if it had been reclaimed from a scrapyard, but the linen was reasonably clean. Again the floorboards were bare and tangled balls of dust and grime had gathered in the corners of the room.

Something caught my eye. In one corner a bright blue piece of cloth. I picked it up. A woman's handkerchief. Lace trimmed but cheap. It was spotted with dark flecks of blood. The flecks were small, some no bigger than pinheads. I dropped the hand-kerchief: the source of the blood had nothing to do with Tam McGahern's wounds. Two shotguns at that range was anything but dainty.

I went back into the living room, found the only other chair and placed it in front of Bobby. One eye had completely shut and that side of his face had ballooned into an ugly red swelling. The sleeked-back side panels of hair now hung like broken wings over his ears. He looked like he was about to start crying. I wanted to hit him again. Really wanted. I lit a cigarette instead.

'Who killed Tam McGahern?' I asked.

'I don't know. Honest I don't. There was nobody here ... I mean in the bar or anything, when it happened.'

'Yes there was. There was the girl.'

'Except the girl.'

'What was her name?'

He looked afraid for a moment. He was thinking about lying to me. He decided not to. 'Wilma. Wilma Marshall.'

'Is she on the game?'

'Not really. She worked as a barmaid in one of his other bars. One of his better bars: Wilma had a bit of class about her. Tam was the kind of guy to take whatever it was he wanted.'

'Where is she now? What's the name of the bar she works at?'

'It was the Imperial, but she's not there now. She only worked there on and off. Since the shooting she's dropped out of sight.'

'Who dropped her?'

'I don't know.'

I stood up and Bobby held up his hands. 'Honest ... I really don't know. It wasn't anybody to do with Tam's crew. Maybe she decided herself. The only other thing we wondered about was if it was the police. You know ... protective custody or something.'

'Did she say anything to anyone about what happened that night?'

'Just what you probably already know. She hid through there in the bedroom when she heard the shotguns go off. Afterwards she peeked over the windowsill and saw two guys with smart suits and sawn-offs get into a car. A couple of other folk seen them as well. Same thing ... smartly dressed. And really fucking calm. Strolling back to the car like they was in no hurry.'

I gave Bobby a cigarette and lit it for him. His hand shook as he smoked. He didn't have what it took. Tam and Frankie McGahern had surrounded themselves with nobodies to make them feel bigger in the scheme of things. Some time soon someone a lot meaner than me would come along from one of the Three Kings to vacuum up what was left of the tiny McGahern empire. If Bobby or his pals got in the way, they would be at the bottom of the Clyde within hours.

'And the police have nothing?' I asked.

'Nothing worth anything. Not on Tam, anyway. Word was they thought it was you that done Frankie. Word now is that the coppers are looking for Jimmy Wallace to talk to. They've been looking for him since Frankie died.'

'Jimmy Wallace?'

Bobby read my thoughts and shook his head. 'It's a dead end. Jimmy didn't do Frankie and he definitely didn't do Tam. It's just that Jimmy dropped out of sight the night Frankie got done.'

'Did Jimmy Wallace work with you? I mean, was he part of the McGahern team?'

'Naw. Nothing like that. Wallace was a wanker. Upper-class wanker. He was always trailing around after Tam. Tam put up with it though. Wallace was never short of a bob or two even though he drank like a fucking fish. Gambled too. I got the feeling Tam saw him all right with cash.'

'Why?'

'I don't know. Tam just seemed to put up with him for some reason. They were supposed to have been in the army together. In the desert.'

'And you reckon Jimmy had nothing to do with either murder?'

'Naw. No way. He was devoted to Tam. Mainly because Tam was his meal ticket. I don't know what they had going on in the past, but it was like Tam felt he owed Jimmy or something.

Tam wouldn't have put up with the shite Jimmy talked otherwise.'

'So why did he do a runner after Frankie was killed?'

'Search me.' Bobby shrugged and smoothed back the broken wings of greased hair. His fingers still trembled. 'When Tam died he lost his meal ticket. Or maybe he thought he was going to be next.'

I thought about it for a second then shook my head. 'Doesn't make sense. If that were the case then he'd have fucked off after Tam was topped. Why hang around until Frankie had his head turned to jam?'

Bobby shrugged again but looked at me apprehensively. He clearly thought I was going to give him another smack for not being able to explain the contradictions in what he had said.

'Where does Jimmy Wallace live?' I asked.

'Sorry, Mr Lennox. I don't know that either.'

'Before Tam got killed, were there any new faces around, or did anything unusual happen?'

Bobby looked at me blankly. I could tell he was trying to think of anything he could give me to avoid another slap. I saw something drop into his memory.

'Jackie Gillespie came around a couple of times.'

'The armed robber? Was Tam planning a robbery?'

'I don't know. But I saw him in the Highlander with Gillespie three, maybe four times. Tight and talky.'

'Gillespie . . .' I spoke to myself more than my new chum. 'Gillespie is a heavyweight. More than a bit out of the McGaherns' league.' I shook the thought from my head. 'Anyone else?'

'There were two guys I never seen before. Tam got me to drive him sometimes and he met with this big fat guy who was staying at the Central Hotel. Jimmy Wallace went with him.'

'Can you remember anything about this man?'

'Naw, no' really. Except I thought he was foreign or something. I only saw him from a distance, like, when he came out of the hotel with Tam, but the way he looked, the way he dressed and that.'

'And the other stranger?'

'He was different. A greasy-looking wee fucker with a droopy eyelid.'

I grinned at the idea of Bobby calling anyone else a greasy-looking wee fucker. 'What business did McGahern have with this guy?'

'I don't know. Honest. But this guy was afraid of Tam. The other guy, the big fat foreigner, didn't seem to be, and Jackie-fucking-Gillespie's scared of nobody.'

I left Bobby in the flat and headed back out onto the street. I thought about what he'd told me. The foreigner and the guy with the droopy eye Bobby had mentioned probably weren't significant. Just business. But Jimmy Wallace intrigued me. It was a name I hadn't heard before, but from what Bobby had said that wasn't surprising. He hadn't been an active member of the McGahern crew, but it seemed as if he'd been on the payroll. I also thought that Bobby had dismissed him too easily as the killer. He may have been a wanker, as Bobby had put it, but as an ex-Desert Rat it was a safe bet that he knew how to handle himself a hell of a lot better than Bobby or his chums could. It was also quite likely that Wallace had killed during his active service. And the question remained as to why he had only cleared out when Frankie died and not when his patron, Tam, had been rubbed.

That wasn't all that jarred with me. The unhurried manner of the killers bothered me. It was professional. If you run or speed off in a car from a killing, people get your number or clock enough to give a description. If you're in no hurry, onlookers tend not to look on, but keep their heads down in case you haven't finished shooting. And if you seem cool and unworried, then potential witnesses are afraid you may come back for them at a later date if they talk.

Very professional indeed. Just like the going over my office had been given.

CHAPTER FIVE

It's difficult to stay lost in Glasgow. Like Jock Ferguson had said to me, it wasn't really a city, just a giant village. But Wilma Marshall was making a decent job of it. I had tracked down her family home: parents and two sisters squeezed into a two-roomed flat in a rat-warren of tenements, with a toilet shared by three more families on the stair landing. The Marshall home could almost have been described as a slum: all it needed was a little fixing up to qualify. Nearly three-quarters of Glasgow's homes could have been described the same way. It was the kind of place a girl would do anything to get away from. It was the kind of place that gave birth to the kind of vicious ambition that had driven generations of Glasgow hardmen and gangsters. And maybe a couple of businessmen.

I didn't approach the Marshall family: the risk of them going straight to the police, if that was who had Wilma, was too great. I couldn't even stake out their flat: Glasgow tenements teemed with life, human and otherwise, and there would be too many eyes watching the constant coming and going and my car, or just me, would stick out like a sore thumb on the street outside.

But, like I said, Glasgow is not a place to stay lost in.

It was a Friday afternoon that I saw her in Sauchiehall Street. Not Wilma Marshall, whom I should have been looking for, but Lillian Andrews, the wife of the nervous little businessman with the damp handshake and the carnation and the unconvincing story to cover up her disappearance and sudden reappearance.

I had studied the photograph Andrews had given me, and I recognized Lillian Andrews instantly. She was tallish with dark hair and a full mouth lipsticked deep red. The expensive cloth of the tailored jacket and pencil skirt cleaved to her deadly curves. The fox-fur stole around her shoulders would have cost more than the average Glaswegian earns in a year. Her features were regular but short of beautiful. However Lillian Andrews was without doubt one of the most sexually attractive women I had ever seen. She oozed sex-appeal from every pore.

She caught me looking at her as I passed her in the street and her full lips twitched a small smile. Not encouragement, but acknowledgement of the only natural response a warm-blooded male could have to her. Of course she didn't recognize me, having no idea that I was the man her husband had hired and then un-hired to find her. But I dodged her eyes. I didn't know why: I was off the case and she was clearly no longer missing, but for some reason I hadn't wanted her to notice me.

Lillian was with a female friend, a shorter woman with gold-blonde demi-waved hair. Lillian Andrews's companion was almost as attractive but not quite as expensively tailored as she was. I turned to look into one of the shop windows, still sparse despite rationing having been almost completely lifted: austerity was a state of mind that seemed to linger with dark comfort in the Scottish psyche. I waited until they were about twenty yards away and a reasonable number of shoppers had curtained me before I started to follow them.

I managed to stick with the two women, unseen, for a couple of hours' shopping. I was able to tail them through the larger stores, like Copland and Lye, but most of the time I hung around outside the stores, standing across the street and smoking, watching and waiting for them to come out of the main entrances. It was taking up my time and it was boring. But there are some things that just ring false and then nag away at you like a dull toothache. John Andrews paying me off was one of them. The other thing was that John and Lillian Andrews were the oddest odd couple I had seen. I knew that women often married for money, but Lillian Andrews could have set her sights much higher, even in Glasgow.

The two women disappeared into Coupar's Furs for an age and when they came out the blonde was gleefully clutching a bulky, ribbon-wrapped package. It was difficult to read from across the road, but her expression conveyed more than joy at a purchase; I got the feeling she had been gifted it.

It started to get dark and I didn't need to worry about having other shoppers to conceal me. The streets began to lurk behind a curtain of dense fog. Glasgow's industry, the million-plus coal fires and its damp, clinging climate made it second only to London for the density and deadliness of its smog. Many babies had been conceived behind the damp curtain of Glasgow's smog, but even more had been smothered in its shroud. The year before had been the worst on record for smog deaths in industrial cities throughout Britain, and the Great Smog in London had killed a thousand. There was talk of a Clean Air Act, but nothing had yet been done. Tonight, as happened every night, the smog descended on the city: more than one soul would depart this world for the want of a decent breath.

I had developed a sixth sense about the smog: I could always feel its grip on my lungs a good half-hour before it really settled in. The streetlights came on but were reduced to grey-wreathed glimmers. I tugged up the collar of my coat and pulled the brim of my hat low. The smog could conceal me, but it could also conceal those I followed. I would need to get closer.

Lillian Andrews kissed her friend goodbye and mounted a

tram. I followed her onto the tram but sat as far back in the carriage as I could and kept the brim of my hat angled in her direction. She dismounted at the Trongate. I waited a few moments and a hundred yards before jumping off the moving tram, the conductress shouting something in unintelligible Glaswegian after me. The smog was now so dense that I could only see a matter of feet ahead. I had to move fast to get close enough to home in on the clacking of her heels on the cobbles, as she headed towards the Merchant City.

I lost her.

I stopped and listened again for the clicking of her high heels, but even that was gone. I walked on a few feet, keeping the kerb edge within sight: it was easy in the smog to wander onto the roadway and lose your bearings completely. She had led me into the Merchant City and I really wasn't too sure which street I was in. I stopped and listened again. Nothing. I cursed, unable to make up my mind whether to go forward or try to retrace my steps through the grey murk. I walked on a few yards. As I passed the end of a narrow alley, something swift and strong grabbed me.

'I saw you earlier,' said Lillian Andrews as she pulled me into the alley. We were instantly curtained by the smog. 'Watching me. You've been following me, haven't you?' She didn't give me a chance to answer but clamped her mouth on mine. Her tongue pushed deep into my mouth. She shoved me away and leaned against the alley wall and unbuttoned her jacket and blouse, exposing her full, milky white breasts in the dim light.

'Is this what you want? Is this why you've been following me?'

I stared at her breasts. Her hand was now on my crotch and nature had given her something to hold on to. I could still smell the perfume she had smeared on me with her kiss. I thought about the small, frightened man who had tried to buy me off.

'Listen . . .' I backed away. 'I—'

'No?' she said with a cold smile. 'I didn't think so.'

Something that felt like a steel hammer smashed into the back of my head and the smog suddenly penetrated my skull. Became even thicker. Darker.

Like so many Glaswegians at the weekend, I woke up on Saturday morning in a ward in the Western General Hospital. A pretty nurse was sitting reading the *Glasgow Herald* at my bedside. I tried to sit up but something exploded in my skull. Bright lights flashed and a searing pain sliced mercilessly through my head. I gingerly explored the back of my head with my fingertips, felt my hair matted beneath my touch and winced as I found an ugly ridge on my scalp punctuated by the hard knots of surgical stitching.

'Now, now . . .' said the nurse. 'We don't want to be doing that, do we?'

I groaned, fighting back a wave of nausea.

'We've got to take things easy.' Nursey maintained her unconvincingly solicitous tone. Through the pain I pondered whether there was some convention, some regulation, that compelled all medical professionals to speak in the first-person plural.

The nurse – small, like most Glaswegians – creased her pretty, perplexed brow. 'I think we should get the doctor . . .'

I looked at her heart-shaped face, crowned with russet hair and nurse's cap.

'Why don't we do that, nurse?' I said.

I watched her petite, trim figure disappear and made a mental note, in my searingly sore head, to make a pass at her later. It was then that the events of the night before came back to me: Lillian Andrews's milky skin; her hot, probing tongue; the blow to my head from her accomplice, hidden in the swirls of smog.

The nurse came back with a young, skinny doctor with bad skin and an artificially authoritative manner.

'Ah, Mr Lennox . . . you seem to have bashed your cranium last night. Perhaps we've partaken of a little too much of the *uisce beatha*?' There was that first-person plural again.

'Let's get one thing straight,' I said. 'Firstly, it's *Captain* Lennox. Secondly, if you had done the most basic of blood tests, you would know that there was absolutely no alcohol in my system. So, before you begin patronizing me, *sonny*, make sure you have the social or intellectual credentials so to do. Now, tell me . . . is my skull fractured?'

'No.' The young houseman's cheeks flushed red. The British were always so easy to manipulate. So ridden with hang-ups about class and authority. There had been a few occasions since being demobbed where I had played the officer-class card. My accent being difficult to place also threw them. I found it funny: so many Brits had talked to me about the British 'healthy disrespect for authority'. Next to the Germans, the British were the most likely to follow, without question, instructions from their 'betters'. And the Germans had learned their lesson.

'Do I have any kind of serious oedema resulting from the blow to my head?'

'Not that I can see, Mr . . . Captain Lennox.'

'Am I fit enough to be discharged?'

'Actually, I think it would be a good idea if you stayed with us for a while.'

'And why is that, exactly? According to what you have said, my head injury is not that serious.'

'It's serious enough for us to want to keep an eye on you.' He struggled to recover some of his lost authority. 'And if this wound was inflicted on you, then perhaps we should get the police involved. But it's not your head injury that is our primary concern at the moment. As you know, tuberculosis is endemic in Glasgow. The National Health Service is keen to eradicate TB in the city. Everywhere for that matter. You were brought in by ambulance. You were found in, well . . . unconscious in an alley. So you can understand why we thought that it had something to do with drink.'

'What's this got to do with tuberculosis?'

'Well, as part of our programme, we routinely do a screen – I mean an X-ray – of the lungs of anyone brought in under such circumstances. Actually, there are plans to bring in a mobile screening service. Anyway, we did an X-ray of your chest. I'm afraid we found what would appear to be a small shadow on your left lung. However, we think it may simply be a faulty film. We'd like to take another X-ray of your chest.'

'TB?' I thought of the morning coughing bouts every time I lit my first cigarette; of the way I could always predict the onset of bad smog.

'I wouldn't be too alarmed, if I were you. There's every chance it's simply a smudge on the film. Have you been prone to coughing fits?'

'Isn't everyone in this town? Sometimes. In the morning.'

'Is it a productive cough? I mean, do you cough anything up? Particularly blood?'

I shook my head.

'I wouldn't worry then. But if it is TB, then we have caught it early enough to sort out. There's a place we can send you. A sanatorium, up north. Clean air. It would work wonders for you.'

'One of these places where they push your bed outdoors overnight? I'd rather take my chances in the smog.'

'It's best to be safe.'

I spent the rest of the day in the ward while the shining machinery of Britain's brand-new National Health Service ground with the efficiency of an ancient steamer. While I waited I used the public telephone in the hall to call Mrs White. I explained I had been taken into hospital for observation and told her that there were concerns about my chest. I left out the fact that for the second time in quick succession I'd been used as a punch-bag. I told her that I would let her know whether or not I was going to have to go into a sanatorium. In any case, I assured her, I would still pay rent to keep my rooms.

'Let me know as soon as you find out, Mr Lennox.' I liked the sound of her voice on the 'phone. It sounded younger. It helped me to imagine her before war and grief had changed her.

I was X-rayed again in the middle of the afternoon and an hour later the young doctor came back to confirm that it had come back clear. He re-examined my head.

'You mentioned a sanatorium . . . where would that be?'

He looked confused for a moment. 'You do understand that we've given you the all-clear?'

'I know that,' I said irritatedly. I wasn't thinking about myself. It was a cheap lace handkerchief spotted with blood I had in mind. 'I just want to know where you would send someone to recover if they presented tubercular or bronchial symptoms. Where are the sanatoria?'

He explained that most TB cases in Glasgow were treated at Hairmyers Hospital, from where they were sent to sanatoria in the countryside. He gave me three addresses: two in Inverness-shire, the other in Perthshire.

'Most patients from Glasgow would be placed in the Perthshire sanatorium,' he explained. 'Easier for family to visit. 'But the demand exceeds the supply. Sometimes they're shunted further north.'

CHAPTER SIX

I had a house call to make before I took the train to Perth. After I got out of hospital I headed straight for my digs. Mrs White intercepted me at the door. I liked the tone of concern in her voice and I told her that I was in the clear. Any warmth dissipated when she saw me wince as I removed my hat.

'Who have you been fighting this time?' Her eyes were hard. This could be the crunch.

'Listen, Mrs White. Someone assaulted me from behind in the smog last night. Hit me on the head. While I was in the hospital they wanted to check out whether I had TB or not. And that's the truth. This is in no way connected to the police coming here.'

'It seems to me that you attract trouble.' She took my elbow and turned me brusquely around and examined the back of my head. 'Elspeth . . .' she called through to her twelve-year-old daughter. 'I want you to go down to Mr Wilson the fishmonger and ask for a bag of ice.'

Mrs White conducted me into the living room and sat me down on the leather Chesterfield while she busied herself in the kitchen making tea. I had only ever seen the living room from the door before and took the opportunity to survey it. The late Mr White had been a junior naval officer in the war and his family had been reasonably well-to-do. The room was well-decorated and furnished expensively. There was a large walnut radiogram against the wall but the new medium of television which had begun to appear in the more well-heeled homes had not yet made its presence felt here. I suspected a recent-past-tense affluence. A glass-fronted cabinet held some glasses and bone-china, as well as a bottle, half-full, of Williams and Humbert Walnut Brown Sherry. A marble and brass clock was the centre-piece on the mantle and was flanked by photographs in deco-style silver frames: a formally posed wedding photograph, each of the girls as babies, an austere-looking older couple with a pretty young girl whom I recognized instantly as Fiona White, standing awkwardly beside them.

She came back in with a large pot of tea and poured me a generous cup. Just then Elspeth, her daughter, returned with an oilskin bag. Fiona White scooped out some of the ice and wrapped it in a cloth, pressing it gently against the base of my neck and instructing me to hold it there. Two beatings' worth of pain started to ease. She stirred two headache powders into a glass of water and laid it next to my teacup, then sat down as far away from me as she could, in a large yielding leather club chair.

'Thank you.' My eyes fell on the photographs again. 'It must be difficult,' I said, and regretted it immediately.

'What?' Flint glinted in her green eyes.

'Bringing up the girls alone, I mean.' I was digging myself a deeper hole and fast.

'I manage perfectly well, Mr Lennox.'

'I know you do. I didn't mean anything . . . I mean, I think you do a marvellous job. It's just that I imagine it can't be easy. Doing everything alone.'

The flint remained in her eyes. The death of Fiona White's husband had been lost in an ocean of statistics. The loss of one junior naval officer counted only in combination with the thousands of other seamen killed. The snuffing out of his life had, by itself, meant nothing to the war effort. But for Fiona White and her two daughters it had been as if the sun had been extinguished. The entire focus of their universe had been annihilated. And with his death, the person Fiona White had been had also died. Much in the same way as the kid who had played on the shores of the Kennebecasis River had died somewhere as the 1st Canadian Army had killed and bled its way through Italian towns and villages with tourist-guide names. We were both victims of war.

'Sorry,' I said. 'I shouldn't have—'

'No, you shouldn't have,' she cut across me curtly. 'How I bring up my children is entirely my affair.' There was an embarrassed silence, then she said: 'What is it that you do, Mr Lennox? It seems to bring you all kinds of trouble. I don't for one moment believe that getting that bump on your head is pure coincidence.'

'I told you when I applied for the flat. I'm an Enquiry Agent,' I said. 'It means that people pay me to find things out for them. Unfortunately other people object to things being found out.'

'So why did the police treat you the way they did that night?'

'Some of the people I work for come to me because they won't or sometimes can't go to the police. The police don't like that. I'm a victim of professional envy.' I smirked, but she either didn't get the joke or chose not to. I decided to get off the subject. 'I will be away overnight tonight, Mrs White. I'm going up to Perthshire. Business. Just the one night. Maybe two.'

I took the powders and drained my teacup. Mrs White took my empty cup but made no effort to refill it. 'Very good, Mr Lennox.'

CHAPTER SEVEN

The journey to Perth was one back in time. The ancient city was not the most cosmopolitan of places and it felt as if it had been untouched by the war or the changes that had happened to the social structure of Britain afterwards. The forties and the fifties had got lost in the mail.

There was only one taxi outside Perth's railway station. It was one of the boxy types from the early thirties. The driver too was surprisingly elderly. I asked him to take me to the nearest half-decent hotel. There was no point in me going up to the sanatorium now. The evening visiting time would soon be over and it was some distance outside town, up in the hills above Perth. Although I had concerns about the vintage of both driver and conveyance, I asked the elderly taxi man if he could pick me up at ten the following morning.

The hotel he took me to was by the Tay, and I had a room overlooking the river. The bed was comfortable enough and the street outside quiet enough but I had trouble sleeping. Every time I closed my eyelids disparate thoughts and images bounced against them. Again I saw Lillian Andrews semi-naked, sensuously wreathed in fog; I saw the desperately off-hand and totally unconvincing demeanour of her ill-matched spouse; the professional manner in which she had used sex as the lure for her ambush in the smog, not knowing the reason for me tailing her, but knowing that I was.

Why was everything so complicated? Why did I *make*

everything so complicated? I knew that I wasn't going to let the Andrews thing go. There was no money in it. No one but me wanted me to push it further. But I would push at it. Until something gave and opened up a picture that made sense to me. Or maybe my inability to let it go was just a case of hurt pride at being bushwhacked from behind. I tried to put it from my mind. For the moment. I had a bigger fish to fry, and one that would pay off. But my head hurt from the blow and the thoughts still crowded in. It took me an age to get to sleep.

My elderly taxi driver turned up exactly on time. When I gave him the address of the sanatorium, far out in the hills above the city, he eyed me suspiciously.

'That's a long way by taxi.'

'I guess so.'

'It'll cost a lot.' It was obvious that he was worried about collecting his fare. I handed him three half-crowns.

'I'll square up with you for the rest afterwards. I'll need you to wait for me until I finish my business at the sanatorium.'

As we drove up into the hills the sun came out as if to show-case the beauty of the countryside for a visitor. The sanatorium itself sat in vast grounds that rose steeply to the plateau on which the vast Victorian edifice sat. The shields of manicured grass exploded into vast beds of rhododendron bushes. It seemed that every window in the building had been thrown open and there were banks of deckchairs ranged around the walls and on the flat part of the grounds. I could understand why. After Glasgow I could feel the difference in the air myself. Breathing is an unconscious act and you never think about the air you pull into your lungs, but up here each breath was like a sip of cold, clear mountain water.

The staff-nurse at reception eyed me with the usual

superciliousness as I explained that yes, I knew it wasn't visiting time but no, I couldn't come back later because my boss had insisted I was back in work that afternoon but I really did want to see my cousin. She checked the name again and told me to take a seat in the garden and they would bring her out to me.

I had expected a frail waif with pale skin coughing Lady of the Camellias-like into a handkerchief. Specifically a pale-blue one with lace trim.

Wilma Marshall was altogether more robust-looking. She was older than I had been told. Twenty-two or -three. She was brunette, about five-foot-one and as far as I could tell through the all-concealing dressing-gown had padding in all the right places. Her face was naked of make-up or lipstick and pretty, not anything outstanding, but I could see what Bobby had meant when he said she had a 'touch of class'. But my guess was she had been little more than a diversion for Tam McGahern. One of the many he could enjoy by dint of his position.

I stood up and smiled as the nurse escorted her across the lawn.

'Wilma,' I said as they approached. 'You're looking so much better.' She looked confused, as you would expect when faced with someone who clearly wasn't the cousin she'd been expecting to see. But she let it go and said nothing to the nurse.

'Thank you, nurse,' I said and waited till she had gone out of earshot before asking Wilma to sit down.

'What is it?' Wilma spoke in a thick Gorbals accent and the 'touch of class' evaporated. Her brow creased and she bit her fleshy bottom lip. 'I thought you people said you were going to leave me alone.'

Now I understood why she had played along: she clearly thought I was someone else.

'We will,' I said, riding the wave for as long as I could. 'It's just that we've got to be careful.'

'I've told you everything I know. And I've said I won't talk to anyone else about it.' Her frown deepened. 'Why are you here?'

'I know you've told us everything, Wilma. And I know that it's an ordeal for you to go through this again.' I talked like a copper: instinct was telling me that was who she thought I was. 'It's just that every time we go through it, there might be something more you remember.'

'What do you mean? What are you talking about?' Her pale brow creased even more. I was asking the wrong questions. Whoever she thought I was or represented, it wasn't the police. Her eyes narrowed with suspicion and then she looked over her shoulder to see where the nurse was.

'Listen, Wilma,' I said as calmly and authoritatively as I could. 'It's my job to find out who killed Tam McGahern. And to make sure you're kept safe and protected.'

I could see all the alarm bells ringing in her head. 'Who are you? What do you want? Are you from the police?'

'I'm a friend, Wilma. I want to help you out. Like I said, it's my job to find out who killed Tam. I just want to ask you a few questions about that night.'

'How did you find me?' Wilma's expression shifted from suspicion to uncertainty to fear. 'No one's supposed to find me.'

'I found your handkerchief in the flat above the Highlander. It was spotted with blood. I didn't think of it then, but later I guessed that it might have something to do with TB.'

'I can't talk to you. You have to go.' She was becoming more agitated.

I placed my hand on hers. 'There's nothing to be afraid of, Wilma. No one else knows that you're here. I'm not going to tell anyone about you. I just need to know who it was that shot Tam.'

'I want you to go.' Wilma stood up. 'I didn't see anything or anybody that night. I just hid until they were gone.'

'That's not what Bobby, Tam McGahern's pet monkey, told me. He said you clocked them from the window. What is it, Wilma? Did you recognize them? Was it someone you knew from the Imperial?'

She looked around as if checking the rhododendrons for spies. 'I can't do this. Not now. I need to think. Come back later.'

'Listen, Wilma, I know you're scared. But I need to know what I need to know. And I can't leave you in peace until you tell me who put you here and what it is you saw or heard that they want to keep quiet. Tell me and I'll disappear. I promise. But if you don't . . .'

Wilma frowned and bit her bottom lip again. 'It wasn't Tam.'

'What?'

'I don't think it was Tam that was with me that night. It was Frankie. It was Frankie that got shot at the door.'

'Wilma . . . it couldn't have been Frankie who was shot. I had a run in with Frankie McGahern five weeks later.'

'They thought it was a big joke.' Wilma's eyes glossed with tears. 'They did it to me before. Swapped places. Pretended to be each other. It started a couple of months before that night. Tam would tell me to meet him at the flat above the Highlander but sometimes it was him, sometimes it was Frankie that turned up. But Frankie'd always pretend he was Tam.'

'And you're sure it was Frankie who turned up that night?'

Wilma nodded. 'Big joke, eh? See if the stupid tart can tell the difference between the identical twins.'

'But you could.'

'Frankie was . . . he was *different* from Tam.' She blushed and a tear ran across her cheek.

'Wilma . . . are you absolutely sure about this?'

'As sure as a woman can be. But I never said. They found stuff in his clothes that proved he was Tam. That's what I couldn't understand. I thought maybe I was wrong. So I played along with it.'

I stared out across the grounds of the sanatorium. Things started to fit together only to fall apart again. Frankie dead in the flat above the Highlander. Tam the one who picked a fight with me and ended up dead later that night in the garage in Rutherglen. Tam was a tough nut with a war combat record to more than match mine. If it had been him that night, then he had deliberately taken a beating to convince the world that he was Frankie. But why? Frankie was a nobody. Only the name Tam McGahern carried enough clout to build a crime empire. Something else struck me: Jimmy Wallace, the hanger-on Bobby had talked about, must have been in on it. He didn't clear off until after the second murder because he *knew*. He knew it had been Frankie, not Tam who had died the first time around. The second killing had been Tam and it had signalled to Wallace that it was time he got lost.

'Who brought you here, Wilma?'

A nurse walked by, looked at us, then at her pocket watch and frowned pointedly. Wilma looked agitated again. 'I don't know who they are, but they paid me money. Told me to keep quiet. They check up on me. You better go.'

'Tell me exactly what happened that night.'

'Not now. Come back.'

'When?'

'Visiting hours are three till four thirty tomorrow. Come back then. But I'm not promising anything. I just want out of this mess.'

'What mess, Wilma?'

She shook her head, clearly very scared. I let it drop.

'I'll see you tomorrow, Wilma.' When I stood up she looked relieved. I decided to temper her relief. 'And Wilma . . . make sure you're here. And no nasty surprises. I expect to be your only visitor. If I see anyone who looks remotely like a goon, then I'll take the next train back to Glasgow and make sure anyone who wants to find you knows where to look.'

I left her sitting in the gardens. I knew there was a pretty good chance that Wilma wouldn't be there when I went back the next day. But I couldn't hang around the sanatorium and I guessed it would be difficult for whoever put her there to arrange her removal at short notice. And she was maybe scared enough to do what I had told her to do.

The last thing I needed was to kill twenty-four hours in Perth. Perth time counted five times longer than anywhere else. My elderly driver dropped me off at the hotel and I had a dismal lunch in the dining room. I was served a lamb cutlet which compensated for its lack of size by having a consistency so resistant to knife or tooth that it could have had industrial applications. I was halfway through the cutlet when a tall and solidly built young man asked with a broad smile and in an accent that was hard to place if he could join me.

'Sure,' I said. 'Help yourself.'

'You're Canadian, aren't you? I can tell from your accent.'

I tried not to make my smile too weary. 'Yes. I am.'

'Pleasure to meet you. The name's Powell . . . Sam Powell.' He extended a tanned hand across the table. Tans weren't something you saw a lot of in Scotland. I shook it. Powell radiated an irrepressibly cheerful disposition. His big smile exposed perfect teeth and he had the big-amiable-lug-type handsomeness of the actor Fred MacMurray. The dislike I took to him was as profound as it was instant. 'I've spent a lot of time in Canada myself,' he explained with an eagerness that was as unstoppable as a runaway freight train. 'Tractors are my business. The company I work for is Anglo-Canadian. I'm in sales.'

'I see,' I said. The waitress came over to take his order. There were only two options for the main course. I sat in malicious silence and smiled as he ordered the cutlet.

'Are you here on business, Mr . . .?'

'Lennox,' I said: there had seemed no need to use anything other than my real name when checking into the hotel. 'Yes. Kind of.'

'What business are you in, if I may ask, Mr Lennox?' No conversational mountain was too steep for this guy to climb.

'Insurance,' I lied. The most boring business in the world usually drops into the path of a conversation like a railway sleeper. Fred MacMurray's younger brother was not deterred.

'Really? Fascinating. General or motor?'

'All types. I deal with claims.' I was rescued by the arrival of his cutlet. His mouth would be fully occupied from now on.

I left untouched the gelatinous grey sludge that was served as dessert and excused myself from Powell's company.

'It was nice meeting you, Mr Powell.' My joviality was genuine. I was free of him. He stood up, shook my hand and smiled his broad, Hollywood-perfect smile. I was happier than I can describe to see a particularly tenacious-looking piece of cutlet gristle jammed between two teeth.

I decided to find another bar in town for a drink rather than risk running into Powell again in the hotel's lounge.

Unfortunately I had to run the gauntlet of Powell's cheeriness at breakfast the next morning. I decided that the hotel proprietress – a stern, joyless, meagre woman of about fifty, who in temperament was the antithesis of Powell – must have been a secret sadist, subjecting me to the twin tortures of the hotel's food and Powell's company.

I dodged his inquisitiveness again and after I checked out stood outside the hotel and smoked. It was a bright sunny spring morning and I left my coat with my bag in the hotel and arranged to pick them up later when my vintage driver and taxi came to collect me again. I walked along the river and thought about Wilma Marshall. It was more than possible that she had put me off until today for a reason; that she needed to get in touch with someone. Whoever that someone was, they had a lot of the answers I was looking for.

I nodded and said hello as I passed a smartly dressed older man in a houndstooth sports jacket with a matching cap and military tie. He walked past mute, as if he hadn't heard or seen me.

My money had been on the police having placed Wilma in the sanatorium, but the police didn't pay witnesses to stay out of sight. Whoever it was had access to a lot of resources, including maybe a compliant doctor. As I walked I considered what she had said about the callous trick the McGahern twins played on her, taking turns to screw her and pretending always to be Tam. It seemed like a senseless, if supremely cruel, subterfuge.

Perth's single cafe was its only concession to modern times and I called in for a coffee before heading back to the hotel to pick up my stuff and meet the taxi. The hotel proprietress was at the counter when I returned. Her shapeless black dress, flat shoes, the keychain around her waist and her unsmiling, weary demeanour made her look more like the governess of a women's prison than a convivial hostess.

'Your friend Mr Powell left something in his room, Mr Lennox. A pen. I have his address. He signed the register with his business address so I can send it on to that, but I thought you might be seeing him soon.'

'I'm afraid you're mistaken . . . I don't know Mr Powell. I only met him at dinner yesterday.'

She gave me her women's-warden look. 'But Mr Powell said he knew you. He specifically asked to be seated with you.'

I frowned. 'Maybe he mistook me for someone else.'

At that point my driver arrived at reception, took my bag and we headed out to the taxi.

'See Uncle Joe's dead,' was the taxi driver's opening gambit.

'Uncle Joe?' I was genuinely confused for a moment.

'Uncle Joe Stalin. Stalin's popped his clogs. It was on the Home Service this morning.' It was the cheeriest I had seen my little driver, but that was about the extent of our conversation during our half-hour drive to the sanatorium.

'Wait here again,' I said as I got out in front of the vast Victorian edifice. I had the feeling I wouldn't be long. It was a prettier, friendlier nurse on the reception desk this time, but she frowned when I asked about Wilma.

'She's not here,' the nurse explained. 'She discharged herself this morning, first thing. I'm surprised you didn't know. You're her cousin, you say?' Her frown darkened with suspicion. 'It was her brother who picked her up.'

'Her brother? Are you sure?'

'I was on the desk myself.' I could see she was on the point of calling someone. She clearly didn't believe I was Wilma's cousin.

'Must have got our wires crossed,' I said and frowned as if annoyed. I thought for a moment. 'You're absolutely sure it was her brother . . . he's a big, good-looking guy . . . looks a bit like a younger version of Fred MacMurray . . . you know, the Hollywood actor?'

The suspicion evaporated from her expression. 'Yes, that's him.'

CHAPTER EIGHT

It was late by the time I got back to Glasgow. The Perth spring had evaporated and Glasgow was shrouded in yet another smog. November through to February was the worst time for smog in the city, but it lurked ready to fall at any time of year and the temperature had taken a dramatic drop during the day.

As I had sat in the train watching the weather through the window change its mood, I had thought about Powell. I was certain he was behind the professional job done on my office and that vague feeling I'd had that someone who knew what they were doing was on my tail. Powell was a professional and I would have been unaware of his involvement if he hadn't flagged it up for me. For some reason that I couldn't quite figure, he had been making me aware of his presence.

After I got off the train I headed, bag and all, to the Horsehead Bar. I needed a little Glasgow cheerfulness after Perth. Big Bob came over and poured me a rye whiskey from the only bottle of non-Scotch they had in the bar.

'How you doing?' he asked without his usual smile.

'Fine. What's up?'

'One of Willie Sneddon's boys was in here earlier. Looking for you.'

'Twinkletoes McBride?'

'No, just some wee bampot they send on errands. He said to tell you that Sneddon wants to see you. If you ask me, Lennox, you play in the wrong part of the playground. I don't know why you get involved with the likes of Willie Sneddon.'

'It's my business, Bob. You know that by now. Sneddon and I are old playmates.'

After I finished my whiskey I headed out to a telephone box and 'phoned Sneddon. I gave him an update on progress so far, which was less than he had expected or I had hoped to give. Mainly because, for some reason I didn't fully understand myself, I wasn't ready to pass on Wilma's conviction that it had been Frankie who had been executed on the stairwell of the flat: all I had was Wilma's intuition and it was a claim that could cause all kinds of shit to start flying. I decided to keep it under my hat for the meantime. When I had finished my report Sneddon reciprocated: he had had practically all his people trying to sniff out something to report back to me. Nothing.

'So you think this punter in the hotel snatched Wilma?' Over the telephone, without the benefit of mock-baronial surroundings and expensive clothes, Sneddon sounded the Govan hardman he was.

'I'm sure of it. Does he sound like someone you know?'

'Naw. He sounds like someone you'd remember. And I make it my business to remember faces. He sounds too smooth for Hammer Murphy's outfit. Could be one of Cohen's mob, but I doubt it. Maybe he's an amateur, though from what you've said it sounds unlikely. Or some out-of-town firm.'

'He's no amateur. He's a professional all right, but something about him doesn't fit with being a gangster. No offence.'

'None taken,' Sneddon said without irony. 'I'll check with the boys, see if he rings any bells.'

There was nothing more to be said but I paused for a moment before hanging up.

'Mr Sneddon, have you heard of a woman called Lillian

Andrews? I don't know what her maiden name would have been.'
I gave him a description of Lillian's knockout looks and figure.
'Like our guy in Perth, she's a real professional. And tough with
it. But not someone that would ever have had to work the streets.'

'There are a lot of sexy-looking girls out there, Lennox. And
I don't know every tart in Glasgow. But from what you're saying,
she's got too much class to be working one of Danny Dumfries's
clubs. She's not working Blythswood Square . . . if she was an
indoor whore, then you should talk to Arthur Parks. I'll tell him
to expect to hear from you.' I smiled. Sneddon preparing Parks
meant that I would get total cooperation. 'Is this woman
connected to the McGahern thing?'

'No,' I said. 'But she is connected to something that's getting
in the way, Mr Sneddon. I appreciate your help.'

'Lennox . . .'

'Yeah?'

'Make sure you keep me up to date on what you find out
about Tam McGahern. I don't like surprises.'

I hung up feeling more than a little uneasy. If Wilma had
been right about Frankie, not Tam, being the first to die, then
I had a pretty big surprise up my sleeve.

CHAPTER NINE

The next evening I was in the one place in Glasgow you were guaranteed a date. If you had enough money on you.

I told a doorman who was all neck that Mr Parks was expecting me and he let me into what had been a drawing room at one time.

Park Circus was in the West End of Glasgow and broke up the otherwise Victorian monotony of Glasgow's architecture with a circle of impressive Georgian townhouses. Most were still single dwellings, occupied by moderately wealthy families, but some had been subdivided into flats. Arthur Parks owned this particular townhouse in its entirety, but had divided it into a large apartment for himself on the upper levels and two smaller flats, one on the ground floor and the other in the basement. From both he conducted one of the most lucrative trades in the world. And, proverbially, one of the oldest.

I was in the ground-floor flat. There were three girls in the reception room I was shown into, all of whom stood up when I came in. One would have been around thirty and the other two were much younger. One looked no more than nineteen. They were all pretty and curved in the right places and all smiled alluringly. I held up my hand.

'Sorry, girls, I'm here on business, not pleasure.' Their smiles disappeared as quickly and mechanically as they had appeared and they sat down again on the sofa, resuming the conversation they had been having when I came in. I sat down in a large

leather armchair and lit a cigarette. A small, bald, bird-like businessman in an immaculate suit came in and they repeated their
performance. I reckoned the businessman was pushing sixty,
but he chose the youngest of the girls.

'Don't trust him if he offers you a lollipop,' I said as they left
the room. The small businessman's cheeks flushed bright red.
I made no effort to disguise my disgust.

The other two girls were scowling at me when another man
came into the room. Not a customer. Arthur Parks was an ugly
fucker. He was about five-eleven and immaculately dressed, but
he wore bottle-bottom glasses that exaggerated the size of his
eyes. His bottom lip curled up, fish-like, over his top and there
was evidence of a badly done repair to a congenital hare-lip.
When he spoke, it was in a camp baritone.

'Ah, Mr Lennox,' he boomed, extending his limp hand theatrically. Everything he did, he did theatrically. 'What can I do to
help you?'

I handed him the photograph of Lillian Andrews that her
husband had given me. Parks took it between manicured fingers.
The flamboyant turquoise ring on his little finger matched his
heavy cufflinks. I wondered if the set was completed with
earrings.

'Recognize her?'

'Mmmm . . . very nice.' It was like a teetotaller commenting
on a fine wine. For all Arthur Parks sold pussy, he had no
interest in it. His last stretch in prison had been for buggery in
the gents' toilet at Central Station. I thought I saw a split-second
of recognition in his expression but then it was gone. Or he
had covered it up quickly.

'Well . . . Do you know her?' I asked.

'No. No, I don't.'

'You didn't look too sure.'

He looked at the photograph again. Made a show of studying it.

'No, I don't know her. It was just that she reminded me of someone. But it can't be her. Who I'm thinking of was blonde. And she's dead.'

'Tell me about her.'

'Forget it, Mr Lennox, it cannot possibly be Margot Taylor. It's just there is a rough similarity. Margot died three years ago. She was one of my girls but I found out she was doing her own thing in her spare time. She got a bit of a slapping for it and then I kicked her out. About six months later she was killed in a car crash. One of her punters was drunk behind the wheel. Served her right. If she hadn't messed me about she would still have been working here. Safe.'

'How alike is this woman to Margot?'

'Not that much. She just kind of reminded me of her. Around the eyes.' He handed me back the photograph. 'Sorry. Can't help you.'

I put the photograph back in my wallet. 'One other thing. Did you ever get the McGahern brothers in here?'

'God no . . .' he laughed. Theatrically. 'Wouldn't let ruffian gobshites like that into my establishment.'

'Do you know anything about an independent brothel that the McGaherns supplied security for? Somewhere in the West End.'

'Not really,' said Parks. 'I heard something about it . . . potential competition and all that. But it didn't seem to last long and as far as I could tell it wasn't taking business from me. Anyway, sorry I can't help you.' Parks nodded in the direction of the older prostitute on the sofa. 'Would you like to spend some time with Lena? On the house.'

The vaguely aristocratic-looking Lena responded by tilting

her head back and parting her red lips provocatively. I've seen that Rita Hayworth movie too, Lena, I thought.

'No thanks, I'll pass.' It wasn't that I didn't find Lena attractive. Parks misread my refusal and gave me his own version of a Rita Hayworth pout. 'I don't fuck whores,' I said. 'Or pansies.'

The next morning a spring sun was trying to break through but an ill-tempered early-morning Glasgow was telling it to fuck off and shrouding it in factory smoke. I had breakfast in a transport caff on Dumbarton Road before heading up into Bearsden about eight thirty. There was a steady flow of commuter traffic in the opposite direction, reflecting the fact that the majority of Glasgow's privately owned cars resided in the leafy driveways of Bearsden.

I parked around the corner from the Andrews residence and loitered in the street as inconspicuously as I could until I saw John Andrews's Bentley slide out of the drive with the sound of water over pebbles.

Lillian Andrews opened the door with the blank expression of someone expecting to see a postman on the threshold. She was wearing a pastel-blue sweater with a double row of pearls tight at her throat, dark-blue Capri pants and low-heeled mules. It was a reasonably conservative outfit, but she looked sexier in it than most women would dressed only in French lingerie. There was the tiniest flicker of recognition in her eyes, then it was swept instantly away. She was good. Very good.

'Yes?' she asked uninterestedly. For a moment she nearly convinced me that we had never before encountered each other.

'Hello again, Mrs Andrews. I'm glad to say that the smog seems to have lifted.'

'I'm sorry,' she said and started to close the door. 'I don't buy anything from door-to-door salesmen.'

I got my foot jammed in the door just in time and leaned my shoulder into it so hard that she nearly fell over backwards. We stood just inside the threshold and her dark eyes burned with hate.

'Get out! Get out now!'

'I need to talk to you, Mrs Andrews.'

'What about?' She backed towards the hallstand and picked up the receiver of the ivory-coloured telephone. 'If you don't get out, then I'm 'phoning the police.'

'You could do that,' I said, taking off my hat. 'But there again, the police know me. They know that the information I give them is pretty accurate.' I smiled, thinking of the ruddy-cheeked farmer's boy who had worked hard to make sure it was. 'So I'm sure they will be interested in why your husband is running so scared and why you ambushed me in the fog the other night.'

'You know my husband?' She put the 'phone down.

'You didn't know that the other night, did you? I know all about your little disappearance and reappearance act. What I want to know is why you bushwhacked me and who it was that parted my hair for me.'

'I don't know what you're talking about. I've never seen you before in my life.'

'Don't mess me about, Lillian.' I closed the door behind me. 'There's something about this whole set up that stinks. If you don't tell me what it's all about maybe I should talk to your husband.'

She laughed. 'Go right ahead.' No bluff.

I grabbed her wrist and dragged her into the living room. I suppose in Bearsden they called it a lounge. It was furnished in *Contemporary* style: sofa and armchairs slung so low that you needed a lift to get out of them; low-level light-wood coffee table; geometric wrought-iron and hardwood room divider; the small grey eye of a brand-new television set watching us from the corner. I threw her down onto one of the chairs. For a suburban housewife she didn't seem particularly perturbed by the rough stuff. She eyed me with the same hate in her dark eyes. Not fear. Hate.

'Listen, Lillian, you can pretend all you like, but we both know it was you with your hand round my dick immediately before the lights went out. All you were interested in was to find out if it was my hard-on following you or whether I had another reason for watching you. Well, I did. A professional reason which I'm not going to share with you. But what started out as professional curiosity became very personal very quickly after your goon tried to fracture my skull.' I sat down opposite her and dropped my hat onto the sofa next to me. 'So, what's the story?'

She stared hard at me but the hate was dissipating. She gave a cynical laugh as if something had just fallen into place for her.

'You're working for John, aren't you? He's been paying you to snoop on me, hasn't he?'

I didn't say anything but she nodded to herself.

'That's what I thought. Okay, I made a mistake. I got involved with someone. Someone who was bad for me. I went away with him. I was going to leave John. But then I saw sense and came home. My ... *friend* ... well, he didn't accept that I was going back to John and he threatened to make all kinds of trouble for me. So I agreed to meet him the other night. To tell him it was all over. I told him that someone was following me. That's why he clobbered you. I'm sorry. But he's crazy that way. That was one of the reasons I broke it off with him.'

'Really? I have to say that he's the most broad-minded jealous lover I've ever come across. I mean, letting you flash your tits at me and put your tongue halfway down my throat.'

She took a cigarette from a packet on the coffee table and lit it with a marble table-lighter. She tapped the packet with slim crimson-tipped fingers.

'You don't understand. Things like that can get complicated. Sex is complicated. When I'm with him I become another person.'

'And this is all over?' I asked.

'Completely.'

'Then you won't mind giving me chummy's address. I'd like to pay him a call. Balance things up a little.'

Her eyes went hard again. 'No. I won't. I want all of this in the past. He's a violent and dangerous man. As you already know. Please, leave it alone.'

'His name?'

She walked over to a sideboard and opened a drawer. She took ten five-pound notes from a wallet and held them out at arm's length towards me. 'Take it.'

'Your husband has already paid me.'

'Now I'm paying you. To forget all about this. I'm back with my husband and he's none the wiser. I feel bad about what happened the other night. Please take this. Consider it compensation.'

I took the money and pocketed it. Like she said: compensation.

I stood up and put my hat on. She showed me to the door.

'Are we agreed that this whole unfortunate episode is over, Mr Lennox?'

'Agreed. Just one last thing . . . does the name Margot Taylor mean anything to you?'

She pursed her full lips thoughtfully. 'No, nothing. Why?'

'It doesn't matter. Someone who looks a little like you. I just thought you might be related.'

She watched me from the door until I turned out of the

driveway. I sat in my car for a while and contemplated the wind-screen. There were three things that were very clear to me. The first was that if the bribe hadn't worked then Lillian Andrews would have fucked me to keep me out of her business. Probably on top of the cash. Second, the name Margot Taylor, coming out of the blue, had sparked a hastily concealed reaction.

And the third thing was that all of my original suspicions about her were true. She had called me Mr Lennox.

I hadn't told her my name.

CHAPTER TEN

I woke up in the middle of the night, my pulse pounding in my ears. The nightmare drifted away before I could capture it, but it had had something to do with a young, frightened face screaming at me. Begging me. In German.

I smoked a cigarette in the dark, its glow painting the walls deep red when I drew on it, then fading again. For some reason I started to think about home. It was my little joke whenever anyone asked me where I was from. My accent had got a little muddled over the years and some people here thought I was American, others that I was English or even Irish. When pushed, which I rarely was, I would say I came from Rothesay and, although puzzled, people generally accepted it. It was actually the truth, but the Rothesay I meant was not the one they thought of: the dismal tourist escape for Glaswegians on the Scottish Isle of Bute. My Rothesay was another. Far distant, in more ways than one: an ocean and a wartime away.

So I lay smoking in the dark thinking about Rothesay and Saint John. About bike rides and canoe trips along the Kennebecasis River. About my exclusive education at the Collegiate School. About the big turn-of-the-century house I grew up in that always smelled of rich, aged wood. About the kid with big ideas and bigger ideals who had died in Europe. A casualty of war.

I hadn't been the only casualty. As I lay in the dark feeling sorry for myself I heard the soft, muffled sound of a woman sobbing. From Mrs White's flat.

The morning sun again struggled to make its presence felt through the grey plumes of mill and factory smoke that drifted over the city. I took the car down to Newton Mearns, to the south of Glasgow. The formation of the state of Israel was still big in people's minds and the latest joke was to refer to Newton Mearns, because of its largely Jewish population, as Tel-Aviv on the Clyde. It took more than a few concentration camps to kill the good old anti-Semitic gag. But, to be fair, one of the things that I liked about Glasgow was the openness and friendliness of Glaswegians. Glasgow was a hard and dark and violent place, and it was always difficult to reconcile this with the warmth of its people. Glasgow was probably the least anti-Semitic city in Europe. But less than ten years after the liberation of the camps, that was a very relative statement.

Glasgow's Jewish community owed its origin largely to deception: many Jewish families, escaping the nineteenth-century pogroms of Russia, had been disembarked at the Port of Glasgow and told by disingenuous ship captains that they had arrived in New York. One such family who had eagerly searched Clydebank for a glimpse of the Statue of Liberty had been the Cohen family, who had learned from bitter experience a fierce and uncompromising toughness. One grandson of the original settlers was Jonny Cohen. Handsome Jonny.

The second of the Three Kings.

I had 'phoned Jonny before coming down to see him. We arranged to meet at his home. Unlike Sneddon's mansion, Jonny Cohen's house was modern, designed by some up-and-coming London architect. It looked more like something you would expect to see sprawling across a lot in Beverly Hills.

There were no drainpipe-trousered hoodlums in Jonny's drive. No hint of anything other than here resided a successful businessman and family man.

I rang the doorbell. The door was opened by a tall, tanned and dark-haired man. His face was big and handsome with a cleft in his chin he could have carried small change in. Jonny Cohen had the kind of looks normally associated with the more masculine Hollywood leading men. They were the kind of looks that women swooned over. Pointlessly. As a husband Jonny Cohen was the model of fidelity; as a father he was loving and fiercely protective; as a gangster he was by far the most intelligent of the Three Kings. Intelligent, ruthless and highly dangerous. But hospitable.

'Hi, Lennox,' Jonny said in his rich baritone and beamed a bright smile at me. 'Come on in ...'

There are some people you come across in life whom you can't help liking in spite of yourself. Jonny Cohen was exactly that type of person: you found yourself putting to one side the fact that he was a violent villain. There was no doubt that Jonny was someone you would be wise not to cross and the Cohen firm had supplied its fair share of custom to the city's hospitals and, on the odd necessary occasion, mortuary. But according to Einstein everything is relative and in Glasgow you couldn't hold a couple of murders against a guy's character. And anyway, Jonny had his own code of ethics. He didn't run loan sharks like the other two Kings; his money came from illegal gambling, prostitution and a string of restaurants and clubs. Most of all, Jonny Cohen was a robber baron: his success lay in the cruel efficiency of the armed robberies he sponsored, planned and on more than one occasion led.

Jonny showed me into a large, open-plan living room. It was populated with Modernist furniture similar to the stuff in the

Andrews's house. Again there was a television in the corner. He caught me looking at it.

'Rachael's idea,' Jonny explained. 'She nagged me to death to get one. A Ferranti T thirteen-twenty-five. Cost me fifty-eight bloody guineas. They're going to televise Princess Elizabeth's coronation. You got one?'

I laughed at his over-estimation of my financial clout. 'No . . . it'll never catch on. I'll stick with the wireless.'

He invited me to sit. That was the kind of gangster Handsome Jonny Cohen was: he invited you to sit. He was an amenable kind of guy, so long as he wasn't standing on top of a bank counter with a stocking mask to hide the film-star looks and waving a sawn-off in your face.

'What can I do for you, Lennox?'

'I'm looking into the Tam McGahern killing. I wondered if you could help me.'

'I heard the police had you pegged for doing his brother.'

'They pegged me wrong. I had a run-in with Frankie the night he was killed. He wanted me to find out who killed Tam. I told him I wasn't interested.'

'So why are you doing it now?'

'I'm contrary. It's what makes me an interesting and complex person. People in blue uniforms kept telling me I should stay out of it.'

Jonny went over to a trolley that looked like it should have been on a spaceship. He poured us both a Scotch whisky and soda. 'So who's paying for your time?' he asked, as if he didn't know.

'Willie Sneddon.'

Jonny smiled wryly. 'If you're working for his outfit you've just increased their brainpower by a thousand per cent.'

'I don't work for anyone's outfit. You know that, Jonny. But he's hired me to do what the police can't or won't do.'

'How can I help?'

I ran through most of what I knew about Tam's killing. I also told him about Wilma Marshall's disappearance from the sanatorium in Perth and the handsome, cheerful lug who had made himself known to me before spiriting her away. I hadn't told Sneddon about Wilma's conviction that the wrong twin had been shot; that meant I had to leave it out of my explanation to Jonny.

He sat for a moment and contemplated his Scotch.

'Tam McGahern was a bad bastard. We all hurt people in this business, Lennox. But that's what it is . . . business. McGahern hurt people, and worse, because he liked it. Really liked it. His brother Frankie was a bampot. Look at him the wrong way and he'd start farting fire. But that's all he was, a nut-job. That's why it fits him coming at you that night the way you said. But Tam was more. Tam had something going on up top. Do you know that Tam never did time? Nor did Frankie. Christ knows how many times they were both questioned but neither was ever arrested, or so much as held overnight.'

'They weren't in a cerebral kind of business,' I said. 'Loan sharking and protection rackets. If they avoided doing time then it was just down to luck.'

Jonny shook his head. 'Luck had nothing to do with it. You would never have guessed it to look at him, but Tam McGahern was as smart as they come. Tam made it to sergeant in the Desert Rats. Got decorated. Believe it or not there was talk of him being made an officer. Story goes that when he was in the army this head-quack tested Tam's IQ and it came out astronomical. But the same psychologist kiboshed Tam's promotion chances by putting on record that he reckoned he was a complete fucking psycho. There again, we all knew that. Tam always enjoyed hurting people that little bit too much and it often got in the way of his judgement. But the truth is he was really sharp and was slowly becoming a bit of a threat. Anyone can be a hoodlum. But some hoodlums *graduate* out of the streets – instead of just kicking the shite out of everything and hoping it bleeds money, they start to think things through. To plan. To come up with schemes. That's what was happening with Tam McGahern.' Jonny drained his Scotch and got up to pour himself another. I shook my head when he nodded towards my glass. He paused thoughtfully before continuing. 'Did Sneddon tell you that the three of us got together to talk about Tam McGahern?'

'No. He didn't,' I said.

'I'm not surprised. I don't want to confuse things, but we did have a sit down to discuss whether we needed to do something about Tam. Something permanent, if you know what I mean. The alternative was to accept that one day Tam might have become powerful enough to constitute a threat to the Kings.'

'What was decided?'

'To leave him alone for the meantime. So long as the threat was contained. Tam knew not to step out of line or he'd get squashed.'

'Maybe one of the other Kings decided to deal with the problem alone.'

'Well, I didn't do it. I don't see Sneddon hiring you to poke about in this if he had arranged it. Even if he contracted a hit from out of town. And Murphy ... Hammer Murphy is incapable of doing anything with discretion or subtlety. If he had done either McGahern, we would all know about it.'

I knew what Jonny meant: Hammer Murphy was the King with whom I least liked having dealings. Much of what Jonny said about Tam McGahern could apply to Hammer Murphy. Except the intelligence. Michael Murphy's nickname suited him;

he was the human equivalent of a blunt instrument: dense and it hurt when you collided with him. Jonny was right though. Murphy always made sure he got full credit for all the brutal acts he was behind. And he was behind many. But I was keeping an open mind: whether it had been Tam or Frankie who had got his head pulped in the Rutherglen garage, it did fit with Hammer Murphy's MO.

'Anyway,' Jonny continued, 'we were all keeping a lid on Tam McGahern's operation. He didn't like it, but as long as the three main firms worked together, he couldn't do anything about it.'

'I hear Tam had a hanger-on of sorts. A guy called Jimmy Wallace. I don't think he was involved much on the business end of things but Tam was supposed to have indulged him.'

'Jimmy Wallace?' Jonny shook his head thoughtfully. 'Can't say I've ever heard of him.'

I sipped my Scotch. It was good Scotch but I would rather have had a rye. I was hearing nothing that I didn't already know. Jonny seemed to pick up on this.

'Not much help, huh? Sorry. I would help if I could ... even if you are working for the wrong people.' He paused. 'There is maybe one thing. Tam McGahern liked his women. This Wilma may have got you nowhere, but McGahern normally liked his girlfriends to be professionals. Experienced, as it were.'

'I've already tried Arthur Parks,' I said. 'Nothing.'

'Arthur Parks is a front man for Sneddon. McGahern would never have gone there. And he was never in one of my places. There was a group of girls working independently somewhere in the West End. What the Yanks would call 'call-girls': everything arranged discreetly for high-paying clients. Classy girls. McGahern provided security for them. He didn't run them, more that they paid him a cut to supply heavies, et cetera. The rumour was that McGahern was pretty cracked up on one of them. The tart that ran the house.'

I thought about what he was saying. Classy girls. In Glasgow, and talking about women who fucked for cash, it was a relative statement. I thought of Wilma Marshall's look.

'You have an address or number?' I asked.

'No. Like I said, it was all done very discreetly and we stayed out of it. Hammer Murphy wanted to force protection on them, but he didn't know where to find them. Added to which, it would have meant a war with McGahern. There were also rumours that these whores were keeping the police sweet. Or that they had high-level contacts. The odd thing is it was almost as if they disappeared from view. Not that they were much in view to start with.'

Jonny made a 'that's it' gesture with his hands. I hadn't told him all I knew and he probably hadn't told me all he knew. But that was the way it worked and I had at least got some new information.

'Listen, Jonny, you can maybe help me with something else. Not connected at all with McGahern. Have you ever seen this woman before?' I took out the picture John Andrews had given me of his wife. 'I think she's a professional too. She's called Lillian Andrews now but God knows what she went by before.'

'What's the deal?' He took the picture and examined it. 'Nice.'

'Only to look at,' I said. 'She's married to a man called John Andrews, who owns a big export business. Something's rotten in the state of Bearsden and there's a smell to the whole set up. Andrews is a scared man and I think it's entirely possible she's blackmailing him or has got some kind of hold on him.'

Jonny looked at the picture again. 'You know something . . . I think I've seen her somewhere before.' He shook his head, clearly annoyed that he couldn't recall. 'Can I hold on to this photograph for a day or two? Do a bit of checking?'

'Sure. But I need it back. It's the only one I've got.'

We switched to general chat for a while and then I thanked Jonny for his time and we made for the door. On the way out I saw a photograph of his parents on the bookcase. They were sitting outdoors at a cafe table under a sun that had never shone on Glasgow.

'How are your folks?' I asked.

'They're fine, Lennox. Thanks for asking. I worry about them. All the trouble with the Arabs.'

'You never fancy it yourself?' I asked.

'Israel? Naw. You can't get a decent fish supper there. Anyway, I was never political. That was my dad's thing. I remember, before the war, he was always talking about the trouble in the Mid East. I could never work out what the fuck was happening in Falkirk that worried him so much.'

I laughed.

'But,' he said, 'God knows I didn't expect them to emigrate at their age . . .' He shrugged, looking at the photograph. 'Just goes to show you never can tell what the future holds.'

I smiled. I was talking with Jonny the devoted son, not Jonny the gangster. The son who had financed his elderly parents' emigration to Israel. The Jewish boy from Newton Mearns who had served with the Second British Army in Germany and had walked through the gates of a camp on the Luneburg Heath forty miles south of Hanover with a name no one had heard of before. Belsen.

'Nope, Jonny. You never can tell.'

I had a clear goal when I left Jonny Cohen's. More a target. And after an hour sitting in my car outside the Highlander Bar I caught sight of it. I crossed the road and intercepted Bobby and his two chums, all of whom were still carrying the signs of our previous encounter, just as they were about to enter the bar. Dougie, the biggest of the trio, obviously still fancied himself as tasty.

'What the fuck do you want, Lennox?' he said, placing himself between me and Bobby and squaring his not insubstantial shoulders. 'We told you fucking everything we—'

I interrupted him with a sharp head-butt to the bridge of his nose. He slumped against the wall of the pub. Pete, ever his loyal companion, turned on his heel and ran. Bobby again was frozen to the spot.

'I cannot abide coarse language,' I explained to Bobby as I grabbed his upper arm and frogmarched him across the road, leaving the still-dazed Dougie propped against the wall.

I shoved Bobby into the passenger seat and drove down to the Clyde. Clydebank was still gap-toothed from wartime air raids and I parked on one of the half-cleared bombsites by the river. I hauled him out of the car and down to the pier. We stood near its edge, the water below black and sleeked with rainbow-swirls of engine oil.

Bobby eyed me sulkily through the eye I hadn't closed. 'One of these days you're going to push the wrong person too far.'

'Oh really? Well, until that day comes I've always got you.' I shoved him and he staggered back towards the edge of the pier. His hideous winkle-picker boots scrabbled on the rough rubble.

'This is very simple, Bobby. You held out on me. I told you I wanted to know everything about Tam McGahern.'

'I didn't hold out,' he protested. 'I told you everything I know!'

I gave another shove to his chest and he tilted precariously backwards. I grabbed a hold of his bootlace tie.

'I can't swim!' he bleated.

I laughed at him. 'This is the fucking Clyde, Bobby. You'll die of heavy-metal poisoning before you have a chance to drown. Anyway, shite floats. Now talk to me . . . what about the whore McGahern used to go to? The one he provided heavies for?'

The hate and fear on Bobby's face didn't leave much room for any other emotion, but for a moment something like confusion crossed it.

'What whore?'

'The classy operation in the West End. The one McGahern was giving one to.'

The penny dropped.

'Oh, aye . . . *her*. I didn't even think about her. I didn't think it was important. I wasn't holding out on you. I just didn't think about her.'

I yanked his bootlace tie and pulled him clear from the water's edge. In a way I was disappointed not to be throwing him into the Clyde. 'What was her name?'

'Molly. I don't know her second name.'

'Tell me about her.'

'I can't. I never met her. Tam had another heavy that he used as a chucker-out. He said me, Dougie and Pete wasn't smart enough for a job like that.' Bobby looked hurt and straightened his tie. 'I don't know what was so fucking special about being a chucker-out for a bunch of whores.'

'Who was this guy?'

'I don't know. Never met him.'

'So you don't know where this brothel was?'

'I didn't say that. One night Tam was supposed to be up seeing this tart, but he got held up at the Imperial. He got me to order him a taxi by 'phone. The address was in Byres Road. Or off it. I can't remember exactly.'

'That's a long road.'

Bobby shrugged. 'It was a long time ago. I can't remember the number. I don't think it would do any good anyway.'

'Why?'

'I heard Tam on the 'phone to Molly one night, about a month before he was killed. I got the impression that she was winding the business up. Or moving.'

I nodded, remembering what Jonny Cohen had said about the operation seeming to drop from view. 'What gave you that idea?'

'I don't know. But I think Tam was worried about him being involved with it maybe causing problems with the Three Kings.'

'I wouldn't have thought Tam would have been too worried about that.'

Bobby shrugged. For the first time I really examined him. He was younger than I had first thought; the twisted face and half-closed eye I had given him made him look almost vulnerable. I found I didn't have the appetite to push him around any more. 'I heard him talking to Jimmy Wallace about Hammer Murphy. Couldn't hear much because they kept it quiet. But I knew that Tam thought Hammer Murphy might take a pop at them.'

I thought about what Bobby had said. 'You told me you couldn't think of anyone who could be behind Tam and Frankie's killings.'

'I can't. Everyone knows it wasn't Hammer Murphy. Everyone knows that Hammer Murphy was dying to have a go at Tam, but that the other two Kings had said no.'

'Tam knew this?'

Bobby nodded.

'Why was Tam talking to Jimmy Wallace about this? I thought you said he wasn't involved with the outfit?'

'He isn't. Or wasn't. But Tam used to ask him things. Talk to him a lot. Like he could give him advice.'

I took a couple of pound notes from my wallet and stuffed them into the breast pocket of Bobby's thigh-length jacket. He took them out and looked at them. His mood lightened.

'What's this for?'

'Get yourself a new suit.'

The biggest immigrant group in Glasgow was the Italians. Some families had been here since the twenties or before, but most had endured repatriation or internment when the war broke out. Now they tried hard to be liked.

The Trieste was a small Italian restaurant near the city centre. I ate there a lot and had got to know the family who ran it. To start with the Rosselis had been surprised at my basic knowledge of Italian. Then they had been distrustful, realizing it was the passing acquaintance the invader – or liberator – has with the culture of the nation he occupies. Now they greeted me with an incurious familiarity that made me feel comfortable. Like the food, the atmosphere was cheap and cheerful.

I sat in the corner, under a tattered but colourful poster extolling the sunny virtues of Rimini, and ate spaghetti and drank a rough red wine.

I tried to get the image of Lillian Andrews out of my head. I had agreed to keep my nose out of whatever sordid business she had going on, but, let's face it, my word carried as little weight as hers probably did. But all of that would have to wait.

In the meantime my progress in getting to the bottom of the McGahern business was less than spectacular. After my meeting with Bobby, I had gone to the GPO main office in Waterloo Street and worked my way through the telephone directories for lawyers and estate agents who might handle sales in Byres Road. There were a few. I 'phoned around them, explaining that I was an American engineer who had moved to Glasgow to help design ship engines. I said that I was looking for a property in Byres Road and if they could give me details and asking prices of properties that had sold in the last three months. Most had been reluctant to help, but I'd ended up with a list of seven properties. I knew Byres Road well; it butted onto Great Western Road about half a mile from where my flat was. Tomorrow I would check the addresses out.

Other than that, I didn't have a thing to go on, unless Sneddon's boys turned something up on Powell, the Fred MacMurray lookalike.

The Italians were supposed to be experts at coffee. It was a skill that seemed to have skipped a generation or two of the Rosseli family and I left my cup half drained and went out into the street.

If there's one thing Glasgow can do well it's rain, and rods of it sparkled in the streetlights as I ran to my car. I was about to unlock the door when a dark-green Riley RMB, so shiny and sleek it looked straight off the production line, pulled up behind me. The door swung open and Jonny Cohen leaned his head out into the rain.

'Lennox! Leave your car there. I'll bring you back for it.'

'What's up, Jonny?'

'I've got something to show you.'

CHAPTER ELEVEN

We drove out of the city centre and headed east. I sat in the front passenger seat but had noticed the two large goons in the back seat as I had got into the Riley. As one of the Three Kings, it was no surprise that Jonny Cohen travelled with muscle. It was true that I genuinely liked Jonny and I came as close to trusting him as you could anyone in his position, but being picked up off the street by a crime boss and two of his goons tended to bring out the over-cautious side of my nature.

'Never mind about the boys.' Jonny read my mind. 'They're not here for your benefit.'

'What's this all about, Jonny?' I asked. We headed out on the A8. Despite Jonny's reassurances, I felt the need to keep track of our whereabouts. He turned and gave me one of his handsome smiles.

'We're going to see a dirty film,' he said.

Just past Shotts we turned off the main road and into the entrance of a small factory. The uniformed nightwatchman raised a finger to the peak of his cap when he saw Jonny and opened the gates to let the Riley through.

I had known that this place existed, but I hadn't known where it was. Jonny Cohen, like the other two Kings, needed a semi-legitimate business to pass cash and other stuff through the rinse. But I guessed there was more to this place than that: Jonny Cohen was well-known to be a major importer and distributor of hardcore, continental pornography. He was rumoured to supply a lot of the stuff sold south of the border, with a fort-nightly truck run to Soho. His enterprising efforts had succeeded in putting dirty magazines and blue movies on the list of leading Scottish exports. And, let's face it, nobody jerked off over whisky and shortbread.

We parked outside one of the factory's warehouses and Jonny led the way in.

There were two other men inside the warehouse. One was middle-aged and short, but had the mean, muscled look of an ex-boxer. The other was even older, nervy-looking and dressed like he worked in a bank. They stood next to an eight-millimetre film projector. A white sheet had been nailed up on the facing wall.

'These two gentlemen are business associates of mine,' explained Jonny. 'If you don't mind, we won't go into names at this point. All you need to know is that we don't just import porn, we make it as well. In Edinburgh, as a matter of fact. My friends here are, well, the wank film industry's equivalent of Sam Goldwyn and J. Arthur Rank.'

'Mr Cohen gave us a rough description of the woman you are interested in.' It was the bank manager type who spoke. 'He also explained how you described her exceptional . . . *magnetism* I suppose you'd call it. But it was when Mr Cohen showed us the photograph . . . May I see it again?'

Jonny nodded and handed him the picture of Lillian Andrews. He examined it for a moment and smiled, tilting it for the ex-boxer to look at. He gave a brief nod.

'No, there's no doubt about it,' he said. 'That's Sally Blane, all right.'

'Sally Blane?' I asked.

In answer the bank manager handed me the photograph while the boxer switched on the projector and turned out the strip lights. A caption, 'Housewife's Choice' came up on screen. The black and white film played mute, so I couldn't hear her voice, but I instantly recognized a younger Lillian Andrews as she opened the door to a door-to-door salesman.

'That's her all right,' I said. 'But she looks different.'

'Younger. We made it about five, six years ago,' explained the bank manager. By this time Lillian/Sally was performing an impressively professional blow-job on the salesman. 'Sally worked for us for about six months. She was a natural. You could say she was custom-made for it. We offered her more money than we have ever offered any of our performers to stay on, but she quit and we never heard from her again. But she was the kind of girl you never forget.'

'Where did you find her?'

'We put the word out that we were looking for new talent. One of our contacts put us on to her. She and her sister came along for an audition.' I tried not to think what an audition for a dirty film might involve. 'I'm not sure, but I think she might have been working in a knocking-shop in Edinburgh.'

I turned back to the screen. Lillian and the 'salesman' were now engaged in full intercourse in what looked like an improbable and certainly uncomfortable angle against a Belfast sink. I remembered the first time I met John Andrews: pompous, brusque, embarrassed; but desperately worried about the woman he loved. This was more than just a marriage for money: it was a set-up.

'Okay,' I said. 'I've seen enough. So Sally Blane is her real name?'

The bank manager turned off the projector and the lights went on.

'I couldn't tell you. All our payments were made on a strictly cash basis. No tax, no names, no pack drill. My guess is that it was a professional name though. Her sister worked for us too and she used a completely different name.'

The boxer placed the film spool back in the can and stacked them with some others. He handed me a brown foolscap envelope.

'These are stills taken from some of the films Sally made for us.' The boxer's voice was cluttered with long, flat Edinburgh vowels. 'We thought you'd maybe need a copy of them. If you need proof.'

'Thanks,' I said. I had a sickening feeling when I thought about the not too distant future: to showing John Andrews photographs of his wife performing sex for money. I should have walked away from this one when I had had the chance. I could still walk away. But I knew I wouldn't.

Jonny Cohen dropped his two heavies at one of his clubs before driving me back to where my car was parked outside the Italian restaurant.

'That was good of you, Jonny,' I said as we parked. 'I mean, going to all that trouble for something that isn't of any concern to you. I appreciate it.' As I made to get out of the car, he placed his driver-gloved hand on my forearm.

'I won't say think nothing of it, Lennox. You owe me. It's a favour I may call in some day.'

I thought about what he said for a moment and then nodded. 'Fair enough, Jonny.'

I stood and watched the deep-green Riley purr into the distance and felt an indistinct unease somewhere deep inside. I was working for Sneddon. I was indebted to Jonny Cohen. I was getting sucked deeper into a case for which I had stopped being paid. I reckoned I couldn't be in a much worse situation.

But I was wrong. I could.

CHAPTER TWELVE

I remember seeing, before the war, a circus film in which a lion-tamer placed his head in the mouth of a lion. I recall thinking it was a pretty stupid way to make a living. Now it was my turn. There was one last King left in the pack.

Hammer Murphy.

A name like Murphy was a badge in Glasgow. It marked you out, made clear your background and allegiances. Your religion. To Glasgow's Protestant majority, a name like Michael Murphy was the name of the enemy. A Fenian. A Mick. A *Taig*. Glasgow may have been the least anti-Semitic city in Europe, but it made up for it in the red-hot mutual hatred between Protestant and Catholic. It wasn't really anything to do with religion, but with origin. The Protestants were indigenous Scots, the Catholics the descendant families of nineteenth-century Irish immigrants.

Hammer Murphy was no more than five foot seven but could never be described as a small man. He gave the impression of being as wide as he was tall. Packed with muscle. Packed with hate. The other two Kings tended to joke about Murphy's lack of brains. He certainly was no scholar, but there was no under-estimating Murphy's vicious animal intelligence.

Everybody knew Hammer Murphy's story. It was the stuff of legends. And knowing the story made you want to avoid knowing the man.

Murphy had learned at an early age that he had been born with the deck stacked against him. He realized that he didn't have the intelligence to learn his way out of the cramped Maryhill tenement flat he shared with his parents, five brothers and two sisters. He also worked out that the British class system strictly rationed opportunity and that as a working-class Glasgow Catholic he didn't even own a ration book. It had been obvious to the young Murphy that he would never enjoy the things in life that others had been gifted by birth outside the tenements. Unless he took them.

All of this had contributed to a dark, malevolent fury that burned deep within Murphy. To begin with, violence had been his way of venting that fury. Violence for its own sake: 'Old Firm' matches between Celtic and Rangers providing the fevered tribal atmosphere. Then he had sought to combine violence with a strategy for survival and success. Productive violence. In his five brothers he had a ready-made gang. The Murphy firm had never been imaginative. It had taken the obvious route: starting with a minor local protection racket, stealing cars, housebreaking. Then they moved into loan sharking. And into another gang's patch.

It had all started as small stuff: a squabble between two insignificant wideboy gangs over a worthless patch of Glasgow turf. But a legend had been born. It was then that Murphy earned his nickname.

The other gang's leader had been Paul Cochrane. The usual way these things were settled was through attrition. Repeated gang battles. Advances made racket by racket, shop by shop, bar by bar, bookie by bookie. But Murphy had suggested to Cochrane that they settle it between themselves. A 'square-go' in front of both gangs. Whoever won would be the leader of both. Cochrane didn't ask what would happen to the loser.

It was expected that weapons would be used and Cochrane had had a set of home-made knuckledusters, a short but lethal spike projecting from its top. Murphy had used his fists, his feet, his forehead. Even his teeth. Cochrane's kicks and punches had made no impact on Murphy's battle-hardened face. When Cochrane had come at him with his weapon, Murphy had broken his arm. The fight had been swift, brutal and very one-sided. Cochrane had gestured his surrender with his unbroken arm.

The triumphant Murphy had then turned to the assembled gang members and told them they were now totally under his control. That now they were stronger. Better. Harder. He promised more money. More power. This was the beginning of something good for them all. Then, in a calm, measured tone, he told them that anyone who opposed him would get the exactly same as Cochrane was about to get.

It was a builder's short-handled, barrel-headed lead mallet.

In front of forty witnesses, Michael Murphy committed murder. More than that, he made it a spectacle: an exposition of extreme, psychotic violence to shock men who dealt in violence every day. When he was finished, he made Cochrane's former deputy scrape up what was left of the erstwhile gang boss's head with a shovel. His point had been made.

Everybody got to know about it. Including the police.

Murphy had been arrested, naturally. He could easily have ended up being hanged. But he had already achieved the status of a legend. The fear that surrounded him bordered on the superstitious. Maybe some thought that if they bore witness against Hammer Murphy, his execution would be no barrier to his returning to exact revenge.

The police knew that he had killed Cochrane. They knew where, when and how. But they couldn't put together a case against him. Murphy was released.

Two more bosses were to meet a literally sticky end courtesy of Murphy's lead mallet. After that, his criminal organization spread like a stain across Glasgow's West Side. It grew to such an extent that the only obstacles to total domination of Glasgow were Willie Sneddon and Jonny Cohen, the two most successful black marketeers in immediate post-war Glasgow.

Things soon got messy. The Second World War had just ended and there were a lot of guns in illegal circulation. The conflict between the three yet-uncrowned Kings had threatened to turn Glasgow into a new Chicago. At the beginning of 'forty-nine, Sneddon and Cohen combined forces and hit Murphy hard. Murphy's bookies were turned over by Cohen's armed robbers every second week. Top men in the Murphy organization were crippled or killed by Sneddon's hardmen. In the meantime Murphy hit both the Cohen and Sneddon operations hard. After Murphy's Jaguar exploded just as he was about to get into it, he called for a truce.

Jonny Cohen had then brokered the Three Kings Deal. In October nineteen forty-nine, over lunch in the elegant art deco surroundings of the Regent Oyster Bar in Glasgow's business district, the three most violent and powerful criminals in Glasgow divided up the city and its most profitable criminal activities. It was the coronation of the Three Kings. The deal struck became a successful and stable arrangement and now, five years on, Glasgow's criminal business was still conducted in comparative peace.

But Hammer Murphy continually strained at the bonds the deal put on him. Of the Three Kings, the bookies' money was on Murphy to be the one to shatter the peace. Whenever a deal was done, Murphy worried that he had been swindled by the other two. He also envied the influence his rivals had with the police, a foothold he had failed to attain. And if one of his firm was arrested, Murphy suspected that Sneddon or Cohen had instigated it through the bent coppers on their payroll.

Murphy was volatile, unpredictable, suspicious to the point of paranoia and the chip on his shoulder was as precariously balanced as it could be. And now I was going to have to find out if he was holding back about Tam McGahern's murder.

There was no way I could simply turn up on Hammer Murphy's doorstep the way I had with Jonny Cohen, or even Willie Sneddon. Instead, I 'phoned him from my office. I only got to speak to one of his goons but left a message explaining in none-too-specific terms what I wanted to talk to him about. I was told to call back the next day for an answer.

But I got my answer within a couple of hours.

After I 'phoned Murphy, I called John Andrews at his office and gave my code name and fake company details again. He didn't take my call. I explained to his secretary that it was urgent and she checked again, but again I got the brush-off. In a way I was glad to put off showing him the stills of his wife. Again I thought about how easy it would be to walk away from the whole sordid business.

God knows John Andrews was a difficult man to like, but it was as if I owed something to myself. To the Kennebecasis Kid. To prove that I could still do the right thing even after all the shit I'd been through. I had encountered another human being who I suspected, somehow and for whatever reason, was being exploited. Manipulated. It could be that I had it all wrong, but I knew that if I walked away, then I was walking away from whatever decency was left in me.

I had a habit of taking lunch in tea rooms that sat on the corner of Argyle Street. There was something about the tea rooms' large picture windows, high vaulted ceiling and black marble that reminded me of a place in Saint John I used to go with my parents when I was a kid back in New Brunswick.

I was on my way there when they took me off the street: two big Micks with busted-up noses and dark business suits.

'Mr Murphy has sent us. He wants to see you. Now. Get in the taxi.' My escorts flanked me and indicated the black cab that pulled up to the kerb. I allowed myself to be guided into it. I tried not to think that this was trademark Murphy; that God knew how many people had been taken off the street in the same manner, probably, given their obvious accustomed expertise, by the same gentlemen. Except the others who had been spirited away had never been seen again.

They took me out to Baillieston. It sat even greyer and uglier than usual under a moody sky and the scrapyard we entered merged seamlessly with its landscape. There was a huddle of Nissen huts in one corner of the yard. Against this backdrop, the honed razor gleam of the parked silver-grey Bentley announced Hammer Murphy's presence like a royal standard on a castle.

My escorts delivered me into the main hut and waited outside. Hammer Murphy sat behind the desk. Like the Bentley, there was the sheen of a sharpened razor about him: all grey mohair and freshly barbered and Brylcreemed. Since the last time I had seen him he had grown a pencil-thin moustache. The Ronald Coleman look sat with his battered Irish spud face no better than the Tony haircut and mohair suit did.

It's often difficult to imagine how some people can resort to the most extreme forms of brutality; to equate the inner violence with the outer appearance. That wasn't the case with Hammer Murphy. He gave you the feeling that he was perpetually on the verge of smashing his fist into someone or something. There was an intense density to his build, almost as if fury was an energy that bound the atoms of his body tighter together.

I considered making a witticism about the new moustache, but decided I would rather survive the encounter.

'Hello, Mr Murphy. You wanted to see me?'

Murphy looked at me with hate in his eyes. I knew not to take it personally. Hate was always there.

'I heard you wanted to talk to me,' he said. His thick Glasgow accent was still tinged with the Galway his parents had left. 'But something's come up. Something I need you to explain to me.'

'If I can.'

'You're looking into Tam McGahern's death. You've been throwing your weight around a bit, I hear.'

'No more than I have had to.'

Murphy stood up. 'Follow me.'

We went out into the yard and across to another of the Nissen huts. I noticed that I picked up my two-Mick escort again on the way. One of the heavies undid the padlock and we entered. This hut was used for storing engine parts and other smaller items salvaged from the scrapyard. There was something bigger on the floor of the hut, wrapped in a stained oily blanket. The package was about the size of a human body. I felt my pulse pick up the pace. Whatever was wrapped up in that blanket, I didn't want to see it. Everyone knew that Hammer Murphy was a life-taker, but no one, least of all me, wanted to be an indictable witness to the fact. That could cut short a promising career.

'Listen, Mr Murphy . . .'

'Shut the fuck up and look,' said Murphy. One of the goons closed the door behind us. I shut the fuck up and looked. The other goon peeled back the blanket from the body's face.

'Fuck,' I muttered.

'You do this?' Murphy asked.

'Me? Fuck no. I thought you . . .'

Murphy looked at me blankly for a moment. 'If we had done this and you was looking at it you would be lying next to him.' I spent a moment considering my promising career while I looked down at the mortal remains of Tam McGahern's erstwhile faithful retainer, Bobby. Someone had adjusted his DA hairstyle with a heavy object. His head was caved in on one side and a lot of what should have been inside was now outside his skull. I tried to dismiss the image of a five-pound barrel-head lead mallet from my mind. Hammer Murphy had no reason to lie to me.

'Then who?' I asked.

'Well, you gave him a hiding. And one of his muckers two hidings.'

'We had a disagreement. We fell out over who should succeed Mr Churchill. He said Rab Butler and I'm a Tony Eden man.' The gag didn't take so I moved quickly on. 'Bobby and his chums didn't tell me everything I needed to know about McGahern. Added to which they had a little party planned for me. I spoiled their surprise. Anyway, I also gave Bobby here a couple of quid. He was pathetic, in a way. A wanker playing at big shot.'

'Could it have been that cunt Sneddon?' Murphy said it as if it was a double-barrelled name. The Wilmington-Smythes and the Cunt-Sneddons.

'No. Sneddon doesn't even know about Bobby. If I had wanted Sneddon to get involved he would have sent Twinkletoes McBride to ease the flow of information. But that would have been about the extent of it. How did you come into possession of the body?'

'Sneddon, Cohen and me are splitting up McGahern's bars between us. Like always I got shafted. Sneddon got the Arabian Bar, the kyke got the Imperial and I get left with the fuckin' Highlander.'

'Good little earner, the Highlander. From what I saw,' I said conversationally, as if we were discussing the comparative merits of models of car and there wasn't the stink of stale blood and spilt brain matter from the Teddy Boy corpse on the floor.

'Anyway,' continued Murphy. 'This piece of shite was lying upstairs from the bar.'

'In the same flat that McGahern was killed in?'

Murphy nodded. 'We didn't want the polis finding out. So chummy here is going to the mincer.'

So it *is* true, I thought. Murphy owned a meat processing plant in Rutherglen, not far from where Tam McGahern had his garage. The rumour had always been that that was where Murphy disposed of any embarrassing reminders of business deals gone wrong. And not just his. He was supposed to have a profitable sideline in processing dead meat for Jonny Cohen and Willie Sneddon. I had become particular about where I bought my Scotch pies.

'I don't get it,' I said. 'He had nothing to give. He knew nothing. Why kill him?'

Murphy shrugged. 'Wee shites like him get killed all the time. By other wee shites like him. You sure you know nothin' about this?'

'Nothing. I didn't expect to see him again.'

'You won't now.' Murphy nodded and the goon covered up Bobby's face. 'You wanted to talk to me about Tam McGahern's killing. He had it coming. He had it coming from me. But I didn't do it or order it. It's like this . . .' He jabbed Bobby through the blanket with the toe of his handmade oxblood. 'All the usual suspects in the clear. There was one thing I wanted to tell you about McGahern. Something that only came up this week.'

'Oh?'

'I have a share in a travel agent. A silent partner, you could say.'

I'll bet, I thought.

'I'm not connected officially with the business,' Murphy continued, 'so McGahern wouldn't have known I would find out.'

'Find out what?'

'Tam McGahern made three trips inside two months. To the same place. Amsterdam. Now what would a wee gobshite like McGahern be doing in fucking Holland?'

'Tulip smuggling?' I smiled. Then I stopped. Murphy's expression suggested he was considering stopping me smiling permanently. 'I don't know. You any idea?'

'None. But it's new gen and I thought it might be useful to you.' He reached into his jacket pocket and pulled out a folded sheet of paper. 'I've got the exact dates here. To and from Holland. No hotel bookings though.'

'Thanks.' I looked at the sheet and pocketed it. 'I needed something new to go on.'

Murphy's taxi took me back to Argyle Street. No goons. I sat in the back as it bumped its way back into the city centre and thought about what I had got. Why had McGahern made so many trips to Holland? It was only once I was in the taxi that I remembered what Bobby had said about McGahern meeting with a foreign type at the Central Hotel. Maybe the big fat guy had been a Dutchman. After the taxi dropped me off I walked back to my office and 'phoned Willie Sneddon. He groaned when I told him about Holland and asked if I needed more money to travel there.

'I've got enough to keep me going for now,' I said. 'It could be nothing to do with him being killed. I'll check things out this end before I start booking boat tickets.'

'Anything else?'

'Not at the moment.' Sneddon was paying the bill, but I wasn't going to tell him about Bobby's new hair parting. There are some things that it's better not to have seen. I considered telling him about what Wilma had said about it being Frankie that night above the Highlander, but still held back. 'I'm not being funny, but you are more connected to the kind of business McGahern was involved in. What would Amsterdam mean to you from a *business* viewpoint?'

'Dunno. Diamonds, I suppose. But McGahern wasn't in that kind of league. Even I would need to get expert help if I got into that. Ask Cohen.'

I said I would and hung up. I tried to get John Andrews on the 'phone again but was given the same brush-off. I considered posting the photographs to him, but there was no guarantee his wife wouldn't open the envelope. I thought about sending them marked 'private and confidential' to him at his office, but all it would take would be a careless or pushy secretary and there'd be all kinds of shit to contend with. Dirty pictures of your wife in a plain brown envelope don't do much for your standing in the business community.

Let it go, Lennox.

CHAPTER THIRTEEN

I took Elsie, the nurse who had so solicitously cared for my clobbered noggin, out to the Trocadero. I usually avoided Glasgow's dance halls. They did big business: these were the mating grounds of the city's working class. And because Glasgow was a resolutely working-class city, the dance halls were filled to bursting every Friday and Saturday night.

My dislike of the dance halls stemmed from the fact that despite the glitz and the sham Hollywood glamour, they had the charm of municipal slaughterhouses. And they frequently became just that. The bouncers often outnumbered the bar staff and nudging someone and spilling their drink by accident could cost you an eye.

But Elsie, my pretty little nurse, was 'keen on the dancing', so our fourth date was to the Troc. I also suspected that she took comfort in a crowd that would keep my dishonourable intentions at bay.

We squeezed through the doors at eight thirty and I was hit immediately by the clammy heat of a thousand bodies condensing against anything from outside. The band was working its hardest to balance volume and tunefulness as it bashed its way through a version of the Ray Martin Orchestra hit 'Blue Tango'. We shouldered a path through the throng and I left Elsie standing on the edge of the dance floor while I got us some drinks. I spotted a table with two free seats and when I came back I steered her towards it. She fell into conversation, as Glaswegians tend to do with any stranger, with the three girls already seated at the table. We danced and drank the whole evening, the alcohol taking no effect in the hothouse of the dancehall.

Shortly after ten the density of the crowd in the Troc intensified as a wave of latecomers poured in, thrown out of pubs and onto the street by Scotland's Presbyterian licensing laws. A group of boys came in, no older than nineteen, with joyously murderous hate burning in their eyes. There was a depressing predictability about what would happen next and my instincts told me it was time Elsie and I should be going.

'There's going to be trouble,' I said when she protested. I was right. We had just made it to the door when we heard the familiar sounds of a gang fight breaking out.

I parked around the corner from the hospital. Glasgow was again wreathed in fog, not as thick as the night I'd encountered Lillian Andrews, but thick enough to give us the feeling of solitude.

After some kissing and fumbling Elsie pushed me away from her.

'That's quite enough of that, Mr Lennox.' She smiled with coquettish reproachfulness but there was a hint of nervousness in her voice.

'What's the matter, Elsie? Don't you like me?'

'I think you're very nice.' She regarded me in the half dark of the car appraisingly. 'In fact you're very handsome.'

'This doesn't bother you?' I laid my hand on my left cheek.

'No. Not at all. The scars aren't that bad and they make you look rugged. How did you get them?'

'I turned the other cheek. Unfortunately I turned it to a German grenade. Actually the scars are from the surgeon patching me up.'

Elsie frowned and traced the small web of thin white scars with her fingertips. I moved in on her again and she pulled back. 'I need to get back . . .'

We got out and I walked her back to the nurses' home.

'I found out what you were looking for,' she said as we walked. 'I couldn't find out everything, but I spoke to a friend who works in Hairmyres. They specialize in TB there.'

'What did you find out?'

'Wilma Marshall was taken by the police to Hairmyres Hospital. They had to collapse a lung and they put her on a course of that new TB drug, streptomycin. She had a bad reaction to it so they gave her nicotine to counteract the side effects. She was in Hairmyres for two weeks and then transferred to the sanatorium in Perthshire. That's all I could find out. My friend wasn't happy about giving the information. You said she's your cousin?' There was a hint of suspicion clouding Elsie's pretty heart-shaped face.

I nodded. 'My aunt is very worried about her.'

We came close to the nurses' home. I pulled Elsie gently into the mouth of an alley and out of the fog-wreathed pool of light from the street lamp. We kissed and then she protested as I hoisted her skirt up. She didn't protest enough. Afterwards, when we stepped back out of the alley mouth, she cried a little and I had to comfort her. She made me promise to see her again and I said I would meet her the following weekend. A promise. It was a lie and we both knew it.

As I walked back to where I'd left my car, the heavy feeling in my chest again warned that the fog was going to congeal into a suffocating smog. I had to drive back along Great Western Road at little more than walking pace, guiding myself by following the ribbon of kerb along the roadside. Fiona White was still up when I arrived home and came to the door.

'Pleasant evening, Mr Lennox?' The air tinted with a hint of sherry when she spoke. The extent of a Saturday night's recreation for a middle-class war widow in Glasgow.

'It was fine, Mrs White. You?'

Her small smile bordered on a sneer. She reached into the hall and handed me an envelope. 'A gentleman delivered this for you this afternoon.'

'Did he leave a message?'

'No. Goodnight, Mr Lennox.'

I threw the envelope down onto my bed unopened, took off my tie and hung up my jacket. I switched the radio on, lit a cigarette and looked out through the window at the street. The smog had closed its grip even tighter on the city. I thought of little Elsie's tear-stained face. There was a time when I would not have used a woman like that. When I would have thought of a man like me as a total shit. There was a time when I would not have done a lot of the things I did now.

I kept my radio permanently tuned into the BBC Overseas Service, the station created to persuade Canadians like me, as well as Australians and New Zealanders, that it was a jolly good idea to stay part of the British Empire. Listening to the Overseas Service had become a habit. Maybe it was because, ironically, it made me feel like I was back in New Brunswick. I listened to the news. Malenkov had succeeded Stalin as Soviet premier. Two members of the Kenyan Home Guard had been murdered in a Mau Mau guerrilla raid. Continued stalemate at Kaesong. More clashes between Arabs and Israelis. Hunt and Hillary had set up base camp in the foothills of Everest. Preparations continuing for the June coronation.

I opened the envelope Fiona White had given me. The note said simply: *Worth looking at.* There was a Chubb key with a tag bearing an address in Milngavie. I turned the envelope upside down and shook it: there was nothing else in it. Nothing to indicate who had sent it. My guess was that it had come from Willie Sneddon, but he hadn't mentioned it when I had spoken to him on the 'phone earlier. Maybe it was from someone else who didn't want to advertise their involvement, should the boys in blue visit me again and find it. I decided I would 'phone Sneddon and ask what it was all about. In the meantime, I had another property to find.

The next day I walked into Byres Road with the list of addresses I had gleaned from my calls to solicitors and estate agents. One was on Byres Road, the others on the streets that ran off it. All densely packed terraces of smaller Victorian townhouses, their faces pushed hard onto the street with only a token skirt of garden to the front. All red sandstone turned soot-black. Some of the houses had been subdivided into flats, the others still intact. Glasgow University was just around the corner and many of the flats and houses were occupied by middle-income academics.

I looked at each property from the outside first. None looked like former brothels. Or maybe they all did. I had my cover story at the ready, but was reluctant to go knocking door to door. There was one house, in Dowanside Road, about three hundred yards from the junction with Byres Road, that looked as likely as any. There was a narrow street to the side of the house that rose steeply away from Dowanside Road. I walked up it and around to the back of the house, trying to look as inconspicuous as I could on a quiet Sunday afternoon. The back of the house was guarded by rails, but I could see that the new occupant had begun renovation of a garden that had been let go. Brothel keepers don't spend a lot of time in the garden.

The affected accent of the Kelvinside area of Glasgow was a remarkable piece of vocal engineering. The socially pretentious Kelvinsiders could not imitate the vowel sounds of Standard Southern English, so instead tried to torture the instinctive Glasgow flatness out of each syllable. Cavalry became kevelry, cash became kesh. The woman who answered the door was the Torquemada of vowels. She was a small, plain housewife in her late thirties with dull reddish-blonde hair and a frosty manner. I could hear the sounds of children from inside the house.

'Ken I help you?' she said.

'Hi, ma'am. My name is Wilbur Kaznyk. I'm over here on vacation from the States and I was hoping to look up an old buddy of mine. War buddy. Frank Harris. I don't have his exact address, but I know it's here in Dowanside Road. Someone told me he'd sold up and moved. I believe you folks've just bought this house.'

For a moment she eyed me suspiciously. She called over her shoulder into the hall. 'Henry ... there's a menn here looking for a Frenk Herris.'

Henry appeared at his wife's shoulder. He was a small mole of a man behind thick glasses. I repeated my fiction about being an American guest.

'It wasn't this house,' he said. 'We bought this house from a Mrs McGahern. She was a young war widow, apparently.'

'Did you meet Mrs McGahern?' I pushed credibility as far as I could. 'I mean, maybe she bought the place from Frank and has a forwarding address.'

'We nayver met Mrs McGeyhern,' continued Henry's wife. 'She hed already moved. Everything was conducted through Mason and Brodie, her solicitors.' It had been Mason and Brodie who had given me the address. 'Perhepps you should ask them. Their offices are in St Vincent Street. Good day.'

She closed the door. So much for hands across the ocean. At

least I knew now that I had the right address. I was also pretty sure that Tam McGahern hadn't had a secret wife. I'd have to work out some way of getting the information from Mason and Brodie.

I thought about heading in to the Horsehead Bar at opening time for the traditional pie and pint but Hammer Murphy's processing plant came to mind, so I decided to have high tea in Byres Road. The overpriced pastries were too sweet. Rationing was being phased out and sugar had only just come off the ration book, so the new badge of affluence was to be liberal with it. I sat at the window and watched the world, or at least Byres Road, pass me by. I drank my tea and contemplated where I was with everything. The sun outside shone on the people and cars that passed with the joyfulness of a Presbyterian preacher: the time I felt most homesick for Canada was the British Sunday.

I made a decision and, after I'd paid, picked up my car and headed up towards Bearsden. Parking where I had before, I walked round to the drive of the Andrews house. A mink-coloured MG TF convertible swished down the drive and out onto the road and I ducked back out of sight, shielded by an overhang of thick bush. I recognized the driver as the blonde woman whom I'd seen Lillian Andrews with that night in the smog, and I was pretty sure it was Lillian in the passenger seat. I waited until they had pulled out into Drymen Road before heading up towards the house.

It was John Andrews who answered the door. He was wearing an open-necked shirt with a cravat and a pale-blue sweater that exaggerated a paunch that needed no exaggeration. Given that he had been avoiding my calls, I expected him to be taken aback, angry even. But he looked startled. And afraid.

'What do you want, Lennox?'

'We have to talk, Mr Andrews.'

'Our business is concluded. We discussed that already. My wife is back safe and sound.'

I held up the envelope. 'We need to discuss what I have here, Mr Andrews. I'm afraid it's important. May I come in?'

Andrews looked undecided for a moment, then stood to one side. I tried not to show that I knew my way into the Contemporary-furnished lounge. Andrews remained standing and didn't invite me to sit. I handed him the envelope with the photographs. After planning this moment for so long, I suddenly found that I wasn't sure what to say. I let him look at the pictures. Halfway through he didn't so much sit down as drop all the way onto the low-slung sofa. He kept looking. When he was finished he looked up at me. There was pain in his eyes. Lots of pain, but no surprise. Or disappointment.

'Are you satisfied now, Mr Lennox?' he said, the hate dull, heavy and blunt in his voice. 'Are you happy that I'm now humiliated before you?'

'No, Mr Andrews. This gives me absolutely no pleasure. I could have left things as they were—'

'Then why the hell didn't you?' His eyes were now glossy. 'Why didn't you leave *things* alone when I asked you to?'

'Because, Mr Andrews, I thought you were a man in trouble. And I think it even more now. I can imagine these pictures are upsetting for you to see, but I also know they were no surprise to you. Are you in trouble, Mr Andrews? Are you being blackmailed or something?'

He laughed a bitter laugh. 'I loved my wife, you know. I still love her. Lillian is so beautiful. So beautiful. I couldn't believe that I could be so lucky at this time of life. My first wife died, you see.'

'I'm sorry. So even then you thought it too good to be true?'

Another bitter laugh. 'Thanks for that, Lennox. Thanks for pointing out how obvious it should have been.'

'Listen, I know you're in trouble. I want to help if I can.'

'I see. Touting for more business . . .'

'I'm not interested in the money. You've paid me more than enough already. I just want to help.'

'Then leave me alone. Just piss off and leave me alone. I'm in trouble all right. I've married a gold-digger and a slut and she's going to take me for everything I've got. That's all the trouble I'm in. And believe me that's enough. Isn't that enough for you, Mr Lennox?'

I picked up my hat. 'If you say so. But I still think there's more to this. If you need my help, 'phone me at my office or on this number.' I wrote down the number of my digs. 'One more thing . . . you maybe aren't aware of this, but Lillian's real name is Sally. Sally Blane. I thought you ought to know. If that still is her legal name and she married you under a false identity, then the marriage is void. You could get out.'

He continued to glare at me with a dull hatred, but took the number anyway.

I stopped off at the Horsehead Bar for a couple. I needed them. I didn't like Andrews. I didn't like his fleshy, ugly face, his affected manner or the way he talked. But once more, somewhere deep inside, I felt pity for another human being in distress. Again it surprised me. I thought that capacity had died in the war along with the kid from the Kennebecasis.

A couple became three or four and I started to think about the little nurse again. And then about Fiona White, my landlady. About her Kate Hepburn eyes. About kissing her to loosen the lips that were always drawn too tight. About how easy it would be for one bundle of damaged goods to get mixed up with another.

About how shit everything and everyone was.

Big Bob asked me if I wanted another but I said no. I was getting into that ugly tinder mood that needs just one drink too many to catch light and then you want to smash a face, any face, just to make someone else feel worse than you do. There was more Scots blood in me than I liked to admit.

I went out into the cold and clammy Glasgow night. I left the car outside the Horsehead and walked all the way back to my flat. It was a long walk and the night air slowly cooled my mood. I stood outside the house. The curtains of Fiona White's downstairs flat were drawn but edged with warm light. The two girls would be asleep in the room to the back, probably dreaming of a father whom they now only really remembered from photographs.

I opened the door quietly and moved quickly up the stairs once I'd closed it behind me. Tonight was not the night to bump into Mrs White. Tonight there was a danger that our mutual need for comfort would be too great.

Or perhaps I was deluding myself.

CHAPTER FOURTEEN

I met Jock Ferguson at lunchtime in the Horsehead Bar. I had arranged it with him earlier by 'phone and given him a rough idea what it was I was looking to find out. But with coppers there is always a price. They are inquisitive by nature. Nosy.

'Why do you need this information?' Ferguson asked. 'Is this something we should be interested in?'

'It's a case I'm working. Something stinks with it. First of all this guy asks me to find his missing wife, then he tries to pay me off, then his wife flashes her tits at me while her buddy cracks my head open.'

'You lead a colourful life, Lennox. Where does this company come in?'

'He owns it. Or runs it. He was none too specific about exactly what it was that they did.'

'Well, I checked it out all right. If your guy is John Andrews, then he owns the company. CCI stands for Clyde Consolidated Importing. The consolidated comes from the fact that Andrews bought a number of smaller companies and formed one big one from it. They have warehouses down on the Clyde and a big office in Blythswood Square.'

'What do they export?'

'Plant, machine parts, that kind of thing. All over. North America, Middle East, Far East . . . You say you had a run-in with the wife?'

'That's one way of putting it. The stitches come out tomorrow.'

'Were they worth it?' Ferguson asked.

'Were what worth it?'

'The tits.' Ferguson came the closest he ever did to a smile.

'I've been able to find out that she's an ex-whore,' I said, ignoring his question. 'Maybe still is. Or at least she used to act in blue movies. You know, the kind you guys like to watch at police smokers.'

He gave me a look. 'Is he crooked?'

'No. That's the thing. Seems a straight Glasgow businessman, if that isn't a contradiction in terms. He obviously didn't know about his wife's past.'

'Until you put him right.'

'Actually, I'm maybe wrong to say that he didn't know. When I showed him the pictures—'

'Pictures? You showed him photographs of his wife fucking? You're quite a piece of work.'

'Anyway . . .' I tried to live with Ferguson's disappointment. 'When I showed him the pictures he wasn't really shocked. More sad. Resigned.'

'A set up?'

'Dunno.' I took a mouthful of pie with more grease than a tractor's axle. Glasgow was not one of the world's culinary capitals. 'That's the feeling I get. Doesn't fit. His wife used to go by another name. However, which is her real and which is her professional name I don't know. But it doesn't fit with blackmail either.'

Ferguson shrugged. 'Well, let me know if you think there's something going on that we should know about.'

We talked about other things until we finished our pies and pints. In fact, Ferguson was making small talk. Or as close to small talk as he could manage. The one thing he was at pains not to discuss with me was the McGahern killing. The one thing that should have cropped up, even if only to repeat his earlier warning.

The next day I went to my local doctor, who removed the stitches from the back of my head. Which was a relief, because they had begun to itch like a son-of-a-bitch. Afterwards I went into my office and it was there that I got the call. It was a young woman. She spoke with an approximation of a middle-class accent, but Glasgow kept reappearing in it, like an unwanted coarse relative trying to squeeze in through the door of a dinner party. She didn't give her name, even when I asked directly.

'All you need to know is that I was a close friend of Tam McGahern. I know you've been asking questions about him. I have information you need.'

'Then just tell me.'

'Not on the 'phone. Meet me down by the river, at the Broomielaw, tonight at ten.'

'You know something?' I said. 'I never understand why people always say that in movies and some mug always goes along with it . . . "Not on the 'phone. Meet me in person in some secluded and dark place where you can get your head bashed in with a tyre iron." Now why should I meet you in a quiet, dark place?'

'Because the people who are mixed up in this are a dangerous bunch. I don't want to be seen talking to you.'

'I've got a better idea. It's called hiding in plain sight. I'll meet you in the main concourse of Central Station. And not ten, nine. I get wrinkles if I stay up late.'

She began to protest but I hung up.

Central Station was just around the corner from my Gordon Street office, but I decided to go back to my digs first and freshen up. I drove back into the city, parked in Argyle Street and walked up to the station to give me a chance to recce every-thing out properly.

I turned up early. About twenty to nine. I stood under the main station clock, looking up at the information board as if planning my journey. There were still people milling about the station. The Edinburgh train arrived and a wave of travellers pulsed through the cavern of the station building. Then it became quieter again. Ten to nine.

I became aware of a smallish figure next to me. Actually I became aware of the odour before the figure. A man of about fifty. Or twenty. Serious drinking had fudged the issue. The lines on his unwashed face where grime had entrenched itself in the creases looked as if they had been drawn in graphite onto grey skin. He looked up at me and bared the ruins of his teeth.

'Y'awright pal?'

'The best. You?'

'Oh you know . . . cannae grumble. Widnae dae much use. Would you have a few pennies to spare?' The tramp spoke with the kind of gutteral Glasgow patois that had confused the hell out of me when I had first moved to the city. To start with I thought the city had a large indigenous population of Gaelic speakers. It took me weeks to realize it was in fact English.

'Let me guess,' I said. 'You've lost your train fare home and you would like me to *lend* you the money, right? And you *promise* that if I give you my address you'll send a postal order to me first thing tomorrow?'

'Naw,' he grinned wider. I wished that he hadn't. 'Naw, I wouldnae say that at all. I'll tell you exactly what I want the money for. Drink. I could lie, mind. But the truth is I would like you to spare me a few pennies so I can get pished.'

'I admire your honesty.'

'Always the best policy, pal. But I'll tell you this and it's no lie: whatever you gie me will be carefully invested. Gie me a couple o' bob, and I can guarantee that of everybody that will ask you for a handoot in the station the night, naebody else will be able to stay drunk for as long as me. Per penny invested, that is.'

'I also admire your pitch,' I said.

'Thanks pal. I'm a leading expert in the field.'

I laughed and handed him a half crown and he was gone.

The station clock struck nine. I glanced around again. No mysterious blonde femmes fatales. No heavies with hands tucked into their jackets. I waited another ten minutes. Nothing. Five minutes more and I left the station. My date had obviously decided Central Station wasn't romantic enough. I walked along Gordon Street past a row of smoking taxi drivers and down Hope Street towards Argyle Street, where I had parked the car.

They jumped me while I was unlocking my car door.

There was a large Bedford van parked close behind me, which I thought suspicious because the rest of Argyle Street was practically empty of parked cars. Because it had pricked my attention I had been half-expecting something and heard them running towards me from the tail of the Bedford. Four of them. Two on either side. Big.

The one who came nearest first swung a length of lead pipe at my head. I didn't have time or room to duck so I jammed forward and into him, weakening the strength of the swing. I brought my knee hard up into his balls. Really hard. And as he doubled over I hooked my fist up and cracked it into his face. I heard him moan and as he went down I grabbed his wrist and snatched the pipe from him. They were all on me now and I swung wildly. I hit two of them. I got one in the face and he screamed as his cheek split open.

I had two temporarily down, one stunned and one uninjured. I couldn't win this fight, but it wasn't a fight they were looking for. They were trying to snatch me off the street and they had lost the element of surprise.

Someone kicked me at the top of my thigh, missing the groin they had aimed for. I took three heavy punches to the side of my face but stayed on my feet. I swung the pipe again and made glancing contact with a head. I was tiring. I took another punch and tasted blood. I hit the pavement and the kicks started to rain in. But then stopped.

I heard the Bedford reverse at speed, a grinding of gears and it sped off. I heard the shrill sound of a police whistle and flat feet running towards me. I dragged myself upright and caught sight of the tail of the van as it swung around the corner into West Campbell Street. A young bobby grabbed my arm and steadied me.

'You all right?'

'I'm okay.' I spat a small puddle of viscous crimson onto the pavement. There was a small crowd gathering around me. A green and orange tram had emerged from the black Argyle Street underpass beneath the huge *Schweppes* sign on Central Station's flank. As it passed most of the passengers on my side gawped at me.

'What was all that about?'

'No idea,' I said. 'They jumped me when I was getting into my car. Maybe they wanted to steal it.'

The young copper eyed me sceptically. 'Who were they?'

'How the hell should I know? Like I said, I was just getting into the car when they jumped me.'

'Did you get the number of the van?'

'No,' I lied. ''Fraid not.'

CHAPTER FIFTEEN

I have an aversion to police stations. As I walked into the St Andrew's Street nick I felt the phantom of a farm lad's fist on my neck. The Station-Sergeant eyed me suspiciously when I asked to speak to Detective-Inspector Ferguson. In my experience, all Station-Sergeants tended to be the same. Most of them were older coppers nearing the end of their careers, or retired to a desk for health reasons. They all wore the same weary 'seen-it-all' expression: it seemed to be a prerequisite to getting that little crown above your stripes that you had to be a cynical fucker. I told this particular Happy Harry that I had an appointment.

Jock Ferguson came out five minutes later and led me into his office.

'I need a favour, Jock. I need to know who the registered owner of this vehicle is.' I handed him a slip of paper with the number of the Bedford truck on it. I knew I was pushing my luck. Ferguson took the note and looked at it.

'I hear you were involved in a bit of a public exhibition the other night. I take it this is the truck involved?'

I nodded.

'Why did you tell the constable you didn't catch the number?'

'Delayed recall,' I said. Ferguson didn't laugh. 'I wanted to keep it unofficial.'

'And why is that? I thought you told the beat man that you reckoned they were after your car.'

'I think it's got something to do with the case I'm working.'

'You know something, Lennox? I think that case is the McGahern case. If it is, you're heading for a shitload of trouble. You were warned.' Ferguson's tone was neutral and I couldn't read any threat into it. 'Have you been poking your nose where it's not wanted?'

'Me? No ... You know me. I'm not the curious type. But maybe someone out there thinks I'm involved because of my run-in with Frankie McGahern. It's just that I was given a beating for some reason and they made off in that truck.' I nodded towards the slip of paper with the number of the Bedford truck on it.

'Okay ... I'll check it out. Give me a day.'

I had lunch at a greasy spoon place and headed back to my office. I felt a bit queasy when I arrived. It could have been the eggs I'd eaten, but it was more likely to have been the sight of an expensively tailored Willie Sneddon and a Burton-suited Twinkletoes McBride waiting for me outside the door to my office. Twinkletoes smiled at me and I felt even queasier.

'We were in town,' explained Sneddon. 'I thought I'd get the latest from you.'

I unlocked my office door and let Sneddon and Twinkletoes go ahead of me.

'There's not much to tell,' I said. I offered them a whisky but Sneddon turned it down for both of them. 'But someone's getting rattled,' I told Sneddon about the botched attempt to snatch me on Argyle Street.

'You recognize any of them?' asked Sneddon.

'No. But if it had been one of the other two Kings, they wouldn't have sent anyone I would recognize. But that doesn't fit. I think this is some independent outfit, maybe even something to do with McGahern's operation. But I smell a new team in town. These guys were big and enthusiastic but really clumsy. Inexperienced.'

'Whoever it is, they're trying to scare you off.' Sneddon was wearing a double-breasted mohair suit, similar to the one Hammer Murphy had been wearing the last time I saw him. He reached into his jacket pocket. For a moment I thought he was going to pull a gun. Instead he took out a gold cigarette case. A gun would probably have weighed less. He lit up.

'No. They were trying to do more than that. They were trying to lift me off the street. Maybe they were as interested in what I could tell them as I am in what they could tell me. Or it could be that it was going to be a strictly one-way trip.'

'That's what I thought,' said Sneddon. He flicked ash onto my floor. 'That's why I'm having Twinkletoes shadow you. Protection.'

'I can look after myself, Mr Sneddon.'

'I'm not offering. I'm telling.' Sneddon's expression darkened. 'People know that you're working for me, even if it's only temporary. No one fucks about with someone who works for me. I let this go and it sends out the wrong signals. For all we know it could have been that Fenian fucker Murphy, just pushing things to see how far he can go. Twinkletoes is watching your back from now on.' Sneddon stood up to go. Twinkletoes didn't. 'But listen to me good, Lennox. If I hear you've tried to lose him or give him the slip, then I'll get him to give your toenails a trim. Hear me?'

'Then I quit.' I took the cash Sneddon had given me out of my wallet and held it out to him. 'Your money's all there. I can't work the way you want me to. I talk to all sorts who would run a mile at the idea of anyone, least of all Twinkletoes, knowing they were a contact of mine. You hired me because I'm independent. Because you know that by buying my loyalty for only a short time, you're buying it completely. I appreciate your interest in my welfare, but what I do is a risky business and I look after myself.'

Sneddon glared at me. A hardman glare. He didn't take the money, so I dropped it onto the desk for him to pick up. We were all three standing now. Worryingly, Twinkletoes had stopped smiling. I felt my toes wriggle involuntarily within my shoes.

'Have it your way, Lennox.' He picked the money up and handed it back to me. 'It's your neck.'

There was a pause. I spoke as much to fill the silence as anything. 'By the way, I got the key you sent. What's the significance?'

Sneddon looked at me blankly for a moment. 'What the fuck are you talking about?'

I took the key out of the desk drawer I had stashed it in, and handed it to Sneddon. The tag with the address in Milngavie was still attached.

'I didn't send you this,' said Sneddon.

I regretted having mentioned it. I had assumed it had been Sneddon, but it could have been Jonny Cohen or even Hammer Murphy.

'My mistake.' I reached out for the key but Sneddon was still examining the address tag.

'But I think I know what this key might be for. Tam McGahern lived with his brother in a flat in the West End. You can't get near it because it's still lousy with cops. But there was a rumour that Tam bought another couple of places. A few months ago. One of them was a house in Milngavie. But the way I heard it was an investment. He was going to rent it out or sell it at a profit.'

'I'll check it out,' I said. I looked across at Twinkletoes, who still wasn't smiling, then back to Sneddon. 'We're clear that I work alone on this, Mr Sneddon?'

'I fucking said so, didn't I?' He stood up. 'But keep me completely up to date on progress, Lennox. Or I swear to God I'll have Twinkletoes make me a necklace out of your toes.'

Milngavie and Bearsden sat next to each other on the north side of the Clyde and were both climbers on the Glasgow social ladder. But Milngavie, bizarrely pronounced *Millguy* by the locals with an odd defensive pride, was one chip-on-the-shoulder rung down from its neighbour.

I waited until evening before driving up to the address on the key tag. The house itself was one of the many anonymous bungalows built twenty years before. In this case, someone had added a dormer window in the roof, obviously converting the attic into a bedroom. If Tam McGahern had intended this to be his home, then its modesty was a comparative statement of his status in Glasgow's crime hierarchy: in contrast to Jonny Cohen's Newton Mearns architect-designed modernity or Willie Sneddon's mock-baronialism, this was humble stuff indeed. It was difficult to equate a flash gangster with this suburban banality.

I parked across the street and back from the house and watched for a while. Dusk turned to dark and the lights flickered on in the windows of its neighbours, but the house remained in darkness. I waited another ten minutes before leaving the car where it was and walking across to the house. There was a wrought-iron gate which protested with a squeak as I opened it, but the neighbouring houses were far enough apart for it not to be heard. I moved quickly up the path that led through a well-tended garden and slipped the Chubb key into the lock. It fitted. I slipped into the dark of the hall.

The first thing I did was to go through the house and draw all of the curtains, switching the lights on in each room as I went. I had brought a torch with me, but there is nothing more certain to bring the police to the door than the report of torch-light in an unlit house.

The house surprised me. This was no investment property: Tam McGahern's personal things were all over the place. The cops hadn't known about this place. No one had known that Tam had built himself a little nest away from the flat he shared with his brother. Well, practically no one: whoever sent me the key had known.

The furnishings were modest and tasteful, not what you would expect from a Gorbals-bred hardman and for a moment I started to doubt if it really was McGahern's place. But it was. The front bedroom had a large walnut wardrobe packed with the kind of exclusively tailored suits you see only on movie stars or gang-sters. A bureau drawer was filled with cash: income avoiding the touch of banker or taxman.

There was also a row of photographs on the living room mantelpiece. Tam with his mother. Tam with Frankie and his mother. All the photographs were of the prosperous post-war Tam with the exception of one. In it, a younger, tanned Tam in Desert Rat uniform with sergeant's stripes on the khaki sleeve stood smiling with a group of other men under a bright and definitely not Scottish sun. The backdrop was a sand-crusted military vehicle. There were five men in the group. Three of them looked foreign. Darker. I took a penknife, prised open the back and slipped the wartime photograph from the frame and pocketed it. As I did, I checked the back of the photograph. It had a single word written on it: *Gideon.*

I also liberated the bureau of its burden, doing a rough count as I stuffed the rubber-banded bundles into my jacket pockets.

I reckoned there was over six hundred quid there. Whoever had sent me the key may or may not have known about the presence of the cash. If they did and had prior claim, then I would keep it safe for them. Lost and found, you could say. But Tam McGahern's tiny empire was being carved up. This could be my little slice.

As I worked my way through the rest of Tam McGahern's house, I was aware it was full of anomalies. Some things were typical of someone like McGahern, others weren't. Like the books. Dozens of them. And not pulp fiction paperbacks: McGahern seemed to have had an interest in history and a couple of the volumes on the bookshelves were heavyweight academic tomes. Others were book-club editions. There was a world atlas, and one exclusively of the Middle East.

I remembered what I had heard about what the army psychologist had said about Tam's intelligence. The evidence of it was all around me. It should have been enough to keep him alive, but the prison quack had also identified Tam's psychotic rage. With Tam impulse always triumphed over reason. He had been killed by his own rage. More than that, he had been killed by someone who calculated that they could rely on his rage to overcome his judgement.

I had the feeling that this was a private space. Somewhere that McGahern spent time alone. It was the only reason that would explain him choosing to do his fucking in that sordid hovel above the Highlander Bar. If there were any hidden secrets, this was where Tam would hide them. I went through the house and switched off all of the lights except the one in the kitchen. I would work through the house a room at a time. There was no need to advertise my presence more than was necessary. I took a heavy-handled breadknife from the kitchen drawer and worked my way on my hands and knees across the floor, tapping the linoleum

CRAIG RUSSELL | 133

with the handle. Solid. I went through every cupboard and drawer and checked the walls for any hidden recesses. Nothing.

It took me a good hour to find it. In the bathroom. The bath was new and built-in rather than free standing, and the bath panel had been recently and expertly tiled, which was why the ragged grouting along the bottom of two of the tiles caught my eye. I used the breadknife to ease the two tiles free and jammed my hand into the void beneath the bathtub. After a bit of scrabbling my fingers closed around a cloth bag fastened with a drawstring. I pulled it out and opened it up. Jackpot.

The bag was about eight or nine inches square and packed tight. I tipped the contents out onto the linoleum floor of the bathroom. It was a criminal's equivalent of a life-raft: the way out in an emergency. It was very impressive. Too impressive for a middle-league Glasgow crook. If things turned bad for Tam then all he needed to make a clean and total break was stowed in this canvas bag. But Tam had gone down faster than the *Titanic* and never did have the chance to use his carefully assembled escape package. There was money, a pocket notebook and three passports: two British and one American. It was only because they all had Tam McGahern's photograph above false names that I could tell they were fake. Other than that, they looked perfectly genuine to me.

Forgeries of that quality took a lot of money, time and the kind of contacts that I could not imagine Tam having. I counted the US dollars; two thousand in total, tight rolls, bound by elastic bands. I remembered McNab asking me if I knew what had happened to the money that had disappeared when Tam had been murdered: this couldn't be it. There was a lot, but not enough for McNab to get physical about. But there was more than enough to get you to the other side of the world. Or, given the presence of a fake American passport, more likely to the other side of the Atlantic.

I carefully re-rolled the money and fastened it with the elastic bands. I put it into my jacket pocket to keep the six hundred quid company. After all, I might need a life-raft myself at some point in the future. It looked like I was going to have to hollow out another volume from the H.G. Wells oeuvre.

After making a note of the fake names, I gave the passports a wipe with my handkerchief before putting them back in the bag, which I then stuffed back under the bath: I thought it best to leave something for any future visitors to find. I kept hold of the notebook. It had a list of initials and numbers, the sense of which didn't leap out at first examination and I wanted to take my time going through it later. I fitted the tiled section back in place, switched off all the lights and made my way in darkness downstairs to the front door. I had just unfastened the Chubb lock when I heard it. The squeaking protest of the gate at the end of Tam McGahern's garden.

CHAPTER SIXTEEN

I eased the Chubb closed again as quietly but quickly as I could. I moved through the darkened house to the kitchen where I used my torch to find the back door. There was a heavy key in the mortise lock. I would let myself out into the back garden, taking the key with me and lock the door from the outside, hoping that whoever was paying a visit didn't feel like taking in the night air.

Slipping the torch back into my cash-stuffed pocket I turned the key. The door didn't unlock: the key half-turned and then seemed to jam. I reckoned that whoever was coming up the path would be at the front door by now. I tried the lock again, turning the key one way then the other, making more noise than I should. Nothing. I heard the sound of the front door unlocking and opening. I leaned my weight against the door, pushing it back in its frame and trying the key again. It turned in the lock with a loud clunk. I slipped out into the dark garden, easing the door shut. I didn't lock it behind me as I'd planned: it would make too much noise and for all I knew whoever was there had already heard it unlock. I eased back from the door. There was no moon and the garden to the rear was hedged in; as far as I could see, I was crouched on a small patio of concrete slabs. I moved like a blind man, afraid I might bump into something and give away my presence. The kitchen light went on. It meant I could see something of my surroundings. It also meant that anyone in the kitchen could probably see me. I scoured the garden desperately for a hiding place, but it was small and laid out as level lawn edged with low shrubs, offering no opportunity to hide.

There were three men in the kitchen, illuminated by the yellow-white ceiling light. I recognized one of them instantly. I rushed forward and ducked under the sill of the window, pressing hard into the wall. I slipped the sap from my pocket, ready to use it should the back door open. There was what looked like a gap between the wall edge furthest away from me and the hedge, suggesting I could get around the side of the house. I started to ease towards it, keeping low and making as little noise as I could.

I was crossing in front of the kitchen door when I heard the handle turn.

I rushed headlong towards the corner of the house. The kitchen door opened and a swathe of yellow light cut across the small lawn, framing the projected shadow of a huge man. I ducked around the corner of the house, hoping that my scrabbling across the concrete slabs had not attracted the attention of the figure in the doorway.

I found myself in a narrow space between the hedge and the wall of the house. I kept my feet planted as if glued: the space had been filled with stone chips and the slightest movement would make a crunching sound and attract the attention of the heavy at the door. There was enough shadow for me to stay concealed while keeping an eye around the corner. A second man came to the doorway with a torch and shone it into the garden. I ducked my head back out of sight. The two men exchanged a few words in a language that I didn't recognize, then closed the door again. The kitchen light went out and the darkness dropped back into the garden.

I edged along the windowless side of the house, trying to

minimize the gravel-crackle of each footstep, and checked the front. The curtains were still drawn but I could see the light from inside leach out at the window edges. I made a quick measure of the distance from the house corner where I crouched in shadow to the gate. There was a Wolseley parked outside the front gate that hadn't been there when I had arrived. I reckoned I could move silently over the grass, but it would be quicker to grasp the nettle and use the squeaking gate, rather than risk entanglement clambering across the chest-high privet. I was just about to launch my run when I saw an amber-red glow in the cavern of the parked Wolseley suddenly swell then diminish. A drawn-on cigarette. They had obviously left a sentry outside.

I drew back and muttered a few words that my mother didn't think I knew. I leaned against the wall and considered my situation. A typical Lennox one: I was crouched in the dark with nearly two thousand American dollars and six hundred English pounds bulging in my pockets, there were four heavies to deal with, one sitting smack bang in the middle of my escape route and another inside whom I already knew to be a real pro. I'd started off thinking that I'd be lucky to get out of here with the cash. Now, I'd consider myself lucky to get out in one piece.

There was nothing else for it than to sit tight and wait until the guys inside finished whatever it was they had to finish or found whatever it was they had to find. The last thought chilled me: what if they were picking up the cash? Maybe they would put two and two together and work out that the cash had gone out the unlocked back door. Then they'd come looking. I pushed at the hedge tight in front of me. With a little effort I could squeeze through it and into the garden of the house next door. But it would be noisy.

I couldn't see my watch but I reckoned I'd been in the house for roughly a couple of hours and out here for twenty minutes. That made it about half past midnight. Not a lot happened in Milngavie at half past midnight and there wasn't even the sound of cars in the distance. I decided to wait it out.

I didn't have to wait long. I heard the front door open and the three goons from inside headed out. No hint of them searching for an intruder. They walked quietly to the Wolseley and got in. The last guy out turned as he closed the gate, trying to minimize the squeaking. His face in the streetlight was shadowed by the brim of his hat but he seemed to look directly at me and my chest went very tight very fast. He turned and got into the car and they coasted down the incline for a hundred yards before starting the engine.

In the sterile Milngavie quiet I could hear the car until it faded into the far distance. Still I waited another ten minutes to reassure myself there hadn't been a fifth goon left inside McGahern's house before I made my way as quietly as possible across the grass, through the gate and back towards where I had parked the car.

While I waited I had thought about the figure I had seen in the light of Tam McGahern's kitchen and the strange language he had spoken to the other two men. They had looked foreign. Dark. But, whatever lingo he had been speaking, it had done nothing to dispel the impression I had of him the first time I'd met him. He still reminded me of the actor Fred MacMurray.

CHAPTER SEVENTEEN

I lit a cigarette to dampen down the cough that had woken me. It was already light and I heard the sound of a draughthorse's hooves outside on Great Western Road. A factory whistle flatly sounded the beginning of a day's monotony for the masses somewhere far across the city.

I swung my legs around and sat on the edge of the bed smoking for a while before I pulled the brown envelope from under my pillow. I had stuffed the cash, the wartime photograph and the notebook I had found at McGahern's into the envelope and hidden it there. It had been after one by the time I got in and I had seen the brief cold glow of Mrs White's light under her door when I tiptoed in, switched on just long enough to let me know I'd disturbed her. There had been no way I could have started lifting the lid on my floorboard hidey-hole and I had been too tired to start hollowing out another book.

I sat stubbornly staring at the notebook, refusing to accept that the meaning of the rows of numbers and letters was never going to leap out at me spontaneously. After ten minutes I soothed my frustration by counting the money again. I had come out of this very nicely. And coming out of it was exactly what I wanted to do. I would give up on the two hundred Willie Sneddon was going to give me for a name. I even considered giving him the hundred back – after all I was well ahead of the game – but I decided against it. Doing that would only signal that, somehow and somewhere along the line, I had scored. I would simply tell Sneddon that I had drawn a blank: that no one was holding out on me, it was just that they really didn't have a clue who was behind the McGahern thing.

Of course I had started the whole thing myself out of sheer curiosity and bloody-mindedness, but a couple of thousand quid did a lot to assuage one's curiosity. Maybe it was time to move on. Or even go home. I now had a reasonable amount of cash behind me, not a fortune, but enough to go a long way in Canada. And, of course, my folks had money.

I had a vague and goofy image of myself buying a place in Rothesay or Quispamsis with a boat moored at Gondola Point, an image that impossibly included Mrs White and her kids. But I was kidding myself: it hadn't been the want of cash that had kept me here. Everybody would be expecting the return of the Kennebecasis Kid: the youth I had been and was no more. Probably the youth I had never been: the truth was that there had always been something in me. A bad seed. The war had just cultivated it. There were a lot of adjectives to describe how men came out of the war: changed, disillusioned, dead. The adjective I used for myself was dirty. I came out of the war dirty and I didn't want to go back to Canada until I felt clean about myself. But the truth was as time went on and I mixed with the people I mixed with I just got dirtier.

I told myself to change the record and while I washed, shaved and dressed I started to think through how I could walk way from the McGahern thing with my new-found stash, which I had now safely stowed under the floorboards. I approached the day in an upbeat mood, determined to put the McGahern business behind me.

It didn't last.

CHAPTER EIGHTEEN

It was Jock Ferguson who pissed on my parade, albeit with the best of intentions. And at my own request.

I offered to buy Ferguson lunch at the Trieste, as thanks for checking out the Bedford van registration. It was as close as I would ever get to bribing him. At first he declined and declared that a pie and a pint at the Horsehead would do fine, but I insisted and he met me there just after one.

'As I've said before, you lead an interesting and complicated life, Lennox.' Ferguson eyed me with the same suspicion as he had his spaghetti when it had arrived. 'I checked out the number of that truck you gave me.'

'And?'

'And it's nothing to do with the McGahern case.'

That's what you think, I thought. Hell of a coincidence that a truck full of heavies is parked behind me after I've been lured out by a call promising information on Tam McGahern.

'So who does the truck belong to?'

'You should think about making a formal complaint about this. There's clearly something rotten going on—'

'Jock . . .' I said impatiently.

'The registered owner of the Bedford is CCI.' Ferguson slid the name and address across the Formica table top. 'Clyde Consolidated Importing.'

'John Andrews's company?'

'The same. Obviously he's not as straight and clean as you thought. You've stirred something up there.'

So there it was. I tried to conceal the jolt that ran through me. Just when I thought I was going to get clear of the McGahern case. The call I got to draw me to Central Station had been specifically about Tam McGahern; then, when it turned into a no-show, I got jumped by goons from a van registered to John Andrews's company. Whatever Lillian Andrews was into – and I knew it *was* Lillian Andrews and not John Andrews – had something to do with Tam or Frankie McGahern. I was convinced that I had been right about John Andrews all along. Lillian was pulling his strings.

'You okay?' Ferguson frowned at me. His chin was tomato-striped where his spaghetti had whipped it. 'You looked a little taken aback.'

'How's the spaghetti?' I nodded towards his chin and he wiped it clean.

'Really good. Never had it before. Never been in an Italian restaurant before, for that matter. You surprised?'

'The cultural poverty of Glaswegians never fails to surprise me.'

'Not that, you clot. Are you surprised that it was one of John Andrews's company vans?'

I lit a cigarette, leaned back and smiled. 'Nothing surprises me these days.'

I had intended to 'phone John Andrews, but thought better of it. Why should he take my call now? Added to which, for all I knew Lillian and her cronies might now be monitoring all his calls, even in the office. I would have to think of a way of getting Andrews on his own. Maybe intercept him on his way into work. I'd have to think it through. I had left Jock Ferguson with not only a new-found appreciation of Italian cuisine but also a growing curiosity about Andrews, CCI and whatever the hell I'd got myself involved with. It would be best to keep a low profile around Jock for a while.

The main thing to come out of my lunch with Ferguson was that I wasn't finished with the McGahern mess. I wanted to forget all about it, but now that I knew the Andrews business was mixed up in it I was sure that there were those who wouldn't let me forget. I spent the afternoon in more stubborn fruitlessness trying to decode the notebook I had taken from Tam's Milngavie retreat. I moved on to studying the photograph I had found. Gideon. Why had a Glaswegian gangster like McGahern written the name of a biblical judge on the back of a snap of wartime chums? Given the infinity of sand in the background, the blazing sun and the desert fatigues, the photograph had clearly not been taken on Mallaig beach. This was the Middle East. And Fred MacMurray and his chums from the night before had been speaking a foreign language that hadn't sounded European to me.

There was something about the whole set up that was making me twitchy. Twitchy was fast becoming paranoid and I was sure that someone followed me back to my digs after I left the office around three forty-five. Glasgow didn't have a lot of cars for a city its size and I should have been able to recognize any tail I had picked up, but the lack of a recurring grille in my rear-view mirror didn't do much to ease the feeling in my gut.

I ate sandwiches and used up the last of my precious supply of good coffee to make a pot. I ate lying on my bed reading, the Overseas Service mumbling in the background as I tried to force myself to relax. Every now and then, however, I felt the need to twitch the net curtain and check there was no movie heavy leaning on a lamp-post outside smoking. It was about eight thirty when Mrs White called me down to the telephone at the bottom of the hallway we shared and wordlessly handed me the receiver.

'Lennox. Is that you Lennox?' I recognized the voice on the other end of the line instantly.

'Is everything all right, Mr Andrews?'

John Andrews gave a bitter laugh. 'I'm a dead man, Lennox. I hope you remember this call for the rest of your life. A conversation with a dead man. Just talking to you means they'll kill me.'

'Who'll kill you, Mr Andrews? Lillian? If you're in some kind of danger you should 'phone the police. Or I can speak to a detective I know, Jock Ferguson at Central Division . . .' I made the offer even though it would mean me having to explain to Jock Ferguson that there was a connection with Tam McGahern and that I'd been sticking my nose exactly where I'd been told not to.

'No. No police. Say nothing to the police.' He was getting agitated.

'Okay, okay. No police. Who's going to kill you, Mr Andrews?'

'They set me up. They had it all planned from the beginning, from the first day I met Lillian . . .' John Andrews sounded as if he'd been drinking and I heard noises in the background that suggested he wasn't 'phoning from home. A pub, maybe. It made me nervous: he was not an impulsive man and certainly not a courageous man, and I had the sense that the nerve it had taken to 'phone me had come distilled.

'Set you up for what?'

'My business. They need my business to make it all work. Not that I know it all, but I've been able to put enough together. And that's another reason for them to kill me. Lillian's been making me forge shipments. Change the details. But that's not why I 'phoned. They set me up and I walked straight into their trap. But so did you. That's why I'm 'phoning you, Lennox. Like I said, I'm dead already, but you could still get out of it all.'

'You're not making sense. Set up for what? And how did they set me up?'

'I'm sorry . . .' he said and I knew that he meant it. 'Through me. They set you up through me. When Lillian went missing . . . when she was *supposed* to go missing . . . they told me to contact you. They wanted you involved.'

I thought about what Andrews was saying. It didn't seem to make any sense but what chilled my gut was that somewhere, deep at the back of my mind, it did.

'Where are you?' I asked. 'I'll come and get you.'

'No . . . no, it's not safe. Nowhere's safe.' There was a pause and I listened to the background sounds of a bar. 'Help me, Lennox. You've got to help me.'

I thought for a moment. I stared at the brownish floral wallpaper on the wall opposite and felt the draft from the gap beneath the front door. 'Listen, Andrews, do you have your car handy?'

'It's outside.'

'I want you to go right now and get in it. Are you sober enough to drive?'

'Think so.'

'Then I want you to get into your car and drive out of the city. North. Take the Aberfoyle road. Don't take Maryhill Road and go through Bearsden and Drymen. I don't want you to go anywhere near your house or your office. Don't stop to pick anything up; don't go anywhere else; don't stop anywhere else. Are you listening?'

'I've got it. I won't.' I could tell he was taking strength from my sense of purpose.

'There's a hotel at the north end of Loch Lomond. It's called the Royal Hotel. Do you know it?'

'I know where it is.'

'I want you to drive up there right now and check in under a fake name. I'll meet you there later tonight. Call yourself Jones ... no, call yourself Mr Fraser, so I know who to ask for. Have you got that?'

'Yes. Royal Hotel, Mr Fraser.'

'Like I said, don't stop for anything: I'll bring a change of clothes and toothbrush and stuff for you. And listen, Mr Andrews, I will get you out of this. I promise.'

'Thank you, Lennox.' I could hear a vibrato in his voice. The guy was as close to cracking as you could get. He had given up and now was struggling to accept that there was maybe some hope. 'I don't know how to thank you.'

'You can start by telling me when I get up there everything you know about what Lillian and her cronies are up to.'

'Why are you doing this? Why are you helping me like this?'

'You're my client, Mr Andrews. Or maybe it's just that I've watched too many Westerns. It's my turn to be the good guy.' I laughed bitterly at my own joke. 'Call me the Kennebecasis Kid.'

After I hung up I ran upstairs, threw a few things into an overnight bag for Andrews and grabbed my keys and jacket. I was halfway back down the stairs when I checked myself. I went back up and unlocked the door of my apartment. I took the bent nail from inside the vase on the mantle and slid under my bed. I used the nail to hook and ease up the floorboard. I reached in underneath and found the oilskin-wrapped bundle, pulled it out and draped my raincoat over it before heading back down the stairs and out onto the street. I put the bundle on the passenger seat and placed my coat over it. I carried out each of these actions quickly and mechanically. I didn't want to think about the seriousness of what I was doing.

But the truth was that John Andrews's 'phone call had spooked me. Whatever the connection between Lillian and Tam McGahern had been, whatever the caper was they had planned, it was big. They had been working on it for months, since whenever Lillian had hooked Andrews, a gullible, lonely widower with a business they needed to control to make their project work. As I drove out of town I tried to think it through as calmly as I could manage. What *was* the connection between McGahern and Lillian? She could have been the 'Mrs McGahern' who had sold on the house in the West End. I had certainly seen the evidence of Lillian Andrews's impressively professional expertise in administering blow-jobs on screen; it didn't take an enormous leap of imagination to envisage Lillian running a brothel. But what didn't gel was Tam McGahern being a partner in whatever scam Lillian and her associates were involved in. It was too big-league for either McGahern. It was more likely that Tam had been involved in some minor way and had started to try to muscle his way in. There was the connection. Maybe. Maybe the connection was simply that whoever Lillian was involved with had killed Tam. And Frankie.

I was now out of Glasgow. It was getting darker and the clutter of the city around me gave way to the increasingly dramatic dark undulations of the Trossachs. It's amazing how you can be in the black heart of Britain's most industrial city and within twenty minutes be driving through a landscape full of drama and empty of people. The road was quiet and I hadn't seen another car for five minutes so I pulled over tight to the verge.

The guys who had tried to snatch me off the pavement in Argyle Street had been enthusiastic for my company. So I had reluctantly taken out a little added insurance. After I parked, I took the tyre iron from the trunk of my car and dropped it into the passenger seat footwell. I thought it fitting, considering my potential opponents had used a tyre iron to pulp Frankie McGahern's head. Although I was now pretty sure that it had been Tam who had been the second McGahern twin to depart this life.

But my main insurance policy lay on the passenger seat, under my coat, wrapped in oilskin. I unwrapped it. It contained a Webley Mk IV revolver and a packet of .38 ammunition. The pistol was identical to the one I had been issued with during the war. But I had liberated this revolver in such a way that it would never be directly linked to me.

I wiped the grease from the Webley, snapped open its top break and loaded it with six rounds then slipped it uncomfortably into my waistband and tugged my double-breasted jacket over it. Again I thought about how much walking around heavy upped the ante: the problem with carrying a gun is that you tend to end up using it. Ten years ago that had not been a problem. In fact it had been expected of me. Encouraged. Now I could end up with a noose around my neck.

The Royal Hotel had a car park that looked out down the length of Loch Lomond. I sat in my Austin with the cold hard edges of the Webley digging into me and watched the clouds scud between the mountains and the inky water glisten. I looked at my watch. It was now past nine. This was my second clandestine meeting in a week. This time there was no Bedford parked behind me and I was more than prepared for any nasty surprises. And I had something better than the Central Station departure board to look at.

I got the impression that the middle-aged woman behind the small reception desk was the owner of the hotel. All the alarm bells started ringing in my head as soon as she frowned when I asked to speak to Mr Fraser. I knew at that moment that John Andrews hadn't made it. Just to be sure that Andrews hadn't been too scared and too drunk to remember the name I told him, I checked Jones. Then Andrews. I explained that they were business colleagues and we had agreed to meet at the hotel. The small woman shook her head concernedly, clearly feeling that she had let me down when she told me that no one had checked in that evening.

I walked back out to the car park. There were two other cars parked, neither John Andrews's Bentley and both seemingly unoccupied. Nevertheless I unbuttoned my jacket and let my hand rest on the butt of the Webley in my waistband. I stood for a few seconds, satisfying myself that there was no menace in the car park other than the hulking shadow of Ben Lomond against a violet-black sky. I turned the ignition key of my Austin and started the drive back to Glasgow, taking the Drymen road in case Andrews had ignored my warning about passing up through Bearsden. Maybe the idiot had stopped off at his house to pick something up. Andrews had been right about one thing: I had had a conversation with a dead man.

It was a skinny young police constable who waved me down with his torch. There was a knot of other police officers and a Bedford ambulance pulled over at the side of the road. I could see from where I had been pulled over that there was a gap in the fencing. I checked that the pistol-butt bulge in my jacket wasn't too conspicuous before winding down the window.

'What's the problem, constable?' I asked.

'Accident, sir. I'm afraid someone's gone over the edge.'

'Dead?'

'Didn't stand a chance. Just be careful as you go past the

other vehicles, sir. You'll have to pull over a little onto the verge.'

'Okay.' I eased the car forward, taking two wheels up onto the grass. As I passed the gap in the fence I looked down. I caught a glimpse of the tailgate of the car that had gone over the edge. It was a Bentley. I turned my attention back to the road and drove on. I didn't need to look any more to know that it was John Andrews down there. The car would be pretty badly smashed up having taken a tumble like that, but I wondered if the police surgeon might, just for a second, be puzzled as to how the driver's head had gotten quite so pulped.

It wasn't a good-mood morning. It was difficult to find real coffee in Glasgow and my supply had run out. I had been forced to buy the locally produced alternative: a bottle of thick coffee and chicory which you diluted with boiling water. I decided to forgo the pleasure and went straight to the office. It was in the Glasgow Herald I picked up on the way: a short piece headed 'Clyde Consolidated Importing chairman killed in tragic accident'. No real detail other than Andrews had been found dead at the scene. I winced as I read it: I am ashamed to say not out of sympathy for John Andrews but because I knew that a certain Detective-Inspector Jock Ferguson was likely to read the same piece in the course of the next day and come knocking on my door. Mind you, it could have been worse: at least it wouldn't provoke a visit by Superintendent Willie McNab and his farmhand. Hopefully.

I still found myself looking over my shoulder and I now had more reason than ever. John Andrews hadn't been killed because he was out for a drive in the country. Whoever killed him would have known he was meeting with someone and more likely than not that that someone was me. Of course, there was always the possibility that it had genuinely been an accident. After all, he had sounded more than a little drunk on the 'phone: maybe the booze and the dark and the sudden bend in the road had been the only conspirators in his death. It was a scrap of a hope to hang on to, anyway. But whether his death had been by accident or design, John Andrews had told me more than enough to shake me up: he had been set up by Lillian and whomever she was involved with, and he had told me that I had been set up. However, he hadn't told me enough to indicate the direction I should be looking in. I decided that I was going to have to go to Sneddon and tell him everything I knew. Sneddon had been right, after all: I needed someone to watch my back.

Sneddon was out when I 'phoned and I left a message that I needed to talk to him. I looked out of my office window and watched people go about their day on Gordon Street. Trams passed. Taxis, like black beetles under a stone, scuttled in and out from under the lattice ironworked canopy of Central Station. It was three in the afternoon. In the Maritimes of Canada it would be eleven in the morning. I never understood why I did that, but whenever I was stressed I thought of what time of day it would be at home. I had done it across Europe, imagining what my parents were doing, what the light in the garden would be like in New Brunswick, while I watched men die.

I unlocked my desk drawer – I had taken to locking it since my office had been so expertly searched – and took out the notebook and the photograph I had found in McGahern's place. I looked again at the list of letters and numbers in the notebook. I noticed that most of the numbers ended in fifty-one and fifty-two. Nineteen fifty-two? Could these be dated shipment numbers? Andrews had said they were using his business to ship stolen goods. But there was no way I could get access to the CCI records now that he was dead.

I looked at the photograph again. There were five men in the picture. Again it looked to me like two, maybe three of them were foreign, too dark to be Scots. Scots are the whitest people on the planet: sometimes they're almost blue-white. The only tans you ever saw in Glasgow were on stout walking brogues. But there again even Tam looked bronzed in the photograph. The last tanned face I'd encountered recently had been the cheery Fred MacMurray lookalike.

I picked up the 'phone and dialled an Edinburgh number. It was time to pull in a few favours.

CHAPTER NINETEEN

Glasgow may have been the Empire's Second City, but much-smaller Edinburgh was Scotland's capital. Edinburgh's inhabitants called it 'the Athens of the North', presumably because none of them had actually seen Athens. If Glasgow could be described as a black city, then Edinburgh was grey. Grey buildings and grey people. It was also the most Anglicized city in Scotland, which is perhaps why its residents were the most Anglophobe you could encounter: what you hate the most is that which you most want to be but are not.

When the train pulled into Waverley station I was greeted with a banner declaring *Ceud Mille Failte*, which I had been told was Gaelic for 'A Hundred Thousand Welcomes'. Having got to know the personality of Edinburgh a little, I would have better believed it meant 'Fuck off, you English Bastard'.

But Edinburgh's ire was aimed at more than the English. The rivalry between Scotland's two main cities was vast and vicious. Much was made of the cultural differences between Glasgow and Edinburgh. In Glasgow they called children *weans* and in Edinburgh they were *bairns*; in Edinburgh they took their fish and chips with *salt 'n' sauce*, in Glasgow with *salt 'n' vinegar*; Glaswegians inexplicably ended their sentences with the conjunction 'but', in Edinburgh with the interrogative 'eh?'.

Sometimes I found myself dizzy from Scotland's cultural kaleidoscope.

I took a taxi from the rank up to Edinburgh Castle and was

dropped at the Esplanade. The officious little corporal on guard was reluctant to let me into the barracks until I informed him that I was Captain Lennox and I was here to meet Captain Jeffrey. He indicated the main office and when I got there Rufus 'Mafeking' Jeffrey was waiting, hatless and dressed in civvies. 'Mafeking' was the nickname I had given him years before and which he resented, although he had no idea why I called him it. Jeffrey was a tall, lanky sort with blond hair frizzily receding. I could tell that he wasn't particularly pleased to see me and, to be honest, I was never particularly happy to be back in a military environment, even the Chocolate Soldier setting of Edinburgh Castle.

'I thought we'd grab a pint down in the Royal Mile, if that's all right with you, old boy.' Jeffrey's smile was as genuine as his mock upper-class English accent, which had come courtesy of an Edinburgh private boarding school.

A Military Police sergeant marched his red cap past us and into the office. He brought back some unpleasant memories. 'Sure,' I said and we headed back down the Esplanade.

We sat in a corner of the pub. The bleak March sunlight from the window behind him sliced through blue smoke and made a halo of 'Mafeking' Jeffrey's frizzy blond hair. We made small talk about the time that had intervened since our last meeting. The smallest of small talk: the truth was neither gave a crap about what had happened in the other's life. I didn't like Jeffrey and he didn't like me, but I had something on him and I had, at one time, pulled his fat out of the fire. He had good reason to be grateful to me. Gratitude is by far the best foundation on which to build a true hatred.

'Do you have the photograph you mentioned?' he asked pleasantly enough. I slid it across the pub table to him. 'Gideon . . .'

he read the back of it. 'I know what this is. And I looked into this Sergeant McGahern for you. He may have started his service as a Desert Rat, but he didn't end it as one. It would appear that Sergeant McGahern was a man of . . . how can I put it? . . . *particular* talents.'

'A natural killer.'

'And then some. But he was apparently quite the tactician and was also a natural leader of men. As you know yourself, Lennox, our last little European conflict required some innovation. You've heard of the SAS?'

'Of course.' Jeffrey's lecturing tone irritated the hell out of me, as did his phoney accent. He belonged to that class of Edinburgh North British who wore kilts to Burns Suppers and Scottish Country Dancing and the Reel Society, but at the same time fought to extirpate any hint of Scottishness from their accents.

'As you know the SAS was set up for special missions behind enemy lines, assassination, et cetera. But it wasn't the innovation it seemed. There was a precursor, set up by mad old Orde Wingate who also created the Chindits.'

'Gideon?'

'The Gideon Force. It operated in Abyssinia. It was an elite force and was made up from the oddest mix . . . British, Abyssinian, Sudanese and Hymies.'

'Jews?'

'Mmm. Strange, isn't it? Don't have time for them myself but apparently Wingate had always been a great supporter of our Jewish friends setting up a state in Palestine. He'd been up to all kinds of shenanigans in what we now call Israel.'

'So what's this got to do with McGahern?' I asked. 'I take it he was a member of the Gideon Force?'

'Forty-three and forty-four, according to what I've been able to find out between poking around in official records and what I've garnered from the grapevine. You do rather owe me for this one, old boy.'

'I don't think we're quite even yet, *old boy*.' I offered him a cigarette to take the sting out of it.

'Anyway,' said Jeffrey, leaning over for the light I offered, 'your Sergeant McGahern was a member of Gideon. But he got quite tight with the Jewboys.'

It was good to know that the small matter of six million dead had done nothing to dampen Jeffrey's anti-Semitism. I thought of Jonny Cohen, who had fought a harder, realer war than this piece of shit, standing in the heart of Belsen. I felt the urge to smack Jeffrey about. Instead I said nothing and waited for him to continue.

'And this is where this precursor of the SAS comes in. When things got out of hand with the Arabs in Palestine in thirty-six to thirty-nine, Wingate set up this unit called the SNS. Stood for Special Night Squads, apparently. They were unbelievably ruthless, encouraged by Wingate, and carried out raids against Arab villages and terrorist groups. Rumour has it that for every ten prisoners they took, they'd shoot one *pour encourager les autres* as it were. You know the Israeli general? You know, the *ghaffir* with the eyepatch?'

'Moshe Dayan. I think you'll find that *ghaffir* is more of a soldier than you'll ever be, Jeffrey.' Dayan had led the Israeli Army with devastating effectiveness in the Arab War four years before. The only war wound Jeffrey had ever risked was a paper cut.

'Well he learned his soldiering from us. Dayan was a member of the SNS. Wingate selected Jews who had been in the Hagganah and the Jewish Settlement Police to serve in the Special Night Squads and in turn there were a number of SNS recruited into Gideon.'

For a moment Jeffrey's attention seemed to wander. I followed his eyes to a slender, effeminate youth at the bar, no older than twenty with a cheap blue serge suit with the open collar of his shirt turned out over the lapels. The youth looked at Jeffrey blankly and turned away. I had Jeffrey's attention again. The old problem.

Jeffrey's predilections were the basis for my personal nick-name for him. Jeffrey had never worked out why I had nick-named him 'Mafeking': it was because he regularly needed relieving by boy soldiers.

It had been Jeffrey's inclinations, no doubt cultivated in the late-night shenanigans in the dormitories of his boarding school, that had gotten him into the scrape I'd gotten him out of: a scrape with an eighteen-year-old pretty-boy conscript. It had been a set up from the start and Jeffrey found himself the victim of blackmail. I didn't much care for Jeffrey's type but he was what he was and I didn't like people being screwed over for something they couldn't help.

Added to which, let's be honest, Jeffrey had had all kinds of contacts in army bureaucracy that would prove useful to me towards the end of my military career and, like now, after. So I had visited the pretty boy and demonstrated how easy it was for me to make him un-pretty. The fairy had handed over the photographs and the negatives and relinquished his hold on Jeffrey. Somehow or other I had never gotten round to handing them over to Jeffrey. Or destroying them.

'Did you find out anything about the other men in this picture?' I asked him.

'Can't say for sure, I'm afraid. But I did get a few names for you. There was one *wallah* who got pretty badly messed up. I've underlined his name . . .' Jeffrey tore a page out of his notebook and pushed it across the table to me. His eyes darted to the boy at the bar and back.

I looked at the names. The first one to leap out at me was McGahern's officer. Captain James Wallace.

'William Pattison.' I read the name Jeffrey had underlined.

'Lance Corporal, according to records,' said Jeffrey. 'Apparently he got himself severely wounded. I thought it might be a starting point because I know where you can find him.'

'Oh?'

'Yes . . . I would have been pushing things too far to get the pension addresses for the others, but it was in Pattison's records that he'd been shipped home and installed in Levendale House.'

'He's still there?' I knew Levendale House, or knew of it. It was a nursing home for disabled ex-servicemen.

'That I don't know, old boy, but I guess he would be. I mean, these chaps who go in don't often come out.'

'Did you find out anything else about the Gideon Force? Or Tam McGahern?'

'Not much. Some of that stuff is still pretty secret. The other thing is, to be frank, that Sergeant McGahern didn't mix in the same circles, as it were. Working-class Glaswegian NCO. And a mackerel-snapper, I believe.'

I frowned.

'Catholic, old boy. Friday fish. But he did seem to be a good soldier. He's dead, you say?'

'Very. Do you know if he served anywhere particular in the Middle East? Before or after Abyssinia?'

''Fraid not. Lots of action in North Africa generally with the Desert Rats, but I don't have details of his postings. I'm afraid I've pushed this as far as I can, Lennox. Any more and questions will be asked, that kind of thing.' As he spoke, his eyes followed the young man who was making his way to the hallway behind the bar.

'Fair enough,' I said. 'Thanks.'

'If you'll excuse me, old boy. Nature calls . . .' Jeffrey stood up. I said goodbye to him and watched as he headed towards the lavatory into which the young queer had disappeared.

Unlike Glasgow, there was no subway in Edinburgh so after I left Jeffrey to his sordid lavatory-conducted business, I walked down the Royal Mile.

The March sky was bright, as it often was in Edinburgh, but chill and joyless, as it also often was in Edinburgh and the castle was squeezed up into the sterile blueness by the city's tight-fisted grip. Edinburgh is basically divided into the medieval Old Town and the Georgian New Town, separated by Princes Street Gardens and Waverley Station. I made my way down The Mound towards Princes Street and the New Town beyond, but gave up on my original idea of walking all the way and hailed a passing cab. The otherwise glum cabbie smiled sneerily when I gave him the address I wanted in St Bernard's Crescent.

Edinburgh is a city of self-righteous primness and was always for me, as an outsider, the counterpoint to Glasgow. Glasgow may have had a black heart, but it was a warm black heart. Edinburgh was all Presbyterian prissiness and ill-founded snobbery; or as Glaswegians were fond of saying, all fur coat and no knickers. It was actually a description that couldn't have been more apt for the address I was about to visit. Despite Glasgow's reputation for hard drinking, hard men and harder women, it was Edinburgh that was Scotland's capital for sex crimes, pornography and prostitution. There was a lot of dark stuff went on behind the twitchy net curtains.

St Bernard's Crescent was in the heart of Edinburgh's Stockbridge: an arc of sandstone Georgian townhouses facing a small tree-filled park. Most of the properties were three storeys above street level and a basement level with windows peering

up to wrought-iron railings. This layout was particularly rele-
vant to the house I was visiting: they said the higher up the
storey you visited, the more you paid.

Edinburgh taxi drivers are noted for having the joie de vivre
of depressed undertakers and this particular cabbie had been
silent throughout the journey. He managed, however, to repeat
his earlier sneer as he pulled up outside the address I had given
him in St Bernard's Crescent and told me how much I was due
him. I usually tipped taxi drivers well, particularly in London
or Glasgow when you could often have the best conversation of
your day in the back of the cab. In this case I counted out the
exact change and not a penny more. My pointed meanness fell
flat as the taxi driver didn't seem to notice or care. This was
Edinburgh, after all.

The house looked just the same as all of the others in the
crescent; in fact the paintwork on the door and windows looked
fresher and the steps better swept than its neighbours, and the
young lady who admitted me was soberly dressed in a blue serge
jacket and pencil skirt and white blouse. She asked me if I had
an appointment and I explained that I wasn't there on business but was a friend of Mrs Gersons. She smiled and led me
into a small office-type room off the reception hall. As I passed
along the hall I noticed how tasteful and expensive the décor
was that Helena had invested in. It didn't surprise me; Helena
Gersons was a sophisticated and elegant lady. Yep, you certainly
got a better class of whorehouse in Edinburgh, I thought to
myself as I made a quick mental comparison with Arthur Parks's
place in Glasgow.

I was a cynical fuck. I admit it. The things I had seen, the
things I had done, had turned me into somebody I really didn't
like and my way of dealing with it was often to greet each day
with a sneer or a joke at someone else's expense. Maybe I was

just becoming acclimatized: attitudes were different here. In America and Canada we'd greet the day with 'Another day another dollar!'; in Glasgow the motto was 'Different day, same shite.' Whatever was going on around me, I was generally too cynical to give a crap.

However, when Helena Gersons walked into the office I felt like someone had given me a punch in the gut. Which, being between my heart and my groin, was appropriate. Helena Gersons was perhaps the most beautiful woman I had ever known. Today she was dressed in a tailored grey suit that hugged her figure in a way that made you jealous. Her hair was black. Raven-wing black and glossy and gathered up behind her head to expose a graceful neck. She had dark eyes and arching eyebrows and her full lips were lipsticked deep red. She smiled at me, but a little sadly.

'Lennox . . .' she said in an accent that was more English than Scottish and was haunted by the vaguest ghost of Europe. 'I didn't think I'd ever see you again.'

'It's a small world, Helena. How have you been?'

She made an open-handed gesture to indicate the Georgian architecture enveloping us.

'I don't mean business. I mean you. How are you?'

'I'm fine. But let's be honest, if you were that interested in my state of mind or well-being then I would have heard from you long before now.' She frowned. 'I'm sorry, that was uncalled for.'

'Probably was called for.' I put my hat on the desk.

Helena dropped ice into expensive-looking crystal and poured me a Canadian Club without asking. She poured herself a Scotch and I waited for her to sit and cross her long silk-sheathed legs before sitting down opposite her.

'I'm a British citizen now.' She took the cigarette I offered.

'No longer a displaced person. I'm now . . . *placed*. Although I just got in under the wire. The police sent in a report about my little enterprise here and I should have been deported as an undesirable alien, but fortunately it got delayed somewhere along the way.'

I gave a cynical laugh. Helena Gersons had a lot of influence with a lot of people in the Edinburgh establishment. String-pullers who had themselves, at one time or other, had their strings pulled within these elegant Georgian walls.

'So business is good?' I asked.

'Okay . . . it's always quieter at this time of year unless there's a ship in. Busiest time is during the Festival.' She laughed and exposed perfect porcelain teeth. 'And, of course, when the General Assembly of the Church of Scotland is in town. The girls are often pushed to deal with so much religious fervour.'

I laughed too. Again I noticed her Anglicized accent and perfect grammar. Just the vaguest hint now of the Vienna she had left behind, little more than a child, in thirty-six.

'You never think about going back? To Austria, I mean?'

'That's another me,' she said and not for the first time shook me up with a statement I could have made about myself. It was good to look at Helena again; to talk to her again. There had been a time, a few years back, when we had talked a lot. Through the night, hushed in the dark. 'And in any case, Austria is still a complete mess. God knows it could go either way and maybe end up a Russian satellite state. Anyway, people like me are an embarrassment. A reminder of past sins.' Her eyes hardened. 'What do you want, Lennox?'

'Is it that obvious that I want something?'

'You always did.'

'We both did. Two of a kind, Helena. Anyway, you're right. Or at least in part. I thought you might know someone I'm checking out. But that's not the only reason I came. I did want to see you.'

She arched an eyebrow. 'I'm guessing you were in town anyway.'

'There's a girl . . .' I ignored the accuracy of her dig. 'She's got a history as a pro. She's been putting the squeeze on a client of mine, but I'm not just sure how.'

I handed her the photograph.

'Why don't you just ask him how she's putting the squeeze on him if he's your client?'

'He's not taking calls. Permanently.'

'Dead?' She pursed her lips and looked at the photograph more closely.

'Very. A staged accident I reckon, and missy here is involved. She calls herself Lillian but she used to go by the name Sally Blane. Did some blue-movie stuff.'

The way Helena stared at the photograph, her brow furrowed, suggested she was looking at a puzzle with a piece missing. She looked up, still frowning. 'I knew Sally Blane. Not well, but she did a few shifts here. I had heard she'd gone off to Glasgow.'

'Is that her?'

'Could be . . . I mean. It looks like her and it doesn't. I know that doesn't make any sense, but her face is different. The same but different. But there again I never really knew her that well. Although she did well with the clients for as long as she worked here. She was an upper-storey girl, if you know what I mean. Higher value, higher income.'

'But she didn't last long?'

'No. I got the feeling she was building her own private port-folio, carving out a little business for herself.' Helena frowned again, beautifully. 'Wait a minute, I remember something else. Towards the end there was a man sometimes used to pick her up after work. Not a client. A boyfriend maybe. Or a pimp. A bad-looking sort. Glasgow accent.'

'What did he look like?'

'A wiry little thug, to be honest. Expensive clothes and a flash car, but they didn't fit with the face, if you know what I mean.'

'I know exactly what you mean,' I said and thought of a Savile Row suit hung on the wrong hanger. 'Was there ever any trouble? I mean with her Glaswegian boyfriend. If he was who I think he was then he was always trying to muscle in on other people's action.'

'No. No trouble. We don't get any here. I don't use muscle and I don't let any gangster push me around. There are no bouncers here because half the time we have a member of the local police somewhere on the premises.'

'It's good to have a bobby on the beat.' I reached for the photograph but Helena still studied it.

'That is strange. I don't remember her this way. Is there any chance it could be her sister? I heard she had one but I never met her.'

'Could be, I suppose. I've had a spate of siblings swapping identities.' I took the picture back. It was certainly the same face as the Lillian/Sally in the blue movie. But it was the second time someone had done a double-take looking at the photograph.

'She had a friend who went by the name Margot Taylor. Might even have been her sister. She worked for Arthur Parks in Glasgow and was up to the same kind of scam. You know, building a little business for herself. Parks was not as understanding, though. I gather she got a hiding and was chucked out.'

'Sorry, the name doesn't ring a bell.' Helena sipped at her Scotch, the glass held in long, slender, crimson-nailed fingers. She had been a pianist, once. Rumour had it that she would sometimes play the piano for her 'guests' and they would be astounded to hear concert-hall-standard Bach and Mozart played in a brothel. Helena had been something of a child prodigy, but that had all been nixed when the Nazis had come to power. Helena and her older sister had both gotten out to an aunt in England just before Anschluss. Her parents had planned to organize their affairs and follow. But when the border between Germany and Austria came down, all other borders became impenetrable for the remaining Gersons family. Helena had found out, after the war, that they had eventually made it out of Austria. But to the East. Auschwitz.

As soon as the war broke out Helena, her sister and her aunt had been arrested by the British authorities and interred on the Isle of Man as hostile aliens. Our paths had crossed imme-diately after the war.

We drank our drinks, smoked our cigarettes and talked about people we had both known for no other reason than to fill the quiet. Any other level of conversation would have taken us too deep.

'I don't work with clients any more. I just run the place. You know that don't you, Lennox?'

'I thought as much.'

'One day I'll sell this place and . . .' She left the thought hanging and looked around herself at the walls. A beautiful bird in an elegant cage. There was a silence. She had taken us too deep. I picked up my hat.

'Better go.'

'Fine. It was good to see you.' The temperature had dropped and she stood up and shook my hand like I was her bank manager.

I felt like crap when I hit the street and decided to walk back through the city to the station. As I walked I let scenes from my past play through my head. I was full of self-indulgent crap after seeing Helena again. I had a coffee in the station cafe before catching the four thirty train back to Glasgow. I wanted to get out of Edinburgh and back into Glasgow's dark embrace.

The Glasgow train was quiet. The next scheduled service would have been full with office workers commuting back to Glasgow and the various stops along the way. I was still in that stupidly melancholic mood and I needed privacy to brood self-indulgently. One of the luxuries I afforded myself at my clients' expense was to travel first-class. I found an empty compartment and settled into it, looking forward to an hour of solitary travel. Unfortunately a short, fat, balding businessman bustled in through the door in a plume of pipe smoke and piled his raincoat, newspaper, briefcase and himself onto the seats opposite.

'Afternoon,' he said.

I grumbled a response and he disappeared behind a fluttered wall of newsprint. At least it looked like I wasn't going to be troubled with small talk. After a few minutes there was a great hiss of steam and the sound of the engine beginning to chug its way into motion and we were under way.

The world outside the window slid by slate-grey. I thought through everything I had on the McGahern killing. Unfortunately it didn't take long. The businessman opposite had now folded his newspaper and set it on the seat beside him and began to read through a *Country Life*. He didn't look like a shootin' and huntin' country type, more like a suburbanite. My idle curiosity cost me dear. He saw me looking at him and clearly took it as an invitation to strike up a conversation.

'It's good to get away before the rush,' he said. He spoke with a Scots burr that was impossible to place as Glasgow or Edinburgh, working or middle-class.

I nodded with a perfunctory smile.

'Through in Edinburgh on business?' he asked.

'So to speak.'

'Now, don't tell me. Sorry, please indulge me for a moment. This is my little party piece: I guess people's occupations and something about them from their appearances.'

'Oh really?' I said. Oh fuck off, I thought.

'Yes . . . now you. You're a challenge. Your accent is difficult to place exactly. I mean you're clearly Canadian, not American. I'm guessing . . . and I could be wrong because your accent has become a little muddled . . . but no, I would say Eastern Canada. The Maritimes.'

'New Brunswick,' I said and was genuinely impressed. But not enough to continue the conversation.

'Now, as to occupation . . .' The little man with the little eyes behind his bank manager glasses was not to be put off by mere indifference. 'What people do, that's usually easy. But with you, I think we're looking at something a little out of the ordinary.' He paused and picked up his copy of *Country Life*. 'Now here's a question that always helps. I go hunting. Shooting mainly. There are two distinct types of people involved in the hunt. Or two distinct types of personality: the hunter himself and the stalker, who leads the hunter to the kill. Obviously sometimes the hunter stalks his own prey. But let's pretend that we are after a deer, you and I. Would you see yourself as a stalker or a hunter?'

'I don't know,' I said without thought. 'Stalker maybe.'

'Yes. Yes, that's what I'd have you down as. Me, I'm a hunter, pure and simple. Mainly wild deer. Magnificent animals. Do you know what the most important quality in a hunter is? Respect for his prey. When I shoot a deer, I bring it down quickly. The trick is a maximum of two shots. To end life as swiftly and painlessly as possible. As I say, out of respect for the animal.'

I smiled wearily just as we passed through the blackness of the tunnel into Haymarket. The train stopped but didn't pick anyone up. The engine exhaled a huge cloud of steam that drifted over the platforms. I felt isolated, trapped in this tiny capsule with the world's most boring man.

'It is remarkable, I think,' he continued, looking out the window at a grey slideshow of Lothian scenery, 'that we often turn out to be someone else. Not who we thought we were at all. Take me – I know what you're thinking: an anonymous little man with no imagination and some kind of bureaucratic job.'

'I—' I started, beginning to feel uncomfortable with the drift of the conversation.

The strange little man cut me off. 'It's all right. That's exactly who – what – I was. Or what I was destined to become. I am not an imaginative person. But what I didn't realize was that, as a child, my lack of imagination wasn't my only deficiency. You see, Mr Lennox, I found out at an early age that I didn't *feel* things in the same way as others did. I didn't get as happy as others, or as sad, or as frightened.'

I straightened in my seat. 'How do you know my name?'

'I'm not saying it particularly marked me out as being different,' he continued, ignoring my question, 'only I seemed to be aware of it, and my life would have followed a predictable course if the unpredictable hadn't got in the way. By which, of course, I mean the war. But there again, you know exactly what I mean, Mr Lennox. You see, during the war, I discovered that my emotional deficiency was compensated for by an ability that others lacked. I could kill without compunction. Without thought or emotion or regret afterwards. I have a talent for it, you see. Just as some have a talent for music or art. My talent is as a killer. Something that is positively encouraged in the context of an armed conflict. I ended up being recruited into the Long Range Reconnaissance Group. I'm sure you're aware of the group's activity.'

'Who *are* you? And how do you know my name?' I started to stand.

'Please, Mr Lennox. Sit down.' With a movement so swift I almost missed it his hand darted into his briefcase. A very slender, very long switchblade snapped out of the knife handle. 'Please, just sit down. And please be assured that, big and experienced as you are, any *physical* contact between us would have unfortunate consequences. I am very, very experienced with this thing.'

I sat down. I didn't need to ask who he was again. I knew. What I couldn't work out was how I could continue breathing with this knowledge. Like he said, I was big and experienced. If it came to it, I would take my chances. In the meantime I sat down and listened.

'It was because of the skills I developed that I moved into the line of business I'm in now. A successful businessman. I have a wife and son you know, Mr Lennox.'

'I didn't. I don't know anything about you, Mr Morrison. Other than your name isn't likely to be Morrison.'

He smiled and laid the knife on the newspaper by his side, discreetly folding it over to conceal it. 'I see ... you think I'm going to kill you because you know too much, because you've seen my face.'

'Something like that.'

'I can understand that. German sailors believe in a small elf called the *Klabautermann*. He is invisible but brings good luck to those he sails with. But if you see the *Klabautermann's* face, you know you're going to die. I have to admit that is the way I've always seen myself. But be assured that that is not the case here. Those I kill – human or animal – die quickly and most often without being aware that they are about to die. That is why I see nothing wrong in what I do. People die all of the time, in terrible pain from injury or illness. You will have seen for yourself the suffering of men in war. The agonies some die in. And not many passings from illness or accident are without great pain. But not my victims. Little or no pain. No foreknowledge and therefore no fear. So you see, Mr Lennox, if it had been my intention to kill you, you would have been none the wiser. You would be dead by now. And anyway, I chose this venue because it is ideal for a chat. If I had intended to kill you, I would have chosen somewhere with more immediate opportunities to distance myself from the act.'

'At the moment I get the idea you're trying to talk me to death. What is it you want, Morrison?'

'This is about what you want.' He smiled and the small eyes twinkled coldly behind his spectacles. I thought of how those tiny, ugly bank manager eyes had been the last thing so many people had seen. I could imagine their deaths the way he had described. A moment of shock. Of disbelief. Then a final gaze into those eyes.

'However,' he continued, 'I do have a proposition of sorts to put to you. But we can discuss that later. Ah . . . our stop. Or at least my stop and I'm afraid I'll have to prevail on you to accompany me part of the way. And, Mr Lennox, please don't be silly. I also have a gun.'

We got off the train, Mr Morrison staying behind me with his raincoat draped over his arm to conceal the knife. It was a small station with two platforms and a siding. It sat on the edge of a small town in the middle of a landscape of unremitting moorland bleakness. It was getting dark now and Mr Morrison indicated the direction we should take from the station.

I noticed we were heading away from the town and towards the empty uplands.

A thousand different images of a thousand different endings to our outing were spinning around in my head. Sure, Mr Morrison was known to be the best in the business, but by his own admission he took most of his victims unawares; I was very much aware of the little shit behind me, the stiletto blade still tucked under his raincoat. And sure, he had all kinds of combat experience, but so did I. And he was a little guy after all. After about fifteen minutes walking uphill we reached an ugly church shaped like a vast stone barn with an undersized steeple. A wrought-iron fence formed a tight square around a clustered churchyard of headstones, some tilted, a few broken. This was Scottish Protestantism given solid form: forbidding, sinister, bleak, hard.

'Kirk o' Shotts . . .' explained Mr Morrison. He was reduced to outlines and shadows in the half-light. I looked around me. No one in sight. This was as good a place as any to do your killing. I cursed myself for not having had a go at him earlier. Now he would be ready for me if I came at him.

'Take it easy.' Mr Morrison seemed to read my mind. 'I know this is a secluded spot for a killing, but that's not why I brought you here. Listen, can I dispense with this?' He raised the sliver of blade and snapped it back into its handle before pocketing it. 'Please don't give me any trouble, Mr Lennox. I brought you here for your benefit, not mine.' He walked across to a corner of the churchyard and eased up a broken piece of headstone that had sunk into the mossy grass. 'I have a particular affection for this place,' he said, retrieving a tobacco tin from the concealed depression under the stone. 'This was – still is – the Great Road between Edinburgh and Glasgow. In the fifteenth century this was a dangerous highway to travel, mainly because of Bertram Shotts. He was a highwayman who was reputedly also a giant. Seven foot tall. Some say eight. He was supposed to have had a hideaway near the Kirk. The place is supposed to have taken its name from him.' Mr Morrison removed a folded envelope from the tobacco tin and put it unopened into his pocket. 'Of course he wouldn't have been a giant, but people like to make their villains larger than life. Literally. I'm sure you'll agree I have a reputation that is more impressive than my physical presence.'

'Why bring me up here? Other than for an I-could-give-a-fuck history lesson.'

'It's a quiet place to talk and I had to pick up my mail. This is how my clients tell me they have a job for me. They leave a time and a telephone number in the tobacco tin for me to call and I call it. I have several such "mailboxes", but this one is a favourite. It's a difficult place for the police to stake out, being so elevated and exposed. Of course some of my clients, the Three Kings for example, have a more conventional and direct line of communication with me.' He pointed across the valley to where a needle of ironwork pierced the almost-dark sky. 'Things are changing, Mr Lennox. They put that up about five years ago. Television transmitter. That's the future, apparently. Things are getting more sophisticated. More technological. The police too.'

'I still don't get why I'm here.'

'First of all, I want you to know how to get in touch with me.'

'Living in Glasgow, I could do with a half-decent tailor. Sometimes it's difficult for my landlady to find a plumber.' I rubbed my chin in sarcastic thoughtfulness. 'But no . . . I don't think I ever really have much call for a contract killer.'

Mr Morrison looked at me blankly. He had described his

sociopathic lack of emotion. It obviously extended to any sense of humour. 'No, no ... I don't mean that,' he said. 'I have a proposition for you, like I said. I wanted you to know how to contact me if you needed. But I'll come back to that.'

'Oh good,' I said, again with undetected irony.

'The main reason I wanted to talk to you is because I have some information which I think you'll find interesting. About a week ago I had a project to undertake for Mr Sneddon. When I was taking the brief he told me that you were looking into the Tam McGahern killing for him. Trying to find out who's behind it. It wasn't me, by the way.'

'If you brought me up here to tell me that you could have spared me the hike. I knew that already.'

'That's not what I have to tell you. About two and a half weeks ago there was a number left in one of my mail collection points. It wasn't one that I recognized. I work for an established clientele and don't tout for business. As I said to you on the train, Mr Lennox, I am a hunter rather than a stalker, but I am more than capable of the odd bit of detection. I have contacts ... people upon whom I can call for paid favours. None of whom, by the way, have any idea what it is I do for a living, although they probably have guessed it's less than legal. Anyway, I had the number checked out by one of these contacts – one who works for the GPO. He told me the number belonged to a public call box in Glasgow. In Renfield Street. Whoever had left the message was being very careful to avoid being traced. Obviously, because it was a call box, they had left a specific time for me to call.'

'Did you?'

'No. Of course not. It could have been a police trap. So instead of calling, I hung around in Renfield Street with a view of the public telephone. Right enough, five minutes before the appointed time a smallish young man went into the call box. It could have been a coincidence, of course, but when another man started to tap impatiently on the glass, the young man opened the door and grabbed the waiting man by the collar and obviously made some kind of threat. The other man scuttled off.'

'Yeah, but you're talking about Glasgow. That's a normal conversation.' I took a cigarette from my case and lit up, offering Mr Morrison one: I thought it best to keep his hands busy. As I lit the cigarette for him his round, fleshy little face glowed in the sudden light. Given all the time in the world to place him in a profession, hit-man would never have come up. That was probably why he was so successful.

'No. This was my man. He hogged the 'phone box for half an hour. He was the person I was clearly expected to contact.'

'Did you recognize him?'

'No. But I recognized his type. He was an underling. Again, another distance that whoever was trying to hire me was placing between him and me. I could tell he wasn't my potential client from the way he dressed and the way he looked frightened when he didn't get the call he had been told to take.'

'What did he look like?'

'Like I said, smallish, maybe a couple of inches taller than me. Cheap suit. Oily hair in what I believe is popularly called a "Duck's Arse" style.'

'Dirty blond?'

There was a pause and I guessed Mr Morrison was frowning in the dark. 'You know him?'

'Knew him. If he was who I think he was, then he's no longer with us,' I said, and had a nauseating thought about Scotch pies. 'I think he may have been a gofer called Bobby. Worked for Tam and Frankie McGahern.'

The sky was dark-blue and velvet behind the looming black form of Kirk o' Shotts. Morrison's face and the mirrors of his spectacles were again briefly illuminated as he drew on his cigarette. 'That would fit. I followed him from Renfield Street all the way back to a spit-and-sawdust place in Maryhill.'

'The Highlander?'

'Yes. I told Mr Sneddon about this little experience and he told me that the Highlander was run by the McGaherns.'

'Doesn't that breach your client–contractor confidentiality?'

'The McGaherns weren't my clients and were never going to be. Like I said, I don't work for just anybody. But, as you know, killing isn't always a refined art. Glasgow is full of men who would take a life for you for twenty pounds. Or less. I'm a specialist and I cost a lot to hire. If the late Mr McGahern had wanted to use my services then it must have been something special. Out of the ordinary.'

I thought about what Morrison was saying. I also thought of John Andrews's faked accident. Maybe that had been planned weeks before. Maybe something was planned for me.

'Mr Sneddon wanted you to know this. He would have told you himself but I said I wanted to talk to you about another matter.'

'This proposition of yours.'

'Exactly. You see, Mr Lennox, we plough parallel furrows. In an odd way we are colleagues, both independent, both working for mainly the same people. The difference is you are a stalker, I am a hunter. As such we could share the kill. As you can imagine, my anonymity is paramount. I do everything I can to remain invisible and the only reason I have exposed myself to you is because I see the potential for partnership. On certain cases, that is. You see, sometimes my observation of marks, following them and establishing patterns of movement, et cetera, exposes me to the risk of discovery. But you are a natural stalker who's at home in the shadows and an expert at tracking people down. My proposition is simple: a fifty-fifty split on any kill we work together on.'

I dropped my cigarette butt onto the ground and crushed the spray of orange sparks with my shoe. I looked at the small, dense silhouette of the bank manager killer.

'Thanks for the offer but no. I'm not interested in that kind of work,' I said, trying to make my tone decisive. 'I don't want any part of your business.'

The silhouette remained silent for a moment. 'Very well,' he said eventually. 'But I think you're making a huge mistake. This is very lucrative work. And, whether you like it or not, you already play your part.'

'What's that meant to mean?'

'Do you remember last year, when Mr Murphy asked you to track down a young couple for him?'

'Yes.' I remembered the job. 'Hammer Murphy said it was a favour for a friend whose daughter had eloped. Murphy's friend just wanted to make sure his daughter was okay.'

'I'm afraid the truth was a little less *domestic*. The young man had, in fact, been an employee of Mr Murphy and had stolen a large sum of money from him. He'd also supplied the police with embarrassing information. Your job was to find them. My job was to lose them again. Permanently.'

'The girl too?' I remembered her. No more than twenty-two or -three.

'The girl too. So you see, Mr Lennox, you have stalked for me before. In any case, I'd like you to think it over. Use the tobacco tin "mailbox" if you need to contact me. Anyway, if you'll excuse me, I'll leave you to get the train back to Glasgow. I won't be travelling with you as I have a housecall to make near here.'

Mr Morrison began to walk towards the black shoulder of the Kirk. He paused for a moment. 'Oh, and I take it I don't need to stress how important it is for you, if you're not going to consider my business proposition, that you do your best to forget my face.'

'No. You don't.' The truth was that Morrison's face had faded from my memory with the fading light. It was that kind of face. Ideal for a killer.

I walked back down what seemed the pitch-black road towards Shotts station. As I did so I had to fight the urge to glance over my shoulder to see if the eight-foot ghost of Bertram Shotts, or the five-foot-five shadow of a sociopathic bank manager, was tracking me.

I telephoned Sneddon as soon as I got back to Glasgow. In fact I 'phoned him from the station and gave him everything I had, including, this time, the fact that Bobby, the McGahern gofer, had had his head mashed in a pretty similar way to whichever McGahern brother it had been who'd had his head pulped in the Rutherglen garage. I told Sneddon that I'd had a cosy chat with Mr Morrison and that we were pretty certain that it was Bobby who had tried to hire him on Tam McGahern's behalf. And I did tell him about my suspicions that it had been Frankie who had been the first to go.

'So it was Tam you gave a hiding?' asked Sneddon. 'I wouldn't have thought that he would have been such a push over.'

'Nor would I. It was a set up. For some reason Superintendent McNab was watching Frankie. I think that "Frankie" was Tam and he made a deliberate exhibition in front of McNab. I started off thinking that it was to set me up as a suspect for the first murder.'

'But you don't think that now?'

'No. What happened that night made me more of a suspect for the second killing which, of course, doesn't make sense. Tam wouldn't frame me for his own murder. It was a set up all right, but I think it wasn't to incriminate me but so that McNab saw me give "Frankie" a hiding. Maybe McNab suspected that it was Frankie who'd been killed the first time round. If I had been in a street fight with Tam McGahern, then I would've had my work cut out, like you say. I think Tam deliberately took a beating to convince McNab that he was Frankie.'

There was a silence at the other end of the 'phone. I guessed Sneddon was thinking it through.

'It doesn't make sense,' he said eventually. 'Why the fuck would Tam McGahern go to all that bother to convince people that he was Frankie and not Tam?'

'Because Tam had been their real target and because of the games he and Frankie played with poor Wilma Marshall, Frankie had been pretending to be Tam that night and ended up getting the lead enema. Tam knew that whoever was after him, they were serious professionals. He was trying to prove that they'd got the right target and leave him alone. He obviously knew enough about me to guess that I would tell him to stuff his job and give him an excuse to jump me and take a hiding in front of a police audience.'

'So who is it that's after him? That's what I'm paying you to find out.'

'With the greatest respect you're not paying me enough. These guys are real professionals, like I said. They gave my office a going over and you would hardly have noticed it. And the way they took out the first McGahern brother was slick. Funny thing is the second killing wasn't. And the guys who jumped me in Argyle Street were more brawn than brains.'

'You saying you don't want the job any more?'

I sighed. I wished that I could say I didn't. 'No. The truth is that there's a connection between this and something else I'm working on.'

'Something I should know about?'

As I fed the pay 'phone with almost all of the change in my pocket, I related the whole story of John and Lillian Andrews to Sneddon. The only thing I had changed slightly in all I had told Sneddon was the chronology to disguise the fact that I hadn't let on right away about Bobby's splitting headache: if Sneddon thought that I hadn't been delivering hot-off-the-press then I might have got a bit of a slap from a couple of his boys. Nothing to put me in hospital, but enough to make me less forgetful in future. And, of course, I thought it prudent not to mention my little bathtub windfall.

I actually felt better for going through the whole story. Saying it out loud even helped me see the whole thing more clearly. Again Sneddon stayed quiet other than the odd grunt throughout. I ended the conversation by retracting my decla- ration of independence. Maybe Twinkletoes would be useful to have on call. It was a call for help: I didn't hold back on telling Sneddon about John Andrews warning me that I had been set up just like him. Sneddon could have gloated – I had been pretty self-righteous about my independence – but he didn't.

'I'll put a couple of guys on your tail. Twinkletoes and another guy you don't know. His name's Semple.'

'Is he more subtle than Twinkletoes?'

Sneddon laughed at his end of the line. 'Naw. Not much. But he's the kind of punter you want around if shite occurs.'

'That's what I need at the moment, to be honest. But tell them to stay in the background unless there's trouble.'

'I'll fix it up.'

'Okay, thanks,' I said.

I was just about to hang up when Sneddon added: 'By the way, what does he look like? Mr Morrison, I mean. I've never actually met him face-to-face.'

'Oh . . . pretty much as you'd expect,' I said. 'Big. About six-three. Hard-looking bastard.'

'Mmm,' said Sneddon. 'Figures.'

CHAPTER TWENTY

Sneddon was as good as his word. I turned in early that night and when I opened the curtains in my digs the next morning I saw a dark Austin 16HP, about seven or eight years old, parked on the street outside, about fifty yards up and on the other side of Great Western Road. One man behind the wheel. Of course it might not have been Sneddon's men, but the vague feeling I had had over the few days before had suggested that if someone was following me, then they were too good for me to catch sight of.

After breakfast I drove west along Dumbarton Road and out of the city. The dark Austin 16HP dutifully followed. It only took me fifteen minutes to reach Levendale House. It was a vast place that had been designed and built as an expression of vast wealth and superiority. It had started life as a stately home: the kind of place you usually saw sitting in the heart of some majestic and beautiful Highland estate. Except it didn't: it sat on the outskirts of Bishopbriggs.

War fucks everything up. More than that, it fucks people up. And that's what Levendale House had become: a refuge for the seriously fucked up.

The funny thing about when the war was over was that everybody wanted to talk about it. Eulogize about it. And when they weren't talking about it they were watching films about it, all of which seemed to star John Mills. It was as if there was some collective desire to convince each other that it had actually been a big adventure that brought everybody together and had brought the best out of even the worst.

Which was, of course, a crock of shit.

What people *didn't* want to see was the shadow of misery the war had cast behind it: the tangle of damaged humans in its wake. But there were people who were prepared to look that truth in the face and deal with it every day. The people who worked at Levendale House looked after the broken bodies and broken minds of boys who had been thrown into the mincer and come back old men. Blind, crippled, mad.

The duty sister at Levendale, a tired-looking woman in her fifties, showed me into a bright day room with a view over the house's vast gardens. I guessed she was the same sister I had spoken to on the telephone. She had asked me what my connection to the patient was and I had explained we had a friend, an old comrade, in common.

'Did you know Billy before . . . well, before he was wounded?' she asked with a concerned look. I got the feeling that her concern was as much for me as her patient.

'No. As a matter of fact I didn't. Like I said, we have a mutual friend who I'm trying to track down. We lost touch after the war. But I never met Pattison before.'

'That's maybe just as well. I think it's best that I prepare you . . . Billy's wounds were severe and extremely disfiguring.'

'I've seen my share,' I said.

The sister left me in the day room. I took in the huge windows opening out onto the gardens, the wood panelling, the ornate cornicing. The Victorian architect of this house had imagined a patrician family spending mornings in this room, secure in their place within the governing machinery of a British Empire on which the sun never set. But two wars had turned the world on its head and the Empire on its ass and now Levendale House and its elegant morning room were home to wounded ex-servicemen who had no place anywhere else.

The sister's warning was not overdone. When she returned she pushed a wheelchair into the room. It was clear that Lance Corporal William Pattison and a grenade had encountered one another at very close quarters. What I couldn't work out was which had taken the biggest bite out of the other. One side of Pattison's face was gone and his mouth had been reduced to a lopsided, lipless slit. Whatever arts and crafts they encouraged here, playing the trumpet was not going to be an option for Pattison. Taut new skin had been stretched over where the right side of his jaw, his right cheek and eye should have been.

The left side of his face was pretty messed up too and gave the impression that someone had pushed all the features around and hadn't managed to get them exactly where they had been before, added to which there had clearly been extensive burning to what was left of his face. Lon Chaney had nothing on this guy. The mask twisted into a grimace and I realized that Pattison was trying to smile at me.

'I don't get a lot of visitors,' he said. You don't say, I thought. His voice was wet, the words chewed in his half mouth. Like I had told the sister, I'd seen my share, but looking at Pattison made me feel pretty sick. I did my best to smile. I consoled myself with the fact that even if my smile was half-hearted, it was twice as good as Pattison would ever manage. 'Sister says you know Tam.'

'Our paths crossed,' I said. I realized that Pattison didn't know that McGahern had died. I decided not to say anything for the moment. I'd see how the conversation went. The poor fuck had enough to contend with.

'What unit were you in?' Pattison asked. I noticed that the right side of his body was limp. Paralysed, I guessed.

'First Canadian. Italy, Holland and Germany.'

'How did you know Tam then?' There seemed to be no suspicion in Pattison's voice. But there again inflection was difficult
when you were half a tongue and sixteen teeth down on the
deal.

'Long story. You were with him in Gideon?'

'And before. Tam was my sergeant. He saved my skin more
times than I can remember.'

'What about . . .' I clumsily indicated the wheelchair.

'Oh . . . that was after Tam was shipped home. My own stupid
fault. Acting the big bollocks. I didn't take cover quick enough.'

'What kind of guy was Tam? I mean back then? To be honest,
I only really caught up with him towards the end of the war.'

'The best. The absolute best. Our unit had this officer – really
good as officers go, and you had to be hard to be part of Gideon,
even if you was an officer. But he was all theory. Tam was the
bloke you wanted running things when shite started to fly. Was
you an NCO yourself?'

'No. Officer. Captain.'

'Oh, sorry sir. Didn't mean no disrespect. About officers, I
mean.'

'None taken, Billy. I came across my fair share of wankers
with pips on their shoulders myself. Anyway I'm not an officer
now.' I pulled a chair up opposite his wheelchair and sat down.
'You and Tam saw a lot of action with Gideon, I take it?'

'Oh aye. We was in the thick of it. Our unit was mainly Jews
and a couple of Sudanese. Won't hear anything against them.
I learned a lot when I was out there. Tough bastards, particularly them Jewish blokes. They had been fighting the Arabs for
years. If you needed them to kick arses then they didn't need
a second telling. Got their own country now, of course. God
help any poor bastard that tries to take it from them.'

'The Jewish men in your unit . . . Tam told me some of them were ex-members of the Special Night Squads.'

'Aye. That's right. Most of them if not all. That's what I meant. They had seen a lot of action before the war. Taking out Arab resistance units. Protecting the Iraqi petroleum pipeline, that kind of stuff. Real hard bastards. And they really hated the Germans. Not many prisoners were taken, if you catch my drift. But them Jewish lads were a great laugh. Tam really got on with them. He was interested in that kind of thing. You know, the history and stuff about the Middle East. That's why he got on so well with our officer. He'd been a journalist or something before the war. Correspondent I think you call them. Middle East was his special thing.'

'Do you know if Tam kept in touch with any of the other members of your unit?'

'I would think so. He looked me up all right. Don't you know that it was Tam who got my face fixed up?'

I was confused for a moment. I did my best to sweep the *that's it fixed up?* expression that must have flashed across my face. 'You've heard from Tam since the end of the war?'

'Oh aye. He visited me four, maybe five times. To start with I had to have a dressing on my face. For months. The wound just wouldn't heal and there was always a danger of me getting infected. They was trying to sort me out with a surgeon who could fix it, but the main man was always booked up. Tam sorted it all out for me. He paid for me to have it done private. The best plastic surgeon in the business. Mr Alexander Knox. I don't know how Tam managed to get him, even paying. But it was Mr Knox who fixed me up. I'm really pleased with the result.'

'He did a great job,' I said and smiled. But don't 'phone Sam Goldwyn and ask if he's looking for a new leading man, I thought. 'When was the last time you saw Tam?'

'About a year ago,' Pattison said and some saliva bubbled at the corner of his slit mouth. Lips must have cost extra. 'He was looking very flash. He's in business now. Doing really well for himself.'

'Did you know Tam's brother at all?'

'No. Never met him, but heard all about him. They was identical twins, you know, but Tam hated his brother. Tam said he could never work out how two brothers could be so alike on the outside but so different on the inside. He said his brother was rotten. Yellow. And a rat.'

'Did Tam talk about him much?'

'Tam didn't talk about anything much. He listened. But when he did say something it was worth hearing. But aye . . . he did talk about his brother a bit. He said his brother was a shirker who'd dodged his call-up. Tam seemed worried that he'd left his brother in charge of the family business, whatever it was they did.'

There was a pause. I looked out of the bay windows again and commented on how nice the gardens were. Truth was I was taking a break from looking at Pattison's face.

'Did you ever come across a Jimmy Wallace in the army?' I asked eventually.

'Not *Jimmy* Wallace . . . *Jamie* Wallace. You know how toffs are with names. That's who I was talking about earlier, when I said about our officer. That was him. Captain Jamie Wallace, the guy who had been a journalist before the war. The Middle East expert. He led our unit and did a pretty good job of it, but like I said it was Tam who was in charge when it came to fighting.'

I thought about what he had said. An officer. Why would an ex-army officer end up as a hanger-on to a thug gangster? 'How did Tam get on with Wallace?'

'They got on all right. Captain Wallace relied on Tam and

Tam was always interested in what the Captain had to say. They was different types, but they seemed to really get on.'

After they wheeled Pattison away I desperately needed to get out of the care home. I stood outside the front door and took a few deep breaths of non-Glasgow air. There was no sign of the Austin 16HP and I guessed it was parked outside the grounds. When I got into my car I sat without starting it for a few moments. I tilted the rear-view mirror so I could see the faint web of scars on my left cheek. Someone like Pattison's doctor had once fixed me up. But that was the difference that being a few feet further away from an exploding grenade meant. I could have ended up like Pattison. Easy. I sat for a moment and thought up a few more gags about his badly rebuilt face, laughing quietly to myself. That way I could maybe kill the ache in my gut and the sting in my eyes every time I thought of the poor bastard.

When you'd had the kind of war I'd had, you learned to laugh at suffering. So long as it wasn't yours. If you laughed at it, then maybe it wouldn't reach you. Get you. And if you believed that, then that was the biggest joke of all.

The Austin 16HP picked me up again and followed me back into town. It stayed about three cars back in an attempt at discretion. I had no doubt that Sneddon's men were handy with a pair of bolt-cutters or cracking open kneecaps with a claw hammer, but surveillance wasn't their strong suit. It didn't matter; I was glad to feel that there was someone looking over my shoulder.

I had a date for that night. I took Jeannie, a small, dark and curvy waitress I had picked up, to see *Sudden Fear* with Jack Palance and Joan Crawford at the Regal in Sauchiehall Street.

Jeannie insisted on the Glaswegian propriety of not sitting in the back row: a public indication of her respectability. The truth was that I was more interested in seeing the film than moist fumblings in her underwear, and we both knew that that would follow anyway in the sweaty, steamed-up confines of my Austin Atlantic.

In Glasgow having a push-bike you paid for yourself rather than nicking it made you flash. Having a car elevated you to Hollywood-level glamour. The fact that my car was a stylish Austin A90 Atlantic Coupe had been more instrumental in winning me pussy than my gentle demeanour, debonair wit and good looks.

'You look a bit like him,' Jeannie commented as we came out of the cinema into night air that was too cold for the time of year.

'Who?'

'Jack Palance. You're better looking, but you do look a bit like him.'

'You think?' I smiled. I looked at Jeannie. I certainly couldn't have compared her to Joan Crawford, or even Gloria Grahame who had, as always, played the cheap good-time girl. When I had first seen Jeannie there had been something about her reminded me of Carmen Miranda: dark hair and eyes, olive skin, full sensual lips. But when I'd picked her up that night I realized that the something about her had probably been the half bottle of rye whiskey I'd drunk and the dim smoky light. As I looked at my little waitress and reappraised the dark eyes, olive skin and full, sensuous lips, the closest comparison I could come up with was Edward G. Robinson with a permanent wave. Suddenly my ardour diminished. 'Yeah, I've been told that before,' I said in response to her Jack Palance remark. 'There's a reason for it.'

'Oh?'

'Long story.'

I was parked further up Sauchiehall Street, closer to the Locarno Ballroom. We walked back.

'It's a great car,' she said as I held the door open for her. Then, come-hither-ingly: 'Could we go for a drive?'

'Sure,' I said. My plan had been to drive Jeannie out of the city, park up on Gleniffer Braes, where there were great views of the city, and trick her into a blow-job. But try as I might I couldn't get out of my head the image of *Little Caesar* chomping down on a cigar. It was then I saw the dark-coloured 16HP parked a few cars back. Sneddon was taking my protection just a little bit too seriously. Take the night off, guys, I thought.

'Gimme a second; some friends of mine . . .' I said to Jeannie and I walked up to the 16HP. I could see it wasn't Twinkletoes and I guessed it was the other thug whom Sneddon had promised to lend me. The guy behind the wheel started his engine as soon as he saw me approach. I noticed that he had a large dressing on his cheek and it was then that I recognized him: he was one of the goons who had jumped me in Argyle Street. Specifically he was the fella whose cheek I had split open with the length of pipe. It was clear he was in no mood for a rematch without his pals and he slammed into reverse, braked, ripped teeth off his gears and sped off down Sauchiehall Street. I ran back to my car and tore out after him.

The 16HP squealed into Blythswood Street and headed down towards the river. He ripped across the junction with Bath Street and just missed being side-slammed by a Rover. I swung around the tail of the Rover but a gap had opened up between us. He reached the Clyde end of Blythswood and swung a left without slowing onto the Broomielaw.

I had to brake hard for a truck which stopped in my path

while the driver bawled out of his cab and accused my mother of all kinds of acts, all indecent, some illegal and at least one of which I thought was physically impossible. I bumped up onto the kerb to navigate round him. It was only when I checked out of my side window that I realized that Jeannie was still sitting next to me. She was staring at me, eyes wide and mouth slack with shock.

'Get out,' I said as gently as I could. 'I have to catch this guy. It's business.'

She still sat stunned. I reached over and opened the door and gave her a shove towards the street. 'Out! Quick!' She got out wordlessly and stood on the pavement still gawp-mouthed. 'I'm sorry, Jeannie ... I'll call you ...'

I floored the accelerator and fired the Atlantic along Broomielaw in the direction of Paddy's Market. The 16HP was nowhere to be seen but I knew if I made the right decisions I could close on him. He had either turned back into the city towards Glasgow Cross or had crossed the Clyde into the South Side. I put my money on the South Side: he would stand more risk of getting snarled up in the city and me catching up.

I swung across the Albert Bridge. Crown Street was empty of cars. From here he could have taken the Carlisle road or headed back towards Govan and the Paisley road. Or he could even have headed off into the Gorbals, but I reckoned that would have been a bad move: actually, anyone heading off into the Gorbals, at any time, for any reason, was a bad move. In his case an Austin 16HP would have looked as much at home in the Gorbals as a priest in an Orange Hall.

On a hunch, I turned towards Govan and followed Paisley Road West. Again I drove as fast as I dared but still caught no sight of the 16HP.

I stopped under the railway bridge, switched the engine off

and rolled down the window. The street was silent except for a Number Nine Corporation tram that trundled its way past heading from Paisley to Maryhill. Sam Costa and his ludicrous moustache grinned inanely at me from a tattered poster, advising me that Erasmic shaving lather was *just right*. The night air had a texture to it, like the cold greasy soot that smeared the railway arches.

He was gone. He could have taken any one of a dozen different directions after I had lost him dumping Jeannie on the pavement. I thought back to that moment and felt like shit, as I usually did when it came to reflecting on how I'd treated women.

There were thousands of Jeannies in this city: uncomplicated girls with crap lives who looked to the dance halls and the cinemas for a scrap of glamour. All they wanted was a few moments while they were still young in which they could pretend that they wouldn't, after all, end up swapping the grey drudgery of working in a factory or at best a shop for the grey drudgery of slaving for a man who would show them little affection and no respect and leave them with an army of kids to care for. The monotony of their week punctuated only by loveless whisky-drenched fumblings on a Saturday night. Or maybe the odd beating.

I thought of poor Jeannie and the meagre dreams and aspirations that she may have had and felt sorry for having dumped her like that. Then I thought of how she had reminded me of Edward G. Robinson and started to laugh as I turned the ignition.

I knew I'd lost the 16HP, but I decided to trace my way back along the river-edge quays just in case. There were a hundred nooks and crannies, alleys and yards where you could lie low. But my thinking was that the driver of the 16HP had used my temporary halt to put as much distance between us as possible.

If Glasgow was the Empire's industrial heart, then the Clyde was its main artery. I drove past Mavisbank Quay, Terminus Quay with its railyards and finally Kingston Dock. As I drove, stark white lights hovered over the ink sleek waters of the Clyde.

Even at this time of night and this far into the city the river glittered with tugs, boats and barges and I could see the occasional fountain of sparks where some nightshift sculpted steel.

I caught sight of a car pulled off the main road into a narrow cul-de-sac between two warehouses. It wasn't my guy. The steamed windows of an ancient Ford told me hasty fornication was the motive for stealth in this case.

I drove on and into King Street, my mind no longer on my quarry but on why I was being watched by Lillian Andrews's accomplices – and I was pretty sure that was who I was dealing with. The man behind the wheel had been the same guy who had been part of the clumsy snatch squad in the Bedford truck. Their lack of finesse didn't fit with the professionalism with which my office had been turned over. Nor did it fit with the uneasy feeling I'd had for the last few days that I was being followed by someone who was too good to be seen. It was true that the guy in the 16HP could have been more obvious, but only if he'd had a sign on his windscreen saying, 'I'M FOLLOWING YOU LENNOX'. Two outfits? It would fit with my Fred MacMurray lookalike and his Middle Eastern pals.

Instinctively I felt they were connected with Tam McGahern in another way, not through Lillian. But everything that Rufus Jeffrey had told me about Tam's military service and connection to the Middle East nagged away at me. That *was* a link that could tie Mr Double Indemnity and his camel-jockeys in with Lillian. I drove back over Glasgow Bridge and back to where I'd dumped Jeannie. A good hour had passed and, of course, she was gone. Everything was fucked up.

I needed a drink.

CHAPTER TWENTY-ONE

By the time I got to the Horsehead Bar it was already an hour after closing time. Which meant this was the time that the Horsehead did its best business. Discreetly. I gave the knock I'd learned and Big Bob let me in. A 'lock-in' was a quaint British custom that made use of a loophole in the licensing laws which allowed the licensee to lock the doors and privately 'entertain' bona-fide friends without charging. In other words, that's when the coppers called for their free drinks and turned a blind eye to the left-open cash till and the other 'bona-fide friends'.

My fucked-up evening stayed true to form. I was greeted by a six-foot-six scowl from the bar.

'Good evening, Superintendent McNab,' I said as un-wearily as I could manage. I thought of asking McNab if I could buy him a drink, but he looked happy with his half of pale ale and his scowl. Also, I wasn't mad on the company he was keeping: there was a capless and chinless army major and a sergeant at the bar with him. The sergeant's cap sat on the bar and it was my least favourite colour: red.

Towards the end of what had been, admittedly, a rather colourful military career I had spent quite some time in the company of the Military Police. In many ways it had been the same kind of experience that I'd had since with the civilian police: sitting in a thick-walled room with a couple of guys who want to kick the shite out of you. The difference with the redcaps was they couldn't, because I had been an officer.

It was as if McNab had been reading my mind. 'Lennox here used to be an officer, you know. Captain, wasn't it?'

I nodded.

'Aye ...' McNab eyed me up and down. 'He used to be a gentleman and an officer. Now he's just a gobshite.'

The little redcap sergeant grinned. I smiled too. What I wanted to do was punch McNab in his big stupid copper moon face. But I smiled. 'If you don't mind, Superintendent, I won't call on you for a character reference.'

'And he's a smart-arse. You know what you are, Lennox? You're a sewer rat. You scuttle around in this city's shite. But the fact is you get to hear things. Things I don't.'

'Is there a point to this, NcNab? To be honest I don't care to be insulted by the likes of you.' I turned square on to him. I started to weigh up the beating in the cells I would get if I busted McNab's jaw and it was becoming an increasingly acceptable bargain. I looked at the little redcap sergeant, then at the major and successfully made the point that if I went for it, I'd make it worth my while and go for a job lot. The sergeant stopped smiling and the chinless wonder with the pips looked like he was wishing he was back in Chelsea. McNab took a step forward.

'Fancy your chances, Lennox?'

'Let it go Lennox ...' Big Bob had moved up to our end of the bar. 'He's not worth hanging for.'

I don't know if it had been the sudden suggestion that he might not survive the encounter, but McNab looked a little less sure of himself. Just a flicker of uncertainty behind the tight expression.

'I'll ask you again, McNab. Do you have a point?'

'Steady on, old chap . . .' The MP major, looking even less sure of himself, eased between me and McNab. He had one of those plummy accents that I thought were only made up for comedy effect by the likes of Basil Radford and Naughton Wayne. 'The Superintendent suggested we come here on the off-chance we could have a word. If you're . . . connected, so to speak, it might be that you have heard something on the grapevine.'

'About what?' I kept my gaze fixed on McNab.

'There was a clothing warehouse broken into last night,' said McNab. 'Not much taken and it wouldn't normally be a major inquiry, but it's what has been taken that's important. The warehouse was used by a company that supplies uniforms. Army, air force and police.'

'So what was taken?'

'They were very selective. They picked up separate items that would account for five police uniforms and three army uniforms.'

'And you think someone's planning an IPO job?'

McNab broke his gaze and sipped his pale ale. 'That's what it looks like. They were just uniforms, mind. No badges or insignia on either the police or the army stuff.'

'I've not heard anything,' I said and McNab gave me a look. 'That's the truth, McNab. But I have to say that I don't think it would be any of the Three Kings. Impersonating police officers gets headlines. Attracts attention and stirs up you boys more than the usual brown envelopes can calm down.'

McNab looked as if he was going to take a poke at me. I grinned: I'd said it to yank on his chain.

'Anyway,' I continued, 'it's not something I think they'd get into. Do a robbery in a police uniform and that's another ten on your stretch if you're caught.'

'I want you to ask around,' said McNab.

'And why should I do that, Superintendent?'

'Because it could make your life easier.'

'And it could make it a lot more difficult if word got out that I was a grass. But maybe I will. I have an idea the Three Kings won't like someone pulling this kind of stunt on their territory.'

There wasn't anything else to say and I moved round to my usual end of the bar without taking my leave. McNab and the two redcaps drained their glasses and left. After Big Bob unbolted the door to let them out he came over to me.

'Listen, Lennox, you're a good customer. And a friend. But if you ever square up to a fucking copper in here again I'll bar you for life.'

'Point taken, Bob. That fucker McNab knows how to push my buttons. I don't think we'll see him in here again. You hear what he was on about?'

'Aye. You're right. The Three Kings wouldn't get involved in an IPO job. This is an outside firm. Or just a bunch of youngsters acting the cunt.'

'I don't think so. Sounds like they had a shopping list.' I drained my whisky and Big Bob refilled my glass without being asked.

'On the house,' he said. 'You look like you need it.'

'It's been a long, long day.'

'There was someone in looking for you earlier. About eight. Didn't leave a name.'

'What did he look like?'

'Fuck . . . I don't know . . .' Big Bob rubbed his chin thoughtfully then an expression of enlightenment lit up his face. 'He was a big ugly cunt. Really big and really ugly. Oh aye . . . there was something else: a big fucking razor scar. Right cheek. Like he'd been chibbed in the past.'

'A big ugly cunt with a razor scar . . .' I repeated. I thought of half of the hard men I did business with, their mothers, even some of the women I'd been with since I'd arrived here. 'This is Glasgow, Bob,' I said. 'You're going to have to be more specific.'

Big Bob laughed. 'You wouldn't miss him. Really, really big fucker. Bigger than me.'

'Any message?'

'Just that he wanted to talk to you. Business.'

I thought for a moment. 'You said he had a scar. Not recent? He didn't by any chance have a dressing on his cheek?'

'Naw. This was old. Hard-looking bastard though. Oh aye, there was one thing . . . he was wearing a pinstripe suit. Like a businessman.'

'Don't they all,' I said and sipped my whisky. Because it wasn't the guy I'd chased all over town it didn't mean it wasn't one of Lillian's associates. I had a funny feeling I'd be hearing from them soon. They hadn't scared me off and I smelt a deal in the air.

He was waiting for me outside: the monster in a pinstripe suit. I had thought Bob's description rather vague but on seeing him I realized that nothing could fit better than 'a big ugly cunt with a razor scar'. He was leaning against a car, presumably his, and it wasn't the 16HP.

I closed my hand around the sap in my pocket. I don't frighten easily and I had been prepared to smack McNab and take the consequences, but this fucker was a whole new ball of wax. He was at least six-seven and comparisons with brick shithouses were totally inadequate: I reckoned he could have killed me just by falling on me. But it wasn't just his build that bothered me. He had the look of a life-taker. A killer. I was glad I had my sap but wished I had had something more substantial, like my tyre iron, or my gun. Or a tank. Mind you, I reckoned that the last time he'd been in a fight he'd been probably been poleaxed by a little Jewish boy with a slingshot. He stood up from leaning on his car when he saw me and I was surprised to see he hadn't dented the wing.

'Mr Lennox?' he asked in a baritone that must have rattled windows in Paisley. At least he was a polite killer.

'Who wants to know?' I asked, trying to work out how tall six cubits was. And a span.

'Mr Sneddon sent me. Me and Twinkletoes is supposed to look after you. I tried to find you earlier but you wasn't at home.' He walked over to me and just kept getting bigger. He was an ugly son-of-a-bitch all right. It looked like he'd beaten up half the population of Glasgow using his face as a blunt instrument. He also had the scar that Bob had talked about: a long and deep crease in his cheek. I was impressed with the reach of the ambitious, and probably now deceased, Glaswegian that had put it there.

'Please tell me you didn't call at my digs?' I imagined Mrs White opening the door and wondering why it hadn't let the light in.

'Naw ... naw ... I seen your car wasn't there. Mr Sneddon told me to be discreet. I'm to let you know that we was watching your back and that if you need any help you's just to shout like.'

I suppressed a smirk at the idea of discretion coming in a six-foot-seven, twenty-three-stone package. 'I could have done with you today. You know anyone who drives an Austin 16HP?'

Goliath shrugged. This was impressive, given the size of his shoulders.

'It's just that I had a run in with someone in a 16HP. He'd been following me all day and I just assumed it was one of you guys.'

'Naw.'

'If you're going to be watching my back, could you keep an eye out for it? Dark blue or black Austin 16HP.'

'Nae problem, Mr Lennox.'

'I'm going home now. I'll be fine tonight.'

'Okey dokey,' Goliath said pleasantly in his Richter-scale baritone. 'But I'll follow you home. Just to make sure like.'

'I take it you're Semple,' I said as I unlocked my car. 'Mr Sneddon told me about you. What's your first name, by the way?'

'Everybody calls me Tiny,' he said without a hint of irony. 'Tiny Semple.'

CHAPTER TWENTY-TWO

There's always a moment, when you first wake up in the morning, when you're temporarily outside your life. Everybody gets it: that feeling of unattributable happiness or contentment or worry or despair. You lie there and think: there's a reason I feel like this but I can't remember what it is.

When I woke up the following morning my gut feeling lay more on the 'different day, same shite' side of the mood fence than 'another day, another dollar'. Then, like comedy bricks falling on Oliver Hardy's head, the crap of the day before fell piece by piece into my memory. I coughed my way through my first Player's Navy Cut of the day without getting out of bed. I lay for a moment considering staying there for the rest of the day, or finding out, at long last, if that ticket to Halifax, Nova Scotia was still valid.

Against my better judgement I got up, washed and put on an expensive seersucker shirt, silk tie and my best suit. I didn't shave but decided to go to 'Phersons and have a shave and haircut. It just felt like that kind of day: there was nothing like having your face scalded with a boiling towel to set you up for twenty-four hours of crap.

There had been a Sunbeam Talbot 90 parked outside my digs and as I passed it Twinkletoes McBride looked up from his *Reader's Digest* and smiled amiably: obviously Tiny was being spelled, presumably resting up on top of a beanstalk somewhere. I got the impression Twinkletoes was grateful for the interruption: a whole page of the *Reader's Digest* at one sitting would probably have given him a headache. It wasn't just that Twinkletoes's lips moved when he read: they moved when someone else was reading. I told him I was walking to 'Phersons for a haircut and asked if he could pick me up in half an hour.

'Pherson's was in the West End, off Byers Road, so not far from my digs. I don't know where the 'Mac' had gotten lost but no one ever talked about MacPherson's, just 'Pherson's. Truth was I really liked the place. A good barber's in twentieth-century Glasgow was the equivalent of the Regency dining room after the ladies had withdrawn: a haven of maleness. I'd heard that the red-and-white barber's pole was the symbol of the ancient barber surgeons: blood and bandages. It wasn't. It was a big stripy dick that stated that this was a man's realm.

'Pherson's reeked of macassar hair oil, spiced unguents, after-shave and testosterone. Which was odd, because old man 'Pherson, a frail, birdlike man in his sixties whose hair was unnaturally black for his age – actually unnaturally black for his species – was himself as queer as a nine-bob note.

This was where I came once a fortnight, as they described two weeks in Britain, and had my hair cut and treated myself to the closest shave you could get in Glasgow apart from calling Hammer Murphy a bog-Irish Fenian fuckface from a speeding car immediately before emigrating to the other side of the planet. 'Pherson's was also where I picked up my supply of prophylactics, known here as 'rubber johnnies'. It was amazing the differences in expression here. I had once tried to explain to a Glaswegian that 'blow-job' was the American and Canadian expression for fellatio.

'Oh aye,' my conversational partner had said. 'That's what we call plating . . . or a gammy. Or a gobble.'

Rubber johnnies. Gammies. Gobbles. I was gradually to become schooled in the quaint charms of the Old World.

During the war I had seen for myself the way the shakes worked on a guy: fingers would tremble and knees would knock at the prospect of battle, but when the bullets started to fly you got too scared and too fired up to shake. It was like that with old 'Pherson: you'd watch the sliver of razor tremble in his thin fingers, feel his other hand's tremulous touch on your face, then, miraculously, the blade would sweep smoothly and decisively across your pulled-taut skin.

'Pherson was giving me a trim, the scissors between cuts fluttering like a bird and snipping at the empty air, when I was aware of someone sitting in the barber's chair next to mine.

'We need to talk, Lennox.'

I looked at Jock Ferguson's profile in the mirror before me. 'Sounds official.'

'It is,' he said. 'But it can wait till you've finished your haircut.'

Twinkletoes looked up from his *Reader's Digest* and reached for the door handle as Ferguson and I passed his car, but I frowned a warning and gave a surreptitious shake of the head and he eased back in his seat.

It wasn't Jock's Morris that waited for us around the corner but a black police Wolseley 6/90 with a uniformed driver. This really was going to be official. Ferguson remained stone-faced and silent.

'What's this about, Jock?' I asked.

'You'll see . . .'

I had worked out that Ferguson wasn't going to return the favour of the Italian meal, and we drove across town towards Glasgow Green and the Saltmarket. When the driver dropped us off at the double-door front entrance of the Glasgow City Mortuary I realized that he didn't have a fun day out planned.

It seemed that we were expected. Glasgow was a city of deficiencies, mainly vitamin, and the inappropriately cheery mortuary attendant who showed us down into the bowels of the morgue had the typical bow legs of someone who had suffered from rickets. It was a common look in Glasgow: a quarter of the population who had lived through the thirties looked like they were riding invisible Shetland ponies.

Glasgow City Mortuary had moved here between the wars and the white-tiled walls reminded me of a municipal bath house. We descended down a starkly lit, wide stairway and into a basement hall.

The smell of a mortuary isn't what you'd expect: no stench of death, more like a mixture of carbolic soap and a faintly stale smell, as if the soap had been mixed with stagnant water. We entered a long, cavernous room. The temperature and Ferguson's mood were both several degrees cooler than they had been at ground level. The cheery attendant with the chimpanzee swagger led us to one of the metal doors that were set in a row into the tiled wall. He slid out the tray and pulled back the white sheet that covered the body stored inside.

'You know who this is?' Ferguson didn't expect or wait for me to be shocked. We'd never talked about it but we both knew that the other had seen the worst a war could throw up. A sort of grim freemasonry.

I looked at what was left of the face. The strange thing was the grey-white hair on the head was still perfectly combed in the over-styled way John Andrews had had it in life. Beneath the hairline, however, there was a deep impression, like a dent in the skull. There were a lot of lacerations across the bridge of the shattered nose, through the now-empty right eye socket and across the cheek. But there was enough of the mouth and the weak, bearded double-chin for me to know for sure that this was Andrews.

'I take it the question is rhetorical,' I said. 'You know damned fine who he is.'

Jock Ferguson gave a curt nod in the direction of the bandy-legged mortuary attendant as a signal to leave us alone. The attendant's smile didn't falter as he made his waddling way back to the door.

'It's good to be happy in one's work,' I said to Ferguson. His expression told me to hold the humour.

'Yes I know damned fine who it is. I also know damned fine that you were attacked by men travelling in one of Andrews's firm's trucks. I know damned fine that you've been sniffing around Andrews and his wife for weeks now. And I know damned fine, even if I can't prove it, that you don't get your face pulped like this crashing a solid-built Bentley into a country ditch.'

I looked at the devastated face again and nodded. 'Maybe he banged his face off the steering wheel. Ten or eleven times. I don't know, Jock . . . but my guess is somebody's gone into bat with a tyre iron.'

'Like Frankie McGahern.'

I looked at him for a moment. There was no way out of this. 'Just like Frankie McGahern,' I sighed. 'There's a link between Lillian Andrews, or Sally Blane as she used to be known professionally, and Tam McGahern.'

'I knew it!' Ferguson lifted his hands and let them fall limply into the folds of his raincoat. 'I bloody knew it. You have had your nose up this case's arse all along, haven't you? I warned you, Lennox . . . I bloody warned you. If McNab gets wind of this he's going to use your arse as a golfbag. I told you to stay out of this case. You don't know what you're messing with here. Trust me.'

'Why don't you tell me?'

Ferguson's normally expressionless face made a good attempt at outraged shock. 'You have got to be fucking kidding. I am telling you fuck all.' He jabbed me in the chest with his finger. '*You* are going to tell *me* every fucking thing you know. If you don't, I'm going to serve you up to McNab on a silver platter.'

I looked down at John Andrews, but he clearly didn't have an opinion on the matter. I could tell Jock Ferguson was serious. I'd lied to him. I'd gotten him to help me while lying to him. He had just cause to dump on me. All he needed to do was tell McNab I'd been running with the McGahern case and holding out on information they needed and McNab and his ruddy-faced farmlad would play bar skittles with my balls.

'Okay,' I said with a resigned tone. I looked at Jock Ferguson. His face was fixed. Determined. I knew I could trust him to be straight with me and I also knew he was pissed because he had thought the same of me. I don't know why people do that.

Anyway, Ferguson was a decent, straightforward guy: that one good cop you know you can rely on. So I decided to lie to him in a decent, straightforward sort of way.

'The truth is, Jock, I did drop the whole McGahern thing. It was looking like far too much trouble and, to be honest, like there was nothing in it for me. So I let it go. Completely.'

Ferguson gave me a sceptical look.

'But I had this other case. He . . .' I nodded to John Andrews's corpse as if he could confirm my story. He certainly wasn't going to deny it. '. . . told me that his wife had gone missing and he was desperately worried about her. I could tell he was genuine, which is more than I could say for his wife's disappearance. I called to see him and he said she was back and everything was hunky-dory and it was all a *big* misunderstanding and sorry to have troubled you and here by the way is about three times the cash that I really owe you so thanks a bunch and go the fuck away. All of which was about as credible as a nineteen-year-old Govan virgin. So instead of doing the sensible thing and forgetting all about it, I see Lillian Andrews in the street and follow her and her friend.'

'Which results in a tit-flashing and head-bashing, as I recall,' said Ferguson.

'Exactly. So one quick feel and twenty stitches later I find out that Lillian Andrews is or was Sally Blane, a whore and blue-movie actress who's as professional with a dick in her mouth as Larry Adler is with a harmonica. Then I hear stories about a high-end, by-appointment-only brothel somewhere near Byres Road in the West End. Just a few girls, but classy and skilled. Story is that the clientele includes many of the great and the good in Glasgow. My money is on Lillian Andrews as madam. None of the Three Kings has a stake in it and my guess, like it or not, Jock, is that they have top cops either on the books as customers or as brown envelope pay-offs. Whatever the reason they're left alone. What I didn't know yet was that Tam McGahern was supplying heavies for security.'

'I thought you said it was independent?'

'It was. McGahern was a sub- not a main contractor. Or at least to start with. I find out later that McGahern was cracked up on the woman who ran the place. Who, like I say, I reckon was Lillian Andrews. But I don't know any of this yet. So then I get a call from a woman who says she has information for me and can I meet her somewhere quiet and secluded where I can get my brains bashed in. I say no go but that I'll be under the clock in Central Station. Time comes and goes but she doesn't. Then I get jumped on the way back to my car by a bunch of thugs out of the Bedford van I gave you the number of.'

'Which is owned by John Andrews's company.'

'Except the woman who 'phoned me and said she had information wasn't Lillian Andrews. Or I don't think she was. And the information she said she had for me was about Tam McGahern's death.'

Ferguson's face clouded again. 'So you were still working the case.'

'No. I've told you,' I lied with indignation. 'I'd dropped it. But when someone 'phones you and tells you that they have information on a murder the cops have suspected you know more about than you really do, you've got to check it out. If I'd found out anything then I'd have got in touch with you straight away.'

Jock Ferguson raised an eyebrow. He was clearly thinking of flying pigs and nineteen-year-old Govan virgins.

'It's the truth, Jock. Anyway, then – and don't ask me how – I get my hands on stills from a blue movie featuring a younger Lillian Andrews slash Sally Blane playing the one-note piccolo. I still don't know what the deal with Andrews is so I confront him with the pictures, like I told you, and it's no surprise to him. Now I know that there's something going on that stinks to high heaven. I actually begin to worry about his safety . . .' I looked down at the smashed face of my ex-client and thought about how much good my worrying had done him. 'Anyway, then I get a call from him and boy is he a scared bunny. He tells me he's as good as dead and Lillian is behind it all. Being the genius I am, I tell him to tell me everything later but to get to safety. I arrange to meet him at a hotel up by Loch Lomond.'

'Except he doesn't make it.'

'Exactly. Oh, and by the way, before you get all holier-than-thou with me one of the options I gave him when he 'phoned me was that I had a cop he could trust. You.'

'If he had he'd still be alive.'

'Maybe. Maybe not. When I suggested getting the police

involved it was like he started to panic. I've got to be honest, Jock, it was as if he knew that Lillian and whoever she was involved with had someone inside the City Police. And that fits with my suspicions about the brothel being left alone because of police contacts.'

Ferguson frowned but his expression revealed that he knew it wasn't impossible: there was a parlour game in Glasgow, usually played in the changing rooms of the Western Baths, called the Manila Envelope Shuffle. The Western Baths were popular with senior police officers, businessmen and Glasgow Corporation councillors.

'Anyway, that's all I've got,' I said as if I'd unburdened all that there was to unburden. It was rather convincing, even if I say so myself. But Ferguson's expression, as always, was difficult to read.

'You should have come to me as soon as Andrews was killed,' he said. Our voices echoed in the cavern of the mortuary.

'I didn't know for sure it was murder. And anyway, you don't have anything to go on.' I nodded to Andrews's body. 'You can't even prove this *wasn't* an accident.'

'But I've got enough from you to start a murder inquiry. A call for help and a declaration that his life was threatened immediately before he was killed. And we know that Tam and Frankie McGahern's deaths *were* murder and now there's a link with Andrews's death.'

I nodded thoughtfully. I knew I hadn't given him enough to make a case. I hadn't told him about the faked shipment manifests that Andrews had told me about on the 'phone. And, of course, I hadn't said a thing about a fourth connected death: Bobby, who was by now probably a better pie filling than he had been a petty crook. I also kept schtum about everything else I'd picked up, including my gut feeling that my Fred

MacMurray lookalike and his chums were completely uncon-
nected to the less than competent mob who'd tried to lift me
from Argyle Street. The truth was I wanted time to dig deeper
myself. Ferguson was a good cop, but he was supported by a
spectrum of policing talents that ranged from the incompetent
to the corrupt. They would either trample all over the evidence
or, if I was right and there was someone on the inside on
Lillian's payroll, they would actively bury it. Anyway, I didn't
work for the interests of justice: I worked for Willie Sneddon.

'You going to question Lillian Andrews?' I asked.

'Got to. Got to get to the bottom of this, Lennox.'

'Listen, Jock. I've shown you mine, now you show me yours.
What did you mean I didn't know what I was messing with?'

Ferguson pulled the sheet back over John Andrews's smashed
face, pushed the body tray into the cubicle and closed the door.
I thought of Andrews's Bentley, his big house and its
Contemporary furniture, his sixty-guinea suits. Now all he had
to his name was a winding sheet and a chilled steel cabinet
and even those were on loan. It made me think of when you
got to know someone in the war who ended up getting killed:
everything they had told you about their lives, all the conver-
sations you had had with them, it all became unreal when they
were lying in front of you, just so much mince.

'Just trust me, Lennox: you *don't* have any idea what you're
messing with. The truth is I don't either. All I know is that it's
political or something. McNab has a bee up his arse because
someone put it there, and I think it buzzed all the way from
Whitehall.'

'What?' I shook my head in disbelief. 'We're talking about
the McGaherns here, not Burgess and Maclean. A couple of
thieves and a whore. What can be political about that?' The
truth was what Ferguson had said had started all kinds of alarms

ringing. Not just politics, Middle East politics. I already had suspicions about where Fred MacMurray's kid brother and his pals had come from, but I couldn't for the life of me work out what they could have to do with the McGaherns' sordid little realm.

'I don't know what the story is,' said Ferguson. 'All I do know is that there have been Special Branch types hanging around St Andrew's Street. The odd military sort too.'

'I bumped into McNab the other night. Or more like he bumped into me ... accidently on purpose. He had a couple of MPs in tow. Some shite about stolen uniforms.'

'No shite,' said Ferguson. 'But not connected, as far as I can see. The MPs are involved because a couple of army uniforms were nicked. It's the police uniforms that McNab is worried about. He's crapping himself in case some outfit is going to pull an IPO job. When crooks impersonate police officers the public get jittery and there's all kind of political bollocks to deal with. And McNab has enough on his plate with the McGahern thing.'

We made our way out of the mortuary hall and back up the stairwell. Once we were out on the street we both simultaneously drew deep breaths of Glasgow air. Hardly fresh, but at least it didn't smell stale or carbolic-rinsed.

'I still don't get it, Jock. I mean, how this thing with the McGaherns could possibly be political.' I was pushing him. It was already beginning to make sense to me: phoney shipments through a company that already dealt with the Far and Near East. But I wanted to know all that Jock Ferguson knew.

'I can't tell you any more. Because I don't know any more.'

'But that's why you warned me off the McGahern thing to start with, isn't it?'

He offered me a cigarette. We lit up and I looked around in

a leisurely way. I saw the Talbot parked on the other side of the street, about two hundred yards up. Please, Twinkletoes, I thought, don't do the psycho-chauffeur thing and come over to pick me up.

'You want a lift back?' asked Ferguson. 'I'll get the driver to drop you. I'm just going round the corner.' He referred to St Andrew's Street, a block away and where the City of Glasgow HQ was located.

'No thanks. I feel like a walk.' The Talbot hadn't moved. Maybe the *Reader's Digest* was stretching Twinkletoes's concentration over three-syllable words like a prisoner on the rack. 'Jock,' I said tentatively, 'I've got a favour to ask.'

'How fucking unlike you.'

'Can you hold off on talking to Lillian Andrews? At least for a few days. Maybe a week.'

'Sure. No problem. And just let me know if you want us to turn a blind eye to an armed robbery getaway car. We could even arrange a points duty bobby to hold the traffic back for it.' Sarcasm is a fine art: Ferguson was clearly a weekend painter. 'Andrews was murdered. Everything points to Lillian Andrews being behind it. Why should I piss about?'

'Okay, gloves off, Jock. Because if you go steaming in now she'll get away with it. I didn't like Andrews. I didn't like anything about him. But I made it my business to help him and I let him down. I want to see that bitch hang for it. You know that I can find out more in a week on my own than a team of your flatfoots would in six months. People talk to me who would clam up if you asked them the time of day. Added to which we've got reason to believe that Lillian probably has contacts inside the City Police. Give me a couple of weeks and I'll give you Lillian Andrews and whomever she's involved with. Gift-wrapped.'

Ferguson took a final draw on his cigarette and dropped the stub onto the mortuary's step. He ground it into the stone with the toe of his shoe and stared at it. 'Okay. Two weeks. But I won't walk away from this empty-handed. If you fuck up and Lillian disappears into the night, then it'll be me gift-wrapping your testicles for Superintendent McNab.'

'Fair enough.'

I waited until Ferguson had rounded the corner before I crossed the Saltmarket and started to walk in the direction of the High Street. After a few hundred yards Twinkletoes pulled up alongside and I jumped into the passenger seat. I felt claustrophobic crammed in next to Twinkletoes's bulk and I imagined how cosy it was going to be sharing a ride with both him and Tiny Semple. I got him to drop me off at my digs and told him to fetch Tiny.

'We're going visiting,' I explained.

CHAPTER TWENTY-THREE

When I was a kid growing up in New Brunswick, I went to Rothesay Collegiate School for Boys, which was as upper as the crust came in Canada. I played in the ice hockey team and was pretty damned good. So good that I started to harbour ambitions about turning professional.

One day we found ourselves playing against another private school: King's Collegiate. King's was based in Windsor, Nova Scotia and we should have taken that as a bad omen in itself, seeing as ice hockey was supposedly invented in Windsor. Anyway, there was this kid called MacDonald, not big enough to be a power forward but as fast as hell, who played the right wing and was my opposite number.

Grace isn't something you usually associate with ice hockey, but MacDonald was truly graceful. Every time I got a run he would come up and dash past me. No checking, no contact, just a flash of red and the puck would be gone. Whatever I decided to do, he'd predict it. Whatever I'd thought of, he'd thought of it first. I felt outclassed and outmanoeuvred. It was a feeling I didn't like.

Now Lillian Andrews was making me feel like that, too.

We arrived at the Andrews house to find it deserted. But this was no hurried evacuation prompted by the unexpected complication of John Andrews's death. The estate agent's sign that we passed on the way into the drive and the curtainless windows told me that there had been a lot of forewarning and planning before this particular coop had been well and truly flown.

I parked on the drive and I could have sworn the Atlantic eased up several inches on its suspension when Twinkletoes and Tiny struggled out of it. I told Tiny to lean against a door at the back of the house and it took us only ten minutes to confirm that it had been thoroughly cleared out. No furniture, no personal items; and I didn't need to lift floorboards or jemmy off bath panels to know there would be no hidden caches of currency and passports.

I stood in the lounge, now empty of low-slung Contemporary furniture and stared blankly at Twinkletoes and Tiny as I tried to work out what to do next. They gazed back at me blankly. I told them there was no point in hanging about. I drove them back to my place, where Twinkletoes had parked the Sunbeam. I told them I was calling it a day and I'd 'phone Sneddon if I needed them again. What I really needed was to be free of my two-gorilla escort for a while. I could do with time to think. The move out of the Bearsden house hadn't been hurried or unplanned. And because an estate agent was involved in the sale of the property, the proceeds had to go somewhere. It was my guess that it had all been part of Lillian's schedule. And maybe John Andrews's sudden detour from the highway had been part of that schedule too.

Again I thought of how Lillian was dancing around me in the same way as MacDonald, my teenage nemesis on skates, who had made me look pedestrian on the hockey rink. MacDonald had been signed by the Ottawa Senators before the war broke out. Then he had had his legs blown off in a mine-field at Anzio. I don't think the Senators renewed his contract.

I was going to have to take the legs from under Lillian.

I didn't feel like the Horsehead Bar, but I stopped off for a couple. Maybe it was because I'd been thinking of Lillian

Andrews's legs that I found myself hankering after some gentler company than I'd find at the Horsehead.

May Donaldson was the kind of woman it's good for a man to know: as obliging as she was undemanding. Most women made you work hard for your entry pass. May, on the other hand, handed you a season ticket straight off. And threw in a few away games as well.

May Donaldson's flat was in the West End, not too far from mine, in one of the ubiquitous Victorian tenements that curled around Glasgow's black heart. I didn't know a lot about May's background, but it wasn't the usual Glasgow working-class story and things had gone wrong for her along the way. I had heard somewhere that at one time she had been married to a farmer. Apparently, he had left her to plough a different furrow.

Being a gentleman, I never asked her age but I reckoned she was in her mid-thirties, maybe a couple of years older than me. Britain's attitude to divorce was the attitude everywhere else had had a hundred years earlier and you could probably deduct a century or two more in Scotland. Being a divorcee here made May spoiled goods and her chances of remarriage were slim. As a consequence, she played the sad and desperate role of the good-time girl. So May and I were occasional playmates. It wasn't the deepest of relationships, but, like I said, it was convenient.

If I sound critical of Scotland's divorce laws, don't get me wrong: I had good reason to be grateful for them. Whenever I wasn't working for one or other of the Three Kings, I helped middle-class couples dance through the legally required pantomime of divorce. It was usually still the husband who sacrificed his reputation, even if he had not been the unfaithful partner. He would fall on his sword, as it were, even if his wife had been falling on someone else's.

May helped me out with my divorce cases. The required

choreography was that I would arrange for May and the husband to book into a hotel together, pull nightclothes over their daywear, get into bed together and I would turn up with a member of the hotel staff to witness that the *delicto* was indeed *flagrante*. The maid or the under-manager would then sign a statement and get their cut of the proceeds and the soon to be ex-spouse would shuffle off. There wasn't a sordid business that wasn't more sordid or more business.

I took a taxi from the Horsehead across town to May's. I would be able to walk back from her place to my digs afterwards. May poured me a whisky as soon as I arrived and we sat down on the sofa together. She wasn't pretty, but she used make-up to make the most of her regular features. From the neck down, however, she was a piece of art. When I arrived she was wearing a white blouse and black pencil-skirt that hugged the most huggable parts of her.

'How are things, Lennox?' she asked.

'Fine. You?'

'The usual. You got a job for me?'

'No,' I said. 'At least not yet. And probably not a divorce when it does come up.'

'So what can I do for you?' she asked. The hint of weariness annoyed me.

'I just came by to say hello,' I said. 'Do I need a reason?'

'Not if you don't say so.' She got up and poured herself another gin. I was still nursing my Scotch. It was something I'd noticed about May: that she always took a couple or three before we got down to business. Not gassed. Just enough for her to take the edge off what we both knew we were going to do. It was a thought that did my self-esteem no end of good.

'Still working in the hotel?'

'Still.'

There was probably some law of physics that prevented the small talk getting any smaller and after my second whisky and her fourth gin, I moved in on her. She led me into the bedroom before heading into the bathroom to fit her cap. I stripped and lay on the bed smoking a Player's. The wallpaper was yellow and floral-patterned, although I guessed it had been white once: May smoked even more than I did. There were scattered attempts at gentility with the furniture and the knick-knacks. Suddenly I felt depressed.

May lightened my mood by coming back in naked except for her stockings and garter belt. She lay down next to me on the bed and we became consumed in our act of heightened apathy. At least I put my Player's out first: in Scotland that made me Rudi Valentino.

Afterwards she made some coffee and brought it through to the bedroom. I lit a cigarette for her and one for myself.

'Do you never feel like a new start?' she asked out of nowhere.

'This is my new start,' I said and blew a wispy circle of smoke towards the cracked plaster of the ceiling. 'I started off life rich and content. There's only so much of that a man can take. My life is so much more colourful now. Mainly black and blue.'

'I'm being serious. I want to get out of this town, Lennox. I want to get married and have kids before it's too late.'

'May . . .'

'Don't get in a sweat,' she said and laughed bitterly. 'I'm not proposing. I didn't come up the Clyde on a banana boat. I know exactly what I mean to you, Lennox. But sometimes I need to talk. Don't you need to talk sometimes?'

'Oh yeah. I talk. I talk myself silly.'

'I want to get out of Glasgow. Get out from behind that fucking hotel bar. Go somewhere where no one knows anything about me. Somewhere cut off from everywhere else. Like South Africa or Australia. Or the middle of the bloody African jungle.'

'You should think about Paisley,' I said. 'It's even more removed from civilization but you can get to it by bus.'

'I'm being serious. This city is shite. My life is shite. Everybody here thinks they know who I am. What I am. They know fuck all about me. Everyone in this ugly fucking city thinks the universe revolves around Glasgow. They just can't see past it. And the truth is this isn't a city: it's a village. Full of petty, stupid, bigoted shits. I hate it. Fucking hate it.' She bit into the crimson of her lower lip.

I stroked her arm. 'Why don't you just leave?'

'And do what?' she said, pulling away. 'I need money, Lennox. The kind of money that working a bar or helping you with your divorce scams doesn't bring. I don't suppose you know any lonely rich widowers?'

The gag startled me for a moment. 'I did. One. But he's not looking in the lonely hearts any more.'

CHAPTER TWENTY-FOUR

There was something nagging away at me. Everything Lillian Andrews did was carefully thought out and planned. A lot of that probably came from her association with Tam McGahern: Mafeking Jeffrey had told me that McGahern's war record showed him to be intelligent, organized and a natural strategist. But what got to me more was what May had said about no one in Glasgow thinking beyond the city's tenement-fringed horizon. It was becoming clear that that was exactly what Tam had been all about.

Everything I had heard about the high-end, West End brothel that no one knew anything much about didn't make sense. I had seen the house they had used. You had to know where to find it. I thought of the affected Kelvinside housewife who had answered the door. I couldn't imagine her type redirecting clients who had lost their way: 'Oh, Eh'm ehfraid you hev the wrong door, the whooorhouse is three along, between the deyntal prehctitioner and the hayccountent . . .' Lillian's well-connected clients knew exactly where to go. So who was pointing them in the right direction?

I used the 'phone in the hall and called Willie Sneddon. I shared my thoughts with him and asked if I could lean on Arthur Parks.

'You think Parky was involved with this other outfit?' Sneddon asked.

'I don't know. But someone was sending the right kind of

client up there. Parks works the top end of the business; maybe he was creaming the best off for this special set up.'

'Naw . . .' said Sneddon after a moment's silence. 'Parky would know that I'd nail him to the fucking floor if he pulled a stunt like that.'

I winced. From what I'd heard of Sneddon's enforcement techniques, he wasn't speaking metaphorically. 'Maybe it was worth the risk,' I said. 'Or maybe the clients he was redirecting wouldn't have been seen in his place anyway.'

'A sideline is a fuckin' sideline,' said Sneddon. 'No one works for me *and* runs their own wee business on the side. Parky's not your man.'

'I'd still like to lean on him. Maybe take Twinkletoes or Tiny with me.'

'No way. Parky's one of my best earners. I don't want him . . . *upset.*'

'Then let me at least talk to him again,' I said. 'Maybe he's not the supplier. I have to admit that when I showed him a photograph of Lillian Andrews, he seemed genuinely not to recognize her, although she did remind him of someone else. But maybe he's heard something more. Or there's something he's not telling me.'

'Like I said, Lennox, I don't want Parky upset. You know how fuckin' antsy these mattress-munchers can be. Just find out what you have to find out without getting him worked up. And leave Twinkle and Tiny out of it. And I wouldn't go round at this time of night. These are his big business hours. Parky shuts up shop between seven in the morning and three in the afternoon. I'll 'phone him and tell him you'll be round to disturb his ugly sleep tomorrow morning. I'll *advise* Parky to be cooperative. That should be all you need.'

I agreed and hung up. I wasn't too happy about the set up.

Whether Parks was involved directly or not, my instinct told me he needed leaning on to spill everything he knew. And Sneddon had just prohibited me from leaning.

I lay on the bed with the lights out and smoked. There was all kinds of crap in my head, buzzing about like bees trapped in a jar. I kept thinking back to what May had said and the desperation with which she had said it. I thought about Lillian Andrews and her dark hair and long legs. Then for some reason I couldn't work out, I thought of Helena Gersons sitting like a beautiful bird in a cage of Georgian architecture. We had had something once. Really had something. But each of us in our own way had been so fucked up that we didn't want anything that made you feel. But that wasn't why I thought of her. I thought of her because if Arthur Parks hadn't been supplying customers to the West End operation, then the next name on the list was Helena's. And, after all, we had a history of lies between us. But most of all, it was what May had said that kept jabbing me awake.

I took breakfast in a cafe on Byres Road before heading off to the Park Circus area. The rain was taking a breather and the sun was trying to fill in, but Glasgow was vomiting its early-morning smoke into its face. I sat at the cafe window eating my ham and eggs – or bacon and eggs as they called it here. I watched the world go by: an older man with rickets worse than the mortuary attendant I had encountered waddled past. He looked under five foot tall but I idly wondered if he would have been six foot, straightened out. He paused, leant over, pressed his thumb to one nostril and ejected the contents of the other in a violent exhalation onto the pavement. A deliveryman pulled up his dray horse and cart outside, spoiling my view of Glasgow's cosmopolitan streetlife. The Clydesdale twitched its tail and splattered the cobbles with dung that steamed in the cool morning sunlight. I said a small prayer of thanks that I hadn't ended up somewhere less sophisticated, like Paris or Rome.

The ancient Greeks were great ones for reading omens. I should have read the augurs in the Clydesdale's shit: it would have saved me a hell of a day.

I walked back along Great Western Road and into the concentric circles of the Park Circus area. When I reached Parks's townhouse, all of the curtains were still drawn across the windows. There was no bull-necked doorman on guard and the deep gloss red of the Georgian-panelled front door combined with the soot-blackened masonry to give the impression of a back door to hell. Or a back door to hell on its tea break. I tugged at the bellpull and rapped the ornate door knocker. After a few minutes it was clear that I wasn't going to get an answer. But when Willie Sneddon told you to expect someone, you expected. I started to get a bad feeling about there being no one at home.

The funny thing about the criminal fraternity is that they are generally very trusting that everyone else will be law-abiding. I walked down the steps to the basement level and found a window slightly open on its sash. I slipped in through the window into a small bedroom. Or rather a room with a bed: I got the impression not much sleeping went on there. It was decorated with red and black Paisley-patterned wallpaper and a vast gilt-framed mirror hung on one wall offering a view of the bed. Romantic. There were two other basement rooms, a hall and the stairs up to the main apartments. I recognized the waiting room in which I'd spoken to Parks before. There were four bedrooms off it. All empty. A vague funk of stale cigarette smoke, scent and whisky hung in the air. A radio played quietly somewhere. From upstairs. I called out for Parks but received no reply. An ornate staircase led up to the next floor, where I knew Parks had his living quarters.

As I reached the top of the stairs the decor became less lurid and more tasteful. The music from the radio was louder: Guy Mitchell informed me that *she wore red feathers*. I walked along the landing and came to a large, light living room. The walls were bright and broken up with framed prints and posters of various theatrical productions. The furniture was modern and tasteful and again contrasted with the contrived lurid Victorian wickedness of the decor chosen for the 'working' part of the house.

'Hello, Arthur,' I said to Parks. He didn't answer. But there again I didn't expect him to. As soon as I had come into the room and my eyes had met Parks's, I knew only one of us was capable of seeing. He sat in the middle of the living room. Someone had pushed the coffee table and sofa to one side to clear enough room for them to go to work on Parks, whom they had tied to a kitchen chair. And go to work on him they had. His jaw sat at an angle to his face that was all wrong. Maybe they had tried to fix his underbite. Most of his face was swollen up into purple puffs of distended flesh. It takes time to bruise and swell like that, and it was my guess that whoever had killed Parks had taken a long time about it.

Parks was dressed only in his vest and underpants and the light-coloured carpet beneath the chair was stained dark with blood and urine. His tongue hung out over the dislocated jaw and his eyes bulged at me, as if emphasizing a point: I *am* fucking dead. I ignored the smell and drew close, examining his neck. Something thick, like a belt, had been used to garrotte him and there were spider webs of blue-black marks where it had crushed capillaries.

Parks's killing had all the hallmarks of a protracted

interrogation under torture followed by execution. Well, to be fair, that was the end of the playground Parks had played in. It was the end of the playground I played in. It was ludicrous to think that Sneddon might have been behind it, but I hadn't seen Twinkletoes since the previous day and I found myself making a quick inventory of Parks's naked toes.

I sat down on the shoved-aside sofa and stared at Parks. It didn't help: he didn't have any ideas about what I should do next. I did get a clue though, when I heard the urgent trilling bells of approaching police cars. Nice. Once more I thought of MacDonald, the teenage ice hockey right forward who could literally run rings around me. I was being framed better than the theatrical posters on Parks's walls. The police bells sounded a street or so away but near enough for a front-door exit to be out of the question. I ran through into the kitchen. It was narrow and had a huge sash window facing the rear. The police would send a car around to the back but their main attention would be on the front door. I slid the window open. There was a pipe angled steeply away from where the kitchen drain branched down to join the main down pipe. Shinning down the main pipe wouldn't be too difficult, but traversing the kitchen wastepipe to get to it would.

Still, shouldn't be a problem, I thought: if they found me in Parks's back yard with busted ankles after trying to escape from the floor on which they would find his tortured and murdered body, it wouldn't take that much explaining.

I eased out through the window and found the steep angle of the pipe with the toes of my Hush Puppies. I took my hat off and threw it down onto the yard below then, scrabbling for a grip on the sandstone, I eased myself down, supporting my weight on the sill. As I inched towards the downpipe, I heard the police car bells ringing more loudly. There was no way I would be able to balance on the wastepipe: I would have to get quick purchase on it and swing over to the main downpipe, hoping that I could grab it firmly enough.

I bent my knees and propelled myself sideways, reaching for the pipe. I grazed my knuckles painfully on the stone wall, but managed to get a decent enough grip. The sleeve of my suit jacket caught on the pipe bracket and I heard the fabric rip. I scuttled down the pipe as fast as I dared and folded into a heap on the flagstones at the bottom. I caught my breath and tried to stand. No busted ankles but my back hurt like a son-of-a-bitch. I grabbed my hat and ran across the small yard, then out onto the alleyway.

I reckoned the coppers would be coming from the direction of Sauchiehall Street, so I headed the other way. I sprinted to the end of the alley then turned right and tried to walk as normally and inconspicuously as possible. I looked down at myself: I was wearing a dark-brown wool suit with suede Hush Puppies. I like to look smart, even if I'm just meeting with homo Glaswegian pimps. However, my choice of outfit today had been particularly fitting: the suede of my shoes and the easily bruised wool of the suit, added to my grazed knuckles, all spoke very eloquently of a recent and rushed descent down a drainpipe. I examined my sleeve and saw that a strip was missing, presumably snagged on the pipe's support clamp.

All it would take would be for a patrol car to pass me, the only pedestrian in the area. Then I'd be well and truly shafted. Only the Belgian rabbit-fur felt of my expensive Borsalino fedora seemed to have survived unscathed. I put on the hat and dusted down my suit as much as possible. Casual, Lennox. Stay cool and casual.

But my mind raced. I decided to get into Kelvingrove Park and cut back up north towards Great Western Road. My guess was that they would send out teams of police on foot to search the area. By the time they got organized, I would be out of the park and sufficiently removed from the scene of the crime. But not necessarily in the clear. If it had been hinted to the police that I was a name to be looked at, then they would find my fingerprints all over the basement and upstairs kitchen sash windows as well as half a dozen door handles.

It could, of course, have been purely coincidental that I happened along just after Parks had been helped to go down a collar size; but there is a wonderful word that only the Scots use, mainly in legal contexts: timeous. Timeous means something like 'within or at the correct time'. My discovery of Parks's tortured body had been *timeous*. The arrival of the police had been *timeous*. All too *timeous* to be coincidental.

My immediate problem was to get away from the area. But there was no way of knowing just how much of a lead the police had been given.

I was now on Park Quadrant. Park Quadrant delineated the outer ring of the concentric terraced circles of Georgian townhouses. There were houses only on one side of the Quadrant: an arc of Georgian terrace. On the other side of the broad, sweeping street was a railing-edged pavement looking out over Kelvingrove Park. Unfortunately there was a drop on the other side of the railings, which prevented me simply vaulting them and disappearing into the park.

I walked as fast as I could without making myself conspicuous. I had just reached the junction of Park Terrace when a black police Wolseley coasted around the sweep of the Quadrant behind me. I dodged behind the meagre cover of the branches of a tree that overhung the railings from the Park below. I squeezed against the row of railings. Beyond them was the drop down into the park, which spread out dark-green under a granite sky.

It was my only way out. If I hung around any longer the place would be teeming with coppers. But until the police Wolseley had passed, I daren't make a move.

The Wolseley crept past me. There would have been no way the coppers inside could have missed me if they looked in my direction. But they didn't. The patrol car drove by, slowly. Just when I thought I was getting lucky, the Wolseley stopped fifty yards further on, on the other side of the street. I prepared to make a run for it.

A tall copper got out of the passenger seat and walked over to the front of the Georgian terrace. He leaned over the railings and looked down and along the basement entries, beneath street level. Again, he didn't even look in my direction. The patrol car inched slowly along the Quadrant while the constable checked every basement court. I was relieved that they weren't coming in my direction, but at the same time they were moving so slowly that I couldn't move on. And that was a problem because very soon there would be more police cars and more flatfoots scouring every nook and cranny.

The copper moved on, still checking basements along the other side of the road. The black police Wolseley prowled beside him at walking pace. I decided to make my move: I climbed swiftly over the railings and eased myself down, my legs dangling above the bushes a dozen or so feet below. Again I spared a thought for my poor ankles, then let go of the railings. I crashed into the undergrowth but not loudly enough for the coppers to hear me. The angry fingers of the bushes scratched at me and I came to a tangled rest. Again no busted ankles, but my back protested with a stab of pain. I struggled through masses of bushes and emerged onto the thankfully empty path. Again I brushed down my suit and bashed the Borsalino back into shape before putting it on my head at an angle that would, hopefully, hide most of my features from passers-by.

I had just finished dusting myself off when I heard voices close by. It would have been perfectly normal to encounter other people in Kelvingrove Park, even on a weekday morning, but an old instinct told me to take cover.

Fortunately the civic authorities had chosen to place a vast commemorative statue directly in front of me. Even more fortunately they hadn't replaced the railings that would have been melted down during the war to supply munitions factories. I ran around the massive rectangular base of the statue and pressed my back against an elaborate heroic frieze on the entablature: gallant soldiers of the British Empire liberating grateful natives around the world from the burden of self-determination. I looked up at the statue mounted above me. A dyspeptic, geriatric general on horseback looked out across Kelvingrove Park to the university and beyond, probably to the Empire that no one had told him was gone. The head of his steed was turned down towards me disdainfully.

The voices stopped but I heard the sound of boots on gravel. More than one pair. I stayed pressed into the entablature and waited until the footsteps had moved on. When I did look I saw the backs of three coppers. Once they were around the corner I headed off in the opposite direction. I had to get out quickly: it wouldn't be long before the park was full with even more Highlanders in uniforms, beating bushes with sticks. I never understood why police searches always involved giving the undergrowth a damned good thrashing. Maybe it took them back to their childhoods in Stornoway or Strathpeffer, beating heather, tugging forelocks and dodging shot for the local grouse-shooting toffs.

I half-ran along the path, slowing down at corners in case I encountered anyone else: people remember a running man. And there was no guarantee that the policemen I'd dodged were the only ones in this part of the park.

I reached the north gate of the park and found a policeman on watch at the Eldon Street entrance. I cut through the trees and kept close to the edge of the River Kelvin, eventually passing under the bridge at Gibson Street. I crossed the river at the old Botanic Gardens station bridge. I climbed the railings and dropped down on the other side, attracting the attention of a couple of pedestrians. I pulled my Borsalino down over my eyes and moved swiftly away, up to where Great Western Road crossed the Kelvin Bridge.

I watched my lodgings from across the street: there were no police cars outside and everything seemed normal. Of course that didn't mean there weren't half a dozen Hamishes waiting for me when I got in. I crossed swiftly and went straight up to my digs. I stripped off and took a hurried bath. The carbolic stung like hell on the scratches that covered my hands and shins. Scratches that would be pretty good evidence of flight.

I shaved again and put on a fresh shirt, tie and suit. Blue this time. I bundled my other suit in wrapping paper and tied it up with string. My Borsalino could be saved and I hung it up, chose a trilby to match the serge and headed out.

I drove to the Horsehead Bar and set about buying Big Bob and a couple of the lunchtime regulars a drink. Parks was long dead but at least I would have someone to say they'd seen me relaxed and not dressed in a brown wool suit: my reckoning was that there was a chance that the two pedestrians who had seen me drop into Great Western Road from over the park railings would have mentioned it when they found a copper guarding the gate.

I forced down a Scotch pie and a pint and left when lunchtime licensing hours were up. I was walking back to the car when the sun was eclipsed. I turned to see Tiny Semple filling my universe.

'Mr Sneddon wants to see you.'

'Okay,' I said. 'I'm parked round the corner. Where shall I meet him?'

'Leave your car. I'm to take you.' I could have been getting paranoid, but I detected a lack of warmth in Tiny's tone. He led me to where he'd parked the Sunbeam that Twinkletoes normally used. We drove in silence. We headed south across the Clyde and down Eglinton Street, eventually turning into a street of dingy houses overlooking the railway. There were already three cars parked outside one of the houses and Tiny parked behind them. The cars were conspicuous because no other house in the street had so much as a stick and hoop outside.

The house looked derelict, but a glance into one of the rooms off the hall revealed stacks of crates. I guessed the house was a store for stolen goods. Sitting in the middle of a street where, no doubt, the neighbours would rob you blind, this little cache would be as secure as Fort Knox. You didn't need padlocks and bolts to keep this lot safe. All you needed was a name. Willie Sneddon. The Robin Hood of the South Side: stole from the rich, terrorized the poor.

Sneddon, Twinkletoes and another thug, DA-quiffed and shorter and leaner than Tiny but every bit as deadly-looking, were leaning against the dilapidated fireplace, smoking. There was a chair in the centre of the room. Cosy, I thought. Like in Parks's flat, enough room to work. Twinkletoes didn't smile at me and I did a quick scan of the room: no bolt-cutters. That I could see.

'Sit down,' said Sneddon. I didn't want to. With four guys

like this in the room, it wasn't good to be the only one sitting. Chances were you'd never stand again.

'Listen, Mr Sneddon,' I said, still standing. 'If this is about Parks—'

'Sit the fuck down,' said Sneddon in a cold, angerless way. I sat the fuck down in a cold, gutless way. I was having déjà vu: my cosy chat in Murphy's scrapyard came to mind.

'Were you round at Parky's this morning?'

'Yes. Like we arranged.'

'Do you remember me telling you I didn't want Parky upset?'

I nodded.

'Maybes I'm a man of too few fucking words. Maybes I should've made myself clearer. Parky upset would have been bad. Parky dead is ever so fucking slightly worse.'

'Listen, Mr Sneddon. I had nothing to do with Parks's death. Or not directly. I think someone didn't want him to talk to me. What's more, I think they wanted him to talk to them. Parks knew something. Or they thought he knew something. When I arrived Parks was already dead. Someone had rearranged his face over a long time and then strangled him.'

'He'd been worked over?' Sneddon drew on his cigarette and dropped the butt on the grimy, naked floorboards before grinding it out with his toe. I worried that he maybe needed his hands free.

'Let's put it this way, he was going to have trouble chewing gum. Whoever went to work on him knew they were going to kill him after. Whether he talked or not. When they got or didn't get what they wanted from him they smashed the fuck out of his face. It wasn't a beating Parks took. It was torture.'

'As I remember, you wanted to lean on him. Aye, that's what you said . . . *lean* on him. I'll ask you this once, Lennox. Did you kill him? And before you answer, I want you to know that I do understand how these things happen. Things get out of fucking hand.'

I bet you do, I thought.

'So, Lennox, tell me the truth,' Sneddon continued. 'Did you do Parky?'

'No. If you'd seen the state his face was in you would know that. I'm not that vicious.'

'Okay, let me see your hands.'

I held them out and felt a chill travel from the chair and into my bowels. The knuckles of both hands were raw from my rapid descent down Parks's plumbing.

'Now listen,' I said. 'I had to make an escape from Parks's place down the drainpipe. Plus I had to schlep through half the bushes in Kelvingrove Park. I didn't get these from torturing Parks.'

Sneddon stared hard at me for a moment. I glanced over at Twinkletoes, who still wasn't smiling. I involuntarily wriggled my toes in my shoes.

'Okay,' Sneddon said at last. 'I believe you. You didn't get those knuckles beating a man to death. Your hands would be all swoll up like fucking balloons.'

Thank God for the voice of experience, I thought.

'That doesn't mean you didn't beat him to death with something else,' said Sneddon. 'But I believe you.'

I tried not to look too relieved.

'Parky made me a lot of fucking money, Lennox. I am displeased about someone killing one of my best earners. Very fucking displeased.'

'I'm sure you are.'

'You've got a new job. Forget the McGahern thing. Find out who killed Parky. And find out quickly.'

'To be honest,' I said, 'I don't think I should forget the

McGahern thing. I think Parks's death is connected. Coincidences make me uncomfortable. I tend not to believe in them, having the logical view of the universe that I do.'

'What coincidences?'

'That we have a conversation and you tell Parks to expect me. I arrive and Parks is freshly dead. Coincidence one. Then I have to make a back-door run for it because the police have been tipped off at that exact moment. Coincidence two.'

'So someone was trying to put you in the frame?'

'Well, you felt you had to ask me if I'd killed him, didn't you? What worries me is that they gave my name to the police. Or they'll give it when they realize that I wasn't caught at the scene.'

'Wait a minute . . .' Sneddon frowned. 'What you fucking mean about Parks getting killed after I arrange a meeting for you? You saying I set it up?'

'No . . . No, not at all.' I held my hands up. 'Parks could have told someone. Or word got out somehow. All I mean is the whole thing fitted together just that little bit too conveniently. I've been getting that a lot, recently. And all to do with Tam and Frankie McGahern and Lillian Andrews. But I need to think it all through. My first concern is not to end up hanged for Parks's murder.'

'You seen leaving?'

'Not that I know of, but all it would take is a couple of public-spirited citizens to have been looking out of their windows while I was doing a Sherpa Tenzing on Parks's back wall. And a couple of passers-by saw me clamber out of Kelvingrove Park.'

'Did they get a good look at you?'

'Probably just what I was wearing. I've got the suit in the boot of my car. But I think I maybe left a strip of it on Parks's drainpipe. I'm going to dump it.'

'When you drop him off back at his car, pick up the suit,' Sneddon said to Tiny. He turned back to me. 'We'll incinerate it. As for this morning when Parky was snuffed, you took your car in for repair at one of my garages. I'll give you the name and address and two mechanics who'll say you were there.'

'Thanks,' I said. But the idea of my avoiding a murder charge based on a dodgy Sneddon-supplied alibi didn't exactly fill me with confidence. And if the police never got the real killers, then it gave Sneddon something on me. I wondered if the suit would be incinerated, after all. But I was in no position to negotiate.

'So you'll find out who snuffed Parky?' Sneddon lit another cigarette. He offered me one and I took it.

'If I can,' I said as if I had a choice in the matter. 'And Tam McGahern. Like I said they're linked.'

Sneddon reached into his jacket and I tried not to flinch. He took out a thick wedge of folded fivers and handed it to me.

'That's on account,' said Sneddon. 'And it's non-refundable. I want a fucking result, Lennox. This is a head-hunt, are we clear?'

I nodded.

'You find who did Parky,' said Sneddon, 'and I'll deal with the rest.'

'Fair enough,' I said, putting the cash, uncounted, into my pocket. I thought of Mr Morrison's post boxes. I had the uncomfortable feeling that I would be supplying a name for one of them. One way or another. Sneddon had made it clear he wasn't going to accept failure.

Tiny Semple drove me back to where I'd left my car parked near the Horsehead. He was much more chatty on the way back.

'It's funny you getting out of Parky's place that way,' he said as we drove.

'How so?'

'He was more used to having some fucker *up* his back drain-pipe . . .' Tiny chuckled baritonely.

I wasn't really in the mood for gags. As we had driven away from Sneddon's secret rendezvous, I could have sworn, looking in the wing mirror, that I saw Twinkletoes come out and put a pair of bolt-cutters in the boot of one of the other cars.

They hadn't been needed, after all.

CHAPTER TWENTY-FIVE

For the next two or three days I kept a profile lower than a fore-skin at a rabbinical convention.

I waited for the knock on the door, or my face, before being dragged down to St Andrew's Street. My experience had been that the City of Glasgow Police found certain inconsequential details, like evidence, totally unnecessary when investigating a case. McNab, like some Solomon with a cosh, had the wisdom and vision needed to decide who was guilty. After that it was only a matter of time and bruised knuckles until the suspect realized they had been wrong all along to think that they had had nothing to do with it.

But no knock had come. And if I had been under surveillance I certainly would have known about it: stealth and subtlety were not Glasgow CID's strong suits.

The Park Circus brothel was closed. It wouldn't have mattered if Sneddon had put a caretaker in and kept it open: the papers were full of lurid headlines about Arthur Parks's death. That meant that the punters it had served wouldn't be seen near it. It also meant that no number of brown envelopes would stop the police being forced to take action and close it down.

It was a tense few days for me, not least because the papers had carried a description of a tall man in a brown suit seen in the area immediately after the murder. That was as far as the description went. But it was enough for me to sweat about. I just hoped that Sneddon had gotten his incinerator fired up.

But I was edgy for another reason. In the same paper that had carried the news about Parks's murder there had been another, smaller article about a death in Edinburgh. In this case, no foul play was suspected, at least from a third party. A leading Edinburgh surgeon had tragically taken his own life. He had shot himself in the head with his former service revolver. He had been one of the leaders in the field of maxillo-facial reconstructive surgery, the article stated. Alexander Knox.

Coincidence three. Within a day or so of Parks being topped, a leading plastic surgeon who had been amenable to doing Tam McGahern a favour or two had just decided to blow his own brains out.

It was over a week after Parks's death that the police did come calling. I was in the Horsehead Bar when Jock Ferguson appeared at my elbow. He accepted my offer of a whisky. A good sign. There's a kind of etiquette with coppers: they don't tend to drink with you before they work you over.

'You got something to tell me?' He raised an eyebrow. I raised my pulse. Maybe he wasn't here to socialize.

'Like what?'

'Come off it, Lennox, you must be up to your eyes in all of this shite.'

'Shite?'

He turned to face me full on, placing his glass down in a businesslike way and leaning on the bar's brass rail. 'Don't fuck me about, Lennox. There's no way that Willie Sneddon hasn't hired you to look into Arthur Parks's death.'

'Oh, that ...' I said and tried to wipe the *and-I-thought-you-were-talking-about-me-being-a-prime-suspect-for-this-murder* expression from my face. I didn't think I had succeeded that well because Ferguson's broad forehead creased in a suspicious frown.

'What else did you think I was talking about?' he asked.

'I wasn't sure, that's all,' I smiled and took a withering slug of the Scotch I'd ordered because Big Bob was out of CC. 'The problem with working in the sewer is that there's a lot of shite to choose from.'

My act of self-deprecation seemed to do the trick and he leaned both elbows back on the bar. 'Willie McNab is trying to tie this one up fast. He has a *theory*.'

'Oh?'

'We had a discussion about homosexuals.' Ferguson grinned, uncharacteristically. 'McNab finds the whole concept beyond understanding. I don't think he likes to admit that there are any in Scotland.'

'I've heard that theory before,' I said. 'That like all the snakes being driven out of Ireland by St Patrick, St Andrew drove all of the queers out of Scotland and they became . . .'

'. . . the English,' we said in unison and laughed.

'I'm being serious though,' said Ferguson. 'McNab has all of these theories about Parks's killing. He thinks it was some kind of sado-masochistic homosexual thing. The only thing he knows about homosexuality is that it's illegal and those guilty of it usually display excellent clothes-sense. His theories are beginning to border on science-fiction. Like they're Martians or something. Do you know, he's like Queen Victoria . . . he *really* doesn't believe there's such a thing as lesbianism. "How's that going to work?" he said. "All sockets and no plugs."'

'Why does he think Parks's murder is sado-masochism?' I asked. 'How did he die?' Clever Lennox.

'Not nice, Lennox,' Ferguson grimaced. I couldn't tell if it was the memory or the Bells that was doing it. 'Someone had beaten seven shades of shite out of him. Tied him to a chair first. His face was battered to fuck.'

'I take it you don't go for the bondage-buggery theory?'

'I knew a guy in the war. A decent guy and a good fucking soldier. He blew his brains out because it came out he was homo and he was going to be court-martialled. Don't get me wrong, I don't swing from those branches myself, but I don't feel the need to persecute people because of the way they were made. And it pisses me off the amount of police and court time that goes into persecuting them. They're not criminals. They're the way they are. That's all. And I don't think they go around howling at the moon or worshipping Satan. And I don't think that what I saw in Parks's flat has anything to do with where he put his dobber.'

'Nor do I,' I said. Not-so-clever-Lennox. 'From what you've said, I mean.'

'So, by my reckoning, Sneddon's hired you to look into Parks's killing.' Ferguson was talking like a copper again. 'But you've got this all tied in with the McGahern thing. Which brings me to the main point.'

'I rather thought it might.'

'I allowed you a little slack on Lillian Andrews. Now she's completely disappeared. I told you, Lennox. I told you I needed to talk to her about her husband's death.'

'Which is still officially an accident?' I asked.

'Which couldn't be more beside the fucking point. You know he was murdered. I know he was murdered. What I want to know is why and by whom. But Lillian Andrews has fucked off. Abroad, I believe, and I don't have enough of a case to persuade McNab she's worth pursuing. So let's start with *exactly* what you have heard about Parks's killing and everything you know about Lillian Andrews.'

'Okay,' I said, as if he'd wrested it out of me. 'Sneddon asked me to sniff about. But it's a non-starter. This is like the McGahern killing – everybody knows it wasn't any of the Three Kings. From what we've heard, there was nothing nicked from the flat?'

'Nothing. But that's meaningless. If you'd seen the state of Parks you'd understand that they weren't interested in stealing from him. It's what he *knew* they wanted. Now that makes me really curious. I don't, for a minute, believe that Sneddon doesn't know what it's all about.'

'He doesn't. Trust me, Jock,' I said without irony. 'This looks more and more like Parks had his own little deal going on somewhere and it all came unstuck.'

'So did his jaw,' said Ferguson. I kept my expression as if I didn't know what he meant.

'As for Lillian Andrews,' I said with a shrug, 'I have absolutely no idea where she has gone or what she's doing. But I feel totally outmanoeuvred. The truth is I'm no further forward than when we last spoke.'

Ferguson stayed for another round, then left. After he left I ordered a double and downed it in one. I felt relieved. Big time. But something nagged at me: why did I feel that I hadn't been exactly pressed as hard as Ferguson could have pressed me?

I left the Horsehead shortly after Ferguson and went looking for a prostitute. Purely in pursuit of my investigation.

Lena, the girl whom Parks had offered me weeks before, was not the kind of girl to work the streets. Too pretty and too 'classy'. Until she opened her mouth to speak, apparently. She had a bad case, Sneddon had told me, of 'Gorbals Gob'. Officially, Lena was taking a sabbatical until things cooled down: she was still under Sneddon's 'protection', whether Parks was around or not. But a week is a long time without business and Sneddon suspected that Lena and a few of the other girls were entertaining some of their established clients in their own places.

The address Sneddon had given me for Lena was over a pub in Partick. I parked the Atlantic across the street from the bar. It sat in a gloomy block of tenements with sooty windows, but had a neon-tube cocktail glass, tilted at a cheery angle, blinking wanly through the Glasgow rain. I could be in Manhattan, I thought.

I crossed the road and walked up the 'close' as the Scots called the narrow alleys between buildings. It stank of urine and reminded me of the set up at the Highlander Bar owned by the McGaherns. I climbed the back stairs to the door of the flat above. The red curtains drawn over the grimy glass of the only window made it glow like a malevolent ember. I didn't knock but turned the handle. It was unlocked and I stepped into a small, clean kitchen. There was a toilet off and I reckoned the door ahead of me led into the only other room in the flat. I swung the door open and walked in on Lena and a fat middle-aged businessman reclining together on her sofa. Lena was dressed as a nurse. Or more accurately half-dressed as a nurse. I could have been wrong, but from what I could see I didn't think she had any medical training, unless mouth-to-dick resuscitation was a legitimate form of life-saving.

'Honey!' I uttered in outrage. 'You told me you got that extra money from taking in sewing!'

They both scrabbled to their feet and fat boy panicked. He pulled his trousers up, grabbed his jacket and rushed past me and out of the flat, giving me as wide a berth as he could as he passed.

Lena wasn't giving me her Rita Hayworth look this time.

'Who the fuck are you?' she screamed. Her voice was thin and scratchy. Like Sneddon had warned, despite her classy looks, Lena had the elocution of a true Gorbals Gal. Then her eyes narrowed suspiciously. 'I know you . . . you was round at the

Circus. You was the guy Arthur was speaking to.'

'That's me,' I said and sat down in the armchair opposite. Lena grabbed a gown and covered her best assets.

'Get the fuck out. Who the fuck do you think you are barging in here?'

'I'm glad you remember me, Lena,' I smiled. 'That night you saw me talking to Parks, I was working for Mr Sneddon. I'm here tonight because I'm working for Mr Sneddon.'

Her face changed. Real fear.

'Listen ... that ... what you saw ... I'm not trying to take business away from Mr Sneddon. It's just I've got to eat ...'

'I noticed that when I came in,' I said.

'Look, I really don't want you to tell Mr Sneddon. I'll do anything ...' Lena took a step closer and opened her gown, pulling it clear of her breasts. I was being invited to play doctors and nurses.

'Put your tools back in their box, Lena,' I said. 'I'm here on business. Mine, not yours. Sit down.'

She covered herself up and sat down. I handed her the photograph of Lillian Andrews.

'Do you know her?'

'Oh, aye. I know that wee fucking whore all right. That's Sally Blane.'

'Did Parks know her?'

'I don't think so, but he knew her sister. She used to work for him for a while.'

'Let me guess,' I said, lighting up. I didn't offer Lena a cigarette: the Royal College of Nursing would have disapproved. 'Sally Blane's sister is Margot Taylor.'

'Aye,' said Lena. 'But Arthur didn't know Sally. Margot dyed her hair blonde. Other than that they looked quite like each other. I only met Sally through Margot. Margot wanted me to work with them. They had their own wee sideline going. But I got the idea Sally thought I was too fucking common for what they was planning.'

'Heaven forfend,' I said and drew on my cigarette.

'Either that or she thought I was too old,' continued Lena, undeterred. 'Sally was a stuck-up wee bitch. Anyways, I wasn't interested. Mr Sneddon wouldn't have liked it. Arthur arranged for Margot to get a hiding because of it.'

I examined Lena. She was probably thirty. Again, she had that vaguely and disconcertingly aristocratic look: not quite beauty, but very attractive. She would have fitted in with a top-end call-girl operation. Until she opened her mouth.

'Where was Sally working?'

'Edinburgh. Some posh fuckhouse. Why d'you want to know?'

'Have you ever heard the name Lillian Andrews? Specifically, do you remember Sally Blane ever calling herself that?'

'Naw. I only met her that time. Once was fucking enough. You sure you're not goin' to tell Sneddon about me having punters here?'

'That's not what I'm interested in. Did you ever see Arthur Parks talk to either of the McGahern twins?'

'No' fuckin' likely. Sneddon would have cut Arthur's balls off if he'd had anything to do with the McGaherns.'

'This operation Sally and Margot were involved in . . . did they tell you much about it?'

'Naw, just that they was going to make three times what we made at the Circus. But Sally shut Margot up. I got the idea that she thought Margot had told me too much. Especially when it was fucking obvious that Sally didn't want me to be part of it.'

'I was told that it was run by a woman called Molly. Do you know if Sally or Margot ever called themselves that?'

'That was what Sally called Margot ... like it was short or something for Margot. Aye, I heard her call her Molly. But there's no fucking way Margot was the boss.' Lena looked thoughtful for a moment. Again, the illusion of refinement was captured, then lost again when she spoke. 'There was something that they said to each other ... about someone else involved. Shite, I can't remember what they said, but I know it was something about a foreigner ... another chippy. You know, a whore.'

'And it was this foreigner who ran the operation?'

'Dunno. Maybes. Or maybes it was Sally. She was always bossing. But this foreign tart was important somehow. Listen, I really don't know anythin'. Like I says, Margot thought I'd fit in. Sally says no. So after that I hears nothin' more about it until Margot's out on her arse and Arthur gives her a hidin'.'

'Did anyone see him give her a hiding?'

'Naw. Well, aye ... one of the boys on the door went with him. But waited in the car. Arthur went in with a barber's strop. It was a few weeks after that that I heard she was dead. The car crash.'

I smoked a little for a moment. I was getting a picture. But it was a made-up scene. And I was pretty convinced it had been painted by Parks, Lillian and McGahern. But I was still looking from the wrong angle.

'Do you have any idea who would have wanted to do that to Parks? Did anything happen in the days before he was killed?'

'Naw. Business as usual. Nothin' special I can remember.'

'I got the feeling you were one of Parks's star turns, Lena. After all, he offered me a free ticket on you. Did he do that with other special guests?'

'Sometimes.'

'Anybody you can remember over the last few weeks?'

'Naw. Nob'dy particular.' She paused and frowned. 'Wait, there was one guy. Fat ugly bastard. I got the feeling he was important. Arthur told me to pull all the stops out. You know what I mean?'

'I can imagine. Can you remember his name?'

Lena laughed a drayman's laugh. 'You fuckin' kiddin'? Nobody leaves their name and address. He was a punter looking for a shag, no' a pen-pal. There was one thing about him though.'

'What?'

'He was foreign. His accent was like a German or something.'

'Could he have been Dutch?'

'I wouldn't know. Dutch . . . where they from?'

'Holland,' I said. 'The one with the windmills.' Lena didn't look enlightened. I got up and put my hat on.

'You sure you're no' goin' to tell Sneddon on me? I mean about my punter.'

'Like I said . . . not my business.' I made for the door.

Lena slipped her gown off. 'You deserve a thank you,' she said. 'Hows about a wee free fuck?'

I looked at her body, naked except for the nurse's hat, shrunken apron, suspenders and stockings. She sure was put together the right way. But, despite the alluring charm of her invitation, I didn't fancy the idea of having to wash my dick with peroxide afterwards. And my ears, if she had talked.

'No thanks,' I said and left.

When I put my mind to it, I clean up pretty well. I had a role to play and I got up early the next morning, bathed, shaved and put on my best business blue. I dressed it up with a pale blue, barrel-cuffed silk shirt, a knitted silk tie in the same blue as the suit, placed a crisp white linen handkerchief in my breast pocket and set it all off with a tiepin and cufflinks in solid gold. I was also a little liberal with my most expensive cologne, which I'd bought from 'Pherson's. I had an expensive gabardine trenchcoat that seldom saw the light and I draped it over my arm on the way out. Mrs White came out of her door just as I reached the bottom of the stairs and we exchanged our usual perfunctory morning greetings.

I smiled as I walked across to the car: Mrs White, despite herself, had cast an approving eye over me. I drove to the office and picked up a few business cards from my drawer. The business cards, however, did not have my name on them. Or my business.

Heading into the city centre, I parked outside the offices of Mason and Brodie in St Vincent Street. The brass plaque told me they were solicitors and estate agents and that they had premises in Ayr as well as Glasgow. Having a place in Ayr meant you had a presence in the nineteenth century.

Everything about Mason and Brodie's offices spoke of Scottish Establishment: the solid oak panelling and sturdy desks, the aged document chests and the smell of pipe tobacco and beeswax that hung in the air, as if preserving the atmosphere of the past. The only thing that didn't fit was the secretary who sat behind the desk nearest the door. She was about twenty and dark-haired with pretty blue eyes. She smiled as I entered and I asked if I could see Mr Brodie, whom I believed was handling the sale of a couple of properties I was interested in acquiring.

She led me into a panelled meeting room and I tried to resist looking at her ass. Resistance turned out to be futile. She offered me tea, which I declined, and asked me to wait for a few minutes while she found out if Mr Brodie was free.

A few minutes passed before a burly man in a business suit appeared at the door.

'Mr Scobie?' he boomed at me. 'I'm Fraser Brodie.' I could tell he was from Ayrshire from his eighteenth-century accent and the fact that he bellowed his hello as he extended his beefy hand. Ayrshire people are by nature one-hundred-decibel speakers: it comes from centuries of shouting across fields or up mineshafts at each other. He had thick, curling dark hair and woolly eyebrows and had the ruddy complexion of a lusty shepherd. I somehow imagined him striding purposefully across the Ayrshire countryside while the more virtuous ewes in his flock ran for cover.

'I believe you are interested in a couple of the properties we have available for sale through our estate agency department.'

'I am indeed,' I said, minimizing my Canadian accent and handing him one of the dummy business cards that supported the fiction of Walter Scobie, of Scobie, Black and MacGregor, Accountants, Edinburgh. 'But I have to point out that the purchase is not for myself, but for one of my clients who is moving his business to the West. I cannot say too much at the moment, but he may have a need for industrial premises in the Glasgow area, also.'

'I see,' Brodie smiled broadly. 'And which of the properties are you interested in?'

'A house you have in Bearsden. Ardbruach House, I believe is the name of it.'

'Oh yes. Yes, of course. Give me a moment . . .' He sorted through some files and handed me a typed-out sheet with a photograph attached. It was the Andrews place, all right. 'Actually . . .' he said thoughtfully, but loudly, 'it is something of a coincidence that your client should be interested in acquiring commercial premises as well; the vendor of Ardbruach House is also about to place a substantial commercial estate up for sale. Offices in the city and dockside warehousing. Would that be the kind of thing your client would be looking for? Or perhaps it would be more manufacturing . . . if so we have—'

I held my hand up. 'I'm afraid I'm not currently at liberty to say, Mr Brodie. Suffice it to say that my client's is a name you would recognize . . .'

Brodie beamed, imagining I represented some Edinburgh financial magnate. He wouldn't have if he had known who my client *really* was. Even here, deep within the comfortable yet unyielding folds of the Scottish Establishment, the name Willie Sneddon would have had the resonance to have him permanently stain some pinstripe. 'I quite understand,' he said knowingly. And loudly.

I read through the particulars of the house.

'Tell me, Mr Brodie,' I said. 'As you can imagine I am *au fait* with property prices across the Central Belt, not just in Edinburgh. It strikes me that Ardbruach House is being offered at a very reasonable price. In fact, this "offers over" figure seems to me considerably underestimated . . . at least a thousand below what I would expect. We will be doing a thorough survey of the property, so it does no one any service not to disclose any potential problems . . .' My mouth was beginning to ache from talking multisyllabic shite.

'Goodness no,' said Brodie, suddenly concerned. I was surprised he hadn't said *heaven forfend*. 'I assure you that there is nothing wrong with the property. The price has been set at a lower starting point because my client is keen to attract as much interest as possible.'

I smiled. 'Do you mind?' I asked and took my silver cigarette case out, offering Brodie one. I lit us both. 'I have to be honest, Mr Brodie. I suspect that your client, for one reason or another, is looking for a quick sale. That is something we may be able to accommodate, and at or around the asking price, subject to survey. But I need to know if that is indeed the case.'

I was good. I was projecting so little personality that I was even beginning to convince myself that I was a bona fide Edinburgh accountant. Brodie stared at me with a frown for a moment. He was working something out. Or he was counting sheep in his head. Finally he said:

'My client is tying up the estate of her recently deceased spouse. It is a distressing time and she is most keen to settle matters as soon as possible.'

'I see,' I said, tilting my head back and blowing a jet of smoke towards the ceiling. 'Then I think we can do business. Would it be possible to talk to your client?'

'I'm afraid not,' said Brodie apologetically. 'I'm afraid Mrs Andrews is out of the country.'

'I see . . .' I said in a tone that suggested it was a problem. He didn't respond: he was clearly concerned that I was going to walk, so I guessed he really didn't know where she was. I let the air between us stew in silence. Then I said, 'My client is also looking for a house for his general manager. He – I mean the general manager – had his eye on a property you had to sell on Dowanside Road. I wondered if it were still for sale.' I took a sheet of paper from my pocket and handed Brodie the address of the former brothel.

'Oh, yes . . .' said Brodie, raising an eyebrow, which given it was as dense and woolly as a sheep's fleece was no mean achievement. 'I'm afraid I can't help you there; it's been sold, unfortunately.'

'Who was the vendor?' I asked. 'That was why the general manager chose that specific house – he thought he knew the people who owned it.'

'Mrs McGahern,' said Brodie. The Neanderthal shield of his heavy Ayrshire brow slid a little over his eyes in suspicion. I guessed why: he was thinking, by my reckoning, that it was a hell of a coincidence that I should name these two properties: one owned by Lillian Andrews, the other owned by a war widow,

Mrs McGahern. Who just happened to be Mrs Andrews's sister. Brodie looked at my business card from beneath the overhang of his brow. I stood up.

'Well, thank you, Mr Brodie,' I said and we shook hands. 'I certainly think we can do business over Ardbruach House.'

The woolly eyebrows lifted a little and he smiled. I promised to be in touch and left.

I 'phoned Sneddon from a telephone box on Great Western Road and brought him up to date. He sounded less than pleased that I was still following the McGahern trail, despite what I had to say to him about Arthur Parks, Lillian Andrews's sister Margot and the big Dutchman.

'Just find out who killed Parky,' he said. 'I don't care how you do it.'

'Listen, Mr Sneddon, I really think we're dealing with something much bigger here. And I think it could be a threat to you and the other two Kings.'

'You saying someone's trying to take over?'

'No. As a matter of fact I don't think they are. I don't think they're even interested in Glasgow. But they're working from here and I think they're going to bring a shitstorm down on you all just by stirring up the police.'

'What's it got to do with Parky?'

'I don't know yet. But he was involved somehow. And I have a bad feeling that these stolen police uniforms have something to do with it. There's a bigger picture than the one we're seeing. I have a sort of half-theory about this that I need to work out. If you were to set up a blackmail operation, I mean compromising people who could afford to pay, who would you use?'

'I'm not into that shite,' said Sneddon. 'It brings civilians into the picture.'

'But if you did, whom would you use?'

'That's the problem. I'd talk to Parky about it. There's that wee shite Danny Dumfries, I suppose. But I wouldn't trust him. He's tied in with Murphy.'

'Oh yeah . . . I didn't think that would be Dumfries's kind of thing.'

'Maybe no, but he gets involved in all kinds of shady shite that we wouldn't touch.'

Sure, I thought, life must be one long moral dilemma for you.

'They must have been hard bastards,' said Sneddon, changing the subject. 'I mean, to do that to Parky.'

'What do you mean?' I said. 'No disrespect to him, but I would imagine a cutting bit of sarcasm would have brought Parks to his knees.'

'That's where you're wrong. It's something that I've been thinking about. You know, with the McGahern thing. There maybe could have been a connection between Parky and McGahern. Parky was hard. Don't let the pansy stuff fool you. He was hard as any of my team. Harder. I know the way he was. Never bothered me. But the army wouldn't take his sort because they thought they would *corrupt* other soldiers, that sort of fucking shite. So Parky disguised it. Pretended to be something he wasn't just so's he could fight for King and country.'

'Parks fought in the war?'

'More than that. I didn't think about it before. He was in the seventh armoured division. Parky was a Desert Rat. Like Tam McGahern.'

CHAPTER TWENTY-SIX

I drove to Edinburgh, rather than take the train again. That way I could avoid rush-hour-commuting contract killers. Before I left I 'phoned to say I was on my way. I parked the Atlantic in St Bernard's Crescent and was shown into the same office as before.

Helena walked into the room and I felt the same kick-in-the-gut reaction.

'I don't see you for years then twice in the space of a couple of weeks.' She smiled and offered me a cigarette from a solid silver box. 'Am I to infer something from that?'

I smiled. 'I'm not here on business, Helena,' I lied, 'if that's what you mean. I wanted to see you again. Maybe we could have dinner together?'

She angled her head back slightly, raised the arch of a perfect dark eyebrow and looked at me with her vaguely imperious manner. Like she was appraising me. Sometimes Helena could look haughty. That was when I really, really wanted to fuck her most.

'All right,' she said. 'We'll eat here. I have a flat on the top floor. Why don't you come back at seven? There's a door at the back takes you into the kitchen. If you ring there I'll come and get you. I don't want you coming in the front . . .' She let the thought die but I knew what she meant: she didn't want me reminded what her business was.

I stood and picked up my hat. 'It's a date. We can talk about old times.'

Her smile flickered. 'No . . . not old times. All I want to think about is the future.'

I drove the Atlantic back into the city centre and stopped at a snobby wine merchants in George Street. The guy behind the counter was thirty at the most but striving hard for middle-age. He wore a pair of those ridiculous tartan trousers, known as *trews* in Scotland, and looked at me as if I couldn't afford the wine. Truth was, it was a push. The Scots were not great consumers of wine, preferring instead their drinks to double as drain cleaner. In Edinburgh, anything potentially exclusive had a web of snobbery swiftly spun about it, and the guy behind the counter made a point of slowly emphasizing the names of the wines, as if it would help me understand. Having been brought up in New Brunswick I could speak French well, so I amused myself by humiliating him by showing off my fran-cophone skills, asking for wines that didn't exist and then looking angry when he said they didn't have them.

I put the bottle of Fronsac in the boot of the car and walked down to a bookstore in Princes Street. A cold wind stirred the dust in the streets and tugged at the raincoats of the glum-faced passers-by. I stopped and looked up at the castle, which towered above Princes Street. There was a flutter in my chest: the same vague feeling of unease. I had had it since I had left Glasgow and at the odd time before that, too. I spun around quickly and startled a young housewife who had been walking behind me, clutching the hand of a pre-school toddler. She passed, as did several others. But I didn't see what my instinct was telling me should be there. I walked on and into the bookstore, trying to tell myself I was imagining things. But it was still there, that feeling that I was being shadowed. Very professionally.

*

After parking the Atlantic in Dean Street, I walked to the back of St Bernard's Crescent. Helena must have been waiting for me in the kitchen, for she opened the door at my first knock. She was wearing a less formal outfit, a deep red dress that exposed her slender arms and long neck, and her hair was loose and brushed her shoulders.

'Come on up,' she said. I followed her out of the kitchen and up a tight stairwell that had obviously been intended originally for servants. It was clear she was trying to keep me from seeing the main business of the house. As if I could forget.

I had half-expected her to bring food up with her from the kitchen, but when we got to the attic part of the house, it was clear it was a self-contained dwelling. Her space. Away from business. The rooms she had would originally have been the servants' quarters but, given the Georgian scale of the house, were still impressive enough. There was a small alcoved section, divided off by a bead screen, behind which something bubbled on a hob and filled the room with a rich, appetizing aroma.

'The only thing I miss up here is having a piano. There's one down in the drawing room, but I seldom get a chance to play it.' I gave her the book I'd picked up for her that afternoon in Princes Street, *Coins in the Fountain* by John Secondari, and she took the wine from me, pouring us a glass each.

While she cooked I looked out of the window. There was a stone pillared colonnade edging the roof and I could see out across the trees in the crescent below. Edinburgh sat mute and grey under a sky shot through with sunset-red silk. I thought of how I'd been here before, in a different apartment looking out over a different city while Helena had cooked and we had chatted and laughed and deceived each other with talk of the future. In my experience, the future was like a seaside day out to Largs: in principle it sounded great, but when you arrived there it just turned out to be the same old shite.

I suddenly felt tired and wished I wasn't there. But I smiled as cheerfully as I could when she came through with two plates of goulash.

'It's almost impossible to find half-decent ingredients here,' she said. 'I don't know what it is the British have against food that you can taste. That you'd want to taste.' She laughed and revealed a hint of the girl she'd probably been before the war. She seemed relaxed and I noticed I could hear her accent more. She had left something of the Helena I'd talked to two weeks before down in the house below. Like a formal coat she wore only for business.

The goulash was delicious. As it always had been. We drank the wine I'd brought and then a second bottle she had. We talked and laughed some more, then fell on each other with a savagery that was almost frightening. She scratched and bit me and stared at me wildly with something akin to hatred in her eyes. Afterwards we lay naked on the rug, drank what was left of the wine and smoked.

'Why don't you tell me why you're really here?' she asked, her voice suddenly cold and hard again.

'I'm here to see you, Helena,' I said, and almost believed it myself. 'After I saw you the other week I couldn't stop thinking about you. About us.' At least that much was true.

'There is no us,' she said, but the chill had thawed a little. She turned on her side and we looked into each other's eyes. 'There never was an *us*. So why don't you save us both a lot of time and get to what it is you want. Unless you've just had it.'

'Don't, Helena. It's not you.'

'What? To be bitter and cynical?' She laughed and rolled onto her back again. She stared up at the ceiling and smoked and I took in her finely sculpted profile. 'We're both cut from the same rotten wood, you and I, Lennox. So cut the crap and tell me what you want.'

'Okay, I did want to ask you something, but I *did* come here to see you. To be with you.' I sat up and took a long pull on my cigarette. 'Listen, Helena, someone . . . a friend of mine . . . was talking to me the other day. About wanting to get away. To have a new start. Why can't we?'

Helena turned to me. The only light was the glow from the fire and the red-gold of it etched the contours of her body. When she spoke her voice was low. 'Stop it. We've been here before.'

'Were we wrong? Why couldn't it work?' I realized that, at that moment, I meant what I was saying. 'My folks have money. I have some money saved. And God knows you must have a bit put away. You said yourself the last time I was here that you dreamed of selling up and starting a new life. We could go to Canada. Away from everyone and everything that's gone wrong in our lives.'

Helena stood up and pulled her dress back over her body. The ice was back in her voice. 'The main thing that's gone wrong in our lives is us. Like I said, Lennox, you and I are both rotten. We blame it all on everything that has happened to us, but the truth is it was always there in us both. It just took a little bit of history to bring it to the surface. Forget what I said before . . . sometimes I talk nonsense. To keep sane. So why don't you just tell me what it is that you want?'

Sometimes you feel more naked than others. I stood up and pulled on my clothes, feeling uncomfortable under her gaze.

'Arthur Parks is dead.'

'I know.'

'I'm to find out who killed him.'

'And what does that have to do with me?' It was fully dark outside and the dying fire was all the light I had to see her face. But I sensed it set hard.

'Okay, Helena, I'll tell you all that I know and what I haven't told my client yet. And it'll tell you exactly what I *think* it has to do with you. Arthur Parks was murdered by someone connected to whatever happened to Tam McGahern, the tough spivvy-type you say you saw Sally Blane with.

'This is the way I see it, or I'm guessing it . . . Tam McGahern sees he can't expand his little empire beyond Glasgow. The Three Kings have him in their sights if he puts a foot wrong. It's true that Tam McGahern may be a psychopath, but he's also smarter than the Three Kings put together. And he's seen that there are opportunities to be had in the big wide world outside Glasgow. So he comes up with a scheme . . . and here's where it gets a little sketchy, because I'm not a hundred per cent on what the scheme was, but it's got to do with the Middle East. So Tam decides to hook himself a few big fish. With me so far?'

'Go on.' Helena's face was suddenly illuminated as she lit another cigarette.

'So Tam conceives this honey-trap operation, gets together a handful of really classy chippies. Not the usual sort, girls with a bit of class and real lookers. He sets them up in a house in the West End, but my guess is that some of the punters who go there don't even know they're whores or that the house is a bordello. Tam was in the Desert Rats and Gideon, so he has an interesting network of friends, including, I think, Arthur Parks. So Tam gives Arthur a cut of the action in exchange for helping him set it all up – creaming off the best customers and sending them to the West End operation. Like I said, I think a few non-punters were also targeted by the girls directly. To start with I thought that this was all a trap-fuck-and-blackmail operation. But they are too selective in their targets. It's a list of names, Helena. A list of names that McGahern needs to make his plan work. One of them is Alexander Knox, the plastic surgeon. Why they need him beats me. But the main target is John Andrews, the poor mug who marries Lillian not knowing she is really a prostitute and porn-film actress called Sally Blane. Andrews seems to be their main target because they need to use his importing business.'

'What for?'

'That I'm not entirely sure of. But I am sure it involves taking things in or out of the Middle East. Anyway, something goes wrong. Tam is targeted by someone who doesn't like his enterprising spirit, so he fakes his own death by killing his brother. But his hunters aren't convinced and they do both brothers. Tam exits stage left under his twin brother's name. But Sally Blane, or Lillian Andrews as she now is, keeps the plan running. Part of that plan is to divert suspicion for the second McGahern death onto me, and then to frame me good and proper for the Parks murder.'

'But that doesn't make sense,' said Helena. She kept the lights out.

'Maybe they fell out. Or maybe getting rid of Parks, just like getting rid of Frankie, was part of the plan from the start.'

'I still don't see what this has to do with me, Lennox.'

'Parks wasn't the only one supplying names and helping set up the West End operation. Parks didn't have the style for it. I got chatting to one of McGahern's former lackeys, a nobody called Bobby who tells me that McGahern was cracked up on the woman who ran the shop for him. Molly. To start with I think that's Lillian, but there's talk of a *foreign* woman.'

'Me.'

'That's what I don't know. I hope to God it's not, Helena. Because if it is, you've got yourself into some serious trouble. Whoever did Tam is a serious outfit. And I don't think we're talking about gangsters.'

'You don't seem to know what you're talking about, Lennox. There are things you don't understand. Will never understand.'

'Are you saying it wasn't you?'

'What I'm saying is you don't know as much as you like to think you know. About me. About anything.'

'Then enlighten me.'

'I think you'd better go.' She stood up and switched the table lamp on. I blinked in the sudden light. Then I saw her face. And I saw in it something I'd never seen before. She looked pale, sad and drawn. But there was something in her expression that was sad and hard and resolute. She handed me my hat.

'For what it's worth, Lennox, it's not me. I told you the last time you were here that I only saw Sally's Glaswegian thug boyfriend once. Don't let tonight fool you: I'm usually particular whom I fuck.'

When I woke up the next day I felt pretty crap. I went to 'Pherson's for a cut and shave and arranged for Twinkletoes to meet me there. Before I went to 'Pherson's I 'phoned Hammer Murphy. I needed his okay for what I was about to do.

'What's to do?' asked Twinkletoes cheerfully as he strained the suspension of my Atlantic climbing into the passenger seat. I smiled back, trying not to think of how easily he would just as cheerfully have used his bolt-cutters to take me down a shoe size.

'Danny Dumfries. That's what to do.'

'What the fuck you want with him? He's one of Murphy's monkeys.'

'I want to talk to him. More exactly I want him to talk to me. I need you to ease the conversation. And don't worry, I've cleared it with Murphy.'

'Okay. Just give me a minute.' Twinkletoes got out of the car, went over to his Sunbeam and took a couple of things out of the boot. He squeezed back into my car even more awkwardly.

There was something long and solid hidden in the folds of his raincoat.

The incongruous golden gleam of six hundred quid's worth of Jowett Javelin parked outside the bleak facade of the club signalled that we would find Dumfries inside. Officially it was a working men's club and run by a committee. That meant the police could only call by invitation, which in turn meant that regulated licensing hours was as alien a concept as men on Mars.

The reality was that Dumfries's club was somewhere between a twenty-four-hour boozer and a brothel. There were a couple of rooms in the back that working girls could rent by the hour. The sexual endurance of Scotsmen meant you could squeeze a lot of business into an hour.

As soon as we entered the club we were plunged into dimly lit gloom. The unventilated room was dense with cigarette smoke, a fume of cheap whisky and the sweat of men engaged in the serious physical toil of around-the-clock drinking.

It was quiet as well as dark. When my eyes adjusted to the gloom, I could see Dumfries standing by the bar with a couple of toughs whom I guessed to be employees. There was a neglected snooker table at the back and five or six expert drinkers sat scattered around the place, oblivious to all but the glasses in front of them.

Danny Dumfries was a small, dark but good-looking man in his late thirties, dressed with impeccable taste. Dumfries and his clubs fell loosely into the orbit of Hammer Murphy's empire, but Murphy allowed him a little more independence than he did his other 'contractors'. If Dumfries had been fully part of the Murphy operation, I couldn't have brought Twinkletoes into his club. As it was I had had to get clearance from Murphy before pulling a stunt like this.

Dumfries smiled when we entered, as much in amusement

as welcome. My bringing along one of Sneddon's heavies was making a statement; Dumfries's smile was the arrogant sneer of someone who feels protected. But, there again, he wasn't to know about the conversation I'd had with Murphy on the 'phone.

'Lennox,' he said, smugly. 'Taking your pet out for a walk?'

'Can we talk?' I said, ignoring the fact that the two heavies had now appeared at our shoulders.

'It's a free country.'

'I mean in private.'

'I'm more comfortable here.'

'This is serious stuff, Danny. And it's as important to Mr Murphy as it is to Mr Sneddon. I'm just looking for some information, but we need to talk in private.'

'Show the gentlemen the way out,' Dumfries said wearily to one of his heavies.

Twinkletoes shoved me to one side as easily as if he were parting curtains. He pushed his face into Dumfries's and pulled the bolt-cutters from inside his raincoat, slamming them down on the bar counter. Several glasses shattered. Suddenly the two heavies looked unsure as to what to do next.

'Tell yer fuckin' monkeys to fuck off, Dumfries, ya wee midget cunt. If you don't, I'm gonna fuckin' kill one of them, just to make a point. Then I'm goin' to shove your fuckin' toes up the other's arse. After that I'll start on yer fuckin' fingers.'

I found myself thinking that if newly appointed General Secretary Dag Hammerskjöld displayed similar diplomatic skills when he took office, the UN would resolve the Korean conflict overnight.

One of the heavies moved in on Twinkletoes, who swung the bolt-cutters backwards and slashed him across the temple. Dumfries's man dropped like a stone while the other made a clumsy move forward. Twinkletoes turned to him and smashed his forehead into the man's face. When he went down, Twinkletoes stamped on his head and put his lights right out.

'Take it easy, for fuck's sake,' said Dumfries, backing away. Twinkletoes grabbed him by his expensive shirtfront and slapped him hard with the flat and then the back of his hand.

'Shut the fuck up,' said Twinkletoes.

'Twinkletoes . . .' I said. 'We don't want him to shut up. We want him to tell us what he knows.'

'Oh,' said Twinkletoes apologetically. 'Sorry.' He slapped Dumfries twice more. 'Tell us what the fuck you know.'

'About *what?*' Dumfries yelled. A trickle of blood dribbled from his nostril.

'Twinkletoes, give the guy a chance. He doesn't know what we want,' I said. I turned back to Dumfries. 'But I'll give you a clue or three. Blackmail. Tam McGahern. Trapping the great and the good with pussy mantraps.'

'I don't know what you're talking about!'

Twinkletoes pulled his hand back again. I stopped him with a gesture.

'Let me try again. Arthur Parks and Tam McGahern. What's the connection?'

'How the fuck would I know?' Dumfries was seriously scared. I understood his fear. I had been scared during my last chat with Sneddon, with Twinkletoes merely lurking in the background. The difference was there was no way I was going to let Twinkletoes indulge his little hobby. The threat should be enough.

I felt uncomfortable about how things had gone. After all of this was over, I would need to operate in this town. For now, I was acting as if I were one of Sneddon's heavies.

'I seriously hope you're not pissing down my back and telling me it's raining, Danny. This is big shit. As you'll have gathered, you don't have Murphy's protection when it comes to this. And if you're holding out you'll have all of the Three Kings on your case.' I turned to Twinkletoes. 'Take a break; watch these two. Danny and I are going to have a chat. Where's your office?'

Dumfries nodded to the back of the club. He showed me into a dingy office and switched the light on. The desk was covered in paperwork and the ashtray spilling over with butts. He still looked scared.

'Take it easy, Danny, for fuck's sake. Sit down. I just need information. I'm sorry about Twinkletoes's *enthusiasm*, but I've been told to travel with him. You okay?'

'Like you fuckin' care.' He slumped into his captain's chair. I sat on the corner of the desk.

'This is simple, Danny, just like I said. Tam McGahern got iced because he was treading on the wrong toes. Just whose toes I don't yet know. But it involved blackmail.'

'It's got nothing to do with me.' Dumfries sniffed and wiped the blood from his nose with a handkerchief. I gave him a cigarette and he lit it with a heavy gold pocket lighter. His hand shook.

'Listen, Danny. I saw what happened to Arthur Parks. And what happened to Frankie McGahern. These guys are pretty handy with a tyre iron and they like their victims to suffer first. Really suffer. If you're involved with this, your only way out is by having the protection of all Three Kings. The other thing is that if I don't give Sneddon what he wants, Twinkletoes out there will give us both a manicure. So tell me the truth and don't hold anything back.'

'I fuckin' swear I'm telling you the truth,' he said. I believed him.

'Okay. But it's going to be difficult to convince my lumbering chum out there. You better start thinking fast and push out a few names I can squeeze. If you were to start blackmailing punters, who would you use?'

Dumfries stared at the wall for a moment, smoking briskly.

'What do you think they were up to?' he asked at last. 'Blackmailing punters with photographs of them on the job?'

'I guess so,' I said.

'There are a few chancers out there who are handy with a Box Brownie. But if I was going to do something like that, there's a guy I would use. Ronnie Smails. His main business is taking dirty pictures, but word has it that if you want someone set up, he's the man to talk to.'

'Does he work for any of the Kings?'

'Naw. He's too fucking far down in the gutter for them to bother with. Trust me, Lennox, you talk to Ronnie Smails for five minutes and you want to have a shower afterwards. He's a low-rent pornographer and all-round creeping-Jesus.'

I nodded, but found it difficult to imagine Danny Dumfries looking down on anyone from the rarefied atmosphere of the flea-pit he ran. 'Where can I find Smails?' I asked.

'He has a *studio* in Cowcaddens. He has a front of doing baby pictures, portraits, that kinda stuff. I don't know if he's your man, but he's who I would go to.' Dumfries wrote down an address and handed it to me.

'I'll pay him a visit. You okay?'

Dumfries nodded, but a sparkle of hate flickered in his eyes.

'Listen, Danny, I'm sorry about the rough stuff, but you shouldn't have called on your heavies. I can't control Twinkletoes. I'll talk to Sneddon and Murphy. Maybe get you a little compensation. Okay?'

Dumfries nodded.

'Just make sure you don't ever fucking come back here, Lennox.'

CHAPTER TWENTY-SEVEN

I didn't think I'd need Twinkletoes to deal with Ronnie Smails, and after the cosy scenes in Dumfries's club, I thought I'd give him the afternoon off. I went back to my digs first, called a buddy in the Port of Clyde and arranged to meet that night at the Horsehead Bar for a pint and a chat.

I drove to Cowcaddens and found Smails's place: a two-roomed shop on the ground floor of a soot-blackened tenement building. There was a printed card in the corner of the grimy window that gave rates for family and wedding photography and provided the last resting place for half-a-dozen flies. Next to it a freshly married couple gap-tooth-grinned out of a yellowing photograph. The bride was a head taller than the groom, and either the dark suit he wore had been borrowed from an even shorter chum, or he preferred his ankles to be well ventilated.

I tried the door but it was locked and no one answered my knock. Smails was out, probably assisting Richard Avedon on an Audrey Hepburn shoot. I decided to come back later.

Jimmy Frater and I had got to know one another through a chance meeting in a bar on a foggy night. I hadn't been in Glasgow long and we both stank a little of the war. It was one of these evenings where light chat reveals a common history, which turns into a gloomy recognition of a similarly damaged soul. The difference between us was that Frater had somehow managed to drag his life back onto some kind of track. He worked for the authority that ran the Port of Clyde and had proved to be a valuable asset on the odd occasion.

I ordered a pint of heavy for Frater and a rye whiskey for myself while I waited for him to arrive. Frater, unlike me, was the dependable, solid sort. I knew I could rely on him being on time for our meeting.

'You get a chance to look at those codes I gave you?' I asked after he had arrived.

'Tell me you're not up to something illegal, Lennox.'

'I'm not up to something illegal,' I said. 'I'd tell you that anyway, of course, but in this case it happens to be true. In fact if I'm right about these codes, then I'll be handing the information over to the police.'

'Okay,' Frater said, but didn't look entirely convinced. 'You were right. All of these relate to CCI shipments from the port. Three different ships, each appearing several times, but different manifests.'

'What was the cargo?'

'Machine parts. Mainly agricultural. Two shipments were oil drilling equipment. The one thing all of the shipments had in common was their destination. Aqaba, in Jordan. That help?'

'Kinda,' I said. Truth was it was a big help: proof of the Middle East connection I suspected.

I drank a few more with Frater, who made his apologies and said he had to get back to his wife and kids. That suited me because I wanted to catch Smails that night. The other reason was that nothing depressed me more than success and happiness.

Ronnie Smails's studio was still in darkness when I arrived back. I guessed that he lived above the premises, but the first-floor flat was also unlit. I tried the studio door again and found it still locked.

I waited until a Corporation tram rattled past and cast a look up and down the street before turning my attention to the panel of four small glazed panes in the door. I picked at the putty around one of them and it crumbled to the touch. I set about easing the pane out of the door with my penknife. Eventually it came away and I squeezed my hand through and un-snibbed the door. With the blinds down, I reckoned it was okay to switch the lights on.

Whatever Smails's talents as a photographer, he was never going to char for me. The studio was filthy and looked as if it hadn't been swept out in a couple of months. I looked through some of the display drawers and found a collection of photographs. Mainly wedding and portrait pics, some of which were ancient. Smails's trade was less than brisk.

I went through to the darkroom. There were several prints hanging on the line. All of them portrayed what tended to happen *after* the wedding ceremony. This was Smails's real business. The commonality between the photographs was that they all illustrated the act of physical union between two or several individuals. The other common factor was that, for some inexplicable reason, the men all had kept their socks on.

I rifled through a steel cabinet and found more of the same predictable fuck and suck shots. But these were posed, not surreptitiously taken blackmail photos. There was one set of photographs that did, strangely, make me a little homesick. It was the most creatively conceived of the scenarios: a Canadian tableau in which a Mountie and a trapper were showing a young lady partially attired as an Eskimo the true meaning of what it meant to spear a beaver. I felt a tear in my eye and had to resist the temptation to burst into a chorus of *Oh, Canada!*

I was about to put the photographs back when I realized that the Eskimo Nell was familiar. To be honest, I hadn't really been examining her face so I took a closer look. She was really quite pretty and I was sure I had seen her somewhere before, but in a completely different context. I pocketed one of the photographs that showed something of her face and put the rest back in the cabinet.

I went through the rest of the place and couldn't find anything that fitted with extortion. Switching the lights out, I climbed the stairs to the apartment above. Maybe there was a hidey-hole up there. Again the flat was in darkness and I flicked the light switch. Nothing. I had to fumble along the hall until I found a standard lamp. It flooded the hall and the rooms off with an insipid, jaundiced light. Smails had obviously opted for a design motif that could best be described as Early Shithole. The place was filthy and smelly and I doubted that this was anybody that McGahern would get involved with.

I was wrong.

I found Smails in the living room. This time there had been no torture, just simple execution. He sat on a grubby clubchair, a long-cold cup of tea on the side table next to him and a cigarette between his fingers that had burned down and scorched unfeeling flesh. A copy of *Spick* magazine had slipped from his fingers and onto the floor at his feet. Smails obviously made a big effort to keep up to date with what was current in his profession.

I examined him more closely. His face showed all the signs of strangulation. He had been choked to death with the same width of garrotte as Arthur Parks. Unlike Parks, Smails hadn't had any information worth torturing out of him and he had been killed swiftly and silently.

He maybe hadn't told his killers anything, but he was telling me exactly what I wanted to know: he was a small man with greasy grey hair long overdue a cutting and his eyes were open and staring, as they would have been in life. But Smails had obviously had some kind of congenital defect: his right eyelid drooped over the eye. Just the way Bobby had described the 'greasy wee shite' he had seen Tam McGahern talking to shortly before he died.

Smails had been my man. I was now certain he had taken the photographs for the blackmail operation but I knew a search of the place would be futile: the pics and the negs would be long gone.

Parks dead. Smails dead. There were two other contacts that Tam McGahern had had before his demise: the fat Dutchman and Jackie Gillespie, the armed robber. I wondered if they were both still breathing.

Remembering my experience at Arthur Parks's place, I decided to get out quick, just in case the cozzers were on their way again, maybe this time without bells and flashing lights. I paused long enough to wipe down with a handkerchief the surfaces and handles that I remembered touching. My fingerprints weren't on record, but they were all over the Parks place and I didn't want my dabs to be the link between two murder scenes. I switched all of the lights off and slipped out into the street.

I had had the sense not to park the Atlantic directly outside, mainly because I didn't want to scare Smails off if he had returned while I was still inside. I was just about to turn the key in the ignition when a taxi stopped outside Smails. Two women got out. I couldn't see them too well but as far as I could tell they were reasonably well put together and I guessed that they were a couple of Smails's 'models'. One paid the taxi driver, while the other rang Smails's doorbell. I had locked the door and hastily tapped the small glass pane into place. The brass at the door called over to her chum, obviously to tell the taxi driver to wait. She rang again and rapped on the door. As far as I could see her knocking hadn't dislodged the pane. She gave up and climbed back into the taxi.

I followed them across town. I had noticed that they weren't cheaply dressed and they certainly weren't concerned about the cost of the taxi. The dark-haired girl I'd seen knocking at Smails's door got off at the Saltmarket. I decided to stick with the taxi. It headed south and we passed Hampden Stadium and eventually stopped outside a tenement in Mount Florida. The girl got out and paid the taxi driver. Bingo: she was none other than Eskimo Nell. And now I remembered where I'd seen her before. She was the woman I'd twice seen Lillian Andrews with. I tried to be as inconspicuous as possible but it was difficult with so few cars on the street.

A number twelve Corporation tram stopped and half a dozen people dismounted. I parked and walked briskly into the midst of the passengers. The blonde disappeared into the communal tenement close. I was just in time to see her turn the corner at the far end of the close and climb the rear stairs. I moved as quietly as I could to the end of the passageway and watched from its cover as she entered her flat. Making a mental note of the number, I headed back out to the Atlantic.

The only reason I didn't make a house call there and then was I did not want her to work out that I'd followed her from Smails's. After all, he would be found over the next day or so and they would work out a rough time of death. Roughly the time that coincided with me being there. And the City of Glasgow Police had a problem with the concept of coincidence.

I drove past Smails's place on the way back. No police cars outside and the place was still in darkness. I tried to 'phone Willie Sneddon to give him an update, but he was out. I headed back to my digs and turned in for the night. But every time sleep started to come it was shouldered out of the way by something big and ugly and frightening. I lay in the dark and thought of Helena and Fiona White and May Donaldson and new starts in Canada. The idea had never been so appealing. I had gotten involved in something a little too deadly this time. I realized that, for the first time in a very long time, I was actually a little scared.

My foreboding turned out to be well-founded. An ill-tempered Mrs White called me down to the shared hall telephone at seven the next morning. It was Willie Sneddon.

'Lennox, don't talk but listen. The polis are on their way to arrest me and I'm going to be here when they arrive. The coppers have lifted Murphy and Cohen. About an hour ago. I was supposed to be lifted at the same time but I wasn't at home. The bastards have lifted most of my team as well, including Twinkletoes and Tiny. I need you to contact George Meldrum – he's my lawyer – and tell him to bail me out. I can't get him on the 'phone and they'll be here any moment. The cops will leave you alone because you're not on any of our teams.'

'What the hell has happened?'

'I don't fucking know. Just get Meldrum as fast as you can.'

'Okay, if it's as big as it seems to be, then they won't let you near Meldrum.'

'Just do it.' He hung up.

I knew of Greasy George Meldrum. I reckoned there was a picture of him on every dartboard in every police canteen in Glasgow. He was known as Greasy George for two reasons: his overly groomed appearance, over-elaborate vocabulary and oiled hair, and the fact that everything he touched seemed to become slippery. Just as the police had a solid case against one of the Three Kings, it would slip from their grasp, thanks to Greasy George.

I got Meldrum's home number from the book and dialled it. No answer. I got dressed quickly, unsuccessfully tried to reach him again by 'phone, and jumped into the Atlantic. I decided it was pointless driving up to his Milngavie home and instead decided to head into my office and wait until nearer nine, when I'd probably catch Meldrum at his offices in Wellington Street.

I listened to the Home Service on the car radio on the way in to my office. One story dominated the news. I pulled quickly over to the kerb and listened intently to the whole report. I muttered *fuck* as all of the pieces suddenly fell into place. Unfortunately the pieces falling into place meant that all hell was breaking loose. I now understood why the Three Kings had been pulled in. I went straight to Meldrum's office and sat outside until his staff started to arrive. I followed them in.

A pretty receptionist greeted me a little disdainfully, obviously annoyed at someone turning up before she could settle into her day. She was also seriously unimpressed that I didn't have an appointment. It was only after I told her I was representing the interests of Mr William Sneddon – and probably those of Mr Michael Murphy and Mr Jonathan Cohen – that she suddenly became very much more accommodating.

I sat for an hour waiting in the reception area trying to work out just how accommodating the receptionist might become. Eventually Greasy George arrived. He was tallish, well-built and balding and wore an expensively tailored blue-pinstripe business suit. I intercepted him as he passed through reception.

'I've heard a great deal about you, Mr Lennox,' he said amiably. 'But our paths have never crossed. Some of our mutual clients speak very highly of you. Please . . .' he held the door open to his office.

'I tried to get you at home,' I said, sitting down.

'I'm afraid I was staying overnight at a friend's house.' He still smiled. It was the type of smile you wanted, for no good reason, to punch. 'My good lady wife and children are away for a few days, so I took the opportunity to visit my friend.'

'I understand,' I said. We both knew I did. 'Have you heard the news?'

'What news would that be, Mr Lennox?'

'The armed robbery. It was the main story this morning. I've no doubt it will hit later editions of the papers. There was an army convoy on its way from the Royal Ordnance Arsenal at Fazakerly in Liverpool to Redford and Dreghorn Barracks. It was stopped by police officers at a checkpoint. Except they weren't police officers. It was a highly organized job, but something seems to have gone disastrously wrong. The result is two dead soldiers, a driver badly beaten and in a coma, and a ton of the latest sub-machine guns gone.'

'I see . . .' The smile faded. 'I'm guessing that this has something to do with those stolen uniforms.'

'You know about the uniforms?' I asked.

'Yes, I do. Messrs Sneddon, Murphy and Cohen have been receiving the attentions of our constabulary a little too persistently over the last while.'

'Well, that's why I'm here. Sneddon 'phoned me this morning. The CID have taken them all in for questioning. Sneddon needs you to head over to St Andrew's Street with a get-out-of-jail-free card.'

'I'm afraid it will be anything but free.'

I smiled. 'I would think you'd want to get all three out of there as quick as possible. After all, between them, the Three Kings must pay more than your tailor's bills.'

'In which case, we're both in the same position, as far as I can gather.'

'True,' I said. 'So I suggest we both work, each in his own way, to free up our revenue sources.'

We left together, Meldrum pausing to tell his secretary to cancel all his appointments for the day. I wondered how many of his clients were on the 'phone. It was quite an achievement for him to get such a large percentage of his clients off: he had a growing word-of-scum reputation and everybody knew that if Greasy George Meldrum was your lawyer, you were as guilty as sin.

We parted company on the street outside his office. He shook my hand and handed me one of his expensive embossed cards.

'Thanks,' I smiled, 'but I don't think I'll be needing your services.'

'You never know, Mr Lennox. But that's not why I gave it to you.' He unlocked the door of his new Bentley R-type and I could have sworn I smelled polished walnut and leather from twenty yards away. 'It is I who may need your services in the future.' He got into his Bentley and drove off. I stared at his card. So far I'd been offered informal partnerships with a professional murderer and the most despised figure in the Scottish legal system. Maybe I should change my image.

I pocketed the card. I'd told him I would never need his services. Truth was that if the police made the link between the Parks and Smails murder scenes, then Greasy George could be exactly who I'd need.

CHAPTER TWENTY-EIGHT

The City of Glasgow Police could not be accused of dynamism. It took Greasy George a full forty-eight hours to get first Sneddon, then the other two Kings out of custody. It also took them that length of time to find Ronnie Smails's body, by which time his cup of tea, and the trail, would be colder than stone cold.

The local newspapers had been a little more lively. Details of the robbery were emerging. It had taken place just north of the border and the trap had been sprung with military precision. There had been three lorries and an army truck escort, because of the nature of the cargo: brand-new Sterling-Patchett L2A1 sub-machine guns, which were being brought in to replace the older Sten guns. There had been an exchange of gunfire, which had left two Tommies dead on the road. One of the drivers was still in a critical condition and had not regained consciousness. The other was providing the police with descriptions of the attack and the attackers. One of the robbers had been wounded by army fire, but had made his escape.

This had been the caper that Tam McGahern had been building up to. And I had a pretty good idea about exactly what was going to happen next.

I had two house calls to make. Both were on the South Side. But first I had to pick up a couple of things from my place. I took my Webley and stashed it under the front passenger seat of the Atlantic. One Saturday night, a couple of months previously, I had gotten into a debate with a thug in Argyle Street.

He had tried to compensate for his lack of guts and skill by pulling a knife on me: a beautiful, pearl-handled Italian switch-blade. We ended the encounter with me up one pearl-handled switchblade and him down several less-than-pearly teeth. I had hung onto the knife. Now I slipped it into my jacket pocket.

Then I went out to play.

First I travelled along Paisley Road West and into the future. The address I had for Jackie Gillespie was near Bellahouston Park. A reasonably new rented Glasgow Corporation semi-detached, Gillespie's house looked clean and bright and opti-mistic. But the real future was looming over it: a spider's web of scaffolding encased a stepped rank of massive, almost complete apartment blocks. Moss Heights. This was where the Glaswegian of the future would live: free from the tenement, free from over-crowding and disease.

Free from any sense of community.

The fact was that Glasgow had swollen like a tumour and was now squeezing against the Green Belt. And if you couldn't build out, you could build up. The geniuses in the City Chambers had decided that the solution to having Glaswegians living on top of each other was to have Glaswegians living on top of each other.

Given my experience of my last couple of house calls, I took the precaution of parking a little away from Gillespie's house. The pavement beneath my feet was pristine, as were the rough-cast and roofs of the houses I passed, their gardens still raw, earth scars, waiting for the first sowing of grass. As I walked, the ringing of heavy tools echoed from the building site in the sky half a mile distant.

Jackie Gillespie, as far as I knew, had no wife or children, yet his bright, new semi-detached council house had clearly been intended for a family. As far as I could see the neighbouring house was yet to be occupied. No one answered my ringing of the doorbell and, after checking there were no neighbours watching, I slipped around to the back of the house. The back door was unlocked. Well, to tell the truth it was *de*-locked. Someone had applied their size tens to it and the wood had splintered. My money was on a Highlander in blue. I had decided to be a little more prepared this time and I took a pair of gloves out of my raincoat pocket and put them on before pushing open the door.

It was fast becoming a bit of a tradition for me to find a freshly strangled corpse in situations like these, and I felt almost disappointed not to find Gillespie sitting in bulge-eyed welcome. Alive or dead, he wasn't here. But whether it had been the coppers or not, someone had given his place a thorough turning over.

I didn't hang around. If it hadn't been the coppers then it would be soon. They were capable of thinking, even if it was a little more slowly than the rest of us. I knew that Jackie Gillespie had been seen talking to Tam McGahern, and I knew Tam McGahern had been planning a big get-out-of-Glasgow job. The police didn't. But they would be working their way through a list of top armed robbers who could have pulled a job like this. And Jackie Gillespie was pretty close to the top of the list.

But whoever had turned over his place had made the connection before me. And that didn't fit with the police.

I got back in the car and headed south, stopping at a callbox on the way to 'phone Sneddon. There was something even colder and harder than usual about his voice.

'Someone's gonna pay for this, Lennox. Someone's gonna pay hard and long. It's been years since a copper's felt he's had the balls to lift a hand to me.'

'McNab?'

'He's a fuckin' traitor. He's supposed to be Orange, for fuck's sake. Instead of hassling me, he should have been kicking the Irish green shite out of that fucking Fenian Murphy.'

'To be fair, Mr Sneddon, I think he's been doing exactly that. And Jonny Cohen.'

'Maybes. You're right about Cohen, though. Word is he took a hammering. The cozzers picked on him special, 'cause armed robbery's his thing.'

I could imagine it. Jonny Cohen would be at the top of the list. But it was the other name I was interested in.

'Have they pulled in Jackie Gillespie?' I asked.

'How the fuck should I know?' said Sneddon dully. Then, after a pause, 'Why? Is Gillespie part of the firm that pulled this stunt?'

'I don't know. I think so. Listen, Mr Sneddon, I think I've put this all together. It's like I said to you before; this could bring all kinds of trouble for you, Murphy and Sneddon. Today was just the start. This has a political element to it. Can you call a meeting? Get the other two Kings together and I can go over what I know. I'm going to need your combined resources to crack this.'

'I dunno, Lennox. The coppers are still sticking to us like shite to a shirt tail. I'll do my best.'

'I'll 'phone back in a couple of hours.'

After hanging up, I headed off for my second house call. I drove down to Mount Vernon and parked around the corner from the tenement block I'd seen the Eskimo Nell go into on the night that Smails had had his collar tightened. There were three storeys of flats above a ground floor of shop fronts. There was an Austin A30 parked outside the close. All of the flats had lights on and I guessed Eskimo Nell was in. I hoped that she was alone. If she had company I could probably deal with it, but it could make things complicated. Slow me down.

I climbed the back stairs and knocked on the door. It was opened by the girl I'd followed back from Smails's place. She looked a little unsure of herself and kept the door on the chain. She had a pretty face. Beautiful, almost. There was no doubt about the fact that she was the woman I'd seen Lillian Andrews with. She had a touch of class about her: just like Lillian, just like Wilma, just like Lena who had been rejected because the class evaporated whenever she spoke.

'What do you want?' she asked.

'I'm a friend of Tam's,' I said, and tried to look both conspiratorial and in a hurry. 'And of Sally's. I've got a message for you.'

I thought the script and the performance were perfect, but it was clear I'd misread my audience. She slammed the door shut. I stopped the snib catching by shouldering the door. The chain held. I rammed my foot into the gap and slammed my shoulder into the heavy teak again. This time the chain snapped and the door flew in and threw the girl backwards. She staggered into the wall and a scream started to rise in her throat. I caught it for her.

'Listen, sister,' I hissed as menacingly as I could manage, pinning her to the wall with the hand I had around her throat. 'This is your choice. You can start screaming and I'll strangle you to death here in your hall, or we can sit down, nice and civilized, on your sofa and chat. But you've got to understand something here and now. You're finished with whatever business you've got with Sally Blane or Lillian Andrews or whatever the hell her real name is. You're playing a different game now. It's called survival. We're going to talk and I'm going to ask questions, then I'm going to deliver you to the Three Kings. And, believe me, if they hand a dolly over to their boys it ends up broken. So whether or not you end tonight raped, tortured and dead depends on how well I can satisfy the Three Kings that you've given me all the answers I need. Do you understand?' I loosened my grip enough for her to gasp a breath and nod vigorously. I tightened it again. 'No funny business. Okay?'

She nodded again. I let her go. She looked at me with wild eyes and rubbed at her throat. I grabbed her arm and frog-marched her through to the living room and threw her down into the armchair. I sure was in a nice business. It was when I found myself pushing women around that I felt most proud of my career choices.

The flat was expensively furnished. And surprisingly tasteful. There was a dining table and chairs against one wall and I dragged a chair over and sat opposite her.

'Are you Molly?' I asked.

She shook her head.

'No. My name is Liz. Molly was Margot . . . Sally's sister. She's dead.'

'You worked for this special set up, didn't you? I'm guessing the name of the game was blackmail?'

Liz nodded. 'I don't know much about what they squeezed out of the punters we set up. I just did as I was told.'

'How did it work?'

'We were given a mark . . . some rich or important bloke. Sometimes the mark would know we were chippies, other times they didn't know they were being set up. But they was always married. Respectable. After a while Tam McGahern would burst in on us, shouting and swearing and threatening the mark. Sometimes he'd soften them up with a wee beatin'. Whichever one of us was working the mark, Tam made out that he was our boyfriend. He'd say he's had a detective on us and then show the pictures. Then he'd say he was goin' to send the pictures to the mark's wife or the papers.'

'Unless the mark did exactly what Tam wanted.'

'That's about the size of it.'

'And John Andrews was Sally Blane's mark?'

'That had been goin' on since long before I got involved. And I only ever knew Sally as Lillian Andrews. I only found out later that the girl what got killed was her sister and that Lillian's real name was Sally.'

'So Margot really is dead?'

'Aye. And because of what we was doing. Tam did his usual angry boyfriend act in the street outside a club Margot and her mark had been at. Lillian was with them. Tam had the photos and everything. He started to pull the guy out of the car but the mark panicked and drove off with Margot and Lillian still inside. In the car, I mean. Tam chased the mark through the city and out onto Paisley Road West. The mark lost control and smashed into a railway bridge. Him and Margot was killed right off. Lillian was in the back. She was knocked about a bit but all right. Except her nose and jaw got busted up. She thought she was going to lose her looks, but Tam got some specialist to take care of it.'

'Who told you all of this?'

'One of the other girls. Wilma.'

'Wilma Marshall?'

'Aye. You know her?'

'We've met.'

Liz rubbed her throat and frowned. 'Can I get a glass of water?'

'Okay. But I'll keep you company.'

We went through to the small kitchen and she filled a glass from the tap. I leaned against the door jamb and smiled at her.

I was feeling pretty smug. We exchanged a look and in that second she knew that I knew who she really was. The fear was gone from her eyes: it made way for a cold, dark hate.

'You've got a great job, Lennox,' she said. I grinned more broadly.

'I don't recall introducing myself,' I said.

'Yeah. A great job. You must spend half your life looking back over your shoulder.'

'Not really,' I said. 'I tend to be a forward-thinking type. I fit in with the new age.'

'Really? Maybe it's time you started looking over your shoulder.' She smiled. A smile that made me think *oh fuck*.

Before I had time to react, something flashed past my eyes as it was looped over my head and around my neck and drawn tight. A thick band that felt like leather. Suddenly breathing became something no longer to be taken for granted and I was pulled back against the body of my attacker. He twisted something at the back of my neck a couple of times and both my head and my chest felt like they were going to explode: one from want of blood, the other from want of air. I was going to get it the same way as Parks and Smails.

I clawed at the strap and then, uselessly, vaguely over my shoulders. The lack of oxygen started a buzz-saw in my head and I started to panic. Something of my wartime training kicked in and instead of struggling I let my legs go from under me and dropped like a stone. I went down so fast that I shifted my attacker's centre of gravity. He maintained the pressure on the garrotte but had to stand with his legs apart and hold me like a sheep being sheared.

I reached into my jacket pocket and freed the catch on my switchblade. I put all of my strength into a sweeping upwards arc and aimed, blind, for a point about a foot above my head.

I guessed that was where his balls would be. I must have been there or thereabouts, because he screamed in agony and the garrotte around my neck loosened. I still had a grip on my knife and I gave it a vicious twist to mash the potatoes. Another scream and I cheered myself with the thought that he wouldn't be passing his strangulation skills onto the next generation.

I scrambled to my feet and spun around to face him. He was about five-eight and dark-skinned and had a Middle Eastern look to him.

I pulled the knife from his groin, giving it another malicious twist as I did so. He sank to his knees, his hands clutched to his genitals, blood spilling from between the fingers. He was retching in great big spasms. He represented no further threat to me, but the bastard had tried to kill me. And he had killed Parks and Smails.

I took my time and made sure the kick I planted hit him square in the mouth, dislodging teeth. I was back in a place I'd been too many times in the war. I got the old tingle, the slowing down of time, the total absence of any kind of feeling for the man you were killing. And I knew that was what I was going to do. I grabbed him by the hair and yanked his head up so that I could get my knife in behind his windpipe before thrusting it forward and out. Then the fucker would know what it was like to fight for breath.

The thing that I hadn't accounted for was that, in the war, there tends not to be a woman in the room behind you with access to heavy cooking implements. I had forgotten about Liz. Mainly because she hadn't done the usual hysterical screaming thing in the background. I was just about to finish my Arab chum off when a train ran into the back of my head.

I went down but wasn't out. She swung some cast iron at me

again and caught me on the temple. This time the lights dimmed so I could enjoy the fireworks that sparkled in my head. I was really dazed but still not out and she knew she'd have to get out quick. I heard her pulling her dusky chum to his feet and rushing him out of the apartment. I pulled myself upright, leaning on the kitchen counter. My head hurt like a bastard, I felt a warm trickle of blood down my neck and the world was still a little tilted on its axis. I looked down to where she'd dropped the cast-iron pan. I counted myself lucky that she hadn't thought to pick up a knife instead. Glaswegians kill each other in the kitchen more than in any other room. Admittedly they usually do it by cooking, but I still considered myself fortunate to get out in one piece.

I soaked a cloth and held it to my head, but still made a stab at catching up with them. There was a smear of blood along the linoleum floor and out onto the common stair. I ran down the steps, my head throbbing with every footfall and out along the close and onto the street. They were gone, as was the Baby Austin.

I half-staggered towards where I had parked the Atlantic and had to stop halfway to vomit. It burned in my crushed throat. There was nobody on the street, but even if there had been, the sight of a Glaswegian hanging onto a lamp-post and making a splash on the pavement was not an out-of-the ordinary occurrence. I felt a little better but every pulse still beat a kettle drum in my head. I'd been clobbered twice now and I knew I wasn't in a good way. Maybe even a fractured skull. I slumped into the driver's seat and sat for a moment, letting the spinning world catch up with me a little before I drove off.

When this was over, I was going to collect big time from the Three Kings and add it to the little nest-egg I'd built up. Maybe, when this was all over and if I was still alive, I would get that boat back to Canada. You never really know where rock bottom lies. But this sure felt like it.

I 'phoned Sneddon from a 'phone box. He had arranged a meeting for the following evening. I asked if it could be sooner but he said that each of the Kings would have to work out how to give the cops the slip. I told him what had happened in the flat.

'The guy who tried to throttle me was the one who killed Parks and Smails,' I said. I told Sneddon what I'd done to the Arab.

'Good. Sounds like the bastard will bleed to death. But I want to be sure. I'll see you at Shawfields tomorrow at eight.'

'Okay,' I said and hung up. I hadn't wanted to tell Sneddon I was in bad shape. Religion and half-baked history meant Sneddon and Murphy hated each other's guts, but they were actually mirror images of each other. Neither was the type you wanted to show weakness to. I redialled.

'Jonny?' I said. 'Can I come over ... and can you get me a doctor?'

CHAPTER TWENTY-NINE

Jonny Cohen's home in Newton Mearns was nearer than any of the other Three Kings, but there was more to it than that. My instinct told me I'd get the help I needed there.

I did, however, feel the need to warn Jonny that I was in a bad way and to suggest that we should maybe meet up somewhere other than his house, but he insisted, saying he'd meet me at the door and get me looked after. He told me that I'd have to accept that the cops would see me arrive: they had him under surveillance, just like the other two Kings and all their chief officers.

It was difficult, but I somehow managed to drive south to Newton Mearns and park the Atlantic three blocks away from Jonny's, hopefully out of sight of the coppers on watch. It was that three-block walk to Jonny's house that took the most out of me. I tugged my hat's brim low over my eyes and pulled the collar of my raincoat up. Two reasons: to hide my face as much as possible, and to conceal the bright red that the collar of my shirt had turned. I walked as straight and purposefully as I could, but now I felt hot and I knew that the sweat I felt in my hatband and trickling down my neck was really blood.

Jonny answered the door and casually invited me in. At least casually from a cop car's distance away. It didn't do me much good to see the shock in Jonny's expression, especially considering his own face was still bruised and swollen under one eye from his encounter with Superintendent McNab and his boys.

'For fuck's sake, Lennox . . .' he said after he closed the door.
I didn't answer: I was too busy hurtling towards the Italian tile
of his hallway.

I came to at about lunchtime the following day. There was a
fat, middle-aged woman sitting reading a newspaper beside the
bed and as soon as she heard me stirring she got up and leaned
over me, placing a hand on either shoulder to pin me to the
bed.

'Not now, sweetheart,' I said weakly. 'I've got a headache.'

'Aye, very funny,' she said in a way that told me she didn't
think it. 'Stay still and don't move your head. I'll go and get Mr
Cohen.'

I lay still and looked up at the ceiling. I felt as sick as hell
and my head still rang with the constant, high-pitched pain.
Jonny came in and leaned over me.

'What the fuck have you been doing, Lennox? I got Doc Banks
to look you over. He's stitched up your head but he was pretty
insistent that you go to a hospital as soon as possible. He says
your skull could be fractured.'

'No time, Jonny. Do you know about the meet tonight?'

'At Shawfields? Aye. I hope you know what the fuck you're
about, Lennox. I have spent the last five years in the middle of
Sneddon and Murphy. Trying to keep the bastards apart. Every
time they meet Murphy starts the wisecracks about the Queen
and Sneddon about the Pope. All of this sectarian shite, it does
my head in.'

'I suppose you're neutral. Being Jewish, I mean.'

'Doesn't always follow,' he grinned. 'You can't just be Jewish
in Glasgow. You have to be a Protestant Jew or a Catholic Jew.
Growing up here I was always being asked if I supported Rangers
or Celtic.'

'What did you say?'

'That I was a Partick Thistle supporter.'

'Smart move ... dodge the sectarian issue and win their sympathy at the same time.'

'Aye, but I still got stick for being Jewish. I remember kicking the shite out of this kid at school who said that us Jews had all the money. It wasn't his insults that got to me ... I was just so fucking furious that my wealthy Jewish parents were making us live in a tenement slum in Newlands.'

I laughed and somewhere in darkest Haiti a voodoo witch doctor shoved a pin through a dummy of my head. The homely, middle-aged woman tutted loudly and told me to lie still.

'Give us a minute, Lizzie,' said Jonny. 'I'll make sure he behaves.'

'I think she fancies me,' I said after she'd gone.

'Lizzie Sharp,' explained Jonny. 'She used to be a matron at the Western General. She had a sideline in helping out young ladies in a spot of bother. Got three years for it. She's pretty handy when someone's banged up. Listen, Lennox, you need to get to a hospital. Doc Banks is worried about you.'

'If Doc Banks had ever worried about anything other than where his next drink came from, he wouldn't have been struck off. I'll be fine.' I eased up into a sitting position to prove I was right, but another stab from the witch doctor proved I wasn't.

Jonny shrugged and tossed me a bottle that rattled in my hand when I caught it. 'The doc says these will kill a lot of the pain. He said they're really strong stuff. But you've to make sure and lay off the booze or they'll make you nuts.'

I'd been tended by a corrupt nurse, medicated by a corrupt doctor who presumably got supplies like these from a corrupt pharmacist. I spilled a couple of the pills onto the palm of my hand. They were the size of horse-tablets; maybe Doc Banks got them from a corrupt vet instead.

'Bloody hell, Jonny,' I said. 'Last time anybody prescribed tablets this size, Moses carried them down from Mount Sinai. Am I expected to run in the four o'clock at Troon after taking these?'

'The doc said you've to break them in half before taking them. Don't worry ... Doc Banks knows not to cross me.' He handed me a glass of water. 'Sleep for a couple of hours, then we can see about losing our cop friends outside before heading up to Shawfields.'

The pills Doc Banks had left did the trick all right. The pain faded enough and I didn't so much fall as plummet asleep. I was plunged into a vivid dreamworld of nauseatingly bright colours and painfully sharp edges. Lillian Andrews, ever the girl of my dreams, was there. She sat in a low-slung Contemporary chair in the middle of a wall-less, infinite room and smoked while all around her men killed each other. The floor beneath her feet was carpeted deep red.

'It's very practical,' she said calmly. 'The blood doesn't show at all.' Her point was illustrated as Hammer Murphy caved in the side of Bobby's head with a swing of his mallet and a spray of blood, the same shade as the carpet and Lillian's lips, spattered her cheek.

'I'm going to kill you,' I said to her without anger or malice as I sat down opposite her on a chair that appeared beneath me. Ronnie Smails and Arthur Parks joined us, each sitting in the chairs I'd found them in. Neither spoke. Parks's lower jaw still jutted at an unnatural angle. I took a glass of red wine from her and we toasted the memory of her husband.

'Are you going to fuck me first,' Lillian asked in a matter-of-fact voice, 'or after?'

'I haven't decided.'

She said something in reply but I couldn't hear it over the screams of the fighting and dying. I sipped the red wine and it was thick and warm and coppery.

I woke up.

The curtains were drawn and the bedroom I lay in suddenly seemed tiny and cramped after the impossible architecture of the room in my dream. I felt sick. I stood up and rushed out of the room. I found the bathroom at the end of the hall just in time. I vomited up all that was in my gut but continued retching for a couple of endless minutes.

I washed my face and looked in the bathroom mirror. The world seemed to still have the hard-edged, harsh hyper-reality of my dream. A pale, drawn face with dark-shadowed eyes stared back out at me. My hair was plastered to my forehead like black seaweed on a beach. I looked old. I felt old. There was a large gauze bundle taped to the side of my head where Doc Banks had stitched me up. Jonny appeared behind me at the door. I looked at the reflection of his bruised face.

'You okay?' he asked.

'I'll live,' I said without much conviction. 'Let's go.'

Lizzie, the matronly abortionist, dressed my head with a more discreet pad and I took another couple of Banks's horse-tablets. Again something appeared turned up in my head and I seemed to see in *Gone with the Wind* Technicolor.

At least my head had stopped hurting.

One of Jonny's minders was about his size and colouring. We waited until he changed into one of Jonny's suits, raincoat and hat. Jonny handed him the keys to the Riley and we watched as the police car outside followed the fake Jonny away.

'I feel guilty, in a way,' said Jonny. 'It's like bemusing children for sport.'

We waited a couple of minutes before going out of the back door, across a couple of neighbours' fences and out onto the street. Jonny brought a couple of heavies with him: it was the expected form for one of these meets. We walked the three blocks to where I'd parked the Atlantic and headed up through Giffnock and Pollockshields before cutting across to Rutherglen. Shawfields Stadium had an art deco, mock-Egyptian entrance that would have done a pharaoh proud – if there ever had been a pharaoh who called his hunting hounds names like *Blue-Boy* and *Jack's-m'Lad* and was partial to placing the odd five-bob bet.

The stadium was packed. We parked in a car park that was ambitiously large and sparsely filled with cars but thronging with punters on foot, taking a short cut to the stands. I followed Jonny and his boys to an entrance marked 'Management Suite' and up into a large room with red carpet, a bar and picture windows out over the track.

Willie Sneddon was already there. Twinkletoes McBride and Tiny Semple lurked malevolently in the corner. Someone had given Twinkletoes a going over and one eye was nearly shut. Copper or not, whoever had given him a hiding like that would be advised to sleep lightly from now on.

Despite his complaints to me on the 'phone, Sneddon's face was comparatively unmarked. Maybe he had managed to keep McNab's hands busy with Masonic handshakes. Hammer Murphy's paranoia was not totally ill-informed. Sneddon leaned against the bar, cradling a whisky glass in his fingers. He nodded in our direction when we arrived.

'You all right, Willie?' asked Jonny Cohen with a smile.

Sneddon grunted. 'Feeling the fuckin' pinch, you might say. You too?'

Jonny joined him at the bar. Behind it, a youth wearing a white waiter's jacket and too much Brylcreem poured Jonny a

Scotch. I held my hand up in response to Sneddon's invitation. I felt like keeping as clear a battered head as I could manage and didn't fancy the party that mixing booze and Doc Banks's tablets would bring on.

Murphy was late. We all knew he would be late. Just to make a point. And an entrance. A roar spilled into the entertaining suite from the terraces below as the traps clattered open to release the greyhounds. It was at that moment that Murphy came in, flanked by the same two hard-looking Micks who had persuaded me into the taxi. Sneddon stood up from the bar and faced Murphy. Twinkletoes and Tiny Semple came over to act as his bookends.

'Murphy . . .' Sneddon's nodded greeting had all the warmth of a Corstorphine landlady.

Murphy didn't answer but something over Sneddon's shoulder caught his eye and he threw a sneer at it. We all looked. It was a portrait of our newly minted monarch hanging on the wall. Oh good, I thought, playtime. In Glasgow's fevered sectarian atmosphere, the reigning monarch symbolized all that was Protestant: a counterpart to the Pope. Depending where you were in Glasgow, you would see either 'Fuck the Pope' or 'Fuck the Queen' daubed on walls. Technically, of course, the Queen was the head of the Church of England and not the Kirk in Scotland. But 'Fuck the Queen' was easier to spell and took less whitewash than 'Fuck the Right Reverend Doctor James Pitt-Watson, Moderator of the General Assembly of the Church of Scotland'.

'You carry them fuckin' pictures around with you and hang them up everywhere you go, Sneddon?' Murphy attempted a jocular smile that turned out simply a baring of teeth.

'You want a drink, Murphy?' Sneddon wasn't rising to the bait. 'We can toast Her Majesty if you like.'

'Aye . . . toast her. That's an idea. I suppose you're all fuckin' geared up for the Coronation?'

'I'll be watchin' it on television,' Sneddon said, his voice even and low. 'You'll have heard of television, I suppose.'

'An' I'll bet she'll be sittin' on one of those big thick velvety cushions, like always.'

'What about it?' There was now a wire taut through Sneddon's voice.

'Now that we're all here,' I said in a let's-change-the-subject-quick way, 'I want to tell you what I've found out about Tam McGahern—'

'You know why she sits on them?' Murphy continued. Apparently my voice didn't carry the way it used to.

'I've got a funny feeling you're going to tell me,' said Sneddon. He put his glass down on the bar and turned to the waiter-jacketed youth. 'You ... fuck off. But leave the bottle.'

Once more, in my head a honky-tonk player stopped mid-tune. The waiter left, but Murphy made a point of intercepting him and giving him a ten-bob tip.

'Don't get me wrong,' said Murphy. 'I've got nothing against her. Nice enough lassie. Not much to look at, mind, but there again I think Phil spends most of his time looking at the back of her head.'

'What the fuck is that meant to mean?' Sneddon's dense frame and hard face seemed to become denser and harder. Jonny Cohen looked over at me with eyes that very eloquently conveyed, *Oh fuck!*

'Listen, boys,' said Jonny. 'This isn't the time—'

'I don't mean nothin',' said Murphy. 'Just that she sits on them big cushions. I just wonder if it's because she's married to a fuckin' Greek. And you know what that means.'

'Why don't you tell me?' said Sneddon. His hand rested on the bar close to the whisky bottle.

'You know, Sneddon ... Phil's a Greek. And them Greeks

like to make their deliveries round the back, if you catch my drift . . .' Murphy turned to his heavies. 'What d'you think, boys?'

'I think it's part of his fuckin' culture,' said one of the broken noses. 'It's probably written into their laws or something.'

'Aye,' said Murphy. 'Or maybes it's in Greek wedding vows . . . "promise to honour and obey and take a roger up the dodger".'

At least, I thought, Murphy was attempting to talk about something that interested Sneddon. And nothing was closer to the heart of Willie Sneddon – ultra-patriotic, Orange Order, arse-painted-blue, Protestant Loyalist – than the new Queen. If I had had a pair of ruby slippers I'd have wished myself back in time to the OK Corral.

'That Pope of yours sits on a big fuckin' pile of cushions himself, you know,' said Sneddon. His hand was now on the whisky bottle. I didn't think he was going to offer Murphy a drink. 'At least Her Majesty doesn't need to be carried around on a fucking chair. I reckon the Pope's always in it 'cause he's too tired to walk after chasin' all them fuckin' altar boys.'

There's an expression 'you could cut the atmosphere with a knife'. Considering the atmosphere was being created by Hammer Murphy and Willie Sneddon, it wasn't the air that would end up cut with a knife. Or smashed to fuck with a hammer. They held each other with unbroken murderous glares. Although, in Hammer Murphy's case, I couldn't remember him look at anything or anybody with anything less than a murderous glare. Maybe, at times of intimacy with his good lady wife, or during tender moments with his children, he would reduce it to an aggravated-assault-with-menaces glare.

'Come on, guys,' I said. 'A joke's a joke. No harm done.'

'Lennox is right,' said Handsome Jonny with a handsome smile. 'Where would we all be if we didn't have a sense of humour?'

'Edinburgh?' I quipped. Sneddon and Murphy turned their murderous glares on me in a way that suggested I was about to quip my way into an early grave. At least I'd gotten them to agree on something. Now was the time to move on.

'Anyway,' I continued. 'Much as I hate to break up this meeting of The Brains Trust, I think we should be talking about what I've found out, instead of tearing lumps out of each other.' As I spoke, Jonny Cohen walked around Tiny Semple and placed himself between Sneddon and Murphy.

'Lennox is right,' he said. 'If we start on each other then we're all fucking doomed. Let's not kid ourselves that there's only the three firms in town. There's a fourth ... the polis. It would suit the coppers down to the ground if we went weak on them. We'd better listen to what Lennox has to say.'

Again the room seemed too bright, the colours too intense, the edges too sharp.

'I gotta sit down,' I said and slumped into a leather armchair. Jonny brought me some water from the jug on the bar.

'Is he fucking okay?' asked Sneddon. I was touched by his solicitous tone.

'I'm fine,' I said. I took a gulp of the water. 'You know what I like about you guys? You're exactly who you say you are. I know that each one of you is you, and a thorough-going crooked bastard.'

'Lennox ...' Jonny said warningly.

'No,' I said as happily as I could manage, 'that's a good thing. I mean it as a compliment. You see every other bastard I've had to deal with has been someone else. Not who they said they were.'

'Lennox, you're not making any sense.' Jonny's tone was now one of concern. Not concern that my health had deteriorated, but that it was about to – suddenly and irrevocably – if I didn't appease Sneddon and Murphy.

'But there you have it,' I said. 'Nothing made sense. Frankie McGahern having a go at me with McNab there to witness it didn't make sense. Frankie hanging around to get the shite mashed out of him in his garage didn't make sense. But it does if nobody is who you think they are. It's pretty obvious when you think about it. Twins. Tam the brains, the decorated Desert Rat, ex-Gideon Force . . . then Frankie the no-hoper.'

'This is your theory that it was Frankie who got it up the ass above the Highlander, not Tam?' asked Sneddon. I was relieved to see him pour a drink from the whisky bottle, instead of brandishing it at Murphy.

'It *was* Frankie. To start with I thought it was a mistaken identity: that it was a simple accident that Frankie was there instead of Tam. They played this game, you see. According to Wilma, the part-time chippy who was there that night, Tam persuaded Frankie to sleep with her every now and then, just to see if she could tell the difference. A laugh. But that wasn't it at all. Frankie was set up just like John Andrews and half a dozen others. Frankie was Tam's twin brother. His flesh and blood. But all he meant to Tam was a face the same as his and therefore his ticket out of a tight spot. Tam had a big job planned: the robbery of all of these Sterling-Patchett machine guns. But because of the buyers he had lined up for them, he was getting heat from a mob who would never give up till they found and killed him.'

'It didn't take them long,' said Jonny. 'If "Frankie" was Tam, then he still got it within a few weeks.'

'Again, no one is who you think they are. Tam McGahern is still very much alive.'

'So who the fuck was that with their face smashed in . . . ?' Sneddon realized the significance of what he'd said and let the sentence die.

'Exactly. Their face smashed in. And Tam McGahern had gone

to extraordinary lengths to make sure that neither his nor his brother's fingerprints were on file. My guess is the schmuck with the caved-in puss was Tam's former commanding officer. A waster called Jimmy or Jamie Wallace. Wallace provided a lot of the intelligence and background knowledge for this deal. He also provided a corpse about the right size and colouring.'

'But this isn't like the twin thing,' said Murphy. 'First time round it's someone who looks fucking identical to the real guy. The second time they're going to see they've got the wrong punter. Or are you telling me they was all fucking triplets?'

'No. But I am telling you that the guys who did the hit above the Highlander didn't do the second killing. That was Tam McGahern himself. He mashed Wallace's face and dressed him up as Frankie.'

'So McGahern is hiding out somewhere?' asked Jonny. 'Or he must be out of town. God knows he couldn't show his face in Glasgow.'

'I was out with this girl the other night,' I said. 'We went to see a Jack Palance film and she said I reminded her of him. I said there was a good reason. Some Ukrainian-American bomber pilot with an unpronounceable surname refuses to bail out of his burning bomber. Very heroic but his face gets burned to fuck. Months of plastic surgery later they still can't get it quite right and the skin is too tight over his face. But it gives him this unique look. Goodbye Volodymyr Palahniuk, hello Jack Palance. The reason I look like him is I took the tail-end of a grenade blast in the face. I end up with a tight-looking face, prominent cheekbones, et cetera.'

'Really?' said Murphy, his eyes wide with amazement. 'That is abso-fucking-lutely fascinating. Now, are you going to get to a fucking point? Because if you don't, I'm goin' to get the boys here to dance on your face. Then you can entertain every cunt with the story of how you ended up looking like Lon fucking Chaney.'

'The point is that Tam McGahern isn't showing his face in Glasgow, because he doesn't have it any more. Tam and Sally Blane, or Lillian Andrews as she now calls herself, set up this honey-trap operation and trapped a lot of important people. Including, I reckon, a top copper. Anyway, one of their targets was a plastic surgeon called Alexander Knox. Tam doesn't hit him for money. Just a new face. He'd already fixed up Lillian's face after a car crash and was dragged into doing a patch-up on one of Tam's army buddies. But I reckon Tam wasn't acting out of loyalty for a comrade . . . he just wanted to see how good Knox was. The point is, Tam McGahern is walking around with a new identity and a new face to go with it.'

'And just how did you come up with all of this?' asked Sneddon.

'What can I tell you? I'm a genius. Added to which I got some of the story from a high-class chippy who calls herself Liz. Except my money is on her being someone else, like every other bastard. Just like Tam played at being Frankie and Sally played at being Lillian, I think Margot Taylor, Sally's sister, is playing at being Lizzie. That, in turn, means that what I got out of her is at least half fiction.'

I paused to take another sip of water.

'I do think there was a car crash and someone's face got mashed up a bit, but I don't think Margot died. But I could be wrong. The important thing is that Margot and Sally-cum-Lillian helped Tam set up this honey-trap. But they weren't alone. Arthur Parks was involved. He was directing customers and a couple of his better girls to the operation. I started off thinking that once Tam and Lillian had got what they wanted out of the operation, Arthur Parks was surplus to requirements, so they killed him. But that doesn't fit with the way he died. Parks was killed by someone who wanted information out of him. It wasn't a quick death. My thinking is that it was either Tam's new business partners or the highly professional mob who thought they'd got him that night above the Highlander. Ronnie Smails got his from the same killer as Arthur Parks.'

'Was Smails tortured?' asked Jonny.

'No. He wasn't. And that doesn't quite fit. Yet.'

'So who is this *highly professional* outfit you keep banging on about?' Sneddon lit a cigarette and looked at me coldly. Sceptically, I thought.

'This is where it gets all very political. And why you guys have been getting the treatment.' I took another slug of water. My head was starting to hurt again and everything still felt unreal, as if I had been detached from myself and was hearing my own words as if they were someone else's. 'You see, I know where these stolen guns are heading. I don't know when, but I know how and can hazard a guess at which ship they'll be on. I have this friend who said she was fed up with Glasgow and the way no one can see past the city boundaries. Well, Tam McGahern did. He served in the Middle East and he saw decades of strife ahead and the opportunities that that strife offered. Tam was ambitious, but every time he tried to fulfil his ambitions he ended on a collision course with the Three Kings. So he decided to go around you. Beyond your horizons. Those robbed guns will soon be on their way to Aqaba in Jordan and my guess is from there straight into the hands of Arab insurgents.'

I gave them a moment to absorb what I'd been telling them.

'I reckon Tam's been at it for over a year,' I continued. 'He started off with ex-army surplus, old and decommissioned guns. But the Arabs are up against one of the best equipped and most disciplined armies in the world. So Tam saw the opportunity to strike it rich. One big deal to get him a new face and a life in a new country. The States. So he planned this robbery with Jackie Gillespie and roped in the extra skills and finance he needed through blackmail. I would reckon that there's at least one British Army top-brass type on the list.'

'This all sounds very fucking elaborate,' said Sneddon. 'A bit too ambitious for a couple of wee *Taig* shites. No offence, Murphy.'

Hammer Murphy didn't reply but continued to gaze his murderous hate at Sneddon. At everybody.

'*Very* ambitious,' I continued. 'These stolen weapons aren't just any old guns. I talked to an army pal of mine; he told me they were commissioned last year to be the army's new small-arm. The Sterling-Patchett L2A1 sub-machine gun, delivering five hundred and fifty rounds per minute. The Arabs are desperate to get their hands on this kind of stuff. Tam has struck gold, but the reason he needed a new face and a new start is he knew that the Israelis were already onto him and would never let go until they got him. That's the *professional mob*, Mr Sneddon. Mossad, if I'm not mistaken. Which is why you three are up to your ears in shite. The City of Glasgow Police will be under enormous pressure to clear all of this up. How much they know about the destination of guns or the involvement of the Israelis, I don't know. But I'm pretty sure they will have guessed that the guns are headed for the Middle East.'

I paused. My head was pounding again and I felt sick. I took some more water. I noticed that everybody was looking at Jonny Cohen.

'What?' he said, his face clouding with anger and disbelief. 'You think because I'm a Jew I've got something to do with this? Just because Murphy here is a fucking spud-muncher doesn't mean he's gun-running for the IRA.'

'Take it easy, Jonny,' I said, and then turned to the others. 'Jonny's right. Mossad would only use its own operatives.'

'And one of them is the guy you ran into in Perth?' asked Sneddon.

'Yeah. Called himself Powell. Looked like Fred MacMurray. He and his cronies have been all over this from the start. It was they who killed Frankie McGahern, thinking it was Tam. But they're not that easily fooled, so they spirited Wilma away and found out from her they'd got the wrong McGahern.'

'So you're saying they tortured and killed Parky?' asked Sneddon.

'Maybe. But I think there's something more to that. There's a Dutchman around. Big guy, rich. I reckon he's brokered the sale of the guns.'

'McGahern's trips to Amsterdam?' asked Sneddon.

'That's my guess.'

'Well,' said Murphy. 'Those kyke bastards have stirred up all kinds of shite for us. I say we get even.'

I laughed at Murphy and he reminded me with a threatening look that he was unused to the experience. 'You don't understand, do you?' I said. 'Just eight years ago there were six million dead Jews across Europe. Maybe more. Millions others left homeless or totally fucked up. All the Jews know now is that a very serious and nearly successful attempt was made to wipe them off the face of the earth. Now, call them touchy, but they seem to have gotten a little pissed about it all. Get this into your head, Mr Murphy . . . all of you . . . the people you are talking about going up against are the toughest, hardest, deadliest, most unforgiving bastards that have ever walked the earth. I don't know what Mossad's motto is, but I can have a guess: *nobody fucks with the Jews any more.*'

'So what do we do?'

'There are three ships that McGahern has been using to ship weapons out to Jordan. All done through John Andrews's shipping company. All I need to find out is when they're planning to move the guns.'

'Then what?' asked Jonny Cohen.

'One of two things. We can tip off the cops so they capture McGahern and company in the act, or you combine all of your forces and hit McGahern together. Then we dump the guns and tell the cops where to find them. My ideal solution would be to get in touch with the Mossad boys. They're more than capable of taking it from there. Unfortunately they seem to have forgotten to put their number in the 'phone directory.'

'Fucking easy choice,' said Murphy. 'We tell the coppers and they take all the fucking risks. *And* they'll maybes start leaving us alone.'

'That would be ideal . . . but, like I said, I've a funny feeling that McGahern's got a copper on the payroll. McGahern could be warned off and we're back to square one.'

'So a fucking bloodbath down at the docks is the way to go. That what you're suggesting?' asked Murphy.

'Listen, the alternative is that you lose your crowns. This has been a four-sided game until now: your three outfits and the police. And let's be honest boys, you've all got at least a couple of coppers each in your pockets. But Tam McGahern's raised the stakes, and the temperature. Because of these guns going missing, Glasgow will be crawling with Ministry of Defence types, Special Branch and Military Intelligence. Added to them there's a Mossad assassination squad out there and, I'm guessing, a few Arabs over here to keep tabs on the deal.'

I leaned back in the chair. My head still swam. I closed my eyes and took another long drink of water.

'The first thing we've got to do is find Jackie Gillespie. One of the robbers is supposed to be wounded and it's my guess it's Gillespie.'

'Why?' asked Jonny.

'Because I'll bet he wasn't wounded by an army bullet. I've seen the way Tam and Lillian work. They don't want partners. Leaving Gillespie dead at the scene would have worked for them. No one associates Gillespie with the McGaherns, but everyone knows that he's worked for each of you at one time or another.'

'Bastard . . .' muttered Sneddon.

'Jackie Gillespie can't stay hidden if all your people are looking for him. He can hide from the police, but not the Three Kings.' I took another sip of water. I felt really sick now and wanted to stop talking. 'I need you three to work together. We need your hardest and most experienced men on this. When we know which ship and when, then we hit the bastards. One more thing. I don't think any of you is the sentimental type, but I've got to make this clear. Lillian Andrews may be a woman, but she's as much the brains behind this as Tam. You've got to see her, and deal with her, the same way. That's it.'

The room seemed to buzz with talk as Sneddon, Murphy and Jonny engaged in heated debate. I sat and felt my head throb with every beat of my pulse. I took another one of Doc Banks's horse tablets and broke it in two, swallowing it in stages with the last of my water. I closed my eyes. There was a rush of sound from outside again as another set of traps opened and the crowd roared. Again, even with my eyes closed, everything seemed bigger and harder and sharper than it should. I imagined I could feel the fall of each paw of every greyhound. Something tidal was going on in my gut. I opened my eyes and stood up. I made my way to the door marked 'toilets', unnoticed by the others because they were still debating who should do what, who was in charge of whom. There was a short corridor then another door, marked 'WC'.

I just made it. Once more I continued to retch, even after my gut was empty. When I was finished I cupped some water from the hand basin and rinsed my mouth. I reckoned that the pill had been puked up so I took another, halved it and washed it down with more tap water. I stood and rested my forehead on the cool porcelain of the tiles. I became aware I could hear the voices from the entertaining suite. Too loud. Not talking: shouting.

I headed back along the corridor and heard glass shattering, furniture breaking. Fuck. I thought I could trust them to pull together and they were ripping each other apart. I opened the door to step back into the suite but eased it shut again as quickly and quietly as I could. No one had seen me, I thought. But I had seen enough. I opened the door again a crack and peered through. Sneddon, Murphy, Jonny and their respective heavies were all on the floor, their faces shoved into the red carpet by burly Highlanders. Batons were arcing through the air and colliding with ribs, arms, heads. I saw Superintendent McNab walk calmly through the carnage. I reckoned there were at least twenty coppers crammed into the room. Half in civvies, the other half in uniform.

I backed away from the door. If I had gone out into the entertaining suite I would have got the same treatment as the others, and I reckoned another stiff blow to the head would probably be enough to finish me off. It would only be a matter of minutes before the police had everybody subdued and handcuffed. Then they would check the toilets for any stragglers.

I went back through the door marked WC and closed it behind me but didn't lock it. There was a tall, narrow window of frosted glass beside the cistern, but high up. This is getting to be a habit, I thought to myself as I braced one foot on the toilet, the other on the wall and eased myself up, undid the catch and swung open the window. It took all that was left of my strength to haul myself up and wriggle my head and right shoulder out through the window. I found myself looking straight down at a two-storey drop onto the car park below. I continued to ease myself through, gripping the wooden frame of the window. I got a leg free and eased a foot down onto the sill. I heard voices in the hall outside the toilet. I pushed through and eased the window closed.

I was outside, but I would still be seen against the frosted glass. The sill extended a foot or so on either side of the window and I worked my way along to its end. There was no downpipe this time; no projection on the stadium's architecture to use as a stepping stone. I turned my back to the window, remained motionless and hoped that no one would pay too much attention to the window. I heard voices in the toilet. Then nothing.

I looked down at the car park. It was getting dark but I could see the police cars and a van parked outside. There were still a few punters milling about. I felt another lurch in my gut, this time from the sight of a figure leaning against the van and smoking, wearing a peaked driver's cap with a City of Glasgow Police chequered band around it. Don't look up, I thought. Whatever you do, don't look up.

I knew the coppers would come out with their captures soon and my chances of being seen would increase to the almost certain. As I was too well-dressed for a window cleaner, I decided the best thing was to climb back into the toilet. I moved as quietly as I could and slid back through the window. I could still hear voices from the entertaining suite, but, having checked the toilet once, I didn't think they would come back.

Not so clever Lennox. The one thing I didn't take into account, of course, was that while my place of hiding may have been checked out, it was, after all, a toilet. I only just managed to duck behind the door as it swung open and a large uniformed figure stepped through and into the cubicle. He had his back to me and was clearly unbuttoning his fly. A man is never more vulnerable than when he's got his dick in his hand and I knew what I had to do. I couldn't let him see me and I couldn't be captured. I cursed inwardly and took the sap from my pocket and swung it at the back of the copper's head. He stumbled forward but steadied himself with his hand against the wall. He wasn't out. I swung again, harder, trying not to think what would happen to my neck if I killed a copper. He went down, his face smashing into the porcelain of the toilet bowl and splashing it with blood.

It had been quiet. Messy, but quiet. But had it been quiet enough? I stood stock still and listened for anyone approaching. Nothing. I went back along the hall. The door at the end was open and revealed the suite was empty. The copper I clobbered had obviously come back to take a leak. But he would be missed.

I moved swiftly across the suite and out onto the stairwell. Making sure that the last of the coppers was heading out of the bottom door, I ran silently down the steps and watched through a crack in the door as the police piled the Three Kings and their bodyguards into the van. The tablet I'd taken earlier had really kicked in and I was back in a Technicolor world. I saw several faces streaked with blood, glistening in the stadium lamplight that seemed to me to sparkle in the dusk.

A small crowd had gathered in the car park and was watching the proceedings. As a group of onlookers passed by the entrance to the suite, I slipped out into their number and walked into the main racing stadium.

I watched three races before I risked going back to the car park. When I did, the police cars were gone and I assumed they had not yet missed their colleague. I found a pay 'phone, made a pithy call to Greasy George and explained he had better get his Bentley and his ass into gear. I made my way to the Atlantic and drove off. I knew that when the copper with his face in the toilet came to, or was discovered, then the Three Kings would each get very special treatment to cough up who had been left behind. But I knew they wouldn't give me up. Not through any sense of comradeship or loyalty – just because I was the only hope they had of getting out of this mess.

Some hope, I thought to myself as I looked at my face in the rear-view mirror of the Atlantic.

CHAPTER THIRTY

I've always considered myself a smart cookie. It's one of these things you get smug about, having brains. Generally, I thought of myself as someone who always had an answer. Tonight, however, that answer must have been moving all over Glasgow, because I found myself driving through the city aimlessly, not seeing the streets, my bruised and drugged brain refusing to give me directions.

But maybe it had. I found myself back in the future. Ahead of me the partly built monoliths of Moss Heights loomed black into the night sky. Again I parked some distance from Jackie Gillespie's brand-new house, although it did little to make the Atlantic, one of only three cars parked on the entire length of the street, less conspicuous.

The back door was still ajar. I made my way into the kitchen and cursed the fact I hadn't brought a torch. I wasn't even sure what I was doing there. I was alone. The Three Kings were out of the picture for God knew how long. No Twinkletoes or Tiny to call on to add muscle. I wasn't even here on a hunch.

I went through to the living room. It was easier to see in there because of the nauseous yellow light cast in from the streetlamp. It was still the tumbled mess it had been earlier. The only difference was the figure sitting in the corner, partly concealed in shadow. I noticed him mainly because of the yellow gleam on the sawn-off double-barrelled shotgun he had pointed at me. I put my hands up but otherwise didn't move.

'Hello, Jackie,' I said. 'You okay?'

'No.' The voice from the corner was deep but weak. 'You Lennox?'

'Were you expecting me?'

'Kinda,' said Gillespie. He lowered the gun and I lowered my arms. 'You're a favourite topic of conversation for McGahern and his tart. You was supposed to sit still for the frame. Like me.'

'Funny thing is I was half-expecting to find you here,' I said.

'Everybody's turned this place over once. They've crossed it off their list. It's the one place in Glasgow I'm safe.' Gillespie moved slightly to the side and his face became etched in yellow. From the look of him, I guessed it would be yellow even without the streetlight. I could see a glistening patch, black in the streetlight, on his shirt and jacket. There was a pool of it on the floor next to him.

'Fuck, Gillespie. Let me have a look at you.' I moved towards him but he hinted I stop by raising the barrels. I took the hint.

'Forget it, Lennox. You're talking to a ghost. You was in the war too. You know when someone loses this much blood, he's fucked. Anyway, I could have gone to a hospital a day ago. What would be the point? Nursed back to health just to be dropped through a fucking hatch at Barlinnie. This way I choose where and when I die.'

'I guess I'm right to think it was McGahern and Lillian who fucked you?'

'Full fucking shaft.' Gillespie lowered the gun again. He nodded when I asked if I could sit next to him. I could see his torso more clearly. He was right. There was no point in discussing it any more. 'McGahern shot me. He executed those fucking soldiers. They didn't die in a firefight. They was conscripts. Kids. Then he turned, calm as fuck, and shot me. But I got a shot off too. Missed the bastard, but he ran for it and drove off in the van. I took the car. Could hardly fucking drive. Dumped the car, waited till dark and walked here. The walk nearly fucking killed me. I was hoping you'd turn up.'

'I kinda guessed you'd be here. Can I get you something? Water?'

Gillespie shook his head. 'The only thing I want you to get me are those bastards. McGahern and his whore. She planned the whole fucking thing.'

'Not McGahern?'

'Naw. His idea. She put it all together. Now shut the fuck up and listen. I don't have a lot of breathing left in me. And remember what I tell you. The Carpathian Queen. She's one of the three ships McGahern's been using. It sails at eleven the day after tomorrow. But the big payoff takes place tomorrow, noon. McGahern gives sight of the goods and gets half the money. Then the other half on delivery. The agent is a big fat Dutch fucker. We only ever called him The Fat Dutchman, but McGahern slipped once when he was talking to Lillian ... he called the Dutchman De Jong. You have to watch the Dutchman: he has a couple of Arabs in tow. Dangerous bastards.'

'One of them isn't any more,' I said. 'We had an *episode*. I've ended his lineage.'

'Watch your back anyway, Lennox. They're all meeting at an empty warehouse on dock thirteen. Like I said, noon tomorrow.'

'Maybe they've changed their plans. After all, you know about the meet.'

Gillespie's laugh turned into a wet cough. 'Dead men don't tell tales. Anyhow, I know more than they think I know. Lennox, promise me you'll get the bastards.'

'I promise. I've got my own score to settle. And the Three Kings have bigger scores to settle.'

It was then that Gillespie said something that jarred with me. Made me feel even more vulnerable and alone. Something he had overheard and couldn't elaborate on.

We sat quietly in the black and yellow geometry of shadow and streetlight. Everything was quiet. No dogs barking, no distant cars passing.

'Lennox?'

'Yeah?'

'I was in Burma during the war. You?'

'First Canadian. Italy and Germany.'

'Then you know too. I mean, you know how this goes.'

'Sure, Jackie. I know how this goes.'

'I always wanted to go to Canada. Read all them comics about lumberjacks when I was a kid. Tell me about it.'

So I did. Gillespie sat quiet, apart from the odd wet cough, and listened as I talked about growing up on the banks of the Kennebecasis. About deep snow winters and hot sun summers. About watching the tidal bore surge up the Bay of Fundy. About the smell of the forest when the snow first melts. I was surprised just how much I had to say and talked on, even after Gillespie stopped coughing.

Like I had told him, I knew how it went.

I left the dead armed robber in his brand-new house, his shotgun still on his lap. When I got back in the Atlantic I sat for a moment and thought back to what he had said and how it had shaken me more than anything else: 'There's one other thing, Lennox. I don't know which one, but one of the Three Kings isn't to be trusted.'

It was four in the morning by the time I got back to my digs. If Mrs White heard me creep in, she didn't signal it by putting on her light. I lay on the bed in my clothes, my exhaustion playing tug-of-war with the nausea and the throbbing in my head. My exhaustion won.

I woke up with a start and a stab of pain in my head. I looked at my watch and saw it was half past nine. I let my head sink back onto the pillow. The pain was still beyond all description of a headache, but I was aware that the intensity had been turned down a notch or two.

I got up and took enough aspirin to rot a steel gut and took a bath, shaved and dressed in a new change of clothes. I wore a black suit with a red pinstripe and a deep burgundy tie. I was dressing up for my coffin. My plan remained exactly the same as it had the night before when I had explained it to the Three Kings. The only difference now was that instead of going in mob-handed with the combined strength of Glasgow's criminal underworld, I was going it alone. I could see the epitaph on my gravestone: *Here lies Lennox: he went it alone. The wanker.*

I drove to the docks and parked the Atlantic. I slipped the switchblade into my jacket pocket, checked the chambers of the Webley, snapped it shut and tucked it into the waistband of my trousers. I found a hole in the fence and dodged between warehouses until I found dock number thirteen. Maybe it would be my lucky number. I could see the warehouse. A Bedford of the same make that had been used the night they attempted to grab me was parked outside, a tarpaulin stretched over its cargo. It started to rain. Something on the other side of the dock began thumping at metal, sending ringing echoes across the water. I ran across to the back of the warehouse and ducked behind its cover. I pulled the Webley out from my waistband and rebuttoned my jacket and coat. I checked my watch: ten before noon. At least it hadn't rained on Gary Cooper.

Two cars arrived, about five minutes apart. They drove round to the front of the warehouse and I couldn't see who got out.

I made my way along the back of the building and round the corner. I found a door on the side but it was padlocked. I was going to have to go in the same way as everyone else. I sprinted the length of the warehouse's side and ducked behind a collection of huge oil drums. I just made it, because a third car, a Nash roadster, pulled up and a red-haired man in a houndstooth jacket and cavalry twills got out. I watched the country-set type, whom I reckoned to be their army connection, disappear into the warehouse. He had the look of someone Lillian and her girls could have compromised.

I hesitated for a moment. I didn't know what I expected the outcome of my one-man crusade to be. Somewhere I still hoped that my chum the Fred MacMurray lookalike and his Mossad pals would come galloping to my rescue, like the US cavalry in yarmulkes. After all, the whole point of our encounter in Perth was to let me know they were there, if I ever got around to working it out for myself.

I looked impotently at the Webley in my hand. Oh well, Lennox, I thought, no one lives for ever. At least my headache would go away. I stole around and pushed the door open enough to see in.

There were two levels to the warehouse and I saw the back of the officer-type disappear up the metal stairs to the upper floor. There was no one on the ground floor, but a couple of crates sat in the middle of the vast space. I guessed they had been offloaded at random from the lorry for the buyers to check the merchandise.

I crept over to the crates, laid my Webley on top of one and picked up the crowbar that had been leaning against them. I was doing well to get this far, I thought. The moment was spoiled by something cold, hard and barrel-like being jabbed into the base of my neck.

'Don't move, Mr Lennox.' I recognized the accent as Dutch. 'I am an expert at executing people with a neck shot.'

I raised my hands. Someone snatched the Webley away.

'Turn around.'

I did as I was told and came face to face with a tall, heavily built man immaculately and expensively dressed. The Fat Dutchman. There was a smaller, darker man next to him. The other Arab. He had my Webley in his hand and was staring at me expressionlessly. He could have been day-dreaming about violating a marquess's daughter, for all I could tell from his face. The unpleasant thought that he might actually be day-dreaming about violating me flashed through my mind and I turned back to the fat boy.

'He isn't your usual stooge, is he?' I asked. 'Don't you usually hang about with Peter Lorre?'

Fat Boy didn't laugh. To be fair, he looked nothing like Sidney Greenstreet.

'You are not half as funny as you like to think you are, Mr Lennox.' The fat man spoke English with a typically sibilant Dutch accent. I had spent quite a bit of time in Holland at the end of the war. Enough to develop one hell of a respect for a people who'd had the crap kicked out of them, been starved half to death, then simply rolled up their sleeves and got on with the business of rebuilding their country. Probably came from centuries of fighting back the sea, as they had had to in the big North Sea flood a few months back. I liked the Dutch. I so hoped I wasn't about to become disillusioned.

'Why don't you and Dusky here put the guns down, Tulip-sucker, and I'll amuse the shit out of you both.' Unfortunately, 'Tulip-sucker' was the best I could do: it's hard to insult a Dutchman and I'd had a trying couple of days. He didn't respond. 'So you're De Jong?' I said. Again no response but I could tell he hadn't expected me to know his name. 'Former Nazi-collaborator and member of the fourth SS Volunteer Brigade Netherlands. Am I right?'

De Jong frowned. I'd hit the target. He was now trying to work out how I knew so much about him. Truth was that I had guessed from his crack about his expertise with the neck shot: there hadn't been enough enthusiastic Dutch collaborators to make up any more than the one SS brigade. In the meantime, his curiosity might buy me a little more breathing time.

'Upstairs . . .' De Jong ordered and nodded towards the metal stairway.

When I got to the top there were three people waiting: Lillian Andrews, the officer-type and a man I'd never seen before. Not that it would be easy to recognize him, the state his face was in. He was blond with prominent ears and that was about all you could see: his nose and jaw were concealed by surgical dressings and what was visible of his face was puffed up in angry swellings. The bandaged man cradled a sawn-off shotgun in his arms. The Dutchman laid a large canvas military holdall on the floor.

'It's all there,' said De Jong. 'Half the money. I've inspected the goods and I'm satisfied.'

'What the fuck is going on?' asked the blond man in the bandages, looking at me through puffy eyelids. I'd maybe never seen him before, but this wasn't the first time I'd heard him speak.

'Nice job, McGahern, or it will be when it heals. Pity about the ears, though . . .' I said. 'Or did radar come as part of the package?' McGahern clearly didn't rate my critical opinion as much as I hoped. He ignored me and looked back at the Dutchman.

'I'll tell you what is going on,' said De Jong. 'Your security is worthless. We found him downstairs sniffing around the samples—'

'*Sniffing* and *samples*,' I said helpfully. 'Not *shniffing* and *shamples*. Whatever you do, don't order me to sit.' Actually, the Dutchman's English wasn't that bad: he was easier to understand than most Glaswegians.

McGahern laughed at my joke. Then he swung the shotgun upwards and slashed me across the face with the barrels. My cheek split and I went down. It was as if all the pain in my head had been asleep and the blow to my face had woken it up. I stayed down but the Arab grabbed me under my arm and hauled me up.

'That's for outside the Horsehead Bar,' said McGahern.

I held the back of my hand to my bleeding cheek and checked my jaw was still working. I examined McGahern. From what I could see through the bandages, the whole architecture of the face had been altered. Even his lips were fuller. But changing someone's eyes was a tougher job and I recognized the same hard, rat-eyed stare from our previous encounter.

'You got what you wanted, didn't you?' I said, but McGahern ignored me.

'What I want to know is how he knows so much about me,' said the Dutchman. 'My name. My background.'

McGahern looked at me then shook his head. 'He doesn't know nothing. Kill him.'

'I know it all. Or almost all. I know about De Jong here and his two Arab pals. Of course he's down to one now. I helped his other dusky chum out with a change of career. He's applying for the post of Chief Eunuch of the Harem now. And I know all about the set up you had running for a year. The shipments to Aqaba. I know about Parks and Smails.' I turned back to the Dutchman. 'That was your handiwork, wasn't it? Or more accurately it was the Son of the Sheik here that did it . . . or his cousin before he started singing soprano. You panicked when McGahern killed John Andrews and then Lillian dropped out of sight. You knew Parks was a partner so you tortured him to find out what was going on. Smails got it afterwards, when you two had kissed and made up. A favour for McGahern to make up for Parks, I'd guess. And I know all about Alexander Knox and your army chum here. How am I doing, so far?'

'You're doing fine,' said Lillian. She had been standing to one side smoking a cigarette and watching. She dropped the cigarette and crushed it with the toe of her black velvet court shoe. 'But this is all guesswork. A yarn you're spinning to save your neck.'

'Oh yeah? Tell that to the Mossad boys when they get here.'

Three blank faces looked back at me. But I could tell that had shaken them.

'We've got Jackie Gillespie,' I said. 'He's making quite a recovery. Your aim ain't what it used to be, McGahern.'

'Bollocks,' said McGahern. 'Now I know you're lying.'

'Really? Then how come I know that the two soldiers didn't die in an exchange of fire? That they were a couple of scared teenage conscripts and you executed them then shot Gillespie immediately after, trying to catch him unawares? You got him in the right side, didn't you?'

Bullseye. McGahern turned to Lillian, as if looking for guidance.

'Where is Gillespie?' she asked.

'Safe. Somewhere you can't touch him.' At least that much was true.

'No . . .' Lillian shook her head. 'No, something doesn't fit with all this. If Lennox knows so much and others know the same, how come he's here alone?'

'I thought you said there would be no loose ends?' The red-haired officer-type spoke for the first time. He had an English accent and his voice was high with fear. 'You promised that no one would see me. That I would be in the clear.'

'There won't be any loose ends,' said Lillian. 'You will be in the clear.' She gestured to McGahern who handed her his sawn-off. It looked like my headache was going to disappear for good. But she didn't aim at me. The sound of the blast was deafening in the warehouse. I was still breathing: Lillian had ruined the army guy's houndstooth. He was on the floor now, blubbering and leaking blood and piss. Lillian walked over to where he lay and fired the other barrel into him. He stopped blubbering.

I looked down at the dead Englishman. 'This is nice,' I said. 'We really should try to get together more often.'

Lillian handed the gun back to McGahern, who plopped two fresh cartridges into the chambers. I heard footsteps coming up the metal stairs behind me. A woman's high heels. The woman came into view and stood next to Lillian, totally eclipsing her looks.

'Hello, Helena,' I said. 'I thought I'd be seeing you here.'

'You never did know when to leave things be, Lennox,' she said, her face genuinely, beautifully sad.

'So you ran the honey-trap operation for them? All along I thought that McGahern here was cracked up on Lillian. But it was you, all the time.'

'I run things here,' said Lillian. 'You weren't smart enough to work that out.' She looked over my shoulder to the Dutchman. 'Go down and get the driver to load the sample cases. But leave the Arab here. I want him to deal with Lennox. Slow and painful.'

I heard the Arab move behind me. I knew he'd loop the

garrotte over my head and strangle me to death. I'd wait until he made his move before I went for the switchblade in my jacket pocket. The Fat Dutchman had been careless in not frisking me. I'd maybe get the Arab and one other before they shot me dead. Like Gillespie, the idea of choosing my departure route appealed to me.

The leather flashed in front of my face. This was it. But then I heard a shot and the Arab dropped the garrotte and crashed onto the floor. I looked up. Helena Gersons was holding an automatic and had it trained on Lillian and McGahern.

'Put the shotgun down,' she ordered McGahern. 'Nice and slow.'

I stood up. McGahern put the shotgun down on the floor. I saw him exchange a look with Lillian. Helena looked at me and smiled an agitated smile. 'Things are never what they seem,' she said. 'Remember I told you that once?'

I moved towards the shotgun. At that moment the Big Dutchman appeared at the top of the stairs. Helena swung her automatic around to bear on him and I made a lunge for the shotgun at McGahern's feet. McGahern threw himself at me and checked my dive. We fell onto the floor. Somehow McGahern got on top of me and sliced at my Adam's apple with the side of his hand. I twisted sideways and his blow hit the side of my neck instead.

There was the sound of a shotgun blast.

We both looked in the direction of Lillian. She was holding the shotgun and Helena was lying on the filthy floor of the warehouse, a great plume of blood and bone and flesh stretching from where her face should have been. I heard myself scream and found the switchblade in my hand. I rammed it under McGahern's ribs and up. He looked into my eyes with an expression of shock. I added to his surprise by giving the knife a one-hundred-and-eighty-degree twist. I felt the heat of his blood on my hand, running down my wrist and under the cuff of my sleeve.

I pushed McGahern off and got to my feet in time for Lillian to let me have it with the other barrel. The blast hit me in the side. Lower left, just above the hip. There wasn't that much pain, but suddenly I felt as if someone had plunged me into a vacuum and I gasped to fill my empty lungs. I fell down beside Helena's body, my cheek on her thigh. It was still warm. I grabbed the automatic lying next to Helena's body and fired wildly in Lillian's direction.

Still clutching the automatic, I hauled myself to my feet. Lillian was gone, but dodging my bullets she'd left the holdall of cash behind. Helena lay with her face gone. The army officer, the Arab and McGahern weren't providing much company either. I leaned against the wall and pressed my hand to where the blood was pulsing out of my side. I tried to catch my breath and listened to the rain and the dull metallic thumping from somewhere across the docks.

I looked over at the Dutchman, who was still standing at the top of the metal stairs.

CHAPTER THIRTY-ONE

It is raining. The entire world beyond the grime-smeared window is as grey and heavy as wet lead. The snappy wind grabs handfuls of rain and throws them like pebbles against the glass, as if trying to draw my attention to just how crap everything outside is. The dull sound of some massive industrial blunt instrument rhythmically hitting metal stretches through the rain, sometimes loud, sometimes muffled, depending on the whim of the wind.

But my attention is pretty much focused on this room. In my life, I have had to explain my way out of a lot of tight corners, but this tops them all.

I am leaning against the wall of an upper-storey room in an empty dockside warehouse. I am leaning against the wall because I doubt if I can stand up without support. I am trying to work out if there are any vital organs in the lower left of my abdomen, just above the hip. I try to remember anatomy diagrams from every encyclopaedia I ever opened as a kid, because, if there are vital organs down there, I am pretty much fucked.

I am leaning against a wall in an empty dockside warehouse trying to remember anatomy diagrams and there is a woman on the floor, about three yards in front of me. I don't need to remember childhood encyclopaedias to know that there is a pretty vital organ in your skull, not that I seem to have made much use of it over the last four weeks. Anyway, the woman on the floor is Helena Gersons and she hasn't got much of a skull

left, and no face at all. Which is a shame, because it was a beautiful face. A truly beautiful face. Next to her is a large canvas
bag that has been dropped onto the grubby floor, spilling half
of its contents, which comprise a ridiculously large quantity of
used, large-denomination banknotes.

I am leaning against a wall in an empty dockside warehouse
with a hole in my side trying to remember anatomy diagrams,
while Helena Gersons without her beautiful face and a large
bag of cash lie on the floor. That should be enough of a pickle
to be in, but there is also the Fat Dutchman looking down at
the girl, the three dead men, the bag and now, at me. And he
is holding a shotgun: the same one that took Helena's pretty
face off. De Jong walks across the floor, swings the shotgun up
and aims it at my head. He pulls both hammers back and
squeezes the triggers. There are two almost simultaneous hollow
clicks.

'Bad luck,' I say. 'Lillian was in too much of a hurry to reload.'
I aim the automatic at his face. He drops the shotgun with a
clatter and puts his hands up. 'That's a good Dutchman,' I say
with a smile, but I am finding it difficult to breathe. 'Now take
two steps back.'

He does what I ask.

'I'm afraid there's more bad luck for you,' I say apologetically.
'What?'

I answer his question by firing the last three rounds from
the automatic into his face. One round pops an eye and he's
dead before he hits the ground.

I look around me. Five dead bodies lying in big sticky pools
of blood.

'If you don't mind, I think I'll join you,' I say to the rest with
a weak smile. I slide down the wall until I'm in a sitting position. I think about Jackie Gillespie and how I'd talked to him

until he died. I would have liked that. At least I got McGahern. And I have stopped the guns getting out. I look at Helena's body and feel like crying. The thing that burns me is that that bitch Lillian has gotten away. She was the brains after all. Truth is, I don't think I really did get all of the answers. The one thing that sticks with me is that Tam McGahern was smart. And he fought alongside Palestinian Jews. He knew how tough they were. That they would never give up. It doesn't fit that he would get involved in smuggling arms to the Arabs. He knew where it would lead. And then there was the way he looked to Lillian for guidance. Yes, she was the brains of the outfit. I looked across at McGahern's body.

'You're not Tam at all, are you?'

He doesn't answer.

'Doesn't matter, Frankie.'

I feel cold. And sleepy. It's not too bad, Lennox, I think. I close my eyes and wait to die.

I am annoyed because someone is trying to wake me. Slapping my face. Someone else is tugging at my clothes where I've been shot. Fuck off and let me sleep. More slaps and someone pulls at my eyelids. I open them.

'Jonny?' I say weakly to the big handsome face pushed into mine. It can't be Jonny Cohen. I think I'm hallucinating. Someone's cutting my clothes. I feel a faint sting as a needle is pushed into my arm.

I look over Jonny's shoulder and see someone else standing there. I decide I definitely am hallucinating: what would Hollywood actor Fred MacMurray be doing in a Glasgow warehouse?

EPILOGUE

I'm standing looking down at a grave. The weather is standing-looking-down-at-a-grave weather: a steel-grey Scottish sky above and a *haar* – as the lyrical Scots call a thick mist – lurking down in the valley. Up here the rain is thin and measly and soaks maliciously into every square inch of clothing it can find.

The summer of nineteen fifty-three turned out to be a record year for sunshine in Scotland, but it still doesn't explain the deep brown tan I've picked up. Three months ago I sat under a sun that had never shone on Glasgow. It had taken a couple of months for me to heal reasonably fully and in that time I had sat, first in a wheelchair, then a hospital deckchair, shaded by palms. The shade didn't prevent me developing this dark tan that makes me stand out even more now that I'm back.

It was Jonny who had fixed it all, but I guess it was his pals in Mossad who had spirited me there and had arranged for my care. I had a visitor while I was there. Actually, there had been a few, including, surprisingly, Jonny who was visiting his parents, 'and dealing with some business' as he put it. But it was Wilma Marshall who surprised me. She was tanned and TB clear. They had fixed her up too, mainly because she had provided so much information about the McGaherns and the operation Lillian Andrews had been running. The funny thing was she had no intention of going home. She had a boyfriend there and a good job and was sending money back to her folks in Glasgow. For once I was glad to see someone change to become someone else.

But it hadn't been all sunshine and happy reunions as I had recuperated. Whenever I thought about all that carnage in Glasgow it made me misty-eyed for the beaches of Anzio. So what happened to everyone?

Well, the police recovered the guns and the cash and decided that it all pointed to a gang fighting amongst themselves. 'When thieves fall out . . .' Glasgow policemen are fond of saying elliptically, as if it explains all things.

Obviously, they took an interest in me as soon as I surfaced again, seeing as I seemed to have dropped out of sight at precisely the same time as the shoot-out at the warehouse. However, my tan backed up my story that I'd been abroad for six months. I even now had official paperwork to explain my absence. It was all just a coincidence, I said. But even I had to admit that it stretched coincidence pretty far that everyone involved seemed to have had some connection to me.

Funnily enough the police didn't push me that far. My conversation with McNab was afternoon tea compared to my previous painful encounter. I got the feeling that he knew more than he was letting on: that word had come down from above not to dig around in my involvement too far. Whatever the reason, I found myself back doing what I had been doing before. I've even been making an effort to increase the number of legitimate clients I work for.

I never did find out for sure who the copper was that Lillian had in her pocket. Maybe it was McNab. Maybe not. There were things, or people, I tried not to think too much about. Particularly Jock Ferguson, the one straight copper I felt I could talk to. I had told Ferguson a fair bit about what was going on as I had stumbled along. Or as much as I could tell any copper. And, like I said, I had always had the feeling that Lillian was constantly a step ahead of me. Funny thing, coincidences. I asked a few casual questions about Ferguson. I always did have the feeling he'd had a tough war. Turns out he had been a Desert Rat.

On the romantic front, I never saw my little nurse again, nor did I ever come across Jeannie, the waitress: although I'm sure it was her I saw terrorizing a hotel owner in the film *Key Largo*. Twinkletoes gave up being a professional heavy and studied chiropody; he now has a peripatetic practice on the Isle of Lewis. Tiny Semple got his big break when Howard Hawks cast him as the 'Thing' in a sequel to *The Thing From Another World*. Hammer Murphy found God, relinquished control of his outfit and last I heard was sequestered in a seminary studying to become a priest.

All of which, of course, is total crap: Twinkletoes still tortures, Tiny Semple still looms menacingly for a living and Hammer Murphy is still the concentrated nucleus of hate at the heart of his violent little empire.

Different day, same shite, as they say in Glasgow.

But I was never free of the image of Helena Gersons lying with her face blown off. No one told me if she had been working for the Israelis or not. But there again, no one told me if Jonny had, either. Not that I think either had been spies or agents or crap like that. I just think that, after what had happened during the war, they had become part of something big that I would never fully understand. But whatever her involvement, I couldn't forget Helena. While I had been recovering in Israel, the pain of what happened to her became anger and the anger became hate. I had burned with the need to get even.

When I got back I didn't tell anyone for a couple of months or so. Other than my landlady, Mrs White, and Jonny, that is. Mrs White had kept my place for me and had even seemed better disposed towards me despite my prolonged and without-warning absence. It turned out that Jonny had called in and explained that he had engaged me at short notice to investigate an urgent security problem he had in one of his distant foreign operations. He had paid six months' rent in advance plus a bonus for the inconvenience. When I returned bearing a tan that was impossible to pick up in Britain, Mrs White had clearly abandoned what doubts she may have had. I think Jonny's handsome outward respectability and the idea of an overseas posting convinced her that my work was, at least in part, above board. And the cash would have helped.

When I got back into my digs I checked that everything was where it should be: my *Niebelungsgold* hoard and the stash of sterling and dollars I'd relieved from Tam McGahern's bathtub hiding place. What I had to do next was expensive, but there was more than enough to cover it. And anyway, for once I don't give a fuck about coming out of this with my pockets lined.

I made sure that it stayed that Jonny and Mrs White were the only people who knew I was back. I steered clear of the Horsehead Bar and I left the Atlantic parked outside my digs where it had been parked throughout my absence and got Jonny to lend me a less conspicuous car. He did so without asking and I think he knew all along what I was going to do.

It took me six weeks to find Lillian Andrews. Not that that was what she was calling herself. As I had expected, the trail had been difficult to pick up. But I did pick it up. I would have found her earlier if I'd not had to keep such a low profile. But as Mr Morrison had pointed out, I'm a natural stalker. Lillian had moved south, to England. The accent had changed as had the appearance, this time without the benefit of plastic surgery. But it's amazing what hair dye and a change of wardrobe can do. I established her movements and kept a detailed log. After a week I drove all the way back to Scotland without stopping.

*

So now I'm standing in the rain in a churchyard looking down at a grave. Whose grave? That I don't know because the name has been abraded by Scotland's corrosive climate. And anyway, it doesn't matter: it's not the occupant of the grave who interests me, you see. Instead I reach down and ease up a broken corner of stone and take out the tobacco tin hidden beneath it. I place a piece of paper in the tin and replace it under the stone. I turn my back to Kirk o' Shotts and head back into the valley.

What's on the piece of paper I have left behind? Just the number of the Horsehead Bar and the day and time I can be reached there. Mr Morrison will know who to ask for. And I still have the cash I found beneath Tam McGahern's bathtub.

Funny thing is, I always considered myself too cynical to go in for revenge.

ACKNOWLEDGEMENTS:

I would like to offer my sincerest thanks to the following people: my wife Wendy for her constant support and advice, Sophie and Jonathan for their patience; my agent Carole Blake, who was, from the very beginning, a total Lennox fan; from Quercus, I would like to thank my excellent editor Jane Wood for making this a better book, Ron Beard for his enthusiasm and Sophie Hutton-Squire for her copy-edits; I would also like to express my gratitude to Louise Thurtell of Allen and Unwin, Australia for her energetic support and invaluable comments; also to Larry Sellyn, Elaine Dyer, Chris Martin and my brother-in-law and friend, Colin Black, to whom this book is dedicated.